JUSTIN S...
WIFE ...
BOUNDED UP THE STAIRS . . .

Frightened, Aidan looped her arms around his neck, tightening them like a vise, not letting go even when they had reached the landing.

For a long enduring moment, violet eyes studied those of silver, then Aidan noticed that Justin's wicked smile had slowly faded. He pulled her arms away from his neck and stepped back. Strangely, Aidan felt an emptiness invade her.

"We survived, madam," he said in an oddly taut voice. "If we are wise, we shall try to work through this in whatever way the law affords."

Recovering from the shock of his nearness, Aidan whispered, "Then you believe that I had no knowledge of my father's plan to marry us?"

"I haven't decided that yet," he said abrasively, realizing his unsteady breathing had little to do with his fast trek up the stairs. "I do not, however, wish to be married to you. Take it as fact."

Praise for Charlene Cross's previous novel,
Masque of Enchantment

"Wonderfully constructed. . . . Ms. Cross skillfully blends all the elements of a classic Gothic . . . with a sweet romance."

—*Romantic Times*

"[A] flawless gem. . . . tightly written, sharp-edged, but filled with warm humor and human foibles. . . . an absolute delight."

—*Rendezvous*

Books by Charlene Cross

A Heart So Innocent
Masque of Enchantment

Published by POCKET BOOKS

A Heart So Innocent

Charlene Cross

POCKET BOOKS

New York   London   Toronto   Sydney   Tokyo   Singapore

An *Original* Publication of POCKET BOOKS

POCKET BOOKS, a division of Simon & Schuster Inc.
1230 Avenue of the Americas, New York, NY 10020

ISBN: 0-671-67700-4

First Pocket Books printing October 1990

10 9 8 7 6 5 4 3 2 1

POCKET and colophon are registered trademarks of
Simon & Schuster Inc.

Printed in the U.S.A.

To my children Dawn, Tracey, and Brian:
You are my pride, my joy, my greatest measure of success.
No mother has been blessed more than I. I love you.

Prologue

15 May 1830

The smell of death clung heavily to the warm spring air. Insects buzzed in a dizzying crescendo, their tiny wings propelling them through the long meadow grasses, then back again around their quarry.

Justin Warfield stood motionless, his tormented gray eyes taking in the grisly sight. Both his parents lay dead, their lives snuffed out by his father's own hand.

Why? he cried silently, angrily.

But he already knew the answer.

His eyes narrowed; then he strode to his mother's lifeless body, where he knelt beside her and removed her jewelry. He tucked her reticule inside his belt, then rose. Moving to his father, he stripped the cold remains of its valuables; the pistol was pried from the dead man's grip.

Shakily he stood; then his icy gray eyes surveyed the spiritless couple again. As he did so he felt his insides quiver; a heaviness settled in his chest. *Love,* he decided, was a wasted emotion. And marriage, a thing for fools.

Turning on his heel, Justin Alexander Malcolm Warfield, the sixth Duke of Westover, strode from the glade. Anguish coupled with hatred burned in the depths of his eyes.

1

"Young lady," Alastair Prescott, the Duke of Atwood, addressed his daughter, his angry voice ringing from the closed library into the halls of the elegant home situated in London's Grosvenor Square, "you've been given ample opportunity to make a suitable match for yourself. Since you've refused to find a husband, I've done it for you!"

Lady Aidan Prescott could not believe what she was hearing. Violet eyes flashed mutinously. Whenever she felt threatened, she always hid behind her anger, using it as a protective cloak. "I'll not marry until I'm ready, sir. And when I do, it will be to a man of my choosing, not yours!"

"Your choosing!" the duke exploded, a furious flush rising up his neck, over his face, to the roots of his silver hair. "You've already denied half the eligible men in England. The other half are either too wise or too cowardly to saddle themselves with the likes of you! And that, dear daughter, narrows the field to exactly naught!"

Thinking she'd won, Aidan resisted the urge to blow on her well-manicured fingernails and buff them against her chest. Instead, she tilted her head, crowned with lustrous red-gold hair, and smiled sweetly. "Well, Father, since you've stated there's nary a man to wed, it seems I shall simply have to remain unattached. A pity, wouldn't you say?"

One silvery brow arched upward, pulling away from its mate. Discerning blue eyes inspected the young woman opposite him. "I beg to differ with you, Aidan," her father replied, a knowing smile splitting his pliant lips. "There's one foolish heart who has offered for you. A man of notable stature and nearly equal wealth to our own. An excellent match, I'd say." He watched the slight widening of his daughter's eyes and purposely prolonged the moment of revelation. Finally, when her exceptional features had settled into a tight-lipped posture, he stated, "The Earl of Sedgewinn."

"What?" Aidan bounded from her chair. Slender hands smacked loudly upon the smooth surface of the duke's mahogany desk. Bracing herself, she leaned toward him. "You must be insane! The man's already outlived two wives and has nearly a dozen children running about. From all reports, they're an incorrigible lot!"

Alastair chuckled. "Their care should occupy your time and keep you out of trouble."

"More like lead me into it, I'd say. I'll not be encumbered with a ready-made family. And as for Sedgewinn, he's a doddering old man. Why . . . why, he's nearly as old as . . . as *you!*"

The insult was too great. Alastair Prescott jerked to his feet, slamming his hands onto his desk. Nose to nose with his daughter, he returned her glare. *"Doddering!* At one-and-fifty, I do not consider myself a palsied, moth-eaten old Methuselah! Had your mother not departed this life when you were but a child of ten, I might have had an easier time of it. As it is, young lady, each silver thread you see atop my head was put there by you!"

When his wife, Anne, had died unexpectedly from a short illness, Alastair had been devastated. Aidan had become his whole life, and he'd admittedly pampered and spoiled her. Yet, despite the fact that she'd been overly indulged, his daughter was giving, caring, a champion for those less fortunate than herself. But, equally so, she was stubborn and rebellious, determined to have her own way— much like himself.

"I'm tired of dealing with your scandalous behavior!" he continued. "So, while I still have a few good years to enjoy before I slip into my grave, I'll let someone else worry over what embarrassing stunt you might pull next!"

Aidan knew he was speaking of her last "shocking display," brought to his attention only a week ago. While riding in Hyde Park with a group of friends, she'd suddenly bounded up in the saddle, planted one foot squarely in the middle of the mare's back, swung her free leg high, imitating a circus acrobat, and headed toward the King's Private Road.

Ignoring the shouts from her friends, she'd cantered along its edge, only to see Victoria and Albert, the Prince Consort, rolling by in an open carriage. With a courteous smile and a polite bow of her head, Aidan had turned her mare back northward, her pose never faltering. Yet, within the hour, the Duke of Atwood had been summoned to Buckingham Palace, and upon his return, a furious Alastair Prescott quoted the Queen's exact words, " 'I am not pleased with your daughter's escapades. They have gone on long enough. Perhaps a husband would tame her wild nature. Don't *you* agree?' " Hence, their ridiculous discussion now.

"Sedgewinn can deal with your antics," her father bit out. "I'm washing my hands of the whole situation!"

"I'll not marry him, Father!" Aidan snapped back.

The duke's fist thumped his desk. "You *will*, Aidan! The contracts are to be signed within a fortnight, and as soon as the banns have been posted thrice, a license obtained, and a minister hired, you'll be married in both a civil and a church ceremony. There will be no question as to its legality! Now, take yourself to your room!"

For a long moment Aidan glared her dissent. Then, in a rustle of lavender silk skirt, she spun and fled the room, slamming the door behind her.

Incensed by his daughter's rebellious disposition, yet frustrated because he could do nothing to conquer that part of her personality, Alastair Prescott fell back into his chair. Cursing his fate, he was by the same token thankful Aidan was an only child. He'd never have survived more than one like her. When she'd been born, nineteen years ago, he'd thought her a gift from on high. But now he was doubtful whence she'd come. Indeed, her beauty could only have been crafted by the angels. But her disposition smacked of Old Scratch himself. Troublesome she was; a constant source of worry. *And* embarrassment, he thought.

"Dear Lord," he wondered aloud, troubled blue eyes searching the stark white rococo ceiling, "what unforgivable sin have I committed to have been burdened with a lone offspring such as this?"

"Aidan," Eugenia Sommers ventured after watching her childhood friend a long moment. "You seem preoccupied . . . disturbed." She set her teacup on its saucer. "Has something happened? Have you and His Grace quarreled again?"

Violet eyes glanced around the cheery drawing room, decorated in soft yellows and springtime shades of green. The reclining sun cast long shadows through the Brussels lace curtains on Portman Square, and Aidan's troubled gaze followed the elongated netlike pattern, stretching across the soft wool carpet to where it stopped at Eugenia's feet. Looking up, she noted her friend's concerned expression. "You know me too well," Aidan stated, her lips trying to lift into a smile, but failing. "I never could hide anything from you."

Eugenia laughed. "Why would you want to? Especially since we've been as thick as thieves from the day we met."

"And in equally as much trouble," Aidan added, her smile finally blossoming. "I don't believe that anyone shall soon forget the pains we have caused over the years."

"Nor do I," Eugenia agreed, her laughter ringing forth again. "Yet, for every hour I spent in my room writing volume after volume on the abominations of unladylike behavior, solemnly swearing I would not commit such repugnancies again, the pleasure I derived from seeing the shocked expressions and raised eyebrows of the stuffy lot we call our peers was well worth the solitude and cramped fingers." She sighed. "But now our youthful follies are only a sweet memory." She noted Aidan's fading smile, then how her friend's perfect teeth worried along her bottom lip. "Aidan, you haven't done something to cause an uproar again . . . have you?"

Since Eugenia and her husband of six months, David Sommers, the Earl of Manley, had returned only this morning from their month-long holiday in Brighton, Aidan knew the latest round of gossip had not yet hit her friend's ears.

6

While the two girls had caused many a stirring among the peerage during their youth, Eugenia had settled into the mold of "proper lady" several years back. Unfortunately, Aidan had not, and she feared her friend's censure should she tell her of the incident in Hyde Park.

"Aidan, I can see it in your eyes. What have you done now?"

Taking a quick sip of her fast-cooling tea, Aidan gulped it down, then laughed disjointedly. "Done?" She shrugged. "Why, nothing."

Eugenia's blue eyes narrowed. "You can't fool me, so don't even try. From the look on your face, I'd say you've really done yourself in this time! Whom have you managed to scandalize now?"

Aidan found she couldn't quite meet Eugenia's gaze. Drawing a deep breath, she admitted in a barely audible voice, "Her Majesty, Queen Victoria."

Although she'd had to strain her ears to hear the words, Eugenia reacted like a cannon had discharged next to her. Her cup clattered around on its saucer, tea sloshing over its rim onto her lap, staining the silk skirt of her blue day dress. Yet she paid it no heed. *"Please,* Aidan," she implored, eyes searching frantically, "tell me you're teasing!"

Violet eyes finally met her friend's wide gaze, and Aidan shook her head. "I wish I were, but it's true." Then, lacking her normal spunk, she quietly told of the incident in Hyde Park, finishing with Victoria's words on the necessity of Aidan's finding a husband to keep her on the straight and narrow.

Despite herself, Eugenia laughed. "Perhaps Her Majesty is right. Maybe you do need a husband."

Aidan carelessly set her cold tea aside. "One who would tame my wild nature?"

"One who would share your passion for life," Eugenia countered, having heard the sarcasm in her friend's voice. "You're not wild . . . simply restless."

Aidan fidgeted in her seat, then sprang from the chair to pace the floor. Why couldn't she be out and about, enjoying herself as usual, instead of worrying over how she could possibly delay her intended marriage to a man she could not—would not!—abide as a mate. She'd do anything if she could only stop the ridiculous event altogether. But there seemed to be no way out—short of running away.

"If you were to find a special someone to love," Eugenia said softly, watching Aidan's to-and-fro motion over the carpet, "I'm certain these feelings of unrest, which you're continually experiencing, will subside. Mine did when I met David. He was the one element of true happiness lacking in my life. Once I found him, everything else seemed to fall into place."

Aidan stopped her pacing; a derisive laugh escaped her lips.

"Do you doubt my words?" Eugenia asked, ready to take issue.

"No. You and David were meant for each other. It was love at first sight for you both. But I've yet to meet a man who sparks even the slightest bit of interest within me. I'm beginning to think there's not a man alive whom I could love." Aidan fell into her seat. "Besides, it's too late for me to even think in those terms."

"Aidan, it's not too late," Eugenia said, holding back her smile. "I'd hardly call you a spinster at nineteen. There's plenty of time for—"

"No, there's not!" Aidan noted Eugenia's questioning gaze. "My father took Her Majesty at her word. He informed me this morning I'm to be wedded."

"Wedded? To whom?"

Aidan nearly choked on the name as she spat it from her throat: "The Earl of Sedgewinn."

"*Sedgewinn!* Why, he's old enough to be your—"

"*Father,* I know," Aidan said dryly, remembering the duke's reaction when she'd stated as much herself. "But, unfortunately, the earl is neither as handsome nor as charming as my father—when His Grace wishes to be, that is."

"Nor as young at heart as the duke," Eugenia supplied, remembering how she'd entertained a schoolgirl's crush on the handsome Duke of Atwood from the moment she'd first met him, eight years ago. "Surely His Grace was only using the earl's name in order to bring you around."

"If it were only true, Eugenia," Aidan said as she came to her feet again. Hands twisting anxiously, she paced the floor anew. "The contracts are to be signed within two weeks. Once done, we're to be married with all expediency."

How could her father do this to her? her heart screamed in painful rebellion. In all her girlhood dreams, Aidan had pictured herself in a marriage very much like that of her parents. Love and devotion had abounded between the pair, and Aidan dreamed of finding a man who would love her equally as much as her father had loved her mother. Suddenly she wondered if her father had forgotten how important the tender feeling truly was.

"I can't do it! I won't do it!" Aidan cried, angry tears brimming in her eyes, yet she fought against their spilling over. "I can't possibly marry a man I don't love. I don't even like him! I can't bear the thought of his hands on me."

A graphic vision of her forthcoming wedding night leapt into her mind, and Aidan shivered through and through. Seeing the reaction, Eugenia hopped to her feet and rushed to Aidan's side. "Calm yourself," Eugenia said, slipping her arm around Aidan's slim waist, leading her to the green-and-yellow-striped silk-covered settee. "There must be a way to extricate you from this mess. If we put our heads together, surely we can come up with something."

"What? Short of running away, I—"

"That's it!" Eugenia exclaimed.

"What's it?" Aidan asked, staring at her friend.

"Running away."

"I've already thought along those lines, but it won't work."

"Why?"

"First of all, with this month's allowance already spent and my inheritance held in trust for two more years, I've barely a farthing to see me past the old London gates."

Instantly Aidan wished she hadn't donated the last of her allowance to her favorite charity, an act which was done with regularity and secrecy. At the time, though, she'd never have imagined herself faced with such a thorny problem as she now was. She quickly swept aside her momentary regret, knowing the orphans' needs were far greater than her own. Besides, if she found it necessary, she could always borrow some money from Eugenia.

"Second," she continued, "once my father discovers I'm

gone, you know as well as I do, he'll come after me. And last of all, once he finds me—and I'm certain he will—I dare not think of the punishment he'd mete out. I'd probably be locked away in my room, only to be let out years from now, when I'm old and wrinkled.''

"True," Eugenia said, a touch of drollness in her voice. "But, still, by running off and publicly rebuffing the earl, you'd be saved from an unwanted marriage."

"With Sedgewinn, maybe," Aidan admitted. "But once the gossips have quieted, I might find myself saddled with someone equally as obnoxious or even less desirable, if that's at all possible."

"I see your point."

"Why, oh, why did the Queen have to make mention of a husband?" Aidan asked, not expecting an answer.

"Perhaps, with her own recent marriage and her first child due in five months, she wishes to see you as happy as she. I hear she's madly in love with Prince Albert—"

"And he's most attentive to her," Aidan cut in. "But Her Majesty's circumstances were far different from mine. No one forced her into an unwanted marriage. In fact, Victoria was the one who proposed to Albert."

Eugenia laughed. "Aidan, I believe that's the correct protocol. With Albert being a prince from the duchy of Saxe-Coburg-Gotha, as well as a second son, and Victoria being Queen of England, it was a trifle difficult for him to bend upon one knee and ask the hand of one whose power far exceeds his own."

"I know that," Aidan conceded. "But it's a bit unfair I can't be allowed to do the same."

"Why can't you?" Eugenia asked, a smile lighting her face and eyes.

Aidan blinked. "What? Propose?" She saw her friend's nod. "To whom?"

"From all the dashing young men you've refused, you can't expect me to believe there wasn't at least one you didn't find favor with."

"That's why I refused them, Eugenia. I found nothing intriguing about any of them. My heart did not a thing."

"I said nothing of love, Aidan. I was thinking more on the lines of compatibility . . . friendship. If there were only one in the lot who's still unattached and whom you think you could abide as a mate, then I'd say he'd be considerably better than the one who awaits you now."

"If I were to find someone, what then?"

"Speak to His Grace. From what you've told me, his main concern seems to be getting you installed under another's protection, freeing himself from his duties. Perhaps he will settle for someone other than the Earl of Sedgewinn to take on his responsibilities."

"Am I such a burden to him that he wishes only to be rid of me?" Aidan asked, then noted Eugenia's look of indulgence. "You need not answer. I'm well aware I've no one to blame but myself for this travesty." She sighed; her shoulders slumped in dejection. "If only I hadn't been so . . . so—"

"Impetuous?" Eugenia asked, her arm slipping around her friend's shoulders, and watched Aidan's bowed head nod in agreement. "It's not a flaw, Aidan. You simply have some girlish ways about you still."

Laughter broke from Aidan's lips. "You sound like someone's persevering aunt. You're only a year older than I, Eugenia."

"And a year wiser."

"A savant, you say?"

"Hardly. But you shouldn't be so down on yourself. There's still hope."

"Convince me."

"Let's say you're able to think of someone to link up with, someone you can abide, and His Grace refuses to change his mind about Sedgewinn. You could always elope, like David and I did."

"A simple solution for you, Eugenia." Aidan rose to pace the room, her lavender silk skirt brushing the highly polished mahogany furniture as she traipsed the area in agitation. "Your father was all for your elopement. Being the youngest of six girls, you saved him the expense of yet another wedding. It simply won't work in my case. The moment my father finds I'm gone, he'll enlist an army to come after me. I know him. No one crosses him and gets away with it. *Ever!*" She stopped and turned toward her friend. "Besides, there's no one to elope with!"

"Can't you think of one man . . . just *one?*"

Inside her head, Aidan quickly ran the list of dandies, fops, and titled gentlemen who'd requested her hand in marriage and scratched an imaginary black line through each. They might still want her, but as before, she wanted none of them. "No, not a one. It's useless, I tell you . . . useless!"

Suddenly the front door was flung open, crashing against the wall; a shout erupted in the entry, startling both women. Eugenia vaulted to her feet and rushed toward the sound of her husband's frantic voice. "What is it, David?" she asked, reaching the doorway, Aidan at her heels.

"There's been an attempt on the Queen's life! Come! Everyone's off to the palace to see if she's all right."

The two women rushed out the door, the Earl of Manley behind them, and swept down the steps into the carriage.

"Does Her Majesty still live?" Aidan asked anxiously. The bays lurched into a gallop, jerking her back into her seat as they rounded the square and turned left onto Portman Street, traveling south. Although she'd been angry with the Queen for suggesting she take a husband, Aidan never wished any evil upon Victoria.

"By all reports, yes," David said, his handsome face quite serious, blue eyes showing uncertainty. The thundering bays whipped the corner and headed west toward Park Lane, then south to Piccadilly. Tossed about in their seats, the trio felt as though they were on a violently pitching ship, caught in the midst of an intense storm, yet they voiced no protest, the Queen's welfare foremost in their minds. "But I wish to see for myself," David finally finished, retrieving his toppled hat from the carriage floor.

"What happened, David?" Eugenia asked as the carriage turned west onto Piccadilly.

"I have little information, except someone took a shot at Her Majesty and Albert. Other than that, I—" The carriage careened left around the corner at the western tip of Green Park to head down Constitution Hill, and instantly came to a bone-crushing stop, almost throwing David and Eugenia into Aidan's lap. "By the gods!" David exclaimed. "Would you look at it!"

Hundreds of carriages congested the street as the anxious

owners inside tried to make their way to the palace. A throng of pedestrians crushed the walkways, heading in the same direction. As their own carriage moved barely inches at a time, Aidan noted a crowd gathered on the opposite side of the street. Anxious questions were yelled to a man who was perched high on the shoulders of several others.

"Was Her Majesty injured?" called a woman's voice above the rest.

"No. Luckily, the fool was a bad marksman, considering he was but six paces away. He shot once and missed, then leveled a second pistol and fired again. Prince Albert shoved Her Majesty down in the seat, covering her with his own body."

"Hear, hear!" several in the group responded.

"Praise the Prince!" a few more harped.

When the crowd settled again, the man continued, "A group of us jumped the dimwit and wrestled him to the ground. When it was all over, the Queen and the Prince went on for their ride as though nothing had happened."

A loud chant rose to fill the air. "Long live the Queen! Praise be to the Prince!"

Aidan, Eugenia, and David joined in the salute until their carriage rolled beyond the joyous throng. Her violet eyes twinkling, Aidan laughed. "It seems the Prince Consort has suddenly gained the approval of the English. But only yesterday, the lot wished to ship him back to Saxe-Coburg."

"Indeed. We English are a touchy lot," David said, smiling. "Had Albert been anyone but another German, we might have accepted him better. But, with his show of bravery in risking his own life for our Queen's, I think the tide has turned in his direction. Perhaps the fates have deemed it so."

"Ho! I say! Lord Manley!" a masculine voice called, drawing the threesome's attention toward a young gentleman who had dashed into the street, dodging other carriages as he ran toward their own. "Might I beg a ride?"

"Certainly, Lord Edmonds. Hop aboard," David replied, stretching out a hand to assist Viscount George Edmonds into the still moving vehicle.

The carriage suddenly gained speed, and the viscount flopped into the vacant seat next to Aidan. He tipped his polished beaver top hat in his gloved hand, exposing a wealth of curly blond locks. "A thousand pardons, Lady Manley,"—he turned his attention to Aidan—"Lady Prescott." He smiled. "Forgive my intrusion, but there was such a crush on the sidewalk, I feared I'd be trampled in the exodus."

"Since we're all going in the same direction and have an extra space to share, you are most welcome to join us, Lord Edmonds," Eugenia replied, noting how the viscount's interested gaze lingered upon her friend. Soft brown eyes seemed to delight in her every move. "You have no objections, do you, Aidan?"

"Of course not," she said, smiling, her amethyst eyes inspecting the newcomer with rising interest.

Not until this very moment had she given much credence to Eugenia's suggestion she elope with one of her former suitors. But, then, she'd forgotten entirely about George Edmonds.

Although he was not overtly handsome, he was, nonetheless, passable. A pleasant young man, three years older than herself and almost a head taller, he had always shown the utmost courtesy to her. When Aidan had gently declined his proposal of marriage this past April while they were in attendance at a spring ball, she'd felt a bit of remorse, for it had been obvious George had been heartbroken. Yet, he'd risen from his knee, where it was bent upon the garden path, and smiled, stating quietly that he understood.

Since that night, she'd only seen him in distant passing. Perhaps her rejection had hurt him more than she'd realized, for it seemed he'd purposely kept himself at bay. She felt it a shame, too. Although she did not love George, she liked him, very much. Enough to marry? she wondered. *Perhaps the fates have deemed it so.* David's words, spoken a second before George's voice had caught their attention, rolled through her head, and Aidan decided perhaps the fates had at that.

"It's good to see you again, Lord Edmonds," Aidan said, her dazzling smile melting George's heart. "You've hurt my feelings by keeping yourself hidden all these past months. I trust nothing has happened to keep you away."

"I . . . I . . ." Suddenly tongue-tied, George fell silent; a spot of red crept up his fair skin, blotching his cheeks.

"Aha!" David interjected, saving an embarrassed George from answering. "We're at the palace. Hendricks," he called to his driver, "see if you can get us closer."

Hendricks looked at the sea of carriages, packed like fish into a tin, and frowned. "I'll try, sir. But I can't promise."

"Do whatever you can." As the carriage wended its way through the narrow avenues, slowly snaking toward the palace gates, David turned to George. "Yes, Aidan's right. You've been keeping yourself a stranger of late."

"I've been at my father's estate in Yorkshire, taking care of some business while he's away. I've only returned to London this past week."

"We're happy you're back, Lord Edmonds," Aidan said, and noted his surprised look.

Their open carriage suddenly snagged the wheel of another, halting their progress. While Lord Manley offered his profuse apologies to its startled occupants, Hendricks backed the team up, untangling them.

"Seems we've come to a standstill," David said, rising to his feet, glancing around him. "And if I'm not mistaken, those are the Queen's postilions over there." He pointed toward some uniformed riders, escorting an unseen conveyance. "They're still a ways off and seem to be having difficulty getting through all this traffic." Cheers erupted, swelling ever louder, confirming his words.

Eugenia stood and craned her neck. "Oh, David, I can't see a thing from here."

"Then, if you feel adventuresome, we can go it afoot. We might make the gates in time to see the Queen and the Prince."

"Oh, yes," Eugenia said excitedly. "Let's try."

"Shall we?" David questioned his guests.

Desperately needing a moment alone with George, Aidan searched for an excuse and found one. "I . . . I find I suddenly feel a bit faint from all the excitement." She noted Eugenia's raised brow, for her friend knew as well as she that nothing could make Aidan swoon. Not even the adder the two had come upon while searching the brush beside a rock wall as they looked for Aidan's riding crop, which she'd dropped when bounding the obstacle on her mare. While Eugenia looked as though she would come unhinged,

Aidan had simply stamped her foot and threatened to behead the creature if it didn't get back into its hole. Apparently the viper had understood, for it had slithered off in haste. "I really must beg off," she said, pressing the back of her hand to her cheek. "But you three go ahead. Don't be concerned about me." Her eyes locked with Eugenia's, relaying a subtle message. Her friend caught it.

"Oh, Aidan," Eugenia said with mock sympathy, fighting back her smile. "We can't possibly leave you here alone." Then disappointment tinged her voice. "We'll simply have to see the Queen some other time."

Suddenly finding his voice, George spoke up. "I will be most happy to stay with Lady Prescott, Lady Manley . . . if that's agreeable with her." He cast concerned eyes on Aidan.

"But, Lord Edmonds," Aidan objected softly, "you'll miss the—"

"The Queen is obviously alive and well. My thoughts lie with you, Lady Prescott. It would be most ungentlemanly of me to desert in your time of need. Likewise, there is no need for all of us to miss the event. Lord and Lady Manley can go without us."

"Well . . . if you insist," Eugenia said warily, feigned concern wrinkling her brow. "But I'd feel simply awful if something—" She noted Aidan's marked frown, warning her not to protest too much, lest George suddenly change his mind. "But, Lord Edmonds, since Aidan is in such capable hands—" A rising chorus grew louder, nearer, apprising everyone the Queen was fast approaching. "Come, David, let's go!"

To Aidan's relief, Eugenia snatched David's hand and began pulling him toward the palace gates. "Thank you, Lord Edmonds," she whispered weakly, offering a tentative smile after the pair had disappeared. "I do so hate that you should miss the excitement because of me."

Gentle brown eyes, filled with longing and concern, gazed deeply into hers. "I would never leave you, Aid . . . uh, Lady Prescott. Never."

Aidan noted the look of adoration in George's eyes, and a shadow of guilt darkened her soul. She could never return his affections, she knew. At least, not to the scope in which he offered them to her. Could she ever love him? she wondered. Only as a friend, she decided, truthfully, for she felt no spark within as she gazed at him, no stirring of her blood as he leaned close to her. Nothing whatsoever. And to ask him to join with her in marriage would be an unconscionable act. Especially when her motives were entirely self-serving. In the end, she very well might hurt George, more so than when she'd originally refused his proposal. He deserved far better than an indifferent wife; he deserved to be loved.

"You seem distressed, Lady Prescott," Lord Edmonds stated, his words breaking through her thoughts. "Are you feeling ill?"

"Yes and no," Aidan answered on a sigh. "In truth, George, I am distressed, but I'm not ill. Nor am I feeling faint. I used that ruse as a means to speak to you privately, but now . . . now I must confess I'd thought to take unfair advantage of you."

George's brow wrinkled. "I don't understand."

No longer able to hold his gentle regard, Aidan turned away. Her fingers plucked at a crease in her skirt. "My father has arranged for me to marry a man I cannot abide," she blurted, not knowing what else to say, or, for that matter, how to say it. "Since you'd asked for my hand once, I thought to propose we might—"

"Marry?" George asked hopefully, excitedly.

"Yes, but—"

"Oh, Lady Prescott, you don't know how happy this makes me," he said, his voice amplifying itself to be heard over the boisterous cries of "God save the Queen." He grasped Aidan's hand, pressing it to his breast. "Lady Pres—Aidan, I'd be most honored to have you as my bride."

"But, George," she shouted, tugging at her hand, yet he refused to release it. "You don't understand. It wouldn't be fair. I don't love you . . . not the way you deserve to be loved. I—"

"You will, Aidan," George countered, pulling her into his lean arms, not noticing how she'd instantly stiffened. "I promise, someday you will love me as much as I love you."

And as his lips lowered over hers, a wave of emotion swept the throng surrounding them, their cheers swelling to a roaring crescendo, rolling through Aidan like a forceful tide. Yet, in response to George, she felt nothing—nothing at all.

2

At precisely half-past eight, a loud knock sounded on the door of Westover House, a highly fashionable home located in St. James's Square. What now? Justin Warfield, the Duke of Westover, wondered, irritated with the lack of solitude he'd found in his own home of late.

Upon his return from France two weeks ago, there had been a continuous influx of well-wishers and curiosity seekers invading his privacy, day and night, half of whom he didn't know. No doubt, Justin thought cynically, the unexpected visitor was yet another eager father hoping to make an alliance between himself, the "much-sought-after" Duke of Westover, and the man's insipid virginal daughter. Would the lot ever leave him in peace?

The knocker fell again, and Justin bounded to his feet, tossing his newspaper aside. "Pitkin!" he shouted to his elderly butler. "Answer the blasted door!" He saw the thin white-haired man scurry past the sitting-room doorway. "I'm not at home—to *anyone!*"

The door gave a slight groan on its hinges, and an emphatic voice echoed through the vaulted entry, sounding vaguely familiar to Justin. A moment later, Pitkin appeared. "Lord Edmonds insists on seeing Your Grace."

Although he would have wanted it otherwise, Justin decided he couldn't very well deny an audience to George Edmonds. If he did so, his great-aunt Pattina, who was also George's godmother, would be furious with him and would undoubtedly make her displeasure known upon discovering his refusal. Not wishing to be the recipient of one of Aunt

Patti's verbal attacks, Justin acquiesced. "Send him in, Pitkin."

"I beg your forgiveness for the intrusion, Your Grace," George said, perusing the tall, broad-shouldered, dark-haired Duke of Westover, who was a half dozen years older than George's own twenty-two. "But it's most urgent that I see you."

Justin's silvery gaze inspected the shorter man through the fine breaks in his long dark lashes. Stalky of build, shoulders obviously padded beneath his gray coat, George appeared extremely anxious. "You seem as though you're on the verge of becoming unhinged, Edmonds," Justin commented while motioning his guest to one of the matching giltwood armchairs. "You weren't, by chance, involved in the plot to kill our Queen, were you?"

George's eyes widened. *"Me?* Never! Why would you ask such a thing?"

Justin fought the desire to roll his eyes. Edmonds never could tell when someone was joshing him. Even from childhood, George had been far too serious. But given his strict upbringing, his stiff demeanor was understandable. "I was merely jesting, George. If I've given offense, I beg your forgiveness."

"No offense was taken, Your Grace."

Justin seated himself; George followed suit. "So, George, what pressing matter brings you to my doorstep?"

"I need to ask a favor of you," George said, coming straight to the point, then watched as one of Justin's dark brows arched over an unreadable gaze. "I . . . I know it's presumptuous of me, but I cannot think of another person I can trust. If her father finds out, he'll have my head."

Justin's lips twitched as he tried to hold back a chuckle. "Are you intimating you've compromised some young maid?"

George blinked. "Heavens, no!"

The throaty chuckle did erupt. "Then, what are you trying to say, George?"

"I . . . I'm in love with a beautiful young lady who has consented, only a few hours ago, to become my wife. Her father, however, has made other arrangements. She's to be pledged to another. If we are to marry, we must elope within the next several days, or she'll be lost to me."

Justin frowned. "Forgive me if I seem a bit slow, but I don't understand how I fit into this."

"To pull it off, I'll need your assistance," George said anxiously, pleadingly.

"George, I'm not one to engage in clever little gambits," he lied, for his half-dozen love affairs had been precisely that. Once the hen was in the coop, he quickly lost interest. "Devices of intrigue are best left to someone—"

"Your Grace, I'm most hesitant about asking, but when I returned to my lodgings a short while ago, there was a message sent from Moorsfield, my father's estate. There's been a fire. The note made no mention how extensive the damage was, but with my father in India, on the Queen's business, I must leave within the hour to see to the repairs— that's if the place still stands. Dash it all!" George exploded, popping from his seat, his fists balled at his sides. "Just when she's finally changed her mind and declared she'll marry me, this has to happen!"

Justin viewed George at length. Collating the sketchy bits and pieces gleaned from the viscount's words, he gathered Edmonds had previously proposed to his intended, only to be rejected. But with an impending marriage, no doubt forced upon her, the young lady had suddenly changed her mind, George now being her matrimonial choice. Was poor, unassuming George simply the more palatable of the two offerings? Knowing George had very little experience with women, Justin feared the man was dashing headlong into disaster. In his eagerness to wed, he might very well be consumed by his ladylove, his heart devoured by the conniving woman. "Who is this . . . this woman?" Justin asked harshly.

Certain his request would be denied, George fell back into his chair, defeated. "Lady Aidan Prescott—the Duke of Atwood's daughter."

Atwood! Justin thought, masking his surprise, for less than two weeks ago Alastair Prescott had been one of the many numbers who'd pressed for a union between Justin and the man's daughter. Although Justin had refused *all* such requests, in as friendly a manner as possible, there were several odd occurrences shortly after his renunciation of Aidan Prescott, making Justin suspicious that Atwood nursed some sort of vengeance toward him.

The first was when, at auction, Atwood had beaten him out of a particularly fine thoroughbred Justin wanted to use for stud with his prize mares, stabled at Warfield Manor, his country home, several hours' drive north of London. The bidding had become heated, the numbers astronomically high. Hesitating a mere second to debate whether the stallion was actually worth the amount last bid, Justin heard the gavel fall. Surprisingly, Atwood, not his agent, signed the draft for the thoroughbred. Later Justin learned the duke had then sold the stallion to another bidder, who had dropped out much earlier, for a lesser sum.

Next came the sale of several pieces of coveted artwork, three Rembrandts included, that Justin wanted for his private collection. The outcome had been the same, with Atwood winning out. If Justin had had any doubts there was some sort of reprisal fixed against him, fostered by Alastair Prescott, those uncertainties were quickly set to rest. While in the midst of negotiating the purchase of a piece of prime land bordering Warfield Manor, suddenly all discussions were ended and the land sold, its new owner unknown. Yet all signs pointed to the Duke of Atwood, and Justin was certain he'd been the target of the scorned duke's ire.

"Do you love this Aidan Prescott?" Justin asked finally.

"With all my heart," George confessed.

Justin viewed Edmonds carefully. "Does she profess her love for you?"

The viscount's gaze shifted. "Sh-she looks upon me with affection. Sh-she—"

"Are you certain she's not simply using you to save her own skin?" Justin asked almost cruelly, and watched George blanch. Did the man have some reservations of his own? he wondered.

"She's agreed to be my wife," George stated firmly. "That's all that matters to me."

"Take care, friend, that she doesn't rip your devoted heart to shreds," Justin warned, his gaze steely. "You might wish to ponder your hasty decision a bit longer. On the morrow, after a long night's rest, things may come into sharper focus.''

"I don't need time to think on it," George stated adamantly, coming to his feet again. "My decision is made. I love her. I want Aidan as my wife. I have since the moment I first saw her. If I can't have Your Grace's help, I shall seek assistance elsewhere.''

Never had Justin seen George react so steadfastly. Yet the man's heart was involved. Foolish as it might have seemed, Justin found he could not deny George's request—whatever it was. "Sit, George, and tell me what it is I'm expected to do.''

"Your Grace, I'm most grateful," George said, a wide smile spreading across his usually serious features. "I was certain I could count on you.''

"On with it, George.''

"Quite. My plan was to elope with Lady Prescott, three days hence. If you could simply deliver Aidan to the inn at Gretna Green, I would be forever in your debt.''

Justin digested George's words. The prestigious Duke of Westover demoted to a mere delivery boy! he thought, smiling derisively to himself. Should his peers get wind of his entanglement in this, he'd be the laughingstock of all London. Yet, it might be well worth the gibes, especially if his involvement were purposely made public—after the fact. By playing the bearer of Cupid's arrow, he could at the same time gain reparation, for the Duke of Atwood's underhanded maneuvers would not go unpunished. "I'm to be entrusted with your bride's care and to safely deliver her into your arms at the Scottish border. Is that all?''

"No. I don't have time to communicate with her. I've hired a coach and it's waiting outside.''

Justin noted George's embarrassment and suspected the man felt somewhat inferior because he didn't own a conveyance himself. Since George's father, the Earl of Coxby, was noted for his niggardly ways, there was a fixed acceptance throughout the peerage of George's circumstances. No doubt, Justin thought, the elder Edmonds still retained the first farthing he'd ever clutched as a lad; but the father's tightfisted manner did the son little good. Justin watched as George slipped a sealed note from his breast pocket.

"If you could give her this"—he handed it to Justin—"it will explain why I had to leave so suddenly. I was to meet her tonight at Lord and Lady Quincy's soiree to finalize our plans. But if you could go in my place and account for my absence, I would be most grateful. The final arrangements must be made between the two of you with utmost expediency. I trust you'll keep this under wraps."

"I'm well noted for my clandestine affairs with the ladies, George. Once found out, I've already moved on to another," Justin said with a chuckle, and observed the surprised look in Edmonds' eyes. "You have no need to worry," he reassured him. "Your lady will be safe with me." Justin tucked the note into his pocket. "You *do* realize Lady Prescott shall have need to stop at an inn along the way so she may rest and refresh herself?" Justin saw George's nod. "It's a rather compromising situation," he cautioned. "If anyone should get wind of this, your bride's reputation might be ruined. As long as you understand the risks and have no qualms, then I foresee no problem."

"I trust Your Grace, emphatically."

Justin's brow arched ever so slightly. Given his reputation with the feminine gender, which in reality was more myth than fact, most men wouldn't allow their fiancées or their wives—not even their mothers!—within a mile of him. Either George truly felt he could entrust Lady Aidan Prescott into the Duke of Westover's hands without any fear whatsoever, or George was an extremely desperate man who hadn't pondered the full magnitude of his request. Although Justin knew, unequivocally, that nothing would happen—for he was highly selective, his personal tastes lending themselves to more experienced women, preferably beautiful young widows—he thought George rather naive. "Your confidence is most reassuring. If all goes well, in a short time you shall be a married man," Justin said, rising. "Now, I suggest you be off to make certain your bride has a place she can call home."

After conferring on the exact day, time, and place where the three would meet near the Scottish border, George vigorously pumped the duke's hand, then bade him farewell.

The door closed and Justin's lengthy strides carried him back into the sitting room, where he folded his long frame into his chair and tried to resume reading his paper. But he found he couldn't concentrate and tossed the thing aside. Springing to his feet, he crossed the room and poured himself a brandy; a dark mood settled over him.

Of all the nights for him to stay home, wanting to escape the crush of London society, he had to choose this one! Blast it all! Why had he consented to help George with this unseemly bit of chicanery. Dispatching young women across the countryside was not his idea of enjoyment! Should anything go wrong, it would be his head, not Edmonds'.

Then, again, this was not just any young woman. This was Lady Aidan Prescott, Alastair Prescott's daughter. Although he'd never had the pleasure of meeting the daughter, he'd certainly had the distinct dissatisfaction of encountering the father. And the thought of thwarting Atwood's noble plans for a lucrative alliance between the man's daughter and whomever Atwood had chosen for her was truly a catharsis that would free Justin of his anger, while at the same time enabling him to exact his own revenge.

"A fair-and-just reward," Justin said in salute, and downed the contents of his glass. "Pitkin," he called, setting the glass aside and angling toward the doorway, "have my coach sent round. I'm going out."

Aidan was seated in the ballroom at Lord and Lady Quincy's stylish home, located on Park Lane, across from Hyde Park, vigorously fanning herself as she watched the doorway for George. On her right sat Lady Manley.

"My hair is suffering from the stiff wind you're creating with that thing." Eugenia's hand caught Aidan's, stopping the strenuous motion. "What has you in such a dither?"

"Nothing," Aidan lied, for she'd not said a word to her friend about George Edmonds' proposal of marriage. Nor that they were to meet here tonight and finalize their plans. "I'm simply in one of my restless moods."

"Well, please don't be tempted to release your pent-up energies by doing something that might cause a stir. You'll only make your father more determined to rid himself of you."

"I promise to behave, Eugenia. You have nothing to fear."

Eugenia's fine brow rose skeptically. "I'll hold you at your word, Lady Prescott. This is one of the most prestigious parties of the season. Should you ruin this one, you'll never be invited to the Quincys' again. Nor, might I add, to any other party in London—ever."

Mischief danced in Aidan's violet eyes. "What do you think it would take to have me cast from the cradle of London society altogether?"

"Not much," Eugenia said blandly. "Why would you even wish for that to happen?"

"If I were a simple maid of common birth, then I could choose the man *I* wanted to marry."

Eugenia laughed lightly. "A misconception on your part, dear friend. Arranged marriages are prevalent among the commonplace as well as the peerage. You're fooling yourself if you believe otherwise. Besides," she said, her gaze running the length of Aidan's ivory satin gown, its low neck and elbow-length sleeves adorned in black Chantilly lace, "you'd look rather silly milking a cow in that garb." Eugenia's smile grew impish; she winked. "And we both know, dearest, your passions for the latest designs from Paris are insatiable. So I doubt you'd much enjoy the more mundane life, Aidan."

Aidan's light laughter tinkled through the air, clear as a bell, though her friend's statement was completely untrue. Actually, Aidan's reputation as a clotheshorse was unfounded. Her continuous shopping sprees were not to appease her boredom, thereby stocking her wardrobe with the latest in fashion, as many of her friends thought. Unknown to them all, her purchases were in the way of serviceable woolens, shoes, mittens, medicines, or whatever else the orphans might have need of. Not even Eugenia was aware of her secret enterprise. After all, Aidan truly believed that one did not find one's way into heaven by touting one's good works.

"A point I hadn't considered, Eugenia," she said, smiling. "You are right, of course." She glanced toward the doorway again, looking for George. "A milkmaid swathed in satin—"

Laughing violet eyes connected with a magnetic silvery gaze across a span of twenty paces, and Aidan instantly swallowed her words. Hopelessly, she stared at the tall, handsome stranger, his long-lashed eyes slowly measuring her, from the champagne-colored miniature rosebuds crowning her intricately styled coppery locks, downward over her creamy shoulders, to linger momentarily on her décolletage, then sweep to her ivory-satin-slippered feet peeking from beneath the hem of her gown.

A light flush crept upward from the erratic pulse that beat wildly in Aidan's throat to spread itself over her hot cheeks. Flustered by the stranger's raw appraisal, she quickly pulled her gaze away from the brazen man. Having noted his impeccable dress—his black evening attire molding itself to his broad shoulders and slim waist—she thought he'd displayed a lazy sort of nonchalance. Worldly and sophisticated, he had a devil-may-care attitude about him and an ego to match! Falsely denying any feminine interest in him, Aidan snapped open her black lace fan and began to cool her flaming face.

"Who is that man?" she whispered to Eugenia, her eyes downcast, for she dared not look at him again. Ridiculously, she still felt herself reeling from his intense gaze; an odd tingling sensation pricked along her entire body. "Do you know him?"

Eugenia glanced over the crowd. "Which one? There are at least eighty men in this room."

"The one not twenty feet from us. He's quite tall, with dark hair and silver eyes."

"Sorry, Aidan. I don't see anyone who fits your description. The nearest man to us is Lord Grimes, and I'd hardly call him tall. He's bald, as well."

"Are you certain?"

"See for yourself."

Aidan chanced a quick peek. Eugenia was right. Portly and short, Lord Grimes stood where the stranger had only moments before. Her confused gaze swept the room. He was gone. A frown marred her smooth brow. Had she imagined him? If so, why did she feel like a fish out of water, her breaths coming in shallow gasps?

"Is that he over there?" Eugenia asked, her closed fan pointing in the direction of the open French doors leading onto the balcony.

Aidan's gaze followed. "Yes," she said, noting how his dark head bent toward a rather striking blond. He seemed to be listening intently to the woman's every word. Suddenly he threw back his head. Deep-throated laughter rose into the air, shooting straight into Aidan's ears; a warm feeling trickled down her spine. "Who is he?" she asked, her eyes narrowing ever so slightly as she watched the coquettish blond tap his arm with her fan and flirtatiously smile up at him. For some unexplained reason, the woman's attentiveness annoyed Aidan. Or was it *his* masculine response to it which actually chafed her?

"Are you somewhere among the clouds?" Eugenia asked, snapping Aidan from her thoughts. "I'd suggest that if you're entertaining any thoughts of exchanging him for Lord Sedgewinn, don't. You'd be far worse off."

"Why?"

"Have you ever heard tell of Justin Warfield, the notorious Duke of Westover?" Aidan nodded, her gaze still on the tall stranger. "Well, my naive little friend," Eugenia said, "you're looking at him."

Just then the Duke of Westover's gaze captured Aidan's. Holding it a long, measuring moment, he glanced away, the blond, once again, the target of his lazy regard. Aidan drew a steadying breath. What was wrong with her?

"The woman with him is the Honorable Mrs. Farley Danvers—Cynthia, I believe. Yes, Cynthia. She's the daughter of Sir John Stone. It's said she *is* or *was* the duke's mistress. No one seems to know which."

"And what does the Honorable *Mr*. Danvers say of their sordid behavior?" Aidan asked priggishly, passing lofty judgment on the couple and their blatant love affair, which normally was unlike her.

"Not much, I suppose. He's been dead nearly a year."

Aidan's head snapped around, her eyes questioning.

"Westover had nothing to do with it. Danvers died of typhoid. According to the gossips, the duke stays clear of married women and virgins. He prefers experienced, unattached females. You might meet the latter requirement, but certainly not the former. Although many a woman has tried to capture his heart, he chooses to remain single. Just look at how they all gape at him." Eugenia indicated the legions of women, their yearning gazes turned on Justin Warfield. Aidan's own gaze stopped momentarily on each one as Eugenia's fan pointed them out. "Given the chance, he'd break all their hearts. Don't tempt fate, Aidan."

"I have no intention of doing so."

"What won't you do?" asked David as he balanced three glasses of champagne in his hands. "Sorry I'm late"—he handed his wife and Aidan their glasses—"but there was such a cram around the refreshment table, I thought to be injured in the press." He flipped the tails of his coat aside and sat next to Eugenia, then sipped from his glass. "Now, Aidan, what is it you refuse to do?"

"I refuse to say," Aidan teased as the melodious strains from the orchestra suddenly filled the grand ballroom.

"Oh, David, a waltz!" Eugenia cried. "Let's dance."

"Dare we leave Aidan unattended?" he questioned, a puckish light entering his blue eyes. "Since His Grace could not be here, we promised we'd keep a watchful eye on his daughter the night through."

Aidan laughed. "I promise I shan't disappear."

"We'd best disappear," Eugenia commented. "The wolves are descending on the lamb." She motioned toward a half-dozen of Aidan's hopeful suitors who were bearing down on them, each from a different direction. "If we're to be spared the nips and snarls as they fight over her, we'd best leave—now!"

"Don't go!" Aidan cried, but Eugenia had already pulled David into the crowd, leaving her to fend for herself.

Like bees drawn to the sweet nectar of a flower, the eager swains swarmed around her, each requesting a dance. Annoyed, Aidan was tempted to swat the lot away. Where was George? she wondered. Was he having second thoughts, the same as she? Her eyes searched the doorway again, while she half-listened to the men's wrangling chatter.

"I asked first," insisted the Honorable Mr. Orville White.

"I beg to differ with you, sir," countered Lord Jeremy Roberts, a lesser son of a marquess. The others joined in, bickering over who had invited her first; Aidan closed her eyes and gritted her teeth.

"Excuse me, gentlemen," a smooth, deep voice interrupted, and Aidan's eyes opened to meet a lazy silver gaze; an odd warmth flooded her body. "I believe rank has its privilege. Lady Prescott, if you will?"

Aidan stared at the outstretched hand. Strong, yet gentle, she thought, surveying the long fingers and the wide, deeply lined palm. "I . . . I . . ." she stammered, furious with herself that she couldn't get her refusal past her lips.

At the flash of indignation in her expressive violet eyes, Justin's chiseled lips cracked into a knowing grin. "I'm honored, Lady Prescott, that you've chosen me as your partner." Without a second's hesitation, he lifted Aidan's gloved hand from her lap, pulled her to her feet and into his arms, and swept her onto the dance floor, all in one swift move. With their mouths agape, the six would-be suitors stared after the pair.

Aidan's feet stumbled over themselves as she fought to break free of Justin's embrace. "What do you think you're doing? Release me!"

"It would be a mistake if I did," he countered with a chuckle, for he'd noted how her feet refused to keep step with his own. He winked, a teasing smile lighting his face; Aidan felt the effects of it to her toes. "You really should take lessons. Your partners' insteps might suffer less, if you did."

Feeling threatened by his male charm, Aidan quickly hid behind her anger. A mutinous glare entered her eyes. How dare he intimate she was a horrid dancer? Especially when she hadn't consented to be his partner in the first place! "Sir, unhand me!"

"If you insist." Justin dropped his arms, and Aidan floundered as her legs buckled. Instantly he grabbed her arm, pulling her against his solid length; his own arm encircled her waist. His familiar touch shocked Aidan; she stiffened. Feeling her resistance, Justin smiled to himself. An untried virgin, he thought, knowing one of his questions had been answered. The pressure of his arm eased, and he smiled. "Now, let's try again, shall we?" Not waiting for Aidan's assent, Justin began whirling her around the floor again. "One, two, three, one, two, three . . . that's it. You do know how to dance."

Feeling the crowd's curious stares upon them, Aidan glared up at the "notorious" Duke of Westover. "Sir, we have not been introduced," she spouted primly. "It's highly improper for us to be dancing like this. I insist—"

"Justin Warfield, the Duke of Westover." Laughter rumbled from his solid chest. "By the look in your eye, I'd say my reputation has preceded me."

Aidan blinked. What could she say? *It most certainly has, Your Grace. By the way, is it all true—the women, I mean? Scores and scores, you say. Upon my word! You must be an exceedingly busy man. When do you find time to sleep?* Instead she mumbled, "I've never heard of you."

Liar, he thought, then said, "But I've heard of you, Lady Prescott." He noted her questioning gaze. "George has sent me."

Aidan missed a step and Justin compensated, their rhythm never faltering. "George? Where is he?" she asked anxiously. "Has something happened to him?"

"Not to him, personally. There's been a fire at his father's estate. He had to leave to attend to the repairs. He's asked that I come in his place and make the necessary arrangements to get you safely to Gretna Green."

"You?"

Justin laughed, drawing the attention of those nearest them. Seeing their raised eyebrows and condemning expressions, Aidan felt like slipping through a crack in the floor. If her father ever learned she'd been held in the Duke of Westover's arms, he'd have her shipped off to a convent on the morrow. Worst yet, he'd probably drive Sedgewinn and herself straight to Gretna Green before the earl got wind of her scandalous behavior! Never mind, she'd done everything in her power to escape the rakish duke's hold!

His laughter subsided. "Then you *have* heard of me," he said, his handsome lips retaining a roguish grin. He twirled her through the open doorway, onto the balcony, and pulled her to a quiet corner. Edging a hip onto the stone balustrade, he released her struggling hand and slipped George's note from his inner pocket. "This will confirm my words," he said, handing it to her.

Breaking the wax seal, Aidan unfolded the note and angled it to catch the moon's rays. "How do I know this is from George?" she asked, suddenly doubting the signature was authentic.

"Who else knows of your plan to elope?" he countered, folding his arms over his broad chest.

Aidan noted how his well-toned muscles swelled beneath the sleeves of his black coat, stretching the material. "N-no one," she said, her gaze quickly climbing to his. It was a mistake.

Lazy eyes assessed her, raking her from head to foot. "George said you were beautiful." The crook of his finger met her chin while he examined her features in the moonlight. High, sculptured cheekbones, a classically straight nose, full trembling lips, huge violet eyes framed with long dark lashes, and flawless skin kissed by moonbeams satisfied his inquiring eyes. "Said he'd fallen in love with you the moment he first saw you. I didn't believe him . . . not until I beheld you myself."

Aidan found herself caught up in his tantalizing words. His deep-toned voice mesmerized her as his magnetic gaze drew her. An odd twitter centered itself in the nether regions of her stomach. Then she felt the touch of his thumb, gliding softly across her parted lips; instantly she stepped back. "You, sir, are no friend of George's."

"And you, Lady Prescott, are not in love with him."

"How dare—"

"I dare because it is the truth. You are using George to save your own hide."

"You know nothing of my feelings for George. What's in my heart is none of your business."

"Isn't it?" Justin asked, coming to his feet, backing her against the balustrade. "I've known George since he was in swaddling clothes. Although we are not the closest of friends, I feel, in some ways, responsible for him. He's had a tough go of it while growing up, and he sees his marriage to you as his one chance for true happiness. I'll not let you destroy him for your own selfish reasons."

Aidan stared at the stranger who seemed bent on chiding her. A dark lock of hair curled over his wide forehead; carved cheekbones slashed upward to his temples, emphasizing the hollows beneath. Steely, long-lashed eyes, topped by dark brows, kneaded themselves into a censuring frown, nearly meeting above his straight nose. Sculptured nostrils flared as if in anger. Chiseled lips, the lower a bit more prominent than the upper, pulled themselves into a tight line above a cleft chin. His strong, firm jaw was set; a muscle worked along its angular lines. "You're mistaken, sir," Aidan defended herself, even though she knew he spoke the truth. "I hold great fondness—"

"But you don't *love* him." He stepped closer to her, almost pressing his masculine length against her trapped form. Before Aidan had the chance to flee, he caught her arms, pulling her hard against him; his clean breath fanned over her face. "I promised George I'd deliver you into his loving embrace at Gretna Green. I will not go back on my word—despite my reservations. However, Lady Prescott, after your marriage, should I learn you've hurt George in any way, you will answer to me. Understood?"

Wide, frightened eyes stared up into his; Aidan nodded.

"Then be in the mews behind your home at midnight on the morrow. One traveling case is all you'll need. And make it small." He released her as though she'd singed his hands. "Until then, Lady Prescott, I bid you good night."

Her voice caught in her throat, Aidan stared after him as he strode into the brightly lit ballroom. Using the stone balustrade for support, she steadied herself; then, on tottering legs she followed. Dared she let this man escort her to Gretna Green? Why, of all men, had George chosen Justin Warfield? Anyone but him! she thought, her stomach suddenly flitting nervously as she paused near the French doors. She took a deep breath, hoping to regain her poise, then smoothed her satin skirt, propped her head high, and crossed the threshold.

Instantly her eyes snagged the wickedly handsome Duke of Westover as he whirled the gorgeous Cynthia Danvers onto the dance floor. His strong arm held the blond improperly close as their feet kept perfect time. Laughter rang from his throat when the smiling blond, her blue eyes boldly flirting, whispered something to him. Its deep timbre ricocheted through Aidan; then, for a brief moment, his gaze met hers. Its silvery sparkle turned to cold hard steel, and Aidan felt she'd been rent in two by a frigid blade.

Severing their gazes, she turned her head and shakily made her way toward her vacated chair, praying her legs would carry her that far. Moments later, Eugenia and David found Aidan seated, quivering and pale, and immediately whisked her from the party. Assessing silver eyes watched with masculine interest as she fled the room.

3

Aidan's unbound hair flowed down her back; her ecru silk dressing gown brushed against her legs as she paced her bedroom floor, the sound of her barefoot tread losing itself in the thick wool carpet. Although the bright morning sunlight blazed through the lace curtains to bound off the cream-colored walls and set the giltwood furnishings aglitter, the cheery atmosphere did little to lighten Aidan's troubled thoughts.

How could she possibly go through with her elopement? she wondered, her hands twisting anxiously. Especially when she was to be accompanied to Gretna Green by the dark-and-brooding "notorious" Duke of Westover! She remembered how his steely gaze had sliced into her while his powerful masculine form had trapped her against the balustrade, the deep timbre of his cold voice threatening her with instant reprisal should she hurt George. Aidan felt the abrupt lurch of her heart. Suddenly she went weak.

Certain her quaking legs would give way, she caught the bedpost and sank onto the down-filled mattress. What was she to do? she silently asked, possibly for the hundredth time in the past half-hour. Her bowed head shook in response to her indecision. Last night, when she'd fled the

Quincys' soiree, she'd been set on calling off her elopement with George. But when she'd returned to Atwood House, Eugenia and David at her heels, she'd come face-to-face with the Earl of Sedgewinn.

"Ah, my dearest child," he'd said, stepping away from her father's side, making Aidan freeze in her tracks as she crossed the marble foyer. His lust-filled beady brown eyes had examined her from head to toe as he moved indecently close to her. "His Grace and I had hit upon a snag in our negotiations. But as I look upon your considerable beauty, I feel compelled to yield on the particular issue which has set us apart. I want nothing to delay our marriage."

Upon hearing his words, Aidan had felt the blood drain from her face; bitter bile surged into her throat as she'd stared at the galling man. He was large-boned and stocky; his ruddy complexion had stood in utter contrast to his thatch of white hair and bushy black eyebrows. His meaty hands grasped the silver knob of his walking cane as he'd leaned on it for support, relieving the pressure on his gout-riddled right foot. He was overindulgent in all he did, and she'd imagined his lovemaking leaned toward brutality, his own lustful needs coming first. Why else had he already outlived two wives and now sought a third?

Without a word, she'd yanked up a handful of skirt, brushed past the leering Earl of Sedgewinn, and fled across the foyer and up the white marble staircase, heading to her room, her father's and Eugenia's words climbing upward behind her.

"Daughter, come back here this instant!"

"Forgive her, Your Grace. Aidan suddenly took ill at the soiree. David and I brought her home as quickly as possible. She seeks her bed so she may rest. I'm certain she will be well on the morrow."

Before Aidan had turned the corner, however, she'd heard Sedgewinn's statement, proclaiming he hoped she was a "healthy broody." Eugenia's shocked gasp and David's harsh admonishment on using such crude language in front of his wife followed, whereupon the duke apologized to Eugenia and David, said good night to Sedgewinn, and had Elsworth show the lot out. Secured behind her locked door,

Aidan had listened in mutinous silence as her father pronounced heatedly, "He's to be your husband, so I suggest you show him some courtesy. It will go better for you if you do!"

Having spent a sleepless night debating what she should do, Aidan found she was no closer to an answer than when she'd arrived home last evening. One thing was certain, though. She would not marry Sedgewinn! Even if it meant she'd have to sell all her clothing and jewels and use the proceeds to flee her homeland, no doubt to live a pauper's life somewhere abroad, she'd do it! She'd do anything! So long as she could escape Sedgewinn's odious clutches! She'd even be willing to endure Justin Warfield's piercing stares and cutting remarks as the reproving duke ferried her overland to Gretna Green. Or would she?

A picture of the arrogantly handsome duke painted itself in her mind, creating a vivid portrait. Devilishly sophisticated, suavely urbane, he had the distinct ability to bewitch the feminine gender with his blatant masculine appeal. Was she any different from the scores of women who threw themselves at his feet?

Yes! she insisted, bounding from the side of her bed to pace the floor again. She disliked him—*immensely!* The arrogant boor!

A knock sounded on her door, and an agitated Aidan called sharply, "What is it!"

"Lady Manley has come callin'," her maid, Penny, answered through the heavy wooden door. "Shall I tell her your ladyship is not acceptin' visitors?"

Aidan traversed the carpet and opened the door with a jerk, startling her maid. "Show Lady Manley up." The maid bobbed her head and curtsied, then quickly turned to do as bidden. "And, Penny . . ." Aidan said softly; the maid swiveled toward her. "I apologize for my abruptness." She noted the maid's accepting smile. "Some hot chocolate would be nice for Lady Manley and myself."

"Yes, ma'am. I'll fetch it quick."

Moments later, Eugenia swept into Aidan's bedroom to wrap her arms around her friend in a gentle hug. "I hardly slept last night worrying about you. Are you still feeling ill?" Eugenia released Aidan. "Come, let's sit." She pulled her friend toward the two chairs angled near the gold-veined white marble fireplace. "Tell me what happened after we left you."

"Not much," Aidan replied vapidly. "My father *politely* informed me, since Sedgewinn was to be my husband, I'd best show the earl some courtesy. It would go better for me if I did."

"Why, the man's nothing but a vulgar lecher," Eugenia returned, incensed. "How can His Grace expect you to show the man anything except contempt?"

"A good question, Eugenia. I had always dreamed of finding my heart's mate—to have a loving relationship like my parents had. But my father's mind is set. I'm to marry Sedgewinn. I suppose he's forgotten the importance of love," she said of her sire.

"Oh, Aidan," Eugenia said, sympathetic tears shimmering in her expressive blue eyes, "I can't believe he's truly forgotten. But just the same, we must find a way to get you out of this terrible fix. Even David said he'd be willing to intercede on your behalf. I've never seen him so enraged. He was ready to call Sedgewinn out for the earl's sheer lack of manners. Since David is more a diplomat than a warrior, I'd never have expected him to react so heatedly. It took me an hour to calm him down."

Surprised by Eugenia's words, Aidan offered a grateful smile and some sound advice. "Tell David I appreciate his gallantry, but he's not to be running off half-cocked, challenging Sedgewinn to a duel. Despite the earl's age and girth, he's purported to be an expert marksman. David should not take the chance, it's true. Not for me, at least."

"Nor for me," Eugenia agreed, willing to forgive Sedgewinn's crude words simply to keep her husband alive. Without David, she was nothing. "But we must find a way to keep you from that horrid man's grasp."

Aidan noted how Eugenia visibly shuddered, her face pinching up like she'd just swallowed a draft of castor oil, and she assumed her friend had envisioned herself, like Aidan had the day before, in the earl's bed.

"How could any woman possibly allow that disgusting man to touch her?" Eugenia asked, her lovely face tormented by the thought.

"I imagine, Eugenia, it was not a matter of their allowing it," she stated of his two previous wives.

"They were forced, you mean," Eugenia said without emotion, and saw Aidan's nod.

"If you'll recall how the last Lady Sedgewinn's frail arms were a multitude of colorful bruises, which she always explained away with a nervous laugh, relaying to all how utterly clumsy she was, I think you'll see she was actually trying to hide the truth."

"Yes. The way she'd suddenly stiffen when Sedgewinn was near. And her eyes had the look of pure fright in them. Until last night, when I . . . I saw for myself the raw look in his own eyes as he beheld you, like you were a tempting morsel he'd gladly devour in one gluttonous bite, I'd never have dreamed him to be so . . . so . . ."

"Barbarous?"

Eugenia nodded, her eyes wide with concern. "Oh, Aidan, I can't allow this to happen to you!"

Aidan quickly slipped from her chair. It was her turn to comfort her friend, just as Eugenia had comforted her the day before. "Don't fret over it," she said, squatting beside Eugenia, her arm encasing the blond's quaking shoulders. "I'll talk with my father today and tell him what I suspect of Lord Sedgewinn. Once he's apprised of the earl's darker side, I'm certain he'll change his mind." Her words had come out steady and were said with much more bravado than she'd actually felt. "He's still angry with me because I haven't yet apologized for insulting him."

"You insulted His Grace?" Eugenia questioned, then wondered why she had asked, for there was nary a time the two didn't quarrel without Aidan upbraiding her sire. Or vice versa. Far and away they were too much alike, each seeing his or her own worst flaws in the other, neither willing to admit they possessed the exact same traits. "What on earth did you say this time?"

"I said the earl was nearly as old as he was."

"That's true enough."

"I called Sedgewinn a doddering old man."

"Aidan! How could you? Especially when your father's so sensitive about his age. You've trampled his ego into the ground. Let's hope there's still a chance of resurrecting it."

"Indeed."

"If an apology doesn't work, then what?"

Then I'll elope with George Edmonds! But Aidan didn't voice her thought, for if her planned *tête-à-tête* with her father should fail, then she didn't wish to involve Eugenia and David. Once her father found she was missing, Lord and Lady Manley would be the first ones he'd question on her whereabouts. If they knew nothing, he couldn't accuse them of being involved and they wouldn't have to suffer his indignant wrath. But first, she had to make a concerted effort to appease her father's wounded pride. Once that was done, surely he wouldn't still wish to marry her off to a wife beater, *would he?*

"Then what?" Eugenia repeated.

"Then I'll take myself off to a convent. Once I've cloistered myself for life, His Grace can't very well find fault with me anymore."

"I pity the poor sisters," Eugenia said, laughing, her spirits rising. "Although patience is a virtue, of which I'm certain the good nuns have in abundance, they are still human. Within a month they will probably boot you through the gates and wash their hands of you."

"You're probably right," Aidan said, her laughter joining Eugenia's. Would she actually run off to a convent? she wondered, just now thinking of that escape route as a viable option. No, she decided, knowing piety belonged to the pious. Her own sins were far too many. She was too vain, too temperamental, too impetuous, too restless, too . . . too *everything!* to take the same vows as the good sisters had. To do so would be out-and-out hypocrisy! It would never work! "But in the interim," Aidan continued, playing the game out, "I'll have time to think of another way to avoid Sedgewinn's clutches—that's if my renunciation, in which I've shown I prefer the nunnery over a marriage to him, hasn't chased him off. I suspect his ego exceeds my father's."

"For your sake, I hope it works." Then Eugenia suddenly blurted, "I never did ask about Lord Edmonds. What transpired when David and I left you?"

"Nothing," Aidan lied freely. "Nothing at all."

Eugenia eyed her a long moment and was ready to question her friend further when Penny came into the room with

their hot chocolate. While sharing their favorite drink together, Aidan proceeded to convince Eugenia that all would
be well once she'd talked to her father. By the time Eugenia
left, a scant half-hour later, Aidan was certain she'd managed to allay her closest friend's fears. Unfortunately, all
her soothing words, stated with the utmost confidence, had
done little to ease her own.

After bathing and dressing, Aidan took the stairs, heading
toward her father's study. But as her feet hit the white
marble floor, she was informed by Elsworth: "His Grace is
out today. He will not be back until supper."

"Did he say where he was going?"

"No, Lady Prescott. Not a word."

Aidan watched as the stoop-shouldered, white-haired man
continued on down the hallway, heading toward the back of
the house. Why, of all days, did her father have to choose
this one to go out? she wondered fitfully. If she weren't
given the chance to speak with him, convince him she was
willing to mend her ways, and beg his forgiveness for being
such a disobedient daughter, she'd have no other choice but
to elope with George.

As she stood alone in the foyer, sunlight glittered through
the large glass cupola, two stories above her, and the area
around her was filled with a mystical brilliance. A knowing
silvery gaze suddenly leapt into her mind's eye, and she
remembered how it had raked her from head to toe. Chiseled, extremely masculine lips cracked into a wide, mocking grin, exposing even white teeth above a strong cleft
chin; a small dimple appeared beside that masterful mouth.
Deep, sensuous laughter seemed to fill her head as she felt
a strong arm encircle her small waist to twirl her around the
floor in an adept, fluid motion. Instantly hot fire raced the
length of Aidan's veins as she envisioned the Duke of
Westover, handsome and sophisticated, looking down at
her; her legs abruptly went all rubbery.

Shaking her head to clear it, she clasped the railing for
support and pulled herself up the stairs, praying with all her
might: *Father, please come home! Please!*

At half-past seven, Aidan sat in the small sitting room
just off the foyer, waiting. Jumpy as a cat that had been

tossed onto a bed of hot coals, she started at every sound. Five times she'd bounded from her chair, thinking she'd heard the front door open, certain her father had returned. But each time she did so proved to be a false alarm, for her overly sensitive ears had been playing tricks on her.

As she sat in the solitude of the room, she again practiced her apology, like she had all day. *Father, forgive my transgressions—* No! That's not right! she admonished sharply, silently. She'd sound as though she were in a confessional, begging for the Lord's forgiveness, and her father would never believe her penance was real. Not using those words.

Father, I know we've had many differences of opinion in the past, mainly because of my lack of forethought, my— The sound of the front door opening interrupted Aidan's thoughts. Voices sounded in the entry, and she hopped from her chair, scurrying to the sitting-room doorway. Her legs abruptly stopped their hasty journey; her bright, smiling face froze into a brittle mask. Warm violet eyes turned cold as ice when they pinpointed her nemesis: Lord Sedgewinn!

"Ah, Aidan, dearest," he said, smiling like a cat that was about to pounce upon a trapped canary, "you look lovely, my dear. Lovelier than I could ever have imagined."

Aidan had bristled at the use of her given name and his familiar tone, for she'd not awarded him permission to call her such or speak to her so. And as far as she was concerned, she never would! *Lecher,* she thought, her stomach suddenly lurching, nausea overtaking her. Then her gaze hit her father's and she caught his stern, unspoken message, which said: *Courtesy, daughter! Remember it!*

Masking the angry light in her eyes, she squared her shoulders, smoothed the skirt of the yellow silk dress she wore, and folded her hands together at her waist, presenting a ladylike stance. If she was expected to play the game, she'd play it well. And to the bitter end, she decided, lifting her smile higher. "Lord Sedgewinn," she said, barely hiding the venom in her voice, "how nice to see you again."

With his hat and gloves handed off to a silent and overly stiff Elsworth, he ambled toward Aidan with the use of his cane. "I trust you've recovered from your sudden illness?" he asked, his raw gaze assessing her from head to toe.

Her back held rod straight, Aidan refused to allow his lewd appraisal to shake her. Although his words seemed a genuine inquiry, filled with gentlemanly concern, his meaning was quite apparent to her. He wanted a strong, healthy body beneath him in his bed. One that would be able to withstand his brutal invasion whenever the urge struck him. Which, no doubt, was several times daily. She'd slit her wrists before she'd ever submit to the likes of him! she decided, her eyes narrowing ever so slightly. "I'm quite recovered, thank you," she said airily. "It was overly warm last evening, and the press of several hundred people in one room at the Quincys' made it unbearable." It was a lie, she knew, for it had been Justin Warfield's threats—and his overpowering masculinity—that had sent her packing. "The heat made me feel a bit light-headed, that's all," she finished, trying to erase the handsome young duke's face from her mind. But the memory of it would not leave her.

"Good . . . good," Sedgewinn answered, obviously pleased to hear her explanation. "I'd hoped it was little else."

"Might I offer you a brandy?" Alastair Prescott asked, coming up beside the earl. His approving gaze settled on his daughter, telling her he was pleased with her actions.

"Supper will be served in five minutes, Your Grace," Elsworth's nasal tone interrupted. "Shall I set an extra place?"

No! Aidan thought wildly, then wondered if she'd actually shouted the word aloud. Realizing she hadn't, she quickly said a round of prayers that the answer would be . . .

"Yes," the duke pronounced, and Aidan's hopes plummeted. If there truly was a God, she was certain his ears were closed to her. Had she been so terribly bad, so terribly wicked, that He wished to see her unduly punished for the rest of her natural life? she wondered. *Hell* could be no worse, she decided as she heard her father's words: "Lord Sedgewinn will be joining us."

In the dining room, framed portraits of her ancestors stared down at her from the mint-green walls as Aidan sat frozen in her seat. Violet eyes watched Lord Sedgewinn as he attacked his third plate, which was heaped to overflowing and covered completely with the rich sauces Cook had prepared. His weak, pudgy chin dripped with the same, for he never bothered to use his linen napkin once, and Aidan found she'd lost her appetite for the delicious fare set before her. With his mouth full, he talked incessantly and Aidan fought to swallow the bile which had, long ago, risen in her throat. It refused to go down.

"I'm certain Aidan will be an exceptional wife," he said to the duke, taking another bite of his food. "She's of sound breeding, good bloodlines, and has a solid frame. We should present you with many grandchildren, Your Grace—the first within a year of our nuptials."

Aidan's gaze bounced off the earl and attached itself to her father, hoping to see his reaction. His face was a blank mask. But she noted how his hand had curled into a tight fist, its knuckles mottled white, where it rested upon the table next to his empty plate.

"Yes," Sedgewinn continued his monologue, bits of chewed food spewing unappetizingly from his loose lips to splash onto the once pristine white tablecloth, "we should have a large brood that will make you proud in no time at all."

Valiantly Aidan fought the urge to shove herself from the table and run, screaming, from the room. Gritting her teeth, she settled her gaze on her own untouched plate. She breathed deeply, closed her eyes, and wondered if the obnoxious man would ever stop eating and talking. If she could only have a private word with her father, she thought, but he seemed content to sit and listen to the ceaseless ramblings of his future son-in-law. How, she could not fathom!

Her eyelids parted and she glanced at the clock on the sideboard. It was nearly ten past nine. In less than three hours Justin Warfield would be behind the walled gardens, waiting for her in the mews, the cobbled alleyway which led to the carriage houses and stables belonging to the grand houses in Grosvenor Square. She considered whether she'd be there herself, then prayed the answer would be no. If she could only speak to her father; apologize to him; swear she'd never disobey him again; fall at his feet and beg his forgiveness. If he would only listen; take her into his fatherly embrace; tell her she was excused, that he would not marry her off to Sedgewinn. Then she'd have no reason to flee with the Duke of Westover. None whatsoever!

Then suddenly another thought hit Aidan. If she could not persuade her father, and she had to follow through on her marriage to George, what would she do if her escort never showed? Given his derision on the elopement, he might very well change his mind. A promise or not, he might go back on his word, determined to save George from the conniving, manipulative little she-devil he believed her to be! Oh, heavens! What would she do then?

"Ah, excellent meal, Your Grace," Sedgewinn said, leaning back and patting his engorged belly. "Excellent, indeed."

Aidan watched as he finally took his splattered napkin from his lap to wipe his mouth, only to leave several unsightly smudges behind. *Pig!* she thought as she looked down to see his plate nearly as clean as when it had been set before him empty.

"Lord Sedgewinn and I will be retiring to the library to finish our negotiations," her father said, eyeing her closely. "Having heard most of the terms, do you have any questions?"

Yes! her mind screamed. *Why are you doing this to me?* Instead, she leveled her subdued gaze on her sire and said, "I'm certain you have my best welfare in mind. I will accede to your wishes on the matter. I'm willing to marry" —she'd almost choked on the word—"Lord Sedgewinn. If that's what you feel will give me the most happiness, I shall do as you ask."

Alastair viewed his daughter a long, searching moment, one silvery brow arched. A pleased look suddenly entered his blue eyes, and he reached out and patted her cold hand as it rested on the table. "Daughter, I promise what transpires tonight will be done with only you in mind." He turned to his guest. "Sedgewinn, shall we?"

The duke rose from his chair, his face a mask of utmost courtesy. For a moment—one brief moment—Aidan thought her father was going to relent, but with his next words, her hopes plunged anew.

"Let's get on with it, Sedgewinn, and see if we can iron

out the few remaining wrinkles in the contract." He cast a bright smile on the man. "Since Aidan is so eager to please us both, I'm certain it won't take long."

"Quite. As you well know, Your Grace, I'm genuinely anxious to bed my new bride. The sooner we're married, the better," he said with a raspy laugh. Then he turned his leering gaze on his intended. "Good night, Aidan, my lovely little dove."

It took every ounce of strength she possessed, but Aidan finally managed to breathe, "Good night, Lord Sedgewinn. It's been a pleasure." Then, as she watched, the duke motioned for Sedgewinn to proceed to the library. Allowing the man to go before him, Alastair followed the earl out of the room.

Cold blue eyes pierced the center of the earl's back, pricking at the man like a sharp dagger, but Aidan had no way of seeing the murderous look in her father's eye. If she had, she'd have realized her soft, pleading words hadn't fallen on deaf ears like she had thought. As it was, though, she felt certain she'd gone down to defeat. Obviously her father cared nothing for her—felt no love at all.

Rising from her chair, Aidan slowly made her way upstairs, where behind a locked door she pulled a small case from the recesses of the oversize clothes press which stood against the far wall of her bedroom. Next, she caught the fine material of her favorite dress: a soft creation made of silk, off-white in color, a multitude of seed pearls beading the entire bodice and edging the hem and elbow-length sleeves. Despite her misgivings, her uncertainties—despite everything!—she planned to be a beautiful bride. George's bride. She'd be a devoted wife to him as well, she vowed silently. Even if she didn't love him.

A feeling of guilt surged through her, but she quickly tamped it down. Regardless of what Justin Warfield might think, she would never consciously hurt George. Never! It made no difference if she had to hide behind a false mask of devotion, concealing her true feelings from her husband—from all of England as well—she'd do it! He deserved no less.

No less? a deep baritone voice mocked her, Justin's harsh, chastising laughter bursting forth inside her head. *He deserves far more, you conniving little bitch! I'd say you've already betrayed him with your deceitful manipulations. All to save your own hide. As promised, you'll now answer to me!*

Aidan quickly shook her head to clear it; her wide eyes darted from corner to corner, making certain the Duke of Westover hadn't, somehow, slipped into her room unseen. Realizing her mind had been playing tricks on her, no doubt resulting from her guilty conscience, she breathed easier. Yet her nerves were still taut, for she dreaded the night ahead. Dreaded seeing Justin Warfield again!

Having packed her small case and changed into a dress she'd filched from her maid Penny, Aidan extinguished the lamp beside her bed, then settled into a chair, waiting in the darkness until the house quieted for the night. With any luck, she'd escape with no one the wiser. *Please, God, for once answer my prayers. Please!*

Downstairs, a frustrated Alastair Prescott leaned back in his chair and wiped his hand over his face. He felt like a man nearly twice his age. With a sudden jerk, he sat upright, slipped the stopper from the crystal decanter on his desk, and poured himself a second healthy glass of brandy. Settling back, he swallowed a good portion of it and prayed the fiery liquid would soothe his nerves and cool his temper.

When he and Sedgewinn had entered the library over two hours ago, the duke had had his mind set. The problem was how he could make Sedgewinn bolt and, at the same time, preserve his honor. In his haste to marry his rebellious daughter off to the first man who would have her, he'd impetuously jumped into negotiations with Sedgewinn without any forethought. Granted, it was a terrible blunder on his part. Yet, once done, he'd misguidedly felt he couldn't withdraw. But, as the three of them had sat in the dining room, Sedgewinn stuffing his flatulent face, Alastair had heard the soft pleading quality of Aidan's voice and the underlying message she'd been trying so desperately to convey, and his hardened heart had melted. Sedgewinn be damned!

At first, the duke had tried to break off their negotiations by placing small obstacles in the earl's path. But the man

seemed willing to agree to anything, so Alastair had quickly
switched tactics. His demands had become more outra-
geous as the minutes passed, even to the point of asking
Sedgewinn for an annual allowance, to be paid directly to
the duke. Then he'd stated a ludicrous sum that not even
the Queen could afford! Hesitant at first, Sedgewinn tried
to arrange a considerably lesser amount, reminding the
duke of all the sturdy grandchildren he'd provide for
Atwood's enjoyment. When the duke had remained stead-
fast, certain Sedgewinn would balk, the man amazingly
conceded. Like a drooling, rapacious hound, he'd practically forfeited his entire fortune. It was obvious that the
earl's acute desire to sink his long fangs into the tender
succulent meat which had been dangled before him had
overridden any common sense the man might have possessed!

Finally, unable to withstand another moment of Sedgewinn's
vile presence, the duke had bounded from his chair and
thumped his desk with his balled fist. "You lascivious bastard!" he'd growled, glaring his distaste at the man. "If you
think I'd ever give you permission to use my daughter to
satiate your satyric lusts, you're sadly mistaken. Get your
overblown backside off my furniture and out of my house!
And I suggest you move with haste, sir, before I boot you
through the door myself."

Taken aback, the earl had opened his beady eyes in
shock; his turgid mouth worked itself like that of a fish.
"But . . . but, Your Grace," he'd blubbered, "I've gladly
conceded everything!"

"You've conceded nothing," Alastair had snapped back,
"except that you're a pompous fool! Now, filth, withdraw
from my presence and never approach me or my daughter
again." Sedgewinn had pulled his considerable girth from
the chair, and Alastair could have sworn he'd heard the
leather cushion emit a sigh of relief. "And Sedgewinn,"
the duke had said in afterthought, his thumb gingerly
testing the pointed tip of the small bejeweled dagger, an
ancestral keepsake that was now used as a letter opener,
"should some unfortunate young woman consent to marry
you and I hear you have abused her, like you did your
previous wives, I'll make certain you never mistreat an-

other woman again—in any way." He nodded toward Sedgewinn's crotch. "Understood?"

The earl visibly blanched, then gulped. "Y-yes . . . quite."

"Good. Now, get out!"

Remembering the look on Sedgewinn's face, the duke chuckled, then tossed down the remainder of his brandy. He glanced at the gilded bronze French clock gracing the mantel. Ten minutes to twelve. Rising, he extinguished the lamp and headed for the stairs and his bedchamber. As he passed down the upstairs hallway, he came to Aidan's door, where he stopped and listened. No sound came from within. Undoubtedly she was asleep. And if she weren't? Either way, his news could wait until tomorrow. Another worrisome night might make her even more submissive and less willing to challenge his every word. A smile crossed his face. He was looking forward to having an obedient daughter. It would be a pleasant change, he decided gleefully. A damned pleasant change, indeed!

Aidan's ear pressed itself to the wooden panel, her breath held tightly in her lungs. It had been five minutes—or was it only five seconds?—since her father's footsteps had stopped outside her door. The house seemed quiet enough. Dared she chance her escape now? In far away tones, she heard the clock in the library begin to chime. *Midnight!* She had no choice. If she didn't go now, Justin Warfield was certain to leave her behind.

Quietly she turned the key; the lock released, sounding like a cannon's fire in the silent house. Nervously she twisted the handle, and again, to Aidan's sensitive ears, the noise was loud enough to wake the dead. Yet, thankfully, no one stirred. With her case in hand, a lightweight cloak draped over her shoulders, she scurried down the hallway on silent feet to the back stairs. Once down them, she peered around the corner, checking the kitchen area, making certain no one was about.

For once, it seemed good fortune was with her. Yanking up a length of black skirt, she fled the house and, like a stealthy feline, bounded down the garden path toward the carriage house. An iron gate stood at the corner of the stone wall, rusting from disuse. Cautiously she lifted the pitted latch and prayed the thing wasn't frozen on its corroded hinges. After several hard pulls, her door to freedom gave way, almost toppling her onto her backside as it did so. With case in hand, she crept down the musty-smelling tunnel, created by the carriage house bordering their own, and stepped through yet another gate and into the blackened, eerie stillness of the mews.

The Duke of Westover's coach was nowhere to be seen. Gazing into the wide cobbled yard, which led from the mews out onto the street, she hoped to see it turning the corner any moment. After what seemed an eternity, Aidan's hopes sank. She'd been only a few minutes late, but apparently he'd left without her. That was, if he'd come at all. Her shoulders drooping, she started to turn.

Suddenly Aidan felt certain she wasn't alone. A dark shadow loomed up only a few feet from her. Its owner stepped from behind the open gate leading back into the tunnel. Aidan's heart leapt to her throat. Garbed in black, the hulking male figure moved toward her, and a scream bubbled to her lips. Instantly a large hand sliced through the air, smothering her cries as he jerked her against his solid form.

"You're lucky I waited, Lady Prescott," Justin Warfield said, his low voice grating along her already trembling nerves. "But more's the pity for you that I did."

4

A heavy cloud stripped itself away from the moon to reveal the Duke of Westover's dark features. Aidan stared up at his shadow-cut face, his brows knit into a heavy frown. Shoving his hand from her face, she quickly pulled from his grasp. "You've managed to take ten years off my life!" she lashed out sharply. "Don't ever scare me like that again!"

"By journey's end, let's hope I haven't snatched several more." Aidan noted the sanguine tone of his voice and stepped back a pace; Justin chuckled wickedly. "Having second thoughts, are we?"

"No," she stated with much more aplomb than she'd actually felt. "I'm simply debating the wisdom of having *you* as my traveling companion. But then, I tell myself you are just a man, like any other."

"Am I?" Justin asked, stepping closer to her, his white teeth catching and reflecting the moonbeams as his lips curled into an immoral grin. "Don't fool yourself into believing I am, Lady Prescott. I might consider it a challenge and need to prove otherwise."

Aidan's eye's widened perceptibly. *"You,* sir, lack the manners of a true gentleman."

"And the term *lady* is a misnomer where you're concerned. You may have inherited the title at birth, but you certainly haven't *earned* the right to be called such."

Incensed, Aidan sputtered furiously, "Why, you . . . you . . ."

"Bastard?" he questioned, his deep rumble of laughter echoing through the silent air. He noticed the shocked look in her wide eyes. No doubt she'd thought to call him such, but like her pretentious sisters within the peerage, would never have voiced it openly. "My lineage is as pure as the driven snows, Lady Prescott." Again deep laughter pealed from his lips. "I assure you I'm not a woods colt; however, I might be considered a miscreant, a rogue, or a scoundrel. The choice is yours."

All three! she thought, glaring up at him, fighting off the odd feelings he evoked in her. "You neglected to include knave, reprobate, and blackguard."

His devilish smile grew wider. "So I did. Thank you for reminding me. Now, since you harbor no illusions about my character, and I hold none about yours, shall we proceed as planned?"

And I hold none about yours . . . The words echoed through Aidan's mind, and as she viewed his mocking features, she wondered how he perceived her. Manipulative, exploitative, selfish, a cunning she-devil? Or did he possibly believe her a close relative to the legendary vampire,

49

certain she was the sort of woman who would drain the last drop of blood from a man's body in order to ensure her own survival?

How dare he think of her in those terms! Especially when it was *he* who held title to being a seducer of women. Woe to all the unsuspecting females who had the misfortune to cross his path, Aidan thought, herself included. No doubt he carefully measured his prey, then, when least expected, quickly pounced, devouring their flesh for his own carnal satisfaction! Certain it was so, Aidan shored up her defenses.

"Yes," she answered finally, her eyes flashing her distrust.

Unveiled, her anger fomented in her huge violet eyes, making Justin take pause. Would he reach Gretna Green alive? he wondered, certain the sentiment he'd read in her scintillating gaze was closely akin to murder. At eight-and-twenty, he found the prospect of being lowered into a gaping black hole extremely unappealing. Puzzled, he thought her animosity would be far more understandable if he'd lain siege to her virginity and had taken it, *not* because he'd consented to help her. Cannily, he decided he'd best protect his back at all times.

Suddenly irritated that he'd agreed to this foolish undertaking in the first place, he snatched the case from Aidan's hand, cupped her elbow, and forcefully escorted her down the mews.

Aidan dug her heels into the cobblestones, fighting against Justin's crushing grip. Not only was he hurting her, they were going in the opposite direction from the street. "Where are you taking me?" He didn't answer. "I demand to know where we're going!"

He rounded a carriage house, which jutted out into the alleyway, and stopped. "To my horse."

"Horse!"

"Yes," he replied in a harsh whisper, pulling her snug against his side. "And keep your voice down, lest you wake the entire neighborhood."

Aidan gazed up at the huge black stallion and blinked. "Surely you don't expect me to . . . to ride with *you?*"

"Unless you'd prefer walking."

"A conveyance would have been—"

"Too noisy. I wasn't about to have my coach driven

down these mews, my ducal crest emblazoned on the door for all to see, just to pluck you from the night and whisk your *ladyship* away in comfort. Now, do you ride? Or do you walk?''

Mutinously she gazed up at his handsome face, her lips pressed into a tight line. The arrogant jackanapes! she fumed, while simultaneously wishing he wasn't so close. The heat radiating from his powerful masculine form transfused her clothing and seared her flesh wherever their bodies touched. It frightened her, yet intrigued her as well.

Hastily Aidan separated herself from his hard length, her eyes again sparking her aversion; again Justin caught their unfriendly message and chuckled. "You should learn to mask your thoughts, Lady Prescott," he said, smiling, "before they lead you into trouble."

Like flint hitting steel, they easily struck sparks off the other. Aidan felt threatened. "My thoughts are my own," she snapped, quickly using her anger as a shield.

But his thick-lashed silvery gaze instantly penetrated her defenses as he whispered, "Not when your beautiful, expressive eyes speak them so clearly, little one. They say much more than you know. A man can hardly refuse what they promise."

The deep, throbbing timbre of his voice shook Aidan to her core. His metamorphosis from disdainful persecutor to gentle persuader, practically in the same breath, nearly undid her. No wonder the majority of her gender groveled at his feet. He was equally capable of evoking both hatred and desire, challenging the feminine heart to tame him or inflame him, whichever it dared. Was she any different from the rest of them? No!

Maddened by the truth, Aidan again pulled her cloak of anger around her and hid behind it. Breaking free of his grip, she hiked her skirts and placed her small hand on the pommel; her foot slipped into the stirrup. As she struggled to lift herself from the ground, the big stallion shied and pranced sideways; his hostile whinny sliced through the still air.

A virulent curse escaped Justin as he grabbed the reins and, with a hard jerk, yanked the stallion's combative head down, silencing him. Before Aidan could protest, his large hands spanned her tiny waist and hoisted her, dumping her sideways on the saddle. In one fluid motion, he settled in behind her. "Hold this," he said, stuffing the case into her hands; then his sinewy arm slipped around her waist, pulling her snugly against him, trapping her between his outstretched thighs. Aidan stiffened at his familiarity and fought to free herself from his taut hold. Again the horse shied. "Be still or we'll both be sprawled on the cobblestones. Like me, Apollo doesn't trust you."

Trust me! she thought, knowing she was literally in the clutches of the most notorious rogue in all of England. Yet, she swallowed her protests. "Apollo? I'd hardly have named him after the god of sunlight when he's as black as midnight."

"Apollo is also the god of prophecy. From his reaction to you, I'd say my stallion was warning me against any further involvement in this tomfoolery. Had I any sense, I'd deposit you back at the gate."

Had she any sense, she'd tell him to do so! "George shall be awaiting us," she reminded. "You've given your word."

"So I have, Lady Prescott," he bit out, wishing to hell he hadn't, for the nearness of her soft form provoked his desire. Turning Apollo, he set the stallion into a steady walk. "But I didn't promise George your trip would be a pleasant one. Such an allowance is entirely up to you. Let it be known, here and now, your actions will dictate the mood of our journey."

The warning vibrated through Aidan like a great bell sounding a death knell, and as they approached the gate, leading back into the gardens, she eyed it at length. Should she keep to the course she was presently on, her nemesis baiting her every inch of the way? Or should she slip from the saddle and fly to the sanctuary of her home?

Guessing her thoughts, Justin reined Apollo in next to the gate. "Last chance, little one. What choice do you make?" He watched as she viewed the iron portal, and was certain her body leaned itself toward it. He smiled to himself, then started to kick his foot from the stirrup and help her down. Abruptly she faced forward; her back stiffened perceptibly. With her head held high, its crown level with Justin's chin, she clutched her case against her, unwilling to budge. "Then a bride you shall be," he said, urging Apollo forward again.

"Congratulations, Lady Prescott . . . or is it best wishes?" he asked, badgering her anew. "I sincerely hope you never regret your decision."

Apollo's hoofbeats echoed through the clear night as Justin guided him down the side streets and through the dark mews and vacant stableyards, keeping their movements as secretive as possible. Slowly he headed them toward Westover House, where his coach awaited them, ready to roll the moment they arrived. As Justin held her in his unyielding embrace, he noted how Aidan's soft hip fitted itself snugly against his groin and how her full breasts innocently brushed his arm. The light scent of lavender wafted upward from her fragrant tresses, which shone like copper in the moonlight, to fill his nostrils, and he fought the hot arousal that suddenly scorched his loins.

Devious and virginal, he reminded himself cynically. And she belongs to another, he silently added, fighting the temptation to set his heels into Apollo's flanks and propel the stallion into a full gallop to end his own agony. They were barely two blocks from his home. If he could only last. Doubting he would, Justin slowly eased back and away from Aidan's soft, appealing form; instantly Apollo halted in his tracks.

Copper curls slashed against Justin's face as Aidan's head spun round. "Why have we stopped?" she asked, eyeing him warily.

In reply, a short derisive laugh escaped Justin's throat. What was he to say: *Because, milady, in order to escape your luscious, provocative little body, I inadvertently commanded Apollo to do so?* Hardly. Dammit all! If he could only be rid of her! His arm tightening unmercifully, Justin slid hard against Aidan and heeled Apollo's sides. The stallion bounded forward, almost unseating his charge, but Justin held her fast. As she bounced between his thighs, he found his agony had increased tenfold, and he gritted his teeth in consternation.

At full speed, they vaulted into the stableyard behind Westover House, where Justin reined Apollo to a jarring stop and dismounted. Grabbing the case from her hand, he dropped it and pulled Aidan from the saddle. "Cool him down," he ordered over his shoulder to the yawning, sleepy-eyed stableboy as he led a scurrying Aidan to the awaiting coach. Silently scoffing at himself, Justin wondered if he'd been referring to Apollo or himself.

Her feet scrambling to keep up with Justin's hard, angry strides, Aidan glared her discontent and opened her mouth to express it, when her foot snagged the hem of her gown. Stumbling, she almost landed on her knees, but Justin quickly righted her. "Why such haste?" she asked, brushing at her dress, then straightening her cloak with a jerk. "The way you've been burning up the earth, one would think someone had set your seat afire." Staring at her a moment, Justin twitched his lips, then let fly his full-throated laughter; Aidan blinked. "I see nothing humorous in the way you've been treating me. A gentleman would never—"

Aidan's words stalled in her throat as Justin scooped her up into his arms and carried her toward the coach. "Woman, you're pressing your luck," he said close to her ear. "We've already decided, once, I'm not a gentleman and you are not a lady." With a flick of his wrist, the door opened and he dumped her onto the leather seat. "My expediency is merely fueled by the knowledge that the sooner I get you to Gretna Green, the sooner I'll be rid of you."

The door slammed shut, and a surprised Aidan watched as the Duke of Westover strode back for her case. Having secured it in the boot, he swung inside the conveyance and dropped the heavy curtains over the windows. With a rap of his fist, Justin signaled his driver, and the coach was set into motion.

In the blackened void, Aidan's remaining senses heightened. Although she couldn't see her nemesis, she heard his indrawn breath and its steady release, smelled his clean, manly scent, felt his overpowering presence. His very being seemed to envelop her in a hard, crushing embrace. The stifling heat in the airless coach suddenly closed in on her. Certain she was about to suffocate, Aidan gasped and reached for the lowered curtain.

"Leave it!" Justin commanded sharply.

Startled, Aidan gazed across the murky cavity at his obscure form. Ignoring Justin's command, she lifted the curtain from the open window to inhale the refreshing night air deep into her aching lungs.

Instantly Justin lurched from his seat. Whiplike, his hand snapped over her wrist. "I said leave it," he ordered barely inches from her ear as he pulled her hand away from the flap.

Aidan struggled to escape his harsh grip. "Let loose of me!" *He's too close*, her mind screamed, her free hand pushing against the solid wall of his chest. "Let go!"

As her pleasing woman's scent rose to fill his nostrils, her ineffectual struggles provoked him, and a sudden wave of masculine lust surged through him. By the gods! Had he gone insane? Certain he had, Justin abruptly released Aidan's wrist and fell back into his seat. "I apologize if I hurt you," he said, his voice strangely tight. "When we've reached the outskirts of London, you may raise the curtains—not before."

Fighting the memory of his nearness, Aidan rubbed her wrist. "What ludicrous reason could you possibly have to keep them closed? By the time we've come upon Islington, we'll be baked alive."

"Secrecy."

"Secrecy! Why, it's as black as pitch in here. No one can possibly see us. Not even with the curtains up."

"Your lovely features, Lady Prescott, might reflect themselves in the moonlight, the gaslights, or the coach lamps—all three, for that matter. To ensure that no one recognizes you, they shall remain closed."

"But I'm suffocating in this unbearable heat."

"Then I suggest you close your mouth and stop adding to the already burdensome atmosphere."

Her jaw clamped shut, and she glared her intense dislike at the shadowy man across from her. Barbarous beast! she thought, wishing there were some way she could make him suffer equally as much as she was, if not more so. Not having a clue as to what manner of torture she could foist on him, she threatened in a mutinous tone, "If I don't get some air this instant, I shall faint!"

A much-used feminine ploy, Justin thought, and chuckled. "Then I suggest you keep your smelling salts close at hand. Or better yet, perhaps you should lie upon the seat so you won't fall and injure yourself."

Each word that escaped Justin's mouth had sounded to

Aidan like it was drifting away from her, instead of toward her. The heat—was it really affecting her? An odd sibilant noise, resembling that of an ocean wave, started in the depths of her ears, to suddenly fill her entire head. At the same time, an unexpected sensation of light-headedness overtook her; nausea instantly claimed her.

"I . . . I . . ." She swallowed hard and shook her head, hoping to clear it. "Your Grace," she said weakly, feeling herself slipping deeper into the chasm which had suddenly opened up before her eyes. "I feel very . . . *strange.*"

With a whispered curse, Justin came up off his seat and shouted, "Potts! Stop the coach!" Scooping Aidan's limp form into his arms, he kicked open the door, splintering the wood, and ducked through it into the cool air. A soft moan drifted to his ears as he bent to one knee, his charge resting languorously across his lap. Her shoulders encased in one arm, his free hand lightly smoothed along her damp forehead. "Rest easy, little one," he soothed gently; then, hearing his driver's feet hit the cobblestones, he ordered over his shoulder, "Find some cool water and a cloth. Be quick about it."

As Potts scurried off, Justin turned his attention back to Aidan. Huge violet eyes stared sightlessly up at him and he cursed himself for not taking her at her word. "Forgive me, little one, but I thought—" A groan erupted from Aidan's throat; she stirred and blinked. "Take a deep breath. Another. That's right."

Aidan's eyes focused and she found herself staring up into a splendid pair of silver eyes. Their tender regard caused a contented sigh to escape her throat; a small smile curved her lips. Then her gaze surveyed the face encasing them; she stiffened. "What . . . where . . . ?" She jerked upright and instantly wished she hadn't. "Ooh . . . I'm going to be sick!"

Swiftly rising, Justin set Aidan to her feet and led her to the gutter, where he gently supported her. After what seemed an eternity, Aidan finally straightened and accepted a cool, damp cloth from Justin's hand and shakily blotted her face. "Better?" he asked, then took the tin dipper from the plump tavern maid who hovered near Potts's side. "Here, little one, rinse your mouth, then drink some."

Aidan took the dipper and followed Justin's bidding. "Thank you," she whispered, handing the empty dipper back to the woman. "I feel much better."

"Ye still look a bit pale, mum," the woman said. "Are ye certain ye be all right?" She turned to Justin. "Ye best see to your missus, sir. And take good care of her. When I was early on, I got the pukes all the time. Wore me out, it did."

Early on? Aidan questioned silently, then suddenly realized the woman thought Justin and she were husband and wife and that Aidan carried his child. "I'm not married," she blurted, thinking to set things straight.

"Oh?" the woman questioned, her brow rising loftily. Her gaze first raked disdainfully over Justin, then Aidan. She dropped the dipper back into the pitcher, sniffed loudly, and set a course for the tavern several yards away. The door opened and a shout of laughter erupted from the merrymakers inside; then the panel banged shut and all was quiet.

Her eyes wide, Aidan remarked, "A bit snobbish of her, passing judgment on us like that. Who does she think she is?"

"A good Christian woman, I suppose," he stated, lips twitching. "Apparently we've given her the wrong impression."

"She should never have spoken out like that in the first place," Aidan snapped, annoyed because the maid had ridiculously paired Aidan with the man next to her. "Wrong impression, indeed!"

Justin chuckled. "Obviously she had no idea we were her so-called superiors. One wouldn't think to find members of the peerage dressed so plainly, milady. Nor would one think to find a duke's daughter relieving the contents of her stomach into the gutter. Nor another duke assisting the lady as she did so."

Aidan fused red. Why did he have to remind her of the indelicate spectacle she'd made of herself? Embarrassed beyond words, she picked up her skirts and marched back to the coach. But when her eyes met the yawning black hole centered before her, she abruptly stopped. A film of perspiration suddenly overlaid her brow. Her hands felt cold, clammy. She gasped for air.

Justin came up behind her, his brow wrinkling in concern. "What's wrong?" he asked, his hands settling on her shoulders.

"I . . . c-can't go back in there," Aidan replied as a violent shudder racked her rigid body. "It . . . it's like a . . . a tomb."

Feeling her fear, Justin again cursed himself for having made her ride in the dark, claustral coach. He had been deliberately cruel, he knew, for he remembered how he'd barely been able to breathe himself. Why had he been so bent on punishing her? Simply because she wished to marry a man of her own choosing, and not her father's? What business was it of his anyway? *None,* he conceded. Except that he'd unwisely gotten himself involved in this unseemly situation.

A vibrating rumble caught his ear and Justin realized it was the sound of coach wheels rapidly rolling toward them. Without hesitation he lifted Aidan into his arms and ducked inside his own vehicle. His backside hit the leather seat, his struggling charge still held tightly in his embrace. As the second conveyance came to a halt beside his, his arm snaked out, catching the splintered door, jerking it shut.

Instantly Aidan felt the oppressive atmosphere close in on her again. Palpable anxiety consumed her, destroying all logical thought. "Let loose of me!" she demanded, fighting her jailer, fearing she'd suffocate. "I'll scream if you don't!" Justin's hand compressed over her mouth just as a feminine voice called his name.

"Justin—Your Grace, are you in there?"

Cynthia! he thought while resisting Aidan's attempts to free herself. Dash it all! Of all streets, she *had* to come down this one. He clamped his jaw and swallowed an expletive as Aidan's sharp teeth sank into the meaty flesh between his thumb and forefinger.

Certain she was about to faint anew, Aidan furiously kicked her legs; her feet thumped madly against the side of the coach. His injured hand still covering her mouth, her trapped protests expelled themselves as softened groans.

As Justin fought to tame the wildcat in his arms, the coach was set to rocking on its springs.

"Justin!" Cynthia's screech shattered the air. "Who's in there with you? Who is she?" his mistress demanded angrily as the coach continued its wild, rhythmic lurch. "Why, you . . . you snake! Cheat! In the middle of a public street—have you no shame at all?"

Cursing all womanhood, Justin hit his booted heel against the floor. "Potts! Go!" he yelled, and the coach bounded forward as thunderous hooves struck the pavement, nearly dumping its occupants onto the floor. As soon as he was certain they'd gained enough yardage between Cynthia's coach and his own, Justin heaved the clawing, biting tigress in his arms upward and tossed her into the seat opposite his.

Aidan gasped. But instead of letting loose her tirade as Justin had expected, she jerked the curtain aside and gulped air into her lungs. Renewed, she turned shimmering eyes on the Duke of Westover. "You, sir, are an insidious repugnant creature," she stated, trying to keep her angry tears at bay.

"I disagree with your depiction of my character," he said, fighting down his own anger. Examining his hand, he gingerly flexed it. Amazingly, she hadn't drawn blood, but it was nevertheless bruised. "Considering the fact that our little scheme was almost exposed by your childish conduct, I had little choice but to restrain you as I did."

Molten silver eyes met flashing violet through the darkness. He was right, of course, but Aidan refused to admit it. At least, not to him. She thought of defending her actions by saying she'd been overcome by the airlessness of the coach, which was partially true. But, more so, it had been Justin himself who had caused her to behave like she had.

Encased in his strong arms, pressed close to his unyielding chest, she'd felt the force of his masculinity. Frightened by it, she'd forgotten their urgent need for secrecy. Oh, God, she thought, knowing the man affected her in ways that no other ever had. Why had she agreed to come with him?

Bolstering her anger, she hid behind the one emotion she was certain would protect her. *"Childish!"* she returned,

determined he'd never know the truth. "Had you not bru-
tally forced me—"

"Yes, *childish!*" he snapped, his patience close to shattering. He jerked the curtains aside, securing them, for they
were almost to Islington; Aidan cringed as his hands cinched
the panels on the window nearest her. She relaxed when he
fell back into his seat. "Had Cynthia seen us, within the
hour all of London would have known I was with Lady
Aidan Prescott, the Duke of Atwood's precocious but nonetheless virginal daughter! As it is, she has no idea what
particular female it was who set my coach to rocking,
subsequently making her think something improper was
taking place inside and 'in the middle of a public street.' "

Aidan's eyes widened; a red stain bled across her face as
Cynthia Danvers' accusing words replayed themselves in
her mind, painting a vivid picture of how the woman and
the outside world must have viewed the scene, and the
erroneous conclusion that was drawn: *The Duke of Westover
and some unknown female had been making love!* "In a
coach?" she asked incredulously, not realizing she'd voiced
her thought aloud.

A snort of laughter erupted from Justin. "Yes, my naive
little innocent—in a coach. And Cynthia, being an experienced woman, *understands* as much," he said without rev-
erence for her sensibilities, and watched as Aidan's blush
deepened. He chuckled. "For a young woman who is about
to marry, you know little of a man's passions." He viewed
her at length, then, sensing the truth, teased, "I suppose
poor unsuspecting George will be made to spend his wedding night alone."

Aidan instantly thought to deny the verity of his statement, but couldn't. She wondered what manner of man he
was, then decided he possessed no decorum at all. "What
transpires between George and myself is none of your affair!" she retorted, then watched as Justin's teeth flashed
white in the dim light.

Perceptive eyes perused her a long, timeless moment.
His knowing smile faded. "As I had suspected, Lady Prescott. You'd never really intended to be a wife to George—a
genuine mate—had you?" He noted how her eyes turned
toward the window, away from his own penetrating gaze.

Perhaps she had a conscience after all. "What is he to be?" he continued his attack. "A mere prop? A piece of scenery to be shoved in and out of your life for theatrical effect?" She didn't answer. "I pity your future husband. And I pity you."

Still no response came forth, and as Justin viewed her perfect profile, bathed in soft moonlight, he indeed pitied her. Stubborn, spoiled, impudent, audacious, she definitely was not the woman for George. Weak, oppressed, insecure, cowardly, George decidedly could not control her. She needed someone who could tame her without breaking her spirit. His harsh rebuke had been meant to chide her into changing her mind about marrying George. Belatedly he realized his words might have done the opposite. Indeed, they might just spur her into becoming "the genuine mate" he'd spoken of, simply to prove him wrong.

Certain George was as untried as she was, Justin feared the man's clumsiness might ruin their naive attempts at lovemaking. He'd cause her pain, pain that could make her unresponsive for all time, and Justin felt his heart cry out: *Little one, you should be loved by a man who can show you what pure pleasure really is. At least once . . . on your first awakening.*

He remembered how she had felt in his arms as they'd danced, as they'd ridden high on Apollo's back, as she'd lain limp and helpless after she'd fainted, as she'd struggled against his hold, fighting him only moments ago. And he remembered how she'd aroused him. Aroused his sympathy, aroused his anger, aroused his *desire*.

Incredibly, as he now viewed her, he imagined himself close beside her, his softly spoken phrases and gentle caresses wooing her, seducing her. Their lips would meet, tentatively at first, then shape themselves into an urgent kiss, thirsting tongues mating wildly. And when he'd kissed her senseless, heated love words whispered in her ear, her anxious pleas filling his head in reply, he'd lower her to the seat, remove her clothing and his, and love her as no other man possibly could. Then, when he was certain she was ready, her hips writhing, begging for his pleasures, he'd enter her secret place, easing slowly upward, his mouth covering hers to capture her momentary cry of pain, and fill her completely. Allowing her time to adjust, he'd wrap her silken thighs around his waist, his tender words reassuring her, praising her, seducing her anew. Then, with his hands molding her rounded bottom, he'd show her the rhythmic movement that would eventually bring them boundless ecstasy. And as their exalted cries finally filled the air, his lips would cover hers once more in a deep, loving tribute to the perfection they'd shared.

Hot desire suddenly racked Justin's body. His eyes closed and he breathed heavily. Virginal and naively sweet, he thought. And he wanted her. Just once. In a coach. *This* coach! *Now!* His heavy lids opened and he gazed longingly at her. "Aidan," he whispered thickly, "you can't let him be your first. I won't let you. Little one, you need a man who knows how to love a woman." He reached for her. "Aidan? Sweet?"

The soft sounds of slumber met his ears, and Justin fell back in his seat, his head hitting the coach wall with a thud. Instantly he shook it, clearing away all residue of his fantasy. What in God's name had he been about to do? To suggest! Sweet Lord! Had he gone mad! He'd never had a virgin. Never wanted one—*until now!* They were a trap ready to spring, inflicting certain death to his freedom!

Frowning, he gazed at Aidan's sleeping form and thought of his mistress. Although their arrangement had been intermittent and unpredictable, the worldly Cynthia gave him satisfaction. His body, at least. But lately she'd begun to press him, subtly hinting at marriage, and he was beginning to think it was time he moved on. After tonight, he might have no other choice!

Justin's lips twitched and broke into a wide grin as he envisioned Cynthia's startled look when his coach, his ducal crest emblazoned across the door, started shaking convulsively. No doubt her shock had quickly turned to indignation, her blue eyes narrowing as an angry flush mottled her fair skin. He could only imagine the curses that would have been heaped upon his head had he not ordered Potts to be off.

Certain the fiery vindictive blond would not hear him out, he decided that perhaps it was best it had ended like this. Although he'd known it to be inevitable from the start, he never did like severing a relationship. Indeed, this way there would be no messy scenes, no angry accusations and heated rejoinders, no tearful pleading, begging him to stay. Perhaps he should thank his charge for making his life a bit easier. Yet, Justin realized that if Cynthia ever discovered who the mysterious woman in his coach actually was, Aidan Prescott's life would be made a living hell. He felt an odd sort of protectiveness well up inside him. Then, instantly angered that he'd felt anything at all, he dashed both women from his mind.

Settling back, Justin folded his arms over his chest and propped his boots on the seat opposite him. In but a few hours, Potts, obeying his master's previous instructions, would pull into an inn, which was a safe distance from London. In the meantime, Justin planned to get some sleep, but as the miles passed, he found himself endlessly gazing at the young beauty across from him, his eyes never tiring from the sight of her. Finally the coach slowed and he glanced out the window. They'd arrived at their destination. Not wanting to wake her, Justin pushed open the damaged door, lifted her into his arms, and stepped out into the night air.

Aidan felt herself floating. Muted voices sounded in her ears, but she refused to rouse herself, content to remain in her state of dreams. Strong arms carried her up the stairs, boots scraping along the worn boards, and she pressed her cheek against the solid chest, snuggling closer. She felt herself drifting downward; a soft feather mattress enveloped her. She purred like a tiny kitten and turned onto her side. Deft hands removed her dress, a cover eased up over her shoulders, and a whiff of breath blew out the candle on the stand near her bed. A light tread moved quietly away from her toward the door, and as though she were still a small child, she called through her sleep, "Good night, Papa."

Justin turned, his brow arching toward a lock of dark hair. A derisive smile cracked his lips, turning itself inward. At the moment, having just removed her dress and having had to physically restrain himself from removing more, he felt anything but fatherly. A long breath escaped his lips, and he finally answered, "Good night, Aidan. Sleep well, sweet princess." Then the door closed behind him.

5

Lord and Lady Manley rushed down the staircase as another fist-hammering knock rattled the door's hinges. David, a half-dozen steps ahead of his wife, nodded his assent to the sleepy-eyed butler who hovered near the entry. The man shifted his nightcap to a more stately position atop his balding crown, then slipped the bolt and threw the panel wide.

"Where is she?" Alastair Prescott bellowed, bursting in the door, his harsh tone causing David to pause momentarily.

"Where's who?" the younger man countered, having recovered to descend the few remaining steps.

"Aidan—where is she?"

Not liking the foreboding look in the duke's eye, Eugenia gathered her robe more securely around her slight form and stopped at her husband's side. "Isn't she at home?"

"If she were, young lady, I wouldn't be here!" the duke snapped with such vehemence that Eugenia cradled closer to David. "Now, where have you hidden her?"

"I assure you," David replied, squaring his shoulders, "she's not with us."

Atwood's gaze raked over the young couple from head to foot. "I'm prepared to search this place from cellar to attic if need be."

Incensed by the older man's suggestion that the couple was lying, David replied heatedly, "And if you attempt to do so, sir, I'll have you arrested."

Observing how the men assessed one another, Eugenia feared they were ready to spring, fists flying. "Your Grace," she said in a rush, stepping between her husband and the duke, "David has not seen Aidan since the night we escorted her home from the Quincys' soiree. The last time I saw her was yesterday, when I stopped to inquire about her health. I promise we've not had contact with her since."

His eyes steady upon Eugenia's, Alastair searched her face. Realizing she spoke the truth, he sighed as his shoulders slumped in defeat. "Then where could she be?"

"Perhaps she went for a canter in Hyde Park," Eugenia offered.

"Before the crack of dawn?" Alastair countered incredulously.

"Are you certain she's missing?" David asked. "Perhaps she's—"

"Sir, my entire staff has searched the house from top to bottom, inside and out. There's not a trace of her. Had not one of the scullery maids risen early and found the kitchen door ajar, I'd still be asleep in my bed and so would you! The maid alerted the butler, who in turn woke me. Thinking a thief had stolen his way in, I went to check on Aidan. Her bed hadn't been slept in. Penny, her maid, found a case and one of Aidan's gowns missing, along with several personal items. Penny informed me that one of her own dresses had vanished from the wardrobe in her room. She'd thought it stolen by one of the staff and had planned to report its disappearance today at a more reasonable hour. Upon searching the grounds, one of my men found the old gate that leads out into the mews open. Now, either she's been abducted by some blackguard to be held for ransom—which I doubt, for no one in his right mind would stop to pack a case if he were relying on stealth and celerity to snatch my daughter. *Or*—which I deem more likely—she's run off!"

As she listened to the duke's account, Eugenia's mind raced. Instantly she connected her missing friend with their discussion over how the two could keep Aidan from the Earl of Sedgewinn's clutches. "George," she whispered, not realizing she'd said the man's name aloud.

"Who, madam, is George?" the duke inquired.

Her gaze snapped to Alastair's face, but she found she was unable to hold his impeaching look. "I . . . I . . . ."

"You know something!" he accused, certain it was so. "Now, out with it!"

David looked from the glowering duke to his wife and noted how her teeth played nervously along her lower lip. "Eugenia, if you do know where Aidan might be, I suggest you tell His Grace."

Her uncertain gaze climbed to David's face. "I . . . I can't be positive, but she may have . . ." Eugenia paused, feeling as though she were betraying her friend. Taking a deep breath, she released it and whispered, "Eloped."

"Eloped!" the duke exploded. "Why in God's name would she do that!"

"Because," Eugenia countered, her tone swathed with indignation, "you were going to force her to marry that lecherous Sedgewinn! Had you been less worried about ridding yourself of her and more concerned over your choice of a potential mate, Aidan wouldn't have felt it necessary to run away!"

Alastair eyed Eugenia at length. Then, hoping to glean as much information as possible, he asked, "And how do you know so much about my plans for Aidan?"

"On the day you informed her of her impending marriage, she came to me for solace. She confided that you two had quarreled. To escape her fate, she threatened to place herself in a convent . . . anything to keep herself from the lecherous hands of the man you'd chosen for her. I suggested she speak with you. But we both know, Your Grace, her words would have fallen on deaf ears, don't we?" Eugenia accused, anger flashing in her eyes. Never would she have spoken so disrespectfully to Aidan's father, but she blamed him totally for her friend's unhappy predicament. "In fact," she admitted without thought, "I was the one who suggested she elope to Gretna Green with one of her suitors. One who would treat her kindly."

"You conspired against me?"

"I would have conspired against the Queen if it meant saving Aidan from Sedgewinn's grasp!"

David's gaze stopped bouncing between his wife and the duke to finally settle on Atwood. "Eugenia's right. You've no one to blame but yourself. Sedgewinn is the lowest of all life forms. If Aidan has run off with George Edmonds, I can't blame her. At least she's chosen a more sensible route and is marrying a man who adores her—not the wife beater you chose! You're lucky she didn't decide to slash her wrists instead!"

Alastair spun on his heel and started toward the door. "I must stop her."

"Why?" Eugenia cried, running after him, catching at his arm. "To prevent an out-and-out scandal so you can still palm her off on Sedgewinn?"

"That arrangement was dissolved last night. You may think me a fool, Eugenia, but I'm not so much the fool as to give the Earl of Sedgewinn the opportunity to abuse my own flesh and blood. When my temper cooled, I realized my mistake and tossed the earl out on his ear. Now, if you'll forgive me, I must catch my errant offspring before she marries a weakling like Edmonds!"

Eugenia and David watched as the duke strode from the house, the door banging shut behind him.

Within the hour, Alastair Prescott had gathered a band of men. Their pockets weighing heavier, they were eager to join his cause. At full gallop, their fresh steeds ate up the miles as the small group headed north toward Gretna Green.

The sun briefly embraced the range of barren hills, then quickly slipped from view. Fingers of light burst across the azure sky, reaching out like a beacon of hope. Instantly they withdrew as the fiery globe sank further beyond the horizon.

Inside the coach, Aidan gazed through the window, staring at the bleak scenery. A wall of silence had divided Justin Warfield and herself from the time they'd left the inn. Growing weary of the cool tacitness, she closed her eyes, her thoughts wandering backward over the day's events.

When she had awakened this morning to find herself in a strange bed, in a strange room, she had jerked upright. Discovering she'd been undressed, she was at first mortified, then fearful. Instantly she'd wondered if something had transpired between herself and her guardian. Somewhere in the dregs of her mind, she'd vaguely remembered efficient hands removing her gown, a cover being tenderly tucked around her, then quiet footsteps moving toward the door. In her confusion, she'd thought she'd heard him call her "sweet princess."

Suddenly frightened that something untoward might have happened to her, she'd frantically searched her memory for a clue which might confirm or deny such a thing. True, she was only partially clothed. But as she'd ruminated over the possibility that Justin had somehow taken advantage of her, Aidan discovered she felt no different than she had the night before. There had been no ghostly sensation of fullness, no lingering soreness which Eugenia had shyly explained a woman experienced after she'd first made love, so Aidan had quickly decided her fears were unfounded. Nothing had happened between the roguish duke and herself. In all likelihood, his endearment had been imagined, as well.

Irritated with herself for having even thought such a thing, she'd bounced from the bed. After she'd washed and groomed herself, donning the same black dress she'd worn last night, she'd descended to the first floor of the inn to find a stoic Justin, garbed in black like the night before, breakfasting alone. Joining him, she had suffered through a wordless meal of cold porridge, the brooding duke's company equally as unpalatable as her fare. As soon as she'd swallowed the last bite of the unappealing gruel, her escort had whisked her from the inn, her one piece of luggage being carted to the coach by Potts, and the threesome were off again, heading in a northerly direction.

The endless succession of miles, stopping only to change horses, which Aidan soon learned Justin had sent ahead the day before so there were no delays in their journey, and which where to be retrieved later by one of his men, had taken their toll on her nerves. Her guardian's continuous silence and assessing stare had annoyed and angered her. To prevent another round of heated words from erupting between them, she'd elected to ignore him, and her gaze had riveted itself to the changing landscape beyond the open coach window. But once they'd hit the Yorkshire moors, it had taken all the willpower she possessed to keep her eyes bent on the desolate terrain. The tedium, both inside the coach and out, had seemed immeasurable.

Slowly Aidan's eyes opened. If only the heather were in bloom, she thought, sighing, her gaze once again affixed to the barren moors. At least then the continuous monotony would have been broken by splendorous splashes of pinkish-purple flowers. Disappointed, she knew it was still too early in the season for its magnificent display. It mattered little, she thought, sighing again, for darkness was nearly upon them.

"Bored, are we?" The foreign sound of Justin's voice made Aidan blink; her gaze skittered his way. "You'd best get used to the bleakness," he continued. "George lives several hours east of here. After tonight, dear lady, so will you." He noted her surprise. "I take it you weren't aware George doesn't reside in London during the season. In fact, he only shows upon occasion, staying with friends just long enough so he won't wear out his welcome. I'm afraid your round of balls and soirees is about to come to an abrupt halt."

Aidan settled an indifferent look upon him. "It matters not."

Justin chuckled. "You lie, little one, and we both know it."

His roguish grin and knowing gaze rippled through her, leaving her feeling somewhat giddy. The man was far too handsome for his own good. She knew it—and he knew it, as well. Tearing his gaze from his, Aidan again stared through the window. She refused to answer him. When her inheritance was settled upon her, she and George would have a place of their own in London. A few missed seasons meant nothing to her. But as she tried to reassure herself of that fact, she found herself unconvinced.

Again the atmosphere froze into silence. Justin's eyes intent upon her, Aidan thought she would surely come unhinged. But soon the horses' hooves struck a different cadence, and the coach turned, heading toward the Lake District, growing ever closer to Scotland and to George.

With that thought, Aidan was overcome by a sudden attack of nerves. Wondering if she could actually go through with her planned marriage, she felt the urgent need to pace, to stretch her legs, extend them into a brisk walk, anything to take her mind from what awaited her. But she was confined inside the coach, and her pride refused to allow her to ask Justin for a brief moment's pause. Instead, she rested her head against the coach wall, again closing her eyes. Before long, she slept.

Justin watched her, infuriated by all the emotion she'd managed to evoke within him. His sullen mood, he knew, stemmed from his refusal to state his opinion of her elopement outright. From the moment he'd left her last night, her soft form snuggled deep in her bed, he'd been fighting the virulent urge to go back to her, take hold of her, and shake some sense into her, in hope of persuading her not to marry George. Her exquisite beauty, coupled with her flaming spirit, would be wasted on the colorless man. George, as dull as he was, could never teach her the ways of love. The man would suffocate her. Justin was certain of it.

Why such knowledge bothered him, he was unable to say. Yet he was in no position to save her from her impending doom. Since she'd taken the step to run off, thereby ruining her reputation, the best he could offer was to set her up as his new mistress. Justin scoffed at the idea, knowing his proposition would be thrown back in his face. Along with the flat of her hand! he thought wryly.

In agitation, he raked his sun-bronzed fingers through his thick dark hair, emitting a low growl as he did so. Damnation! How had he gotten himself into this mess? Stupidity, he conceded, his rapt attention turning away from the slumbering beauty across from him to view the dimming scenery outside his window. He was a fool for caring about what happened to her. She'd made her decision, freely, and she should be made to live with it!

He remembered a long-ago spring day and a sunlit meadow, which lay on the edge of Warfield Manor, his country estate. The revived image filled his mind with the gentle sway of long grasses mixed with a vivid array of sweet-smelling wildflowers. And the pungency of *death,* he thought, its graphic memory piercing through him. Had he had a normal boyhood and had that boyhood ended differently, perhaps he could open his heart to a young woman, like Aidan, and realize the so-called joy of love. But in reality, he was immune to the emotion, his jaded heart frozen in time.

As the miles passed, Justin found no solace in his thoughts, and as the sky darkened, so did his mood.

Aidan finally stirred from her nap, surprised to see it was dark. A full moon hung in the sky, cloaking the panorama with its silvery light. Gnarled black fingers stretched over the roadway and across the landscape as tree limbs cast their eerie shadows. Stifling a yawn, Aidan turned toward Justin, his face shaded from view. "What time is it?" she asked, sleep still tinting her voice.

"Nearly midnight." Her gaze shifted from him. She did not respond, only stared through the window, as usual, and Justin viewed her at length. "You seem rather pensive, Lady Prescott," he stated after a while. "Might it be you're having second thoughts?"

"No," she snapped untruthfully, violet eyes settling on him anew. "I'm simply anxious to get this over with."

"The journey? The marriage ceremony? Or both?"

"The journey, naturally. I'm anxious to see George." It was a lie, but she couldn't very well admit she dreaded seeing her intended. At least, not to Justin Warfield. "How much longer before we reach Scotland?" she asked, trying to ignore his constant taunting manner.

"Probably another half hour." In that instant, a moonbeam spotlighted her features, and Justin saw Aidan's eyes widen; he grinned. "Of course, if you are experiencing a sudden change of heart, I could always have Potts turn us around—"

"You'll do no such thing!" she cried, her taut nerves finally shattering. "I . . . I can't possibly go back. Not now. Not when—" She swallowed her words and tried to eradicate the vision of the Earl of Sedgewinn, his face suddenly looming up before her eyes, his sharp gaze leering, his vulgar mouth curving into a lascivious grin. "You don't understand. I simply can't go back."

Justin noted the desperation in her voice. "I suppose you fear your father's wrath. Or perhaps it's the thought of seeing the jilted bridegroom you left behind. Who is the miserable fellow, anyway?"

Abruptly, Aidan's eyes misted over. While she traced her sudden tears to her emotional distress, she fought to keep them at bay. Then, with enmity punctuating each syllable, she finally said, "The Earl of Sedgewinn."

Instantly Justin stiffened. A hard edge set itself along his firm jaw. Had he reserved the least bit of respect for the Duke of Atwood, it now lay dead. "Your father tried to pair you with that whoreson?" he questioned, wanting confirmation.

"Yes."

Justin strained his ears to hear her whispered reply. The word, having pitifully torn itself from her lips, caused a strange lurch in his chest. "By God! Is the man insane!"

"I've caused him too much worry," she admitted; then her teeth tormented her lower lip as she again stared through the window. "My father wishes to be rid of me. But I couldn't make myself marry Sedgewinn. He's . . . he's . . ." She fell silent.

The smallness of her voice, confessing that she felt unwanted, unloved, produced another jab at his heart. Suddenly an unfamiliar feeling overtook him, and Justin moved across the small space to Aidan's side. Oddly, he experienced an uncontrollable need to comfort her; his arm slipped lightly around her shoulders. "And that's why you chose George?" He watched her nod. "Did you think him merely the lesser of two evils?"

"George isn't evil," she quickly defended, gazing up into silver eyes that were amazingly filled with compassion. "He's nothing like Sedgewinn. George is kind, gentle, courteous . . . a true gentleman."

"But you don't love him, do you?"

Had not his tender regard mesmerized her, his gentle tone soothed her, Aidan would have denied his words. But his sudden transformation into a caring protector had caught her off-guard. "No," she confessed, then quickly added, "but, just the same, I plan to make him a good wife."

Justin's hand rose. Long fingers framed the oval of her face as he gazed deeply into misty violet eyes, eyes that questioned him, lured him. "Little one, you're willing to give too much." His gaze shifted to her softly parted lips, their dewy sheen reflected in the moonlight, and his breath caught in his chest. "You can't marry a man simply because he's known to be a gentleman. There needs to be some sort of emotion . . . a magical feeling which passes between you and the one you choose. You could never be happy without it."

Fascinated by the mobility of his mouth, she found she was unable to answer immediately. Here, under the cradle of his arm, his gentle fingers lightly caressing her cheek, her heart skipped erratically. Strangely, she felt an unexplained magnetic pull, drawing her ever closer to her guardian. The sensation frightened her, excited her, and she wondered if what she was now experiencing resembled the magical emotion he'd mentioned.

"Could you be happy, little one?" he asked, his searching gaze running over her face. "The truth."

"I . . . I don't know," she whispered, her gaze casting itself downward, away from Justin's, for his intent regard made her feel rather . . . *odd*. "But I have little choice. My father will never forgive me. He'll marry me off to Sedgewinn the moment I return." She shuddered distastefully. Noting her reaction, Justin tightened his hand on the crest of her shoulder, easing her closer to him. Aidan made no protest. "I already committed myself to George. I can't back away now. He'd be deeply hurt."

"George will survive," he said, not caring one way or the other if the man ever recovered from her rejection. At present, it was his ward's mental anguish, the grief she was suffering over her father's coldheartedness, that concerned him most. The man's lack of sensitivity in choosing a suitable mate for her infuriated Justin. If Atwood were within his reach, he'd thrash the man soundly.

"Then what shall I do?" she inquired, her tone defeated.

Liquid violet eyes stared up at him while moist lips trembled softly beneath his gaze, and Justin reacted with a force so strong it jolted him. His restraint snapped. All his latent desires, those which he'd purposely held in check from the moment their eyes had first met while he'd strongly denied they even existed, surged through him. Overpowered by his emotions, he was unable to resist her. "Little one," he whispered huskily as gentle fingers brushed the fine wisps of hair away from her face. "I'll protect you . . . keep you safe. You'll want for nothing. This I promise."

With each word, his head slowly lowered, his gaze riveted to her tempting lips. Entranced by their beauty, he wanted to taste their bounty, explore their mysteries, teach them to respond to his own.

Her heart beating wildly, Aidan thought to stave him off, but she could find no convincing reason to do so. Enthralled, she watched as the masculine curve of his lower lip separated itself from its mate, the pair growing ever closer. Overwhelmed by the riot of emotions that were hammering through her, every nerve in her body set on alert, she moaned softly. Her eyelids fluttered shut. Long lashes rested lightly against the delicate skin above her cheeks as she waited with anticipation.

Then she felt his first tentative touch as his mouth brushed silkily over hers. A whimper of protest escaped her when it withdrew. Hearing the wordless entreaty, Justin emitted a groan of longing; his lips captured hers, molding them to his own. Slowly she opened to him, like a rose unfurling in the morning sunlight, and hot fire raced through his veins as she surrendered completely to his mastery.

Sweetly naive, he thought, refreshed by her untried attempts to please him. Following his lead, her tongue traced his lips, imitating each movement he made; then it chased and played a wild erotic game of passion. Raw desire ripped through him. His breath caught; a shudder racked along his hardened body. This was one virgin he would gladly take to his bed. Yet, he knew, she must be gentled into submission, slowly, expertly, and he realized if he didn't stop this madness now, he would, undoubtedly, lose control here in the coach.

With a will of steel, Justin fought down his rampant desires. Placing one last tender kiss on her lips, he withdrew. Gentle fingers smoothed her coppery tresses, stroking her like she were a small kitten. "We must not rush into anything, little one," he said, his desire still vibrating in the low timbre of his voice. "When we are back in London and I've settled you into your own place, there will be time enough to show you what pleases me and to discover what pleases you."

Feeling as though she'd fallen into the Thames in the dead of winter, Aidan instantly stiffened. "Pleases?"

Foolishly Justin ignored the sudden glacial look in her eye. "Yes," he said, a sportive grin splitting his face. "I've never taken a virgin as my mistress before. I—"

"Mistress," Aidan screeched, shoving at his chest, trying to dislodge his arm from her shoulder. "You pompous boor!"

Surprised by the vehemence in her voice, Justin frowned. "What else, little one? I thought you understood. I offered you my protection, not marriage. Wedlock is for fools," he stated emphatically. His parents' marriage attested to that!

Narrowed eyes spewed purple fire as Aidan's lip curled contemptuously. Whatever had made her think the rogue would condescend to taking her as his bride! And why she would have considered such a ludicrous proposal in the first place, she was unable to say. He was a dangerous scoundrel, a womanizer who lacked scruples. Eugenia had warned her as much. Yet, stupidly, like so many of her gender, she'd found herself falling under his spell.

Angered that she'd almost become one of his willing victims, Aidan instantly sought revenge. As Justin had predicted, her arm raised to swing in an arc, but quick reflexes allowed him to catch her wrist before her hand connected with his face. "You arrogant ass!" she hissed, venom lacing each word as she struggled to free herself from his grip. "I'd no more lie with you than I would a . . . a goat!"

Hard gray eyes assessed her as Justin fought the heated urge to drag her back into his arms and prove her wrong. His lips broke into a cold smile. "You may live to regret your decision, little one. George might be willing to share his name, but he'll be able to share little else. I, on the other hand, would have given you all your heart could have possibly desired—all, that is, except my name."

A murderous glare lit Aidan's eyes, and she would have pronounced her acidic retort, but the coach suddenly lurched as the horses were whipped into a full gallop. The abrupt motion threw her off-balance, and she swallowed her words.

"Highwaymen!" Potts yelled from above as he snapped the whip in quick succession, driving the team onward.

Justin released the fuming Aidan to quickly shift into the opposite seat. His fist hit the coach wall, and a hidden panel sprang free, revealing a set of matched pistols. "Get down," he ordered as he grabbed one and poured powder down its barrel, then rammed the lead ball home. Aidan obeyed without hesitation and curled herself up like a cat, her cheek hugging the rich leather seat as she held on for dear life.

The coach pitched wildly as Justin tried to prime the

weapon. Fine powder spilled across his hand onto the floor. A vibrant expletive escaped him as he cursed his luck. His grip on the weapon tightened, and the job was completed in short order. The cocked pistol was slipped beneath his sinewy thigh, its barrel pointed toward the door.

While Justin worked furiously to load the second pistol, thundering hooves drew alongside the careening coach. "Halt!" a masculine voice shouted, but Potts paid him no mind. "Stop, I says," the man commanded, "or I'll blow yer bloomin' head off!"

The coach swayed crazily, then jolted to a sudden stop, tossing Justin sideways. The cocked pistol slid from the seat and hit the floor. Powder flashed as the weapon exploded. Another curse erupted from Justin's lips as Aidan simultaneously cried out in fright. Both were drowned out by a screech of pain, while as it sheared through the night air, just beyond the coach window.

The ball rammed into the second pistol, Justin flipped it around to pour the priming powder. Forthwith, the door flew wide, a bevy of weapons aimed at his head. Assessing the group, several lit torches held high among them, Justin decided there was little chance he could bluff his way out of his predicament. Slowly he lowered his own pistol, setting it aside.

"Let me at him," one of the men snarled, fighting his way toward the forefront of the pack. "The coward! He put a hole in me, he did!"

"Shut up," the man closest to the door said, his pistol now leveled at Justin's heart. "Quit yer complainin'. Ye'r only scratched."

His senses attuned to every sound, every move, Justin smiled. "You've caught me low on funds, gentlemen." He slipped a gold ring from the little finger on his right hand. The large ruby, surrounded by diamonds, winked in the dim light. "Perhaps this ornament will suffice." He held it out to the man who appeared to be the group's leader.

"We ain't after yer money or yer jewelry, mister. So keep that bauble on yer pinky."

An odd feeling settled over Justin; his eyes narrowed suspiciously. "Then if you aren't intent on robbery, do you mind explaining why you've detained my coach?"

The man jerked his head. "It's her we're after."

All eyes turned toward Aidan, who now huddled in her corner. "Me! Why me?"

"Ye'r the Duke of Atwood's daughter, ain't ye?" the man asked, and Aidan quickly turned anxious eyes toward Justin. "Well, yea or nay, girlie?"

"Sir," Justin intervened, his gaze scanning the field of men. Not seeing Aidan's father among them, he edged forward in his seat, his body making a partial barrier between Aidan and the man in the doorway. The man's lax pistol swung to attention. "There's no need to be so jittery. I'm unarmed and outnumbered." Justin's hand rose slowly, the tip of his finger gently easing the barrel aside. He relaxed when the man allowed it to remain in its new position. "The lady is whom you say," Justin continued. "You seem like a man who understands the ways of love. Without regard for her health or safety, this young woman's father plans to force her into a marriage she does not want. The man to whom she is to be betrothed is depraved, perverse—a wife beater. Instead of subjecting herself to such cruelty—a life of unending torture—she travels to Gretna Green with me. Certainly you understand our haste. We are—"

"In desperate need of a marriage agent, I'd say," a cold voice interrupted.

"Father!" Aidan cried incredulously. Her heart tripped wildly as Alastair Prescott stepped into view, his stern gaze first raking over his daughter, then settling on Justin. Disbelief written on her face, she croaked, "How did you—?"

"In your haste to leave, daughter, you forgot to close the kitchen door behind you," he answered, his hard gaze riveted to Justin's. Two sets of narrowed eyes, one blue, one gray, carefully assessed the other, each pair refusing to look away. "You caused quite a stir, Aidan. We'd thought a thief had stolen you away. But Eugenia managed to set our fears to rest."

"Eugenia! How? She knew nothing of my plans."

Alastair finally turned his attention to his daughter. "She knew enough to set me in the right direction!" he snapped, his gaze shifting back to Justin's. "Your Grace," he said on a sarcastic note. "Might I join you inside the coach? The night air grows chilly."

Justin's lips split into a cool smile. "Please accept my invitation to do so, Your Grace." The lofty form of address was stressed with equal sarcasm as he waved the older man inside. "You must forgive me for not asking you sooner. My excuse being: at the moment, I was given cause to forget my manners. I do hope you'll understand."

Inclining his head, Alastair returned the cool smile. "I do, sir." When he'd seated himself next to Justin, he turned his attention to the man in the doorway. "Mr. Thompson, please join us, if you will." The man seemed startled by the invitation; then he turned to hand his weapon to one of his companions. "I'll have need of your pistol as well," Alastair stated, and Thompson pulled his girth through the doorway, weapon in hand.

"Miss," he said with a nod as he sat next to Aidan. His gaze turned itself on his employer. "There be a problem, Yer Grace? I thought everythin' were settled—ye all bein' so civil to one another and the like."

Alastair chuckled. "All's well, Thompson. You're simply my insurance it stays that way."

Upon hearing her father's words, Aidan suddenly feared some harm might come to Justin. So far, she'd remained virtually silent, first from fear, then from confusion, but she quickly found her voice. "Father, I must explain. The Duke of Westover—"

"There's no reason to explain, Aidan," he said, waving her off. "Everything is quite apparent. His Grace has already admitted the two of you were on your way to Gretna Green. I'm just making certain your elopement proceeds as planned."

Aidan breathed easier. But had she seen the contented look in her father's eye, closely resembling that of a fat cat after it had just ingested a small bird, she'd have realized she'd misinterpreted his words. "Then you know about George?"

"George?" Alastair questioned, pretending ignorance as a frown marked his brow. "Ah, the best man. Since he's not here, we'll have to proceed without him."

Aidan blinked. "Best man! Father, he's—"

"Not important, daughter. Your marriage to Westover, here, will simply have to go unattended."

"Marriage! But, Father, he's not the man . . ."

Frozen into a human statue, Justin sat silently, listening to the exchange between father and daughter, cold eyes appraising both. From the moment the man called Thompson had mentioned Atwood's name, Justin had suspected he was doomed. When Alastair Prescott had stepped forward, he *knew* it.

Not seeing the man initially, he'd thought the band of men had been sent toward Gretna Green with instructions to stop all coaches in hopes of catching the errant Lady Prescott, her father having remained in London. Foolishly, he'd tried to enlist the leader's sympathy, but he now realized his words had served only to trap him. Or had they? Perhaps he'd been the intended bridegroom all along!

As he thought on it, Justin was certain, from the moment he'd declined Atwood's proposed alliance between Aidan and himself, the man had become instrumental in maneuvering all the players to their present end, like actors in a play.

No doubt poor destitute George had been paid a tidy sum to portray the part of anxious bridegroom, moving on- and offstage just quickly enough to say his lines and be gone. The ruse he'd used to excuse himself now seemed a bit contrived. What legitimate bridegroom would actually leave his ladylove in the hands of another while he rushed off to patch up an old house? None that Justin knew of.

Aidan Prescott, on the other hand, had undoubtedly rehearsed her part to perfection. She'd certainly fooled him with her instant show of dislike, her immediate defense of George and their forthcoming marriage, and her feigned swoon in the coach. Angered that he'd been duped, Justin conveniently disregarded the memory of how ill she'd been afterward.

Then, he thought, there was her softly whispered "Good night, Papa," which had instantly tugged at his heart and gained his sympathy, causing him a sleepless night. Her sudden bout of tears and quick surrender into his arms—too quick, he realized, as he looked back on it—were all a ploy to throw him off-guard. Undoubtedly, though, when he'd mentioned the word "mistress," her reaction had been genuine. From the start, marriage had been her game, and she'd been unwilling to settle for less.

"Say something!" Aidan demanded of Justin, breaking through his dark thoughts, hoping, praying he could somehow persuade her father this was all a terrible mistake.

Steely eyes turned on her. "What is it you want me to say? That I refuse to marry you? I think not, sweet Aidan. The cards are stacked against me. Should I balk, Thompson will blow my head off." Hard eyes snagged Aidan's father's. "Right, Your Grace?"

"Very perceptive of you," her father replied.

Gray eyes pivoted toward the daughter. "So you see, Aidan, it seems I have little recourse but to marry you."

Her eyes round with disbelief, Aidan stared at Justin; then her slackened jaw instantly snapped shut. Her fiery stare singed the Duke of Westover from head to toe, making known her discontent. How could he take this so calmly? Anger filled her, for he'd refused to put up a fight and had simply lain down like a whipped dog. Quickly she thought to grab the pistol and fire at him herself. Coward! she silently railed, then immediately turned on her father. "I'll not marry this . . . this *miscreant,* no matter what you say or do! I'd prefer death, any day!" Without warning, she seized the pistol barrel, aiming it directly at her heart. "Shoot, I say!"

Alastair's own heart seemed to pop into his throat, while Thompson's eyes bulged from his head. Fortunately the man was steady of hand or there would have been certain disaster. "Here, girlie, take yer hand away."

"No! Shoot me!"

"Aidan!" Alastair commanded. "Do as you're told!"

Abrupt laughter filled the coach, startling the two Prescotts, plus the duke's hired man. All eyes slowly turned toward Justin. "Bravo!" he piped, applauding. "Nice touch! You nearly had me convinced." Astounded, Aidan relaxed her hold, and Justin watched as the weapon was quickly lowered. "There's no need for theatrics, Aidan," Justin stated, his sarcasm evident. "I know my fate is sealed."

Slapped with the realization that Justin somehow thought she was involved in her father's plot to bind them as man and wife, she fell back against her seat; her eyes searched his face. "Surely you don't think—"

"I do, *sweet* Aidan." His sharp gaze sliced into her like honed steel. "Now, enough has been said on the subject."

Certain she'd been rent in two by his cutting stare, Aidan realized nothing she could say or do would change his mind. He'd pronounced her guilty without benefit of trial. Slowly her gaze fell from his. Admittedly, both their fates had been sealed.

Alastair had watched the exchange between his daughter and Westover with interest. When he and his men had first come upon the coach, he'd been ready to pull the blackguard he'd found inside through the door and trounce the man soundly. But when his eyes had caught sight of Westover's ducal crest, he'd instantly thought better of it.

Lying back, he had waited, making certain it was indeed Justin Warfield within. When the man's voice had confirmed it, Alastair could hardly contain his glee. What a stroke of luck! To think that his first choice in the way of a suitable husband for his daughter—the only man he knew could control her, tame her wild nature, and produce a horde of physically and mentally sound offspring for Alastair to indulge—would fall so easily into his hands! Fate had surely smiled upon him. But now he wondered if he'd perhaps erred in his judgment.

No, he decided as his gaze ran over his daughter, then Westover. The two were a perfect match. Though neither of them realized it now, they would—eventually. Alastair was certain of it. "Thompson," he ordered abruptly, "have one of your men take the reins. Tell the others to stay close behind. Within a short time we'll all be on our way home."

The coach was backed from the shallow ditch, where it had landed, and was soon set into motion. The stern mode of silence which cloaked the foursome inside the rolling vehicle, heading ever closer to Scotland, seemed to Aidan like a shroud of death. Her death, she thought, knowing her carefree life and the freedom she'd once enjoyed would soon lie buried. As she peered at Justin, bathed in dim moonlight, she was certain her body would soon follow. A lust for blood seethed from his gaze, sending an instant chill down her spine. May God help her when they were finally alone!

All too soon, the coach stopped in front of a small white-washed cottage topped by a thatched roof. The sign hanging above the front door indicated that nuptials were performed inside. With the marriage agent quickly routed from his bed, the unhappy couple was escorted through the door, the Duke of Atwood and several pistol-bearing men playing the part of attendants.

When the agent nervously asked if Justin had a ring to give his bride, Justin quickly slipped the ruby ring from his little finger and shoved it onto the third finger of Aidan's left hand. Their vows exchanged—Justin's in clipped tones, Aidan's barely choked through her lips—the agent then informed Justin he could kiss the bride. A quick peck settled itself on her forehead.

"Satisfied?" Justin asked of his new father-in-law as he stepped away from Aidan's side.

"Completely," Alastair answered with a cool smile. "Just remember, my son, she is to be cared for in the manner to which she is accustomed. Also, her health has never suffered in the past. I don't expect it to now."

The duke's message received, Justin inclined his head. "She will be taken under my protection. No harm will come to her, I assure you."

"Then I see no reason why the happy couple can't be on their way," Alastair said at large, and his men lowered their pistols. He stepped to Aidan, folding her into his embrace. Immediately he felt her stiffen.

"How could you?" she whispered accusingly.

"He's far better than Sedgewinn, daughter. With time, you'll understand why I did what I did."

"Never," she countered, her hurt evident, and pushed from his arms.

Ignoring her new husband completely, Aidan marched toward the door, feeling in desperate need of some fresh air. Tears stung the backs of her eyes and she fought to control them. Yet, despite her determination, several spilled over when she heard one of the men say, "Ain't never seen a bride who wore black to her own weddin' afore."

Certain she was about to flood the cottage, she quickly slipped outside into the night. A bride in mourning, she thought as she brushed her tears aside, breathing deeply. And she'd married a man who'd acted more like a pall-bearer than a groom. His elegant silk shirt, tight-fitting trousers, and fine leather boots, all the same shade as midnight, had fitted the occasion perfectly. She was doomed! Trapped in a void where she was certain no love would ever shine. And she'd never forgive her father for striking the final nail into her coffin by marrying her off to a black-guard like Justin Warfield, the "notorious" Duke of Westover! With an angry scuff of her shoe, she decided she hated them both!

Moonlight suddenly reflected off the center stone of the ring gracing her left hand, flashing like fire in her eye. In a fit of temper, she pulled the gold circle from her finger, intending to toss it into the woods, beyond the road. Instantly a strong hand clamped over hers, startling her.

"That ring, sweet wife, is probably worth more than your dowry and three others combined."

"What dowry?" Aidan snapped, hoping he'd think her destitute.

"Precisely. So I suggest you reconsider your deed. That trinket may very well be the only thing of value you ever receive from me."

Aidan shoved it into his hand. "Keep it. I have no use for it." She turned on her heel, intent on heading for the coach.

Infuriated by Aidan's shrewish tone, mainly because he was now trapped in an unwanted marriage, Justin took off after her. His hand snagged her arm, spinning her around. Her wrist trapped in his long fingers, he pushed the ring back onto her finger. "Never take it off again. You're mine now, Aidan, and all the world shall know it. Consider it a token of my *love*."

The sarcasm that dripped from his words angered her further. "You insolent buffoon!" she berated him, fighting against his hold and her tears. "You wouldn't know what love was, not even if it were to slap you in the face."

Thinking she intended to retaliate, as she had tried to do in the coach, Justin quickly caught hold of her other wrist and jerked her against him. "A bride can hardly leave the wedding chapel without the proper signature of marriage. Can she, sweet?"

Justin let loose her wrists, and before Aidan could react, his arm slipped round her waist, molding her snugly against his hard length; his mouth covered hers in one fell swoop. Momentarily, she stood stunned. His harsh lips became more insistent, his hard, angry tongue forcing its way between her lips, and she began to fight against his strong hold and the wild emotion which had suddenly rocked through her entire body.

In desperation, the heels of Aidan's palms shoved against Justin's shoulders, only to slide off the silk-clad sinew beneath them. His hold tightened as his fingers splayed across the back of her head, forcing her to be still. His lips opened more fully, his deepening kiss branding her, burning her, consuming her. Then, when Aidan thought herself all used up, Justin suddenly released her. "Consider that another token of my undying love. One that will not be repeated." Without warning, he swept her up into his arms, deposited her inside the coach, and slammed the door.

As Alastair Prescott watched the entire episode from the doorway of the small cottage, the couple's words lost to him, he thought better of allowing Justin Warfield to take immediate leave with Aidan, alone. Acute anger emanated from the young duke. One misstated word, one false step, and the man's weak hold on himself was bound to snap its restraints. Once unleashed, his fury would, no doubt, erupt with a ferocity that would rival any beast's. Alastair hoped Westover's tenuous hold on his temper would stabilize with time. And the older man meant to stay close at hand until he was certain it had. Then, to his surprise, he watched as Justin climbed atop the coach to settle next to the driver.

"My men and I will follow along with you back to London," Alastair informed Justin upon reaching the coach.

"The road is open to all who wish to travel it," Justin replied coolly. "However, Aidan and I are headed only as far as my estate. You'll be on your own from there." With that, Justin snatched up the reins and, by way of a quick flick of his wrists, set the coach in motion.

Alastair surveyed the vehicle, dust kicking up from the road in its wake, and he wished he'd been much less impetuous and a good deal more prudent in his original assessment of things. Perhaps Justin Warfield was the wrong choice for his daughter, after all. With a frown marking his brow, Alastair quickly mounted his horse, then followed, never falling far behind.

6

Aidan stepped from the interior of the coach, her neck craning backward as she gazed up at the huge three-story brick-and-stone mansion known as Warfield Manor. To her eye, the beautiful structure exuded wealth. Smoothing the wrinkled skirt of Penny's black gown, she waited nervously while Justin instructed Potts to bring her small case when he came.

"Are you ready, my lovely bride, to make your grand entrance as Warfield Manor's new mistress?" Justin asked, his intent gaze upon her.

Aidan noticed his somewhat cordial tone did not match the hard glint in his eyes, and it unnerved her. From the moment they'd left Gretna Green, he'd purposely distanced himself, either by riding atop the coach with Potts or by exchanging places with one of the ever-present group of hired men, who kept vigil on the conveyance, to ride horseback for a while. Not once had he entered the coach, and Aidan had been relieved he hadn't.

She was now alone with him, her father having said his farewells where the roads to London and Warfield Manor had forked. Again she viewed the huge structure. Her new home stood before her. *His* home, she corrected, sure she would never be able to consider it her own. Oddly, a deep sadness settled around her heart, for she thought of the lovely place, not in the terms of ownership, but in the sense of welcome and belonging. Never would Justin extend those simple, yet pleasant courtesies to her. Of that she was certain.

Aidan felt a hand at her elbow, and her husband guided her up the stone steps, across a level plain of slate, toward two massive doors that were artfully carved, the Westover ducal crest set in stone above them. As the pair reached the entry, one panel abruptly swung inward.

"Your Grace," the elderly butler said, alarmed by his employer's unexpected appearance. "We were not fore-warned. No message—"

"Relax, Ridley, before you suffer a bout of apoplexy. No warning came because I hadn't planned on being here."

"I'll have the banner raised," Ridley stated, referring to the display of arms which flew on a pole atop the house whenever the duke was in residence.

"Don't bother. I'll be gone before it can be hoisted."

Her huge violet eyes taking in the grandeur surrounding her, Aidan had missed the exchange. At her feet, pink-veined marble flowed across the great hall to sweep up the walls, several stories, to a massive glass cupola, its beveled panes acting as both protection and opening to the blue heavens beyond. A huge chandelier, secured by a sturdy chain and anchored in an iron beam which ribbed the glass, dropped from its domed center. A multitude of candles graced the gilded sconces, waiting to be lit at nightfall.

Straight across from the entrance, where Aidan stood, was a wide staircase, also of pink-veined marble, that climbed upward into the core of the house. Framed by at least a dozen marble columns and a carved marble balustrade, the area beyond was secreted from her view. On each side of the huge foyer were a half-dozen rooms, their gilt-trimmed white doors tightly closed, all except one.

"Ridley!" a woman's voice impatiently called through the open panel. "Who goes there?"

Aidan watched as an elderly woman appeared in the doorway. Hair the color of polished silver, she stood regally for one of such small stature; an arthritic hand gripped the gold knob of her walking cane, lending her support.

"Westover!" she cried in surprise. "What brings you here?"

Justin's lips spread into a wide grin which sparkled in his silvery eyes. "Why, you, of course, Aunt Patti," he said as his long strides carried him toward his great-aunt's side. "I've missed seeing you."

One silver brow arched skeptically. "A likely story, nephew," she said, presenting her lined cheek for his light kiss. "Soon enough, the truth will be out." Her faded blue eyes latched on to Aidan. "Another servant girl? Ridley, take her to the kitchens and have her fed, then show her to her new quarters."

Justin's aunt waved a dismissal at Aidan, making her blink. "Servant girl!" Aidan exclaimed as she shook free of Ridley's hand, which had somehow attached itself to her arm. She marched toward the woman. "I beg your pardon, but—"

"Silence, you insolent chit!" Aunt Pattina snapped, emphasizing her words with a thump of her cane. She squared her sagging shoulders. "Such impudence will not be tolerated in this house, young woman, and never in the presence of your superiors. If you expect to remain employed here, you shall remember those rules. Now you may take your leave. Ridley will show you the way."

Aidan bristled; violet eyes instantly clashed with blue. Never before had a member of the peerage spoken to her in such condescending tones. Little did it matter her appearance confirmed the older woman's assumption that she was nothing more than a servant. If the positions were switched, however, Aidan knew she would never have uttered such a sharp command to anyone, no matter what her status in life.

Drawing a breath, Aidan was about to pronounce who she was when a burst of laughter rang through the air. Startled, both women turned curious eyes toward its source.

Justin's merriment settled into a deep rumble within his chest. "Forgive me," he said, having regained his composure, then tried to make a formal introduction, a social amenity which he hated and paid little heed in doing correctly. "Aunt Patti, uh . . . Pattina Warfield Wadsworth, the dowager Marchioness of Falvey—Lady Falvey—may I present my new bride. Aidan holds the title that nearly all the single women in England have coveted. She is now known as Her Grace, the Duchess of Westover."

Aunt Patti's chin dropped, then instantly snapped to. Recovering from her initial shock, she quickly found her voice. "Have you lost your mind, nephew? Whatever possessed your to marry a common maid?"

Aidan had had enough. "Madam," she addressed Justin's aunt, "it may come as a surprise to you, but I am not a common maid, as it were. My father is Alastair Prescott, the Duke of Atwood. For the sake of argument, however, let's say I were indeed the daughter of a lowly chimney sweep. I need not remind you, or any of the peerage, that as the Duchess of Westover, I deserve the respect my rank affords me." Inwardly Aidan was surprised by her own words, and the haughtiness in which they were said, but she continued on. "With your rank being one mark lower than mine, I am now *your* superior. But since I do not hold much stock in the pretentiousness of our social structure, I shall not require you address me in the formal manner in which one might expect. Please call me Aidan."

Aunt Patti's brow arched anew as she reassessed the newcomer into the Warfield fold. Frisky little baggage, she thought, her respect for the girl growing with each passing second. Yet she purposely held her admiration in check. Instead she emitted a self-righteous sniff. "Christian names are reserved only for those individuals who have gained my affection. You, madam, have yet to do so."

Again Justin laughed. "I can see the two of you will get along nicely. Knowing as much, I shall take my leave."

"Leave!" Aidan cried. "Where are you going?"

"Back to London, of course, to resume the life I've always enjoyed."

Aidan watched as he turned on his heel, heading for the door. Suddenly she was certain he intended to desert her, allowing her to wither and die. Hiking her skirts, she quickly followed after him and snatched at his sleeve, catching it. "You don't mean to abandon me here . . . alone?"

"Sweet Aidan," Justin said, a smile teasing his lips,

"you won't be alone. Aunt Patti shall be here to keep you company." He removed her insistent fingers from his sleeve.

"I won't stay . . . you can't make me!"

"You will, dear wife. Orders shall be issued that the farthest point you may go is the boundary of this estate and no farther. As I promised your father, you will be fed and cared for in the manner to which you have been accustomed. As the Good Book says, 'Ask and it shall be given.' You can have anything you desire. All you need do is behave yourself and follow my rules."

"Which are?" Aidan asked.

"You are to stay at Warfield Manor until I say you may leave."

"You act as though I'm some paltry criminal who's been given a life sentence for some odious crime that was perpetrated against all mankind. I've done nothing wrong. You have no right to imprison me here."

"Don't I?" Justin asked, his thumb and forefinger catching her defiant chin. He tilted her head up and Aidan's eyes met his hard gaze. "You wanted to be the Duchess of Westover, and so you are."

"That's not true! I didn't want to be your wife. I had nothing to do with our being forced to marry. You must believe me. My father's plans were of his own making. I had no part in it. I knew nothing about it."

"Such a pretty tale, sweet. But I fear I don't believe a word you've said. As your husband, I have every right to say what you can and cannot do, where you will and will not live. Believe me when I say it won't be in London. I don't wish to be encumbered with an unwanted bride." He dropped his hand. "But remember, sweet, when I have decided the time has come for me to sire an heir, you will see me again—not before. Until then, lovely Aidan, I bid you farewell."

Aidan would have started a new round of protests, denying she ever wanted to be his wife—an encumbrance, as he'd put it—but her husband snatched her small bag from Potts's hands and shoved it into her own; the door slammed in her face. Justin was gone.

Hopelessly she stared at the door; then her shoulders slumped in defeat. Turning, she noted Justin's aunt was

inspecting her closely. Too weary to listen to another Warfield's slams, she headed toward the stairs. Rest and privacy were what she wanted, desperately needed, and she
cared not where she found them, just as long as she did so.

"Ridley," Aunt Pattina called as Aidan placed her foot
on the first step, leading to who-knew-where. "Show Her
Grace to the suite next to the duke's. Draw her a hot bath
and have a tray sent up. Afterward, she is not to be disturbed by anyone."

Gratitude shone in Aidan's eyes as she turned her gaze
on Justin's aunt, but the woman had already turned away
and, with the aid of her cane, was headed back into the
sitting room.

As she followed Ridley up the stairs, Aidan caught sight
of the ruby ring on her finger. The fire in the stone seemed
to brand her hand. Justin had ordered her never to remove
it, but defiantly she slipped it from her hand, vowing never
to wear it again.

Bright light filtered through the windows of the morning
room making its blue decor glitter like sapphires. Its serenity
did little to appease Aidan, who sat pretending interest in
her embroidery. Angrily she jabbed the needle into the
fabric and pulled the thread through, only to have it knot.
She paid it no mind and continued the routine stitching
through the cloth, until finally she thrust the needle into her
thumb.

Her silver brow arching, Aunt Patti watched as Aidan
winced; then in a fit of temper the younger woman tossed
her needlework across the room. "At least you are wise
enough to admit when you have no talent for fine stitchery.
Many young women would have continued with their task,
believing they were creating a beautiful work of art. I ad-
mire your truthfulness."

As Aidan sucked the drop of blood from her thumb,
fearing it would fall onto her off-white gown—her only
gown for the time being—she turned a surprised look on the
woman, for Aunt Patti had barely spoken a dozen words to
her since she'd been abandoned at Warfield Manor by her
husband four days ago. "I could outsew fifty women should

I have a mind to do so,'' Aidan answered. "Right now, my patience grows thin.''

"I suppose that sampler was merely a facsimile of my nephew's heart. The way you were plunging the needle into it, I'd say, if it were the real thing, Westover would be lying dead somewhere by now.''

"I care not where he is,'' Aidan lied, soothing her tender thumb. "Dead or alive, it makes little difference to me.''

"Then why are you so restless? It would seem to me, if you cared little about your husband, you'd be quite content sitting in the lap of luxury, as you are now. But that doesn't seem to be the case. Obviously, something is troubling you.''

Aidan came out of her chair to pace the floor. "I'm being held prisoner. Every time I come within twenty paces of the main gate, someone pops from the bushes and sets me on a course back to the house. I'm not allowed near the stables for fear I'll snatch a horse and bolt. I resent such treatment. I have no money, no transportation. So how do they expect me to escape this place? I'm being watched every moment of the day. No doubt my door and windows are guarded at night.''

"They are,'' Aunt Patti admitted, drawing a look of disbelief from Aidan. "I have no say in the matter, child. Westover left orders to have you watched. You are not to leave the grounds under any circumstances.''

"But why?'' Aidan asked, feeling confused and hurt over her confinement. "I've done nothing wrong. Why does he treat me so?''

"You tell me,'' Aunt Patti countered, then waited for an answer.

Violet eyes surveyed Justin's aunt. The woman was always watching her, as though she were looking for a flaw. Undoubtedly, Lady Falvey had found many, Aidan decided, for indeed Aidan had not been on her best behavior. Depressed and moody, she had withdrawn into her shell. Even the brisk walks she took daily did little to relieve the tension that was building inside her. Eyes were always following her, spying on her every move, and she was about to come unhinged from the continuous feeling of oppression which surrounded her. To be free, that's all she wanted. Free of Warfield, both the estate and the man.

"I have little information on what transpired between my nephew and yourself to know precisely how the two of you managed to be saddled with each other," Aunt Patti said, drawing Aidan's attention. "Would you like to elaborate? Perhaps then I can tell you why my nephew wants you kept out of his hair."

Aidan sighed. There was no reason why Justin's aunt should not know of the events that had led up to their forced marriage. Taking her seat, she explained how it all came to pass. She started with the episode in Hyde Park and ended with the so-called marriage ceremony in the small cottage at Gretna Green, leaving nothing out. "So you see, for some ridiculous reason, he believes I was part of a conspiracy to trap him. I swear I had nothing to do with it. Why, I'd rather have joined a convent than to be strapped to the likes of him. He's the last man I'd have chosen to marry!"

Lady Falvey surveyed Aidan at length, just as she had over the last several days. In that time, she'd been able to read the girl and had discovered that Aidan was much like herself when Pattina was of the same age: intelligent, high-spirited, independent, restless, and stubborn. As stubborn as her nephew—obviously a Warfield trait.

Pattina Warfield Wadsworth quite liked Aidan; however, she believed Aidan's story only up to a point. The concluding part of her niece's statement was definitely false. Aidan might believe Justin was the last man she'd have ever chosen to marry, but Pattina did not. The problem was how to make the chit realize it. Her nephew, as well.

To Pattina, it was obvious that they were meant for each other. And there had to be a way to maneuver these two headstrong individuals into a position where, once they discovered the unmistakable truth themselves, they would willingly fall into each other's arms. A deception, perhaps. Whatever it took, she had to get the newlyweds together. And the sooner, the better, she thought, knowing she'd enjoy welcoming yet another generation into the Warfield family.

"What? Isn't he handsome enough or rich enough for your tastes?" Aunt Patti baited.

Aidan stared at Justin's aunt. "It has nothing to do with his physical appearance or his wealth, Lady Falvey. Your nephew is extremely handsome—too much so—and by the looks of this place, I'm certain he holds a great fortune. It's because we don't love each other."

"Is love important to you?" the dowager asked, her gaze studying the girl carefully.

"Yes . . . very," Aidan said, her eyes misting over. "Ever since I was a small child, I had dreamed of having a marriage very much like my parents had. I remember the affection, the caring, the laughter. Even after my mother died, I held on to that dream. But apparently my father has forgotten what love means in a marriage, for he tried to pair me with that hideous Lord Sedgewinn. He didn't even ask what I wanted."

"Was the secret alliance with my godson, Viscount Edmonds, what you wanted?"

Aidan blanched. "George is *your* godson?"

"Yes, he is. Undoubtedly, that's how Westover became involved. My nephew knew I'd be displeased if he had turned George away." She shrugged. "Well, it seems Westover's desire to forgo a confrontation with me has gotten him into a bit of a spot—you too." She sighed effectively. "Have you notified George of your marriage yet?"

"No. I don't know how to tell him," Aidan said in a small voice, aware she hadn't done so because she was a coward. "Or, for that matter, where he might be."

"Well, I doubt that he's still at Gretna Green."

"I never intended to hurt George, Lady Falvey. And I never intended to marry your nephew. He's the last man I would have chosen for a husband," Aidan repeated, trying to convince herself it was so. "Why didn't I save us all the worry by running off to a convent?"

Pattina's light chuckle erupted, startling her new niece. "A convent? I doubt that, sincerely. And most women would have named him their first choice in marriage. You are quite unusual, Aidan. Quite unusual, indeed."

Aidan had noted the use of her Christian name and realized Lady Falvey had apparently come to feel some form of affection for her. "What am I to do?" she asked of Justin's aunt.

"Sitting around moping certainly isn't the answer. As I see it, my nephew wishes to keep you under wraps so he can continue his wandering ways. Out of sight, out of mind, so to speak. And you, my dear, are strapped to the rogue, whether you like it or not. For better or for worse, the bonds of matrimony shall hold the two of you together until at least one of you departs this life."

"Certainly you're not suggesting I shoot the blackguard?" Aidan asked incredulously. "Though I'd gain a certain amount of satisfaction in doing so, I don't relish the thought of leaving one prison, only to be cast into another."

"I was suggesting no such thing, dear. Although it may seem the only plausible route to travel at the moment, I think perhaps, if you take a hard look at the situation, you may discover that gaining your husband's affection is the better way of dealing with it."

Aidan's jaw dropped. "Gain his affection! Why, you must be insane! That's the last thing I want from the man!"

No sooner had the words left her mouth than Aidan wondered if they were true. Despite what she might state to his aunt, over these past several days Aidan had found her every waking thought to be of Justin Warfield. She couldn't eradicate the insufferable rogue from her mind! Moreover, each night, he managed to steal his way into her dreams, his molten-silver eyes hotly traversing her body, his pliant masculine lips kissing her senseless, and Aidan would awaken with a start, her heart pounding wildly, her whole body aching for the unknown. Far or near, he tormented her constantly. Would he ever leave her alone?

The sound of Lady Falvey's voice snapped Aidan from her reverie. "Has he not stated, when he feels it is time to sire an heir, you will see him again?" Aunt Patti watched as Aidan blushed. A frown settled on the girl's brow; then she nodded. "If there is affection between you," Aunt Patti continued, "then the inevitable will be met with far less difficulty."

"You don't think he'd use force, do you?"

Pattina laughed lightly. "Force? He'll have no need to

use force, dear. He is known to be very persuasive. He's charming, tender, intriguing, potent, and extremely handsome. He's the best the male species has to offer. And from what I hear, no man is purported to be a better lover." Pattina saw Aidan blush anew. Satisfied, she continued her onslaught. "And although, at first, you may vow to resist him, I'm quite certain, in the end, you will break that promise." Pattina sighed. "Indeed, he will come for you, Aidan. And in view of my nephew's lusty appetites, it will not be long before he reappears to take possession of what is rightfully his."

"Ridiculous!" Aidan scoffed with false bravado. "He has nearly all the women in London falling at his feet, offering themselves freely. Why should he come for me?"

"That's precisely why he'll come for you. There is no challenge with the others. All men have the inborn desire to give chase and the need to conquer. History states as much, from the caveman on upward in time. Westover becomes bored easily, as is evidenced by his past affairs. As he makes his rounds in London, it won't be long before he begins to think of the young beauty, his virginal bride, whom he's left behind. From what you've told me, I gather you've made it quite clear that you despise him, that you don't wish to be chained to him, that he's the last man you'd willingly give yourself to. Once his temper has cooled over being caught, he'll start thinking about those words of rejection. His ego won't allow them to go unanswered. Take it as the truth. He'll be back—soon."

Aidan blanched. Fear rippled through her. "But . . . but I don't want him here. I . . . I don't want anything to do with him! Isn't there some way I can stop this from happening?"

"Escape is all," Aunt Patti said, her head shaking with mock hopelessness. "But I see little chance of your doing so."

The thought of Justin's coming for her upset Aidan more than she would have liked to admit. He frightened her, for, just as Aunt Patti had said, he was far too masculine, far too magnetic. Indeed, he surrounded himself with an air of mystery which made most women want to break through the layers of secrecy and discover the man hidden beneath. Unfortunately, she was no different. Knowing she lacked the strength to fight him off for long, she realized she'd eventually succumb to his persuasive charms. But once she'd given herself to him, Aidan feared he'd cast her aside, the chase ended, his conquest made. She knew she'd be left wanting, desiring him, in a womanly way. She'd be lost to him forever. To allow Justin Warfield anywhere near her, Aidan knew, meant certain doom.

"Aunt Patti, isn't there some way you can help me?" Aidan asked as she sprang from her chair to settle at the dowager marchioness's feet. Pleading violet eyes gazed upward, seeking an answer. "I won't allow myself to be made his slave—like some concubine he can use at will. No woman should be made to submit to a man in that way. It's degrading . . . wrong."

Aunt Patti noted the sudden sheen of tears in Aidan's wide violet eyes and smiled to herself. "You speak of my nephew as though he were some sort of barbarian."

"Isn't he?" Aidan countered. "What else would one call a man who has made his wife prisoner against her will? Please, there must be some way I can escape my fate. An annulment, perhaps. I can petition—"

"Do you really think the Queen will allow it?" Lady Falvey asked, trying to dissuade Aidan from such thoughts. "I expect it highly unlikely Her Majesty will turn aside your marriage, especially when it was she who suggested you find yourself a husband."

"Then what am I to do?" Aidan asked, feeling despondent.

Lady Falvey pretended to study the possibilities. "Well . . . if we're careful . . . No! I doubt it would work."

"What? Please tell me!"

"Well, in the afternoons, I usually take a short drive in the phaeton. Today I'll delay my outing until early evening. If we're careful, I might be able to smuggle you through the gates and off to the nearest coaching inn. You'll have to curl up under my feet as tight as a cat. My skirts and the lap robe I use for warmth to keep my legs from stiffening up should provide sufficient cover to hide you."

"How do you propose I escape my guards?" Aidan asked, not certain it would work.

"I'll send several of them on fictitious errands. As for the few that will remain, I'll create a diversion of sorts. I'm not certain what, but by the time we're ready to leave, I'll have thought it through. All you'll need worry about is meeting me at the stand of trees where the drive curves toward the gates. Wear the dress you arrived in. The less conspicuous you are, the better. If you look like a maid, they might think you're a maid. Be there at half-past six.''

"Do you think it will work?" Aidan asked, needing reassurance.

"We can only give it a try."

"And if we fail?"

Pattina laughed. "I've never failed at anything in my life, dear. Why should I do so now?"

Aidan believed Justin's aunt. The woman was indeed crafty. Aidan could only imagine Pattina in her younger days as being the most-sought-after catch in all of England. She was nearing seventy, and her beauty might have faded, but her wit and charm had not. And she was still smart as a steel trap. Strange, Aidan mused, that Justin's aunt had suddenly taken an interest in her plight, especially when the woman had treated her so coolly when she'd first arrived. But she quickly swept the thought from her head and began to wonder, should Aunt Patti's plan succeed and she did make it back to London, where could she possibly stay? Certainly not with her father. It would be a long time before she forgave him, if ever. Besides, he'd probably pack her up and ship her back to her husband, no questions asked.

"Do you have relatives in London?" Aunt Patti inquired, and Aidan wondered if the woman had read her mind.

"Only my father—but I refuse to have any contact with him. He betrayed me, his only child. Your nephew, as well. I shall not forgive him for it, ever."

"You can't very well sleep on the streets, dear girl. If we succeed, where shall you go?"

Aidan's teeth played along her lower lip. "There's always Eugenia."

"Ah, the young woman who suggested you elope. Since she was the one who put the idea into your head in the first place, I doubt she could very well turn you away. Should she try, play upon her guilt. It never fails."

"We are the best of friends. She would never refuse to help me."

"Good, good. Then I won't have to worry over your safety," Aunt Patti said, smoothing Aidan's coppery locks. "Should your possessions arrive, I'll redirect them back to London to . . . ?"

"Lord and Lady Manley's residence on Portman Square," Aidan supplied.

"Portman Square. I shall remember. In a very short time, you'll be able to change your clothing at will. Now, up with you." Lady Falvey motioned Aidan to her feet. "Pack your few belongings and have yourself ready. Don't forget. You're to meet me at half-past six. Until then, do and act as you always have. We don't wish to draw suspicion. A sour look will go a long way in throwing the lot off."

Aidan rose. "Lady Falvey, I can't thank you enough—"

"Don't thank me yet, child. Our plans haven't proved out. When they do, then I'll accept your praises. Now, off with you, and don't forget to look glum."

"I'll try," Aidan replied, a bright smile lighting her face, the first in nearly a week. Her freedom was at hand, and she couldn't help but be happy. As she reached the door, though, a frown settled on her brow. "Will this do?" she asked, turning toward Justin's aunt.

"Excellent," Aunt Patti replied, then watched as Aidan slipped through the panels, closing them behind her.

Quite pleased with herself, the dowager marchioness leaned back in her chair. She'd pulled it off. By restating the facts with a few well-placed misrepresentations, she'd convinced Aidan to head off to London, straight into her nephew's arms—and his bed, she hoped. Although she knew Westover would turn up for his bride eventually, Pattina also knew that would be a long time in coming. Why should the man rush back here when he believed his wife was being kept captive, safe from other men's eyes and arms? There was no need to hurry on his part that she could see. And when his temper did finally cool—in a year or two, she guessed—and he'd decided it was time to start a family, her arrogant nephew would slowly make his way back to his estate.

"Sorry, Westover," she said to the portrait of her nephew which hung over the marble fireplace, "but I don't have time for you to dawdle. What is left of my life grows short, and if I had waited for you, I'd be dead and buried well before you swallowed your pride and realized the woman you were forced to marry was the only one who would ever do." She rose from her chair to lean on her cane. "So, dear boy, I've hurried up that which cannot be escaped. Someday you'll thank me for it."

Then, with a regal bow of her head toward the portrait, Justin's aunt left the room.

At twenty past six, Aidan, who was dressed in Penny's black gown, waited in a darkened niche just outside the kitchen area, where Aunt Patti had instructed her to be. Not long after their talk, a note from the dowager marchioness had been slipped under Aidan's door, informing her that her escape route would be via the kitchen door. She was to listen carefully and take her cue when given. There was no hint of what Lady Falvey's directive might be, but Aidan knew she'd have only one chance, and she'd best act quickly.

Earlier in the afternoon, while taking her daily walk, she'd scouted the area near the rear of the house, then on toward the gates, searching for places to hide as she made her quick dash toward the stand of trees at the bend in the driveway. Several shrubs, the trunk of a two-hundred-year-old oak, and a short hedge, near the gardens, were miraculously placed to her advantage, allowing her a quick, speedy jaunt from one to the other, before she hit a longer stretch which led across the lawns and into the copse. With luck, she'd make it, with no one having spotted her.

So far, her fortune had been good. She'd been able to escape down the spiraling stairs, which led to the kitchens, without being detected. The opening and closing of several doors in the hallways had set her heart to pounding. And at one point it seemed to slip clear up into her throat when she thought she'd heard footsteps climbing the stairs toward her. Whoever it was had changed his mind and begun descending again. As soon as she thought it safe, Aidan had done the same.

Now, while pressed from sight, Aidan felt herself growing impatient. Time was quickly passing, and she wondered what was keeping Lady Falvey. And what should she be waiting for, listening for? Instantly she received her answer.

"All of you—snap to!" the dowager marchioness ordered with a thump of her cane as she entered the kitchens, surprising those within. "Line up over there. No, not there . . . there!" Lady Falvey pointed her cane toward an area meant to ensure that the entire staff would have their backs to Aidan's hiding place. "Excellent," she said, once everyone had scurried into position. "Now, eyes forward." The bevy of maids and servants quickly complied. "I've decided to conduct an impromptu inspection. Since we have the new Duchess of Westover living under this roof, I want everything in tiptop condition. That pot," she said of the thing as it hung from a hook on high. She hit her cane against its tarnished copper bottom and everyone, including Aidan, jumped. "I want it polished until it shines like a mirror."

The loud tone, which had rung out like a steeple bell, still rebounded through Aidan's head, and she wondered if that had been her signal. Chancing a peek, she espied the marchioness, her silver brow arched; the woman gave her a slight nod.

"Now, hands out!" Pattina stated brusquely. "I'll tolerate no filth—anywhere."

As the staff mumbled among themselves, a few secretly wiping their hands on their clothing, Aidan slipped from her nook and sneaked toward the back door, praying no one would notice her movement from the corner of his or her eye. Unfortunately, it was not to be.

"Hey, she's tryin' to slip off, she is," one of the scullery maids announced, and Aidan stiffened.

"So she is," Aunt Patti said in a frigid tone. "Thank you for noticing."

With her case in front of her, her back to the staff, Aidan stood frozen, waiting for the ax to fall, should someone recognize her.

"Eyes forward, I said!" Pattina commanded, and was instantly obeyed. "You, girl, since you probably wouldn't have passed inspection anyway, head out that door and keep going. I'll tolerate no deception from anyone. You may collect what's due you, along with your belongings, on Friday next. Now, be gone with you!"

Aidan breathed a sigh of relief and quickly headed for the door, only to smile at the marchioness's next words.

"Any further insubordination from anyone, and that person may follow straight after the chit! Now, let me see your hands."

Once Aidan's feet had hit the crushed stone beyond the small yard just outside the kitchens, she fairly flew across the back drive toward the first shrub, then on to the next and the next, until she scurried behind the huge oak. Resting a moment, she spotted the hedge, then glanced out over the lawns toward the copse. Checking to see if anyone was about, she then dashed to the safety of the hedge and across the lawn into the stand of trees.

Winded, she leaned back against a small tree for a brief respite to catch her breath, then made her way toward the main drive. Horse's hooves crunched in the stone, followed by the roll of wheels. Justin's aunt would be here any second, Aidan thought, smiling with relief.

Suddenly a man's voice rose up, and Aidan ducked behind a bush. Too late she recognized it as being sumac. As the gentle breeze lifted a poisonous leaf ever closer to her face, she stared down her nose at it, listening to the exchange just beyond.

"I'm sorry, yer ladyship, but the duke said I was to check all vehicles leavin' the property. Even yours."

"Get on with it, then!" Pattina snapped. "I'm already late for my outing." Nervously the man peeked inside the phaeton, then lifted the lap robe covering Lady Falvey's legs. "Satisfied?" Aunt Patti asked snappishly.

"Yes, ma'am," he answered, ducking his head.

"Then move on to the gate and open it for me," she ordered, and the guard loped off to do so. As soon as he was out of earshot, Aunt Patti called in a whisper, "Aidan, get out here, quick."

Lady Falvey guided the horse and phaeton off the road as close to the trees as she could possibly get them. Backing away from the bush, Aidan breathed a sigh of relief that it hadn't touched her, then bolted from the stand of trees and into the phaeton, beneath Aunt Patti's feet. Before she could get settled, the horse was on its way, Aunt Patti's feet resting on Aidan's ribs.

Curled into a ball under the lap robe, praying she was all tucked in tight, Aidan bounced along for what seemed an eternity. Finally the phaeton slowed, and Justin's aunt let out an audible sigh. "We're clear. Out from there, now."

Aidan pulled herself up from the floor to sit next to her fellow conspirator. Her light laughter erupted to sail high on the breeze. "Aunt Patti, you're an absolute wonder. You should give lessons in stealth to the Queen's own army."

The marchioness's laughter joined Aidan's. "Perhaps I should. It would be rather nice to have a flock of young men around me again, hanging on my every word. I'll consider your suggestion, Aidan dear. Yes," she said, smiling, her blue eyes dancing with merriment. "I will, indeed."

Before long, the phaeton pulled into an inn. The stage to London was already loading its passengers. Lady Falvey took several large bills from her reticule and handed them to Aidan. "This is to purchase your ticket, and the rest is for whatever you might need."

"I can't possibly take all this," Aidan said, her eyes wide as she realized just how much she had in her hand. "What will you do for funds?"

"Westover sends me a monthly allowance, of which I spend little. What you hold in your hand is actually yours. Take it. I'll send more as you need it. After all, your husband is responsible for your welfare. He's promised to keep you fed, clothed, and housed in the manner to which you are accustomed. I heard him say so myself. Now, no further word on the matter. The coach will be leaving any moment."

"Thank you, Aunt Patti. You are a godsend." Aidan hugged her husband's aunt, then placed a light kiss on the woman's lined cheek.

"Make certain you write to let me know how things are going," the marchioness ordered with a wave of her cane as Aidan rushed off to catch the public coach.

"I will," she called. "I promise."

With her space secured, Aidan climbed inside the stage, then waved to the dowager marchioness until the woman became a small spot in the distance. Settling back, she hugged her suitcase to her. In only a few hours she'd be back in London, free to do as she wished. Until Justin Warfield discovered she was in town, that was.

Frowning, Aidan began to wonder what exactly her husband's reaction might be. Volatile, she decided, and she determined to keep herself from his sight and out of his way so he wouldn't know she was there. They could lead two separate lives, as they had before. It was apparent that in the past they'd belonged to two different social circles, for she'd never had the opportunity to meet him until the night of the Quincys' soiree. As long as she kept to her own close companions and away from those with whom he associated, she'd be just fine. Yes, that's what she'd do, she decided, a smile lighting her features, pleased with her plan.

7

Shortly after midnight, a bored Justin Warfield walked through the front door of Westover House. Handing his gloves, hat, and walking cane to Pitkin, he dismissed the man for the evening, declaring he was going to bed himself.

After rummaging through a stack of calling cards and notes, which had been left on a silver tray atop a table near the entry, and deciding the round of visitors was again nothing more than eager fathers intent on making an alliance between their daughters and the already married duke, he headed for the stairs. Eventually a notice placed in the newspaper, announcing he was no longer available, would put a stop to the perpetual parade to and from his door, but at the moment, he preferred to keep the information about his marriage secret.

Yet, it seemed strange that no one appeared to have any knowledge of his state of wedlock. He'd have thought that Atwood would have spread the word all over London by now, laughing at how he'd trapped the Duke of Westover into marrying his daughter. While at his club this evening, not a word had been mentioned, not even a whisper, so apparently the man had remained silent. Why, Justin was at a loss to say. Unless Atwood thought the news would start a round of gossip in which his daughter's reputation might be sullied.

That had to be the reason. To their peers, her sudden elopement would have meant only one thing. She'd fallen victim to the notorious young duke and found herself in the family way. Scandalous behavior, they would say, and Atwood realized the ramifications should anyone discover the couple were wed. His daughter would be ostracized, made an outcast among those who were her equals, and Atwood didn't wish for that to happen, hence his secrecy.

All the better for himself, Justin thought, entering his room. With Aidan securely tucked away at Warfield Manor, he could enjoy the pleasures he'd heretofore known: late nights, beautiful women, fine wines, a large wager on a hand of cards, or a quick trip to the Continent. All these were formerly and presently his. He had to answer to no one. Least of all a wife.

So why was he bored? he wondered as he stripped from his clothing to lie naked upon his bed. Nothing seemed to hold any interest for him. He'd been home these past several nights well before midnight, with the exception of tonight. But that was only because he'd forced himself to stay at White's.

Determinedly he'd joined in a dull round of conversation, played a game of cards, in which he'd quickly lost interest, along with his money, and by ten o'clock he'd found himself fighting off his urge to yawn, a rarity indeed. Still he'd stuck it out, until he'd nearly cracked his neck when he'd dozed off in his chair. Perhaps it was simply the thought of being married which had made him want to settle in like an old house husband, awaiting his slippers and pipe, desiring nothing more than the sound of a crackling fire and a good book to entertain him until bedtime.

Ridiculous! Justin turned on his side and punched his pillow, then looked at the empty one beside him. His hand moved lightly over its down-filled volume, and he envisioned coppery tresses fanning outward over the satiny material covering it. Smiling violet eyes stared up at him, teasing him, enticing him to move closer and take what was rightfully his. His hand curled in the pillowcase, wanting to touch the shiny locks he was certain he saw. Suddenly he realized he'd been hallucinating.

Damnation! He was going daft! Certain his delusions were caused from the intense desire to have a woman beside him and nothing else, he quickly decided that tomorrow he'd pay a call on Cynthia Danvers. With a few words of attrition, plus an expensive bauble or two, he was confident Cynthia would willingly return to his arms. And once his manly appetites had been satiated, he was certain his violet-eyed fantasy would disappear, like a wraith in the night.

Indeed, he needed a woman, but never a wife. Positive this was so, Justin jerked the covers up over his long body and settled in for what became a disturbing, yet fulfilling night of dreams. Sweet visions of a pair of haunting violet eyes chased through his slumberous mind until dawn. Unfortunately, he had no memory of them the following morning.

At nearly one o'clock in the morning, Lord and Lady Manley swept into the foyer, quietly closing the door behind them. "Seems Winston decided he couldn't wait up for us," David said, urging his wife toward the dimly lit sitting room, its door open.

"So much the better for us," Eugenia whispered, then laughed seductively.

The moment the couple passed through the panel, David shut it, then drew his wife into his arms and settled a fiery kiss upon her waiting lips. From the corner where she sat, a blushing Aidan first thought to remain silent, but as the kiss became more heated, she could no longer stand to be the voyeur. She cleared her throat, the sound instantly breaking David and Eugenia apart.

"Aidan!" they both cried in unison. While Eugenia nervously patted her hair, David straightened his jacket, then hid himself behind his wife's skirt and smiled sheepishly.

Aidan fought down her urge to laugh. "I hope you don't

mind, but I sent Winston off to bed," she said of their butler. "I wanted to speak to the both of you, alone."

Recovering from her embarrassment, Eugenia found her voice. "Tell us what's happened. Did your father find you? Are you married? Where's George?"

"I will. Yes. Yes. And I have no idea," Aidan said in response to Eugenia's rapid-fire queries.

"If you're married, why don't you know where your husband is?" Eugenia asked, a frown marking her brow.

"I have an inkling as to his whereabouts. At this moment, he's most likely abed with Cynthia Danvers."

"Cynthia Dan— You don't mean . . . Aidan, tell me it's not so!" Eugenia cried, rushing to her friend's side. "Not Justin Warfield!" She saw Aidan's nod. "But how? I thought you were to marry George Edmonds."

"So did I."

"Then how did the Duke of Westover get involved?" Eugenia asked, pulling a chair close to Aidan's; David followed suit.

"As you already know, I took your suggestion, Eugenia, and had planned to elope with George," she began, playing on her friend's guilt as Aunt Patti had proposed she should do. Eugenia's gaze fell from Aidan's, and Aidan instantly wished she hadn't used the ploy. The final decision had been hers, and hers alone. She felt it unfair to place the blame on Eugenia. "I should not have said that." Aidan laid her hand over Eugenia's, giving it a gentle squeeze. "You are not responsible for my folly."

"I feel accountable, nonetheless," Eugenia said.

"Well, don't. In the end, I'd never have married George. Everything would have been fine if my father hadn't caught up with us."

"Westover, how—?"

"The night of the Quincys' soiree, he was sent by George to tell me there had been a fire at the Edmondses' home. George felt it necessary to leave at once and see to the repairs. In his stead, he'd sent Justin Warfield. The plan was for the duke to deliver me to Gretna Green and George. But my loving father caught up to us. Instead, Justin and I became the unhappy couple who were united in wedlock. He's furious at being caught. He's even accused me of being involved in some sort of plot to trap him. Hence he dumped me at his estate, with orders that I was never to leave, and headed back to London. Oh, Eugenia, it was terrible. I was guarded day and night, like some felon."

Eugenia's hand tightened around Aidan's. "How were you able to find your way back here?"

Aidan explained how Justin's aunt had created a diversion to help her escape. "She slipped me out to the nearest coaching inn. I can't thank her enough."

"It seems you've found a friend in Lady Falvey," David said, finally entering the conversation. "But from what you say, are you certain her motives were purely selfless?"

"I don't know what you mean," Aidan stated, confused by David's words. "She risked a lot by sneaking me out as she did. I'm almost certain she relies on her nephew for her complete support. Had we been caught, Justin might have turned the full force of his fury on his aunt. Undoubtedly, he would have cast her out of his home. Her health is not the best. As it is, she can claim she knows nothing of my escape. She's even devised a plan to keep the wolves at bay by telling everyone at Warfield Manor I've taken to my bed and I wish for no one to attend me except Lady Falvey. Justin won't even know I'm gone."

"A rather ingenious plan," David replied, still uncertain the marchioness was doing all this solely to protect Aidan. For some reason, he felt the crafty woman's intent was to throw the newly married couple together, not keep them apart. If so, he wanted nothing to do with such chicanery. Justin Warfield was one man he didn't wish to have as an enemy. "Now that you've managed to escape, where do you plan to stay?" he asked.

"I can't stay with my father, so I was hoping I might impose on the two of you—but only for a while," she quickly added, espying David's marked frown. "Aunt Patti will be sending me an allowance, and I will be more than willing to pay for my keep. As soon as I've saved enough, I plan to lease a place of my own."

David shook his head. "Aidan, I don't think it's such a good idea—"

"Aidan, will you excuse us for a moment?" Eugenia interrupted. "I'd like to speak with David alone."

"Certainly." Aidan rose and walked toward the door. Opening it, she stepped into the foyer, where Eugenia's words filtered into her ears.

"David, we can't simply turn her out onto the streets. Especially when I feel responsible for what's happened to her."

"Eugenia, I don't wish to play the ogre where Aidan's concerned, but should Westover get wind of the fact that we've taken her in, it will be our heads. You know he has the power to cause us much grief. He could very well strip us of everything except our titles."

"It matters not. Aidan's welfare is at stake. First it was Sedgewinn, now it's Westover. I won't allow her to be set upon by that rogue. There's no telling what he'll do to her."

David chuckled lightly. "The man's purported to be a lover, not an abuser, Eugenia. The most he could possibly do is make her swoon over the excitement of his experienced lovemaking."

Outside the room, Aidan fused red. Like it or not, eavesdroppers always managed to hear the truth about themselves, she thought, which was exactly what she'd done. Knowing it, she also knew that was precisely why she had to stay free of Justin Warfield. She wanted nothing to do with the man. Nothing!

"David . . ." Eugenia sternly drew her husband's name out, then waited.

"All right. We'll give it a go. But if Westover shows up to claim her, I won't attempt to stop him. As long as that's understood, then she may stay."

"Oh, thank you, my love!" Eugenia cried; then there was a long silence.

Aidan imagined the two were sharing a somewhat torrid kiss; then, as the pair exited the room, she was certain of it. High color slashed across Eugenia's cheeks, and David's eyes were a smoky blue, while his eyelids appeared weighted with unfulfilled passion. Feeling as though she were an intruder, Aidan fidgeted nervously. Her gaze kept itself plastered to the wall behind them.

"Aidan, you are welcome to stay," David said, a bit huskily. "But if Westover shows up—"

"I know. You will not attempt to interfere with what transpires between Justin and me, and I won't expect you to. Besides, I doubt if he much cares where I am, so long as it's far away from him. Thank you, David . . . Eugenia. I appreciate your kindness. And I promise I shall keep out from under foot. The two of you are to pretend I'm not here," she said in a rush, heading for the stairs. "Winston has already shown me the guest room, so I'll be off to bed."

"An excellent idea. Eugenia and I were thinking of doing the same. And the sooner, the better," David said after the fleeing Aidan, only to receive an affronted look from his wife. But the suggestive appeal in her husband's eyes quickly melted Eugenia's heart. She took David's hand and pulled him up the stairs.

Inside her room, Aidan couldn't help but overhear the lighthearted laughter and tender words the couple shared as they made their way to their quarters. Momentarily struck with envy, Aidan wondered why she couldn't have made a love match like her friend had. Thankfully, Eugenia's and David's rooms were down the entire length of hall from Aidan's, affording both hosts and guest their respective privacy.

As Aidan slipped out of Penny's dress, she stifled a yawn. Tomorrow she would see about her belongings. For now, she just wanted some sleep. Not having a night dress, Aidan slid her naked form beneath the covers. Stretching languorously, she was certain she would have her first good night's sleep since she'd left London. Within minutes she was locked in a world of dreams, Justin Warfield drifting in and out of each fantasy, allowing her little if any rest.

The next morning, with the use of Eugenia's hand, Aidan composed a note requesting that Penny come at once to Lady Manley's. Within the hour, Aidan's maid was standing on the doorstep on Portman Square. To her relief, Aidan discovered the last of her things were being packed at this moment and were to be shipped to Warfield Manor this afternoon. Instead Aidan instructed they were to be sent to Lady Manley's and Penny was to come with them.

"I don't know, ma'am. It's your father who employs me. He thinks you're in the country. If he finds out—"

"I shall be your new employer, Penny. In addition, I'll give you a raise in salary." The maid's spirits perked up. "All you need do is make certain my things are sent here. No one must know their destination. Do you think you can do that?"

"It won't be a problem," Penny said, smiling. "Bob, the liveryman, will bring them himself. He's sweet on me, you know. He'll do most anythin' I ask. And he won't tell a soul."

"Good," Aidan said, rising from her seat. "I shall see you both this afternoon." She slipped a sealed note into her maid's hand. "This will be your confirmation that I've requested your presence at Warfield Manor. Of course, you will come here instead. Bob is to dawdle about town so it appears he's been gone on a long journey. I shall give you the afternoon off, and the two of you may spend it however you wish. Just make certain he understands he must return to Atwood House in the appropriate length of time it would take him to travel to Warfield Manor and back."

"I will. We don't get to spend much time together," Penny said, "and Bob will be real pleasured to hear what you're doin' for us."

As soon as Penny left, Aidan asked Eugenia if any parties were being given this evening. As luck would have it, the Rothschilds were hosting an intimate gathering.

"Do you think it wise to place yourself out in public so soon?" her friend asked, quite concerned.

"I'll not be made to sit at home for fear of discovery. Besides, the duke doesn't attend the same social events we do. From what you've told me, outside of my father, my husband, David and yourself, no one knows Justin and I are married. I'll simply keep a low profile and attend only the intimate gatherings, like the one at the Rothschilds' tonight."

"Still, you're taking a chance, Aidan," Eugenia cautioned. "The duke may not attend the same social functions we do. But that doesn't mean he has not been invited. One day the two of you are bound to meet. Then what shall you do?"

Aidan thought a moment. "I'll pretend I don't know

him," she said, unable to really say what she'd do when the moment came. She noted her friend's doubtful look. "Eugenia, please don't fret. When it happens, it happens. And when it does, I'll deal with it. Until then, I won't allow myself to worry over it."

"So you say," Eugenia responded as she poured herself another cup of tea. "I can tell you this, my friend. I'm certainly glad I won't be the one who's in your shoes when the Duke of Westover discovers his wife is in London. And although David and I are on your side, we won't be able to help you. So I suggest you think long and hard on what you're doing. Ask yourself one thing, Aidan. Is purposely flaunting your freedom worth the repercussions? I think not, dear friend. I think not."

Aidan carefully measured her friend's words. Was she actually flaunting her freedom, as Eugenia had accused? Indeed, it was quite possible she was doing precisely that. Admittedly it was her way of thumbing her nose at her father and her husband, the two men who, at the moment, she despised most. A risky business, she thought, knowing she could very well lose the one thing that mattered most to her: her independence. She wished for no man to tell her what she could and could not do, especially when the man cared nothing for her. But her husband apparently was of a different set of mind. She'd been told by Justin he expected her to obey him—it was his right!—and if she played by his rules, all would be fine. Fine for him! she thought, feeling hurt at the way fate had treated her.

"Aidan," Eugenia said, breaking into her friend's thoughts. "I have an appointment shortly at my couturiere's. Would you like to come along?"

"If you don't mind, I'd prefer to stay here," Aidan said, then sighed. "I need to do some thinking."

"A good idea." Eugenia rose and smiled. "I'm certain you will find the right answer, if you give yourself some time."

"I hope so."

"You will," Eugenia said with encouragement. "I shall see you later."

Aidan sat quietly in the sitting room, studying her options. Since neither Justin nor she wished to be married, perhaps they could strike a deal. They could lead separate lives, doing as they wished, so long as they did so privately and inconspicuously. Oh, if only she could convince the Queen that her marriage should be annulled. Yet, like Aunt Patti had said, it was Victoria who had suggested she marry in the first place.

But, she thought, perhaps Justin could persuade Her Majesty differently. He could play upon the woman's sympathy, explain he had been forced into a marriage he did not want, tell her he did not wish to be linked to a flighty, simpleminded creature such as Aidan Prescott! He could call her anything he liked, so long as it worked!

Excited by the prospect, Aidan felt certain Justin could solve their problem with ease. And if his appeal to the Queen fell through, then she'd strike her deal with him on leading separate lives, something she was positive he'd agree to. Convinced one or the other would work, she decided, when they finally did meet, she'd offer him her solutions. At the moment, however, she wasn't in favor of searching him out. To her way of thinking, when they came face-to-face would be soon enough. Pleased with the answers she'd derived, Aidan rose from her chair and made her way upstairs to prepare for the arrival of her belongings.

Justin left Buckingham Palace, a dark scowl marring his brow. Upon rising this morning, he'd been certain he'd found the solution to his problem, and within minutes he'd sent a note off to the Queen, asking for an audience. A matter of urgency, he'd stated in his request, and less than an hour later he'd received word back that Her Majesty would see him at eleven o'clock, sharp. Striding up to his carriage, Justin glanced at his timepiece. It was now half-past that hour. With a snarl, he ordered Potts to set a course for Cynthia Danvers's house; then he settled into the seat with a disgusted thud.

Dammit all! He'd been certain his appeal for an annulment would be granted. But to his surprise, Victoria had expressed her pleasure that he and Aidan Prescott were now man and wife. In fact, it seemed as though the Queen had been laughing at him behind a mask of cordiality as she listened to him plead his case. Her lips had twitched several times as a glint of merriment had entered her royal eyes.

"Although I disagree with the way in which it was done, Westover," Victoria had told him, "I feel the Prescott girl and you are well-suited. Two fine families have been united, and your children will be of sturdy stock, not to mention exceptionally good bloodlines. I'm sorry, sir, but I can see no reason to dissolve the marriage. Your request is denied."

Had she been anyone but his Queen, he would have argued the point, but as it was, he had little choice but to obey her command. With a deep bow, he had left her presence.

As the carriage rolled down one street, then another, Justin's mood grew darker and darker. His driver turned the corner of the street on which Cynthia lived, and Justin called out, "Keep going and take me home!"

Potts did as directed without question. As they passed Cynthia's modest brick home, Justin kept his eyes forward. Because of his black mood, nothing would come of seeing her, he knew, except an argument. He'd see his former mistress later, when his temper had settled and he had decided what other course he might take to secure his freedom from Aidan Prescott—legally.

At least the chit was safely tucked away at Warfield Manor and not underfoot nor out flaunting the fact she was now the Duchess of Westover. How much longer his marriage would be kept quiet, he had no idea. But he suspected by this time tomorrow all of London would know. With a growl, Justin closed his eyes and shook his head. How in blazes had he gotten himself in this mess in the first place? Stupidity, he conceded, as always. Plain, unadulterated stupidity!

That evening, a line had begun forming outside the Rothschild mansion long before Aidan had arrived with Lord and Lady Manley. "I thought this was to be an intimate affair," she commented to the pair, somewhat confused.

"It was last year. No more than twenty-five or thirty people at best," Eugenia replied as they waited their turn to enter the grand house.

"Perhaps Rothschild has fallen into a bit of good fortune

and decided to open the party to more guests," David said as they passed into the foyer, then headed toward the wide marble staircase which led up to the grand ballroom.

Eugenia glanced at Aidan, noting her hesitation. "Would you prefer we didn't stay?"

Troubled violet eyes turned toward Eugenia. "We are here, so we shall not leave," Aidan said with much more courage than she felt. Then, as the gathering moved up the stairs, she prayed that Justin Warfield wasn't among them.

Finally, after what seemed an eternity, she placed her card on the silver tray. The servant gazed at the card, then respectfully bowed. Aidan thought his manner odd and nervously waited to be announced.

"Good luck," Eugenia whispered as Aidan stepped forward.

Squaring her shoulders and smoothing the skirt of her blue satin gown, which she'd chosen from her newly arrived belongings, she listened for the words: The Right Honorable Lady Aidan Prescott. Instead she heard: "The Most Noble Duchess of Westover."

Hot fire surged up Aidan's neck as her head snapped around with force. Eyes wide, she stared at the man who had just announced her. In the ballroom, the music stopped; a discordant rise of whispers swept through the crowd to roar in Aidan's ears.

"Obviously the word is out," Eugenia said from close behind her. "I suppose the servants were told to be on the look out for you and to announce your true title. Hold your head high, smile, and face the lot of them. Now, go!"

Feeling like an automaton, Aidan woodenly descended the three steps into the ballroom. Her face frozen into a tight smile, she waited for Eugenia and David. Once they had joined her, the three tried to make their way to a secluded spot on the opposite side of the large room, but it was impossible. A crowd instantly surrounded her, offering their congratulations and inquiring why the duke was not with her.

"So you're the one who's captured him at last," one young woman stated peevishly, her assessing gaze raking Aidan from head to foot. "I was given to believe he preferred *true* redheads." She ran a critical eye over Aidan's coppery tresses, then patted her own fiery locks, which Aidan realized were no more natural in color than a raven was red. With a sniff, the girl turned her back on Aidan and retraced her steps through the crowd.

After ten minutes of fielding question after question, which became more personal as each second passed, only to be followed by deliberate glances at her stomach, Aidan had had enough. "Excuse me," she stated sharply, then turned on her heel and exited the Rothschild mansion, Eugenia and David close behind her.

"Of all the nerve," Aidan said as their carriage slowly headed back toward Portman Square, her fan working vigorously as she tried to cool her flaming face. "The lot are nothing but a tribe of gossipmongers."

"Well, at least now we know why there was such a crush at the Rothschilds'," David said blandly. "They came to see you, Aidan. Or should I say, they came to see the woman who finally snared the evasive Duke of Westover."

"I wish you wouldn't say anything at all," Aidan commented caustically. She noted David's arched brow. "I'm sorry, David. I shouldn't have spoken to you so sharply. It's simply that I cannot believe what's happened. I won't be able to go anywhere, ever again."

"I wonder how the word got out," Eugenia said. "No one knew of it this morning. And Madame Sophie knows everything," she said of her couturiere. "Practically everyone who's anyone goes to her. She mentioned nothing about it."

"Well, someone let the bird out of its cage," David said, "and I'm certain it won't be long before Westover discovers his wife is in London. The gossips won't be silent over this one."

Frightened by the prospect of seeing her husband again, Aidan felt the blood drain from her face. All her bravado failed her as she imagined the rage that would greet her. No doubt he would blame her for the ballyhoo which had arisen over their so-called secret marriage. "I can't face him," she whispered, fearing what might transpire between them, realizing none of it would be good. "I can't."

Seeing Aidan's sudden pallor, Eugenia turned to David. "We have to get her home." As Eugenia quickly switched seats to comfort Aidan, David commanded his driver to head home, fast.

"I'm sorry I've ruined your evening," Aidan said in a small voice, tears glistening on her lashes.

"You've ruined nothing," Eugenia replied, hugging her friend closer to her. "Heaven only knows why we attend these horrid things to begin with."

"To show off our new gowns, I suppose," Aidan said with a sniff and a small smile, eliciting light laughter from Eugenia.

"And David probably makes his appearance so he can place a wager on a horse," Eugenia countered, winking at her husband, hoping to keep the light banter going and ease Aidan's fears.

"What ho! Rather cheeky of you!" David cried, pretending to be peeved at his wife's faked effrontery. "You've exposed me, completely! With the truth out, I suppose you will henceforth check my pockets each time we go to one of these gatherings."

"Indeed I shall, sir," Eugenia said with mock severity. "Especially since your bets produce little, if any, reward."

"Can I help it if the last nag I bet on pulled up lame only yards from the finish line?" he asked, his brow rising.

"No, dear. But if you had wagered on the horse I chose, you would have won."

"And how much did you win, wife?"

"Fifty pounds sterling."

David frowned. "From now on, I shall defer to your judgment."

As Aidan listened to the young couple's repartee, which she knew was for her benefit alone, she wondered why she couldn't have found a mate similar to the one her friend had. David was kind, witty, and he loved his wife beyond life itself. Instead, she'd found herself linked with a rogue: arrogant, self-centered, and faithless. Undoubtedly he was at this moment with his mistress, enjoying himself immensely. The blackguard! she berated him silently, losing some of her fear and regaining her former anger at the man. Although it was her husband who deserved censure, she was the one who had become the talk of the gossips, eyes inspecting her to see if she had fallen victim to the duke's masculine allure.

Her reputation had been sullied. Never mind there was not an ounce of truth to the prattle. A vicious seed had been planted, which would grow to enormous proportions. Time would prove them all wrong, she knew, but until then, she alone would be the one made to suffer from the maliciousness, the looks, the innuendo.

Her indignation renewed, she decided whatever it took, she'd make the Duke of Westover release her from this farce of a marriage. And soon!

Justin felt a forceful finger poking at his shoulder. He peeled open one eye to see Cynthia standing over him.

"You say you are married, and now I believe you," she railed at him. "I leave you alone for a minute and come back to find you dozing like some old dog in the heat of the day."

Rolling his head from side to side, trying to release the kink that had settled in his neck, Justin smiled derisively. "You're right. I am behaving like some feeble old cur."

He rose from the chair situated in Cynthia's parlor. Stretching, he glanced around him, trying to get his bearings. The last thing he remembered was Cynthia's suggestively saying she was going to slip into something less restrictive. As he gazed at her, he noted she had.

"You look lovely," he said, his voice husky with sleep, and the blond ran her hand over the whisper of material she wore, the low-cut silk nightdress clinging wickedly to her voluptuous body. As she did so, he envisioned a different beauty in the flimsy thing. The violet-eyed siren beckoned to him, and he instantly felt a stirring in his loins.

Justin shook his head, clearing the vision from his mind, then stifled a yawn. Immediately he noted Cynthia's narrowed gaze.

"Have I become that boring to you?" she asked irritably. "If so, perhaps you should take your leave."

In truth, Justin was bored, but he refused to admit it. "The fault lies not with you, but with me, Cynthia. I have a lot on my mind, lately—mainly, how to extract myself from my marriage. Forgive me if I seem disinterested."

"Perhaps I can change your mood," she said, moving against him, trying to inflame him.

Her arms crept upward around Justin's neck, pulling his head ever closer to hers. As her full lips took possession of his, Justin tried to respond. Nothing happened. After a long moment, in which he felt as dead as a fallen tree, he pulled back. "I'd best be leaving," he said, unwrapping her slender arms from his shoulders. "I have an early morning ahead of me," he said, gathering his cane and hat. "I'll be out of London for a few days and will call on you when I return."

Cynthia followed him to the door. "I suggest you inquire first," she said snappishly. "You may find I'm out with someone else."

"If that's what you want, Cynthia, then so be it. I don't ask that you wait. The decision is yours." Justin placed his hat on his head, saluted her with his cane, and was out the door before the blond could respond. The hard thud of wood and a rattle of glass met his ears as he strode to his waiting carriage. "Home, Potts," he said, settling in his seat.

Why he had gone to Cynthia's in the first place, he did not know. But he was glad to be away from her. As they'd shared an intimate candlelight supper, he'd begun to notice her flaws. Not in her features, for there were none.

Peevish, self-centered, frivolous in nature, she had nothing to offer in the way of intelligent conversation. Did any woman? he wondered, feeling exceptionally disagreeable toward the feminine gender at the moment. Even more disrupting to him was the fact that he'd seemed to have lost his masculine vitality. Never had a woman been unable to rouse him, nor he, her. But tonight, as Cynthia had practically laid her ripe body at his feet, he was amazed to discover he felt nothing. Had his usually healthy male appetites suddenly been sucked dry? No, he quickly decided, for when he'd thought of a violet-eyed vixen, he'd responded with vigor.

Dammit all! he swore inwardly. She was ruining his life! Somehow he had to rid himself of her. But how? Unable to find an answer, short of murder, Justin stared at the starless sky, cursing his fate, and Aidan Prescott, as well.

8

"She refuses to go anywhere," Eugenia said to David as the couple viewed Aidan from the window while she sat in the gardens reading. "The most she's done is post a letter to Westover's aunt. Otherwise, she simply sits."

"Can you blame her?" David inquired. "If it's not the dread of hearing what the gossips are saying, it's the fear of running into Westover. Either one is enough to make her burrow in."

"What shall we do?" his wife asked, her concern evident.

"Give her time," David replied. "It's only been two days since her encounter with the quarrelsome lot at the Rothschilds'. If I know Aidan, she'll bounce back in no time at all."

Eugenia turned clouded eyes on David. "How can you be so certain?"

"Because Aidan is not a quitter. At the moment, she's licking her wounds, but as she does so, she's also steeling her courage. Before we know it, she'll be in the thick of the social whirl, boldly challenging anyone who questions her rank or her dignity. With the title she holds, and the power it affords her, the talk will soon stop."

"But her husband is not of the disposition to support her on this. Without his backing, her title means little."

David chuckled. "It's not Westover's support that matters here. Those who continue to malign her will risk censure from our Queen."

"Victoria knows of all that has transpired?" Eugenia asked incredulously, and watched as David nodded.

"In fact, my love, as I've heard tell, it was she who

announced the duke and Aidan were married. Hence the fiasco at the Rothschilds' the other evening.''

Laughter bubbled forth from Eugenia's throat. ''With the Queen on her side, Aidan can't possibly lose.''

''I'd say the likelihood of her doing so is precisely zero,'' David replied, smiling. ''And since you need not worry over your friend any longer, how about showing some concern for your husband?''

Seeing his boyish pout, Eugenia smiled up at him. ''I'd be most happy to,'' she said, then pulled him toward her waiting lips.

Sunlight danced through the leaves of the ancient elm as a light breeze languidly lifted and settled the foliage like a thousand fans in as many maidens' hands. Absentmindedly Aidan flicked a loose tendril of hair away from her cheek, then moved restlessly on the stone bench where she sat. Having stared at the same page for the last ten minutes and not knowing a word it said, she shut the small book with a snap. Her eyes refocused as she took in the profusion of color surrounding her in the garden, but its beauty did little to lift her flagging spirits.

There had to be a way to extract herself from this terrible dilemma. After experiencing the disastrous turn of events at the Rothschilds', she knew she could never face anyone again. Oh, what she would give to be able to walk among them, her head held regally high, and to disdainfully stare down her nose at them all. But that was an impossibility and would remain so, until things were settled between her husband and herself. And the only way to arrange that was to meet him head-on. For the past several days, she realized she'd been hashing and rehashing that thought in her mind, never finding the courage to take action. Short of strangling her, what could he possibly do?

Aidan's hand climbed to her throat, covering it protectively. Knowing Justin Warfield's hot temper, she feared he just might follow through. Ridiculous! They were two adults who had found themselves in an unwanted marriage. Surely they could work together to find a way to dissolve the thing! Yet, she realized that telling herself as much and mustering the heart for an encounter with the man were two different things entirely. Sighing, Aidan had to admit, until she'd found the courage to face him, she'd have to remain content in keeping herself hidden.

Aunt Patti reread Aidan's letter for the third time, primarily the passage which stated her niece had managed so far to evade Justin's detection.

London is abuzz with the news of our marriage. How the whole came into the information, I have no idea. Since your nephew has not made his appearance, I can only assume he is unaware I am here, and not at Warfield Manor. But after last night, I fear he may show up, and soon. What shall I do then?

"Fall into his arms, you twit!" Aunt Patti railed to her bedroom walls. "Seduce him! Whatever it takes so I might look upon my *great-grand*nephew before I die!"

Deciding that talking to herself did little good, the dowager marchioness ambled over to her writing table, whereupon she withdrew a sheet of paper and took pen in hand. She dipped the point into the ink, then wrote: *The chit has managed to escape! You might find her at Lord and Lady Manley's, Portman Square, London.*

With her falsely dated note sealed, she called for a servant. "Have this delivered to Westover House, and be quick about it!"

When the man had left, Aunt Patti settled into her rocking chair. With her nephew having sent word two days ago that he would be away from London for close to a week in search of a stud for his mares, she was convinced he would have no idea when he'd received her letter. And since her nephew's aging butler was showing signs of senility, she was certain Pitkin wouldn't remember when it had arrived either. Positive her part in the matter would remain hidden, at least for the time being, she smiled with satisfaction. "A little nudge in the right direction will undoubtedly bring about the appropriate results," she said, thumping her cane for emphasis. "And you, nephew, had better comply!"

Persuaded she had done all she could do at present, the dowager marchioness picked up her needles and painfully set to finishing the mate to the small pair of bootees she was knitting.

At Portman Square, Aidan stood in her bedroom, carefully viewing herself in the mirror. All morning long, she'd sat in the walled garden behind Lord and Lady Manley's, continually worrying over her predicament, until, like the rosebushes, she'd felt certain she was about to take root herself. Now, with Eugenia and David having gone out for the afternoon, she'd become bored with her self-imposed exile and decided it was time she stop playing the coward.

Settling a plain straw bonnet atop her head to hide her coppery tresses, which were pulled back and netted into a bun, Aidan tied the blue satin ribbons beneath her chin. She stepped back and ran her hand over her skirt, her eyes never leaving her image. Unadorned, the simple blue muslin gown provided her the appearance she'd hoped to achieve. To her own eyes, she looked no different from any other woman who traveled along the streets of London. And in no way did she resemble a member of the peerage—much less a duchess!—which pleased Aidan considerably.

Satisfied she wouldn't be recognized, she snatched up her reticule, containing only a few shillings, draped a light shawl around her shoulders, and left the house. With determination in her step, she walked several blocks from the house, where she hailed a passing cabby.

Upon hearing her destination, the man arched a surprised brow. "Ye sure ye wants to go there, miss? Ye ain't exactly escorted, and—"

"Sir, I'm quite certain of my destination. Escorted or not, I am paying you to take me there. Now, let's be gone."

Frowning, the man tipped his hat. "It be yer hide, missy," he grumbled beneath his breath, but Aidan had caught the words.

"Indeed, sir, it is. And I'll take full responsibility for it." She settled into her seat and the driver shut the door. Within moments the hired cab was headed toward London's East End.

Shod hooves clicked smartly against the cobblestone street, wheels rumbling along on a rhythmic drone. Inside the vehicle, Aidan gazed through the small window. As they neared her intended destination, she noticed how the buildings became shabbier-looking with each passing block, the smells more repugnant to the nose. Finally the hired conveyance stopped in front of a modest structure which stood behind a tall stone wall. The old place was greatly in need of repair.

Handing over her fare, Aidan walked up to the rusting iron gate, its latch broken. The small yard beyond was devoid of grass; no flowers bloomed in the unattended garden area, only weeds. Traveling the cracked stone walkway, she ascended three worn steps to knock on a scarred wooden door. As her violet eyes took in the sights around her, Aidan decided that feeling sorry for herself was extremely foolish, especially when there were those who were in far worse straits than herself.

The huge door squeaked on its abraded hinges and the face of a plump white-haired matron peeked around its edge. "Why, Miss Prescott," the woman said, not knowing that Aidan was titled. A smile lit her tired face as she opened the door fully. "I didn't expect to see you until the week after next. Apparently the good Lord saw our need and has sent us an angel."

"An angel?" Aidan questioned, laughing. "I'm certain you're mistaken, Mrs. Hampstead."

"I'm not mistaken. Just this moment, I finished saying my prayers, and here you are."

"Is there something wrong?" Aidan asked as she stepped through the doorway. Instantly the stench of sickness overwhelmed her. "The children, are—?"

"They've all come down with smallpox. The poor little things are in such sad shape, running a terribly high fever and vomiting too."

"Where's Dr. Brenner?" Aidan asked, quickly slipping from her shawl to hang it on a peg behind the door.

"He's upstairs in the sick ward, tending to the worst of them."

Aidan headed toward the stairs and ran their length, her skirts hiked above her knees. Reaching the second level, she noticed the odors were far stronger. She shuddered and swallowed hard as she traversed the gloomy hallway, its walls in great need of new plaster and a coat of paint.

Stopping at a partially open door, she pushed against its wood. The action revealed cot upon cot of seriously ill children, some moaning deliriously, others retching violently.

A weary-looking man, whom Aidan knew to be barely thirty years old, but appearing nearly twice that age now, stood over a child's sheet-draped body. Placing weights over the boy's sightless eyes, he completely covered the once cherubic face that was now badly pockmarked.

Although she didn't know the lad, for he was new to the fold, Aidan's heart lurched painfully. These poor little souls had suffered more than their due already. Orphaned, cast out onto the streets to fend for themselves, living fist to mouth, they had found a savior in Dr. Brenner, who had searched them out, bringing them here, offering them some stability. Dear God! Why were they being made to suffer even further?

Giving some instructions to a nurse, the tall, slender man rubbed the back of his neck, then looked up. "Miss Prescott, you shouldn't be in here!" he admonished, quickly striding toward her.

"But I want to be here," she countered, fighting the hand that had settled at her elbow. "You obviously need help, Dr. Brenner, and I've come to offer mine."

Despite Aidan's attempts for him to do otherwise, Dr. Brenner moved her out into the hallway and closed the door behind them. "Smallpox is highly contagious, Miss Prescott, and unless you've had a case of it yourself—which I doubt, for there's not a scar on your face—I won't allow you to set foot in that room."

"Considering the need, I'm willing to take the chance," she stated firmly, placing her welfare behind her. "They're little more than babies. They know me. I've read to them, played games with them, helped bathe and feed them. There must be something I can do to ease their suffering."

Dr. Brenner sighed. His hand raked through his thick blond hair as his tired eyes settled on her. "You've done a great deal already. And for that I thank you. But I'm sorry, I can't have you chance it."

"But—"

"No, Miss Prescott!" he snapped in uncharacteristic anger. "And that's final."

Surprised by Dr. Brenner's harshness, Aidan watched as he stepped several paces away from her, stopping at the window which stood at the end of the corridor. Shoulders slumped, he stared through the clouded pane, smudged with years of soot and grime. To Aidan, he seemed on the verge of physical and emotional collapse.

"Why does everything happen at once?" he whispered, as though he were speaking to no one in particular. "Oh, God, it's all my fault."

Aidan came up behind him. "What is your fault?"

His head pivoted toward her. "The boy who just died—I brought him here nearly three weeks ago. I'm certain he carried the pox with him."

Aidan placed a comforting hand on his forearm. "Dr. Brenner, you couldn't have known that at the time."

"No, but had I been here the instant he'd taken ill, I would have quarantined him. Instead, I was off with some pompous duke's business agent, trying to renegotiate the lease on this ancient relic"—his hand waved about him, denoting the shoddy building—"hoping to keep a leaky roof over their heads! It was a futile attempt, and by the time I'd returned, the others had been exposed. Now, besides fighting to keep them alive, we'll all be on the streets in a week."

"The owner is throwing you out?" she asked incredulously, then saw the doctor's nod. "Surely there's some way to gain a reprieve."

"Since the man has seen fit to double our rent, I doubt there's much anyone can do. I could barely meet the payments as it was."

A sudden foreboding riddled through Aidan. "Who is this duke?" she asked with caution, praying it wasn't her father. *Or* her husband! She doubted it was Alastair Prescott, for she knew his properties were kept in good repair. As for Justin, she could not say what he owned or what condition it was in. Even if this particular building belonged to her husband, were she to intervene on Dr. Brenner's behalf, asking Justin to reduce the price of the lease, she was sure her pleas would instantly fall upon deaf ears. If Justin Warfield displayed such heartless contempt for a passel of needy orphans, then undeniably, he would show her no kindness at all. He'd never grant her any concessions, not when he abhorred her as he did!

A cynical laugh escaped him. "Do you hope to change this lofty personage's mind?"

"I can always try."

"Then his titled name is Westover."

Aidan's knees nearly buckled, for her worst fears had come true. Violet eyes narrowed, and she began to seethe inside. Not only was he a seducer of women, he was an abuser of small children as well!

The door flew open, and one of the nurses called out, "Dr. Brenner, we need you, quick."

He started for the room, Aidan after him. "You can't come in, Miss Prescott. If you feel such a strong need to help, you can search out this Westover fellow and persuade him to show some mercy. If accomplished, that in itself would be a miracle."

Before Aidan could respond, the door closed firmly in her face. Following the hallway to the stairs, she descended them and left the house, her thoughts on the orphans. Miracle, indeed! she fumed, certain she'd get nowhere with Justin Warfield. Besides, she was afraid to approach him, fearing he'd send her straight back to Warfield Manor, Dr. Brenner and his wards no better off than they presently were.

If only she had the money, she thought, traveling the cracked walkway to the gate, exiting through it. There was very little left of what Aunt Patti had given her. Asking Eugenia and David for such a large sum was out of the question. And so was approaching her father. That meant she had to find the resources herself. All she had were her clothes and her . . .

"Jewels!" she exclaimed aloud, startling several poorly dressed individuals who were passing close by her.

"If ye be lookin' fer baubles, girlie," one woman commented with a sniff, "ye'd best be takin' yer business where a man can afford to pay ye such, fer ye ain't gonna find nothin' like that around here."

Realizing the woman viewed her as little more than a lowly but pretentious strumpet, Aidan stared after the departing figure as she waddled away. Finally Aidan snapped her mouth shut, which had dropped in astonishment. Quickly she picked up her stride, her mind turning to the one item she'd willingly sell without a second thought. After a short wait on the corner, she flagged down another cabby and was on her way back to Portman Square.

Fortunately, upon her return, Aidan discovered that Eugenia and David were still out. Going straight to her room and her jewel case, she opened its lid. The item she wanted was the most prominent piece of all—the large ruby. The eye of the devil, she thought, snatching the ring from its velvet bed, stuffing it into her reticule. Before she could change her mind, Aidan fled the house and climbed into the waiting conveyance.

A short time later, her reticule was fatter by far. Now all she need do was find out the name of Justin's business agent. As she settled once again into the waiting vehicle, she wondered how she could possibly do it. *White's!* she thought, knowing she might spot one of Justin's acquaintances at the prestigious men's club. But precisely who were his friends?

"Well, miss, are we gonna sit here all day?" the cabby asked.

"Take me to White's."

"They won't let ye in, miss."

"Just do as I say," Aidan snapped, suddenly weary of being questioned at every turn.

Before she could draw another breath, the conveyance lurched forward, heading toward White's. Deep in thought, Aidan reviewed the episode with the clerk inside the jewelry house. When she'd walked into the establishment, she'd been all set on selling the ring, but as she pulled the ruby-and-diamond circlet from her reticule, she heard Justin's ominous voice: *That trinket may very well be the only thing of value you ever receive from me.*

As she gazed at the magnificent ring, she'd felt saddened. If there were feelings of affection between them, she would have gladly worn the beautiful token. But she'd realized that her husband cared nothing for her, and likewise, she cared nothing for him. Besides, the orphans needed the proceeds from its sale, she'd defended silently, insisting she was doing the right thing. Justin could buy himself a hundred such rings. This one mattered little.

But in the end, when she'd handed it to the clerk, the word "pawn" had passed through her lips, not "sell." The clerk had examined it and offered her what he deemed to be his best price. Knowing it was worth twice the amount cited, Aidan had tried to barter him upward. The two haggled, until they finally compromised, Aidan promising to make a set monthly payment until the loan was paid in full and the ring was hers again.

While she presently thought about it, Aidan wondered why she hadn't sold the thing outright. Not doing so, she now had to worry about making the payments. Oh, bother!

The hired vehicle stopped outside White's, and Aidan instructed the driver to wait at the curb. She opted to remain inside, watching the sidewalk, praying she would soon recognize someone. Before long, a short, foppishly dressed man sauntered up the street, his walking cane tapping smartly alongside him. Aidan instantly remembered him from the night of the Rothschilds' party, and she was certain he would recognize her. What was more important, he knew Justin, for the man had informed her as much while offering his best to her on their marriage. To Aidan, he seemed the type who knew something about everyone.

"Sir Percival," she called, waving at him through the open window; blinking, he turned toward her voice. "Might I request a word with you."

Sir Percival Filbert frowned, then slowly stepped to the conveyance. Finally placing who Aidan was, he bowed. "Your Grace."

"Please forgive me, Sir Percival, but I was wondering if you could help me. I feel simply witless—"

"How may I be of service?"

"Well, my husband . . . His Grace asked that I drop some papers off at his business agent while I was out doing my regular errands, but I seem to have misplaced the man's name and whereabouts. Would it be possible for you to tell me whom His Grace employs?"

"Certainly. His name is John Dawson. He's located just off Pall Mall." Sir Percival stated the street and number. "By the by, when is Westover due back in London?"

Aidan blinked. "He's gone?" she asked incredulously, yet relieved to hear it. Instantly she realized her slip. "Uh, he's been gone far too long already," she corrected with a sigh. "I do miss him so."

"Well, if someone were to ask me, I'd tell him. His Grace is a fool for leaving his lovely bride alone."

"Thank you for your help, Sir Percival. And I agree. He *is* a fool." With that she instructed the driver to take her to Mr. Dawson's, and the vehicle rolled away.

By late that afternoon, Aidan was wearily but happily ensconced in the sitting room on Portman Square. She'd just sent word to Dr. Brenner that he'd been relieved of one his worries. Having presented herself as Miss Addison, she'd negotiated a six-month lease with Mr. Dawson on Dr. Brenner's behalf, paying the full sum due with the proceeds from Justin's ring. Now the orphans had a home until winter, and by then she hoped to have enough money of her own to extend the contract for another six months. Right now, she'd done all she could possibly do. Except pray for the swift recovery of all Dr. Brenner's children.

The front door opened, and Eugenia and David swept inside, their laughter rising into the air as usual. Hearing it, Aidan again felt a fleeting pang of envy, but she quickly shoved it aside. After relaying their day to their guest, Eugenia and David proposed they all dine in this evening and have a round of charades afterward. Content to stay at home and relax, Aidan agreed wholeheartedly with the couple's suggestion.

A furious Justin Warfield stormed through the door of Westover House, nearly knocking Pitkin down as he did so. Steadying the man, he handed over his hat, gloves, and walking cane, then marched to the table and retrieved a letter from the ever-present silver tray. Tearing open the seal, he read his aunt's note.

"When did this arrive?" he asked cryptically.

"Today, I believe. Or was it yesterday?" the man questioned himself, scratching his head. "Or was it the day you left?" Pitkin looked around the huge entry. "Let's see. I was coming from the back hallway—"

"Never mind," Justin said, a hint of irritation in his voice. From the date inscribed at the top of his aunt's letter, he decided it had arrived the day he'd left. If so, then why hadn't it been on the tray when he'd returned this afternoon?

Knowing he'd get no logical answer from Pitkin, he let the issue drop. Although the man's lapse of memory had become highly exasperating of late, Justin hadn't the heart to dismiss him, especially when Pitkin had served three generations of Warfields. To put the man out to pasture would certainly cause his demise, he knew. And Justin didn't wish that on his conscience. Besides, the word from his aunt wasn't news to him at all.

Frustrated over not being able to find the right stallion for his mares, he'd returned to London earlier than expected. Deciding he needed to relax, he'd taken himself off to White's, where he'd planned to engage in a game of cards. But when he'd entered the establishment, he'd found himself overrun by the lot who had instantly offered their congratulations, some in a ribald manner. At first he'd thought nothing of the round of congenial remarks, for he'd assumed the announcement of his marriage had come down from his Queen. Then he'd learned his wife was in town.

"We were wondering why you weren't with your new bride at the Rothschilds' the other evening," one man had said, slapping Justin's back. "Rather foolish of you to let her out of your sights so soon. I'd never have expected you'd be off somewhere trying to match your mares to a stallion when you had a lively little filly to take care of at home. In fact, it seems rather bizarre you're here with us now."

Shouts of laughter had met Justin's ears, while some jovially chided: "Yes, Your Grace, what *are* you doing here?"

"Good question," Justin had said, hiding his anger at discovering his wife was in London behind a false mask of cordiality. "It seems, gentlemen, I've been a bachelor for so long that I sometimes forget there are other matters which should claim my attention. If you'll forgive me, I shall take my leave and attend to my new bride." With that Justin had spun on his heel, heading for the door, several good-natured guffaws following him out into the night.

Portman Square, he thought, weighing his aunt's note in his hand. He turned and retrieved the articles he'd handed

Pitkin. "I'll be late. Don't wait up," he said, opening the door. With a shout, he called for Potts to stop the carriage, which had rolled several yards down the street. In a long-legged lope, he caught up to it. "Portman Square," he ordered with a sharp edge to his voice as he climbed inside. Then he settled into the seat, his black thoughts on a certain violet-eyed witch.

David, Eugenia, and Aidan had no more stepped from the sitting room, their laughter chiming gaily in the foyer as they teased one another over the round of charades they'd just finished, when the brass knocker on the front door fell under a heavy hand.

"Who could be calling at this late hour?" Eugenia asked, her eyes instantly turning toward her husband.

David nodded to Winston. "We'll soon see."

Frozen in her tracks, a fearful Aidan watched as the panel swung inward. Instantly a cold voice cut like a knife into her breast: "I have reason to believe my wife has taken refuge here. Inform Lord Manley I've come to claim her."

Aidan immediately thought to flee, but her legs refused to cooperate. Then, as Justin crossed the threshold, her wide-eyed gaze clashed with that of her husband. Dark and foreboding, his cold stare beheld her a long, seemingly endless moment, and Aidan could tell his anger was held in tight restraint. Dread slithered down Aidan's spine. Noting her reaction, Justin slowly turned his attention toward David.

"Forgive the intrusion, sir," he said in clipped tones. "My stay shall be brief. Since my wife has taken it upon herself to burden you with her care, I've come to relieve you of such responsibility." Justin slipped a leather wallet from his coat pocket and removed several large bills, whereupon he placed them on the small table beside him. "This should cover her expenses."

Rebounding from the shock of seeing the duke on his doorstep, David finally found his voice. "Keep your money, sir," he said, his tone implying he'd been insulted by the man's actions. "I won't accept it."

"Nevertheless, you shall have it." Justin returned his gaze to Aidan. "Madam," he said, extending his arm toward her for the placement of her hand on his sleeve, "it is time we take our leave."

Although she'd tried to prepare herself for the moment when she and Justin would finally meet, she realized she wasn't ready for it at all. Frightened eyes shot back and forth between David and Eugenia, pleading for help. Noting her distress, Eugenia protectively stepped to Aidan's side, while David opened his mouth in protest. But before his words could leave his lips, Justin spoke with cold authority: "I suggest, Lord Manley, you do not attempt to interfere in this matter. By law, I have every right to remove my wife from your home. She is to obey me without question. Only our Queen can absolve her from doing so, and I can promise you that won't happen. Now, either she comes with me peacefully, or she comes by force. If the latter is chosen, I assure you what ensues will not be pleasant."

Aidan noted the instant squaring of David's shoulders and the narrowing of his eyes. Surely he wasn't foolish enough to take Justin on! Belatedly she remembered David's words on how the Duke of Westover could possibly strip both Eugenia and him of everything they had, except their titles, and realized she could never allow such a thing to happen to her friends. Quickly she stepped between the two men. "I shall go without issue," she blurted, her anxious gaze switching from one man to the other, praying one of them would back down.

Justin retreated a step. "A wise choice, madam," he said, a lazy smile splitting his previously stony face; the change made Aidan's breath catch. Justin noticed her feminine reaction; his smile broadened knowingly.

Furious with herself for allowing his magnetic charm to draw a response from her, she returned his discerning look with a hostile stare. "I need to fetch a few things—"

"You will come as you are—*now*."

Deciding he believed she might try to escape—a thought which had indeed crossed her mind—Aidan presented him with an overly sweet smile. "As you wish, Your Grace," she said airily, trying valiantly to mask her feelings of contempt—contempt that had grown even darker the instant she'd discovered him to be the owner of the horrid building that housed the orphans.

Justin shrewdly realized her buoyant rejoinder was not meant for him, but for her friends. Not wishing to contribute to any further feelings of ill will, whereupon he might find himself in an actual battle of fists with Lord Manley, he offered Aidan one of his heartrending grins. "I do wish, madam," he said most pleasantly, extending his arm again. "Shall we?"

Almost as though she feared a bed of hot coals lay beneath its innocent-looking surface, Aidan looked at his arm, then cautiously placed her hand on his sleeve. Fire instantly blazed through her fingertips and shot up her arm. Ridiculous, she thought, denying the hot sensation existed. The urgent need to remove her hand swept through her, yet she resisted doing so. Only solid flesh and hard bone lay beneath the black material, she knew. Nevertheless, her hand felt as though it were burning.

Justin's hand slipped over hers, trapping it; Aidan's gaze skittered to his face. "A bit of insurance so when we step through the door you won't bolt," he whispered for her ears alone. He tightly wrapped his fingers around hers, then looked at David and Eugenia. "Again, I apologize for the intrusion. Good night."

With long strides, Justin began escorting his errant wife toward the door. Aidan's feet scrambled wildly to keep up with him.

"Wait!" Eugenia cried, drawing the departing couple's attention. "Aidan, are you certain this is what you truly want?"

"Yes," Aidan lied freely. She could say little else or she'd risk harming her friends. How, she was unable to say, for she doubted Justin Warfield would resort to physical violence. But just the same, she didn't wish to chance it. "Don't fret, Eugenia. I'll be all right."

"Lady Manley," Justin said, his tone conciliatory, "I assure you no harm shall come to Aidan. If you know anything of my reputation, you will realize I am quite the opposite of Lord Sedgewinn. Please understand that my wife and I have some urgent matters to settle. Once done, Aidan shall be allowed to communicate with you." With his pledges made, Justin guided his wife through the door and into the darkness.

* * *

Surrounded by the cool night air, which was not half as chilly as Justin's mood, Aidan stared blankly at the array of buildings along the route the carriage was taking toward St. James's Square. With her arms crossed over her youthful bosom, her heart jumping fearfully beneath, her hands rubbed along her bare flesh near her elbows. Seeing the movement, Justin leaned forward in his seat, opposite Aidan's, and removed his coat.

"Put this around your shoulders," he said, stretching the thing toward her. "It will keep you warm."

Aidan's gaze centered itself on him. "Keep it. I'm fine just as I am."

One dark eyebrow arched. "Put it on, I say, or I shall wrap you in it myself." Aidan cast him a rebellious glare while declining to accept it. "Of course," he continued, a frosty smile pulling at his lips, "should you take a chill and fall gravely ill, all my problems will be solved. But I doubt very much you will enjoy lying in the grave, for that's precisely where you might find yourself if you refuse to listen. The choice is yours."

Aidan hesitated a brief moment, assessing him. Undoubtedly he'd be as pleased as Punch should she catch her death. Not wanting him to be relieved of his misery in a way that would only add to her own, she snatched the coat from his outstretched hand and pulled it around her shoulders, a decided mistake.

Justin's alluring masculine scent clung to the material and floated upward, instantly stimulating her senses. Visions of their coach ride to Gretna Green filled the field of her mind, as did the remembrance of his heated kiss. Stop it! she silently admonished herself. He was a rogue, a charlatan, and an abuser of children, who wanted naught to do with her—nor she, him! She pushed the coat downward, keeping her arms covered, then glanced at Justin. "Satisfied?" she asked waspishly.

"Not until I've found a way to be rid of you legally. Then, and only then, will I be satisfied."

Aidan decided not to comment on his statement, yet she wondered if he'd considered other ways to free himself of her, besides those which were deemed within the law. Probably, she concluded, knowing she'd fleetingly thought of several ways to unburden herself of him. The problem was, how not to get caught. Yet, the way fortune had been frowning upon her of late, she feared half of London would stand at her trial to bear witness against her. Murder was obviously out of the question. But she wondered if Justin had considered similar methods himself.

His cool calculating manner, coupled with his sole determination to be free of her, told her it was highly possible. Realizing it, Aidan suddenly felt very apprehensive. "Why did you come for me?" she blurted in a strident voice.

"Right now, I'm wondering that myself," Justin replied flatly. "Until less than two hours ago, I thought you were still safely tucked away at Warfield Manor. But I soon discovered differently. Tell me," he said almost casually, while rolling his head on his shoulders, trying to relieve the tension which had settled there, "how did you manage to escape your guards?"

As Aidan watched the taut sinew flex beneath his white shirt, she could not deny that he was a fine male specimen. Strong, lean, and muscular, he was broad of shoulder and narrow of hip, not an ounce of undesirable flesh anywhere. Nor was he corseted, as was the custom these days for fashion's sake.

His long fingers moved over his flat belly, massaging it; then they went to his throat, removing his cravat. The scrap of white material fell across his knee; then the studs were slipped from his shirt front, halfway down his chest, exposing a mat of dark hair. Instantly Aidan wondered if he planned to disrobe completely. Unconsciously, she pulled his coat more securely around herself.

Justin emitted a sigh. "Forgive me, but I've been trussed up long enough. Now, madam, how did you make your escape?"

"If I told you, I'd be sharing a secret that could very well be of use to me in the future," she retorted haughtily, not wanting to say anything which might implicate his aunt. "You'll just have to be satisfied with the knowledge your security measures were not all they might have been."

Justin eyed her closely, then was certain he'd found a way to break her imposed silence. "I can only assume you bribed one of my men. But since you had no money, it would seem highly improbable—unless, madam, you offered him what you had no right to give." He paused and waited.

"And what might that be?" she asked without thinking.

Justin smiled indifferently. "That which I alone hold claim to—your own sweet body."

Insulted, Aidan sputtered with indignation. "Why, you . . . you . . . you braying ass! How dare you suggest—"

"Ah, we've arrived," Justin cut in, trying to contain his laughter. The instant the carriage had stopped, he stood and stepped down. His cravat and shirt studs held in his right hand, he offered Aidan his left. She ignored it and swept from the carriage and up the steps, stopping at the entry to Westover House.

Justin noted her stiff form and smiled to himself. For some evil reason, he enjoyed nettling her. Perhaps, he admitted, it was because she'd been part of the conspiracy to trap him. If he could not find a way to escape his marriage, then he was going to make her suffer for her transgressions. And since she'd elected to come to London, against his express wishes, her heartaches were about to begin. Indeed, he needed to teach her a lesson in obedience. And until she learned who was master, she would be made to pay—dearly.

A frown marked his brow as he wondered what exactly he was to do with her. He could lock her in her room and discard the key. But then there would be talk and innuendo. The little that he'd suffered earlier in the evening at White's had been more than enough for anyone's comfort. He did not wish to be the brunt of their jokes again. Blast it all! The vixen was fast becoming a thorn in his side, one he wanted to remove, and quickly. Unfortunately, he didn't know how to go about it. Short of murder, that is.

As he stepped to her side and reached around her to open the door, Justin's hand automatically settled at Aidan's waist to guide her through. Strangely, the act seemed quite natural to him. Then his fingers drew themselves more firmly around her middle, trying to explore more of her feminine softness, but the cumbersome material of his coat blocked his way. Suddenly she broke free of his hold, as though his caress repulsed her, and stepped into the foyer.

Perplexed by his odd feelings, he decided his unexplained desires had erupted merely because she was female and he was male—nothing more.

Aidan's eyes scanned the entry. Westover House appeared to be a miniature replica of the house at Warfield Manor, pink-veined marble flowing outward and upward. Except where Warfield Manor had a central staircase leading up into the great hall, Westover House had dual staircases, a span of a dozen feet separating them. His and hers? she wondered, knowing, whichever one he used, she'd employ the exact opposite.

"They were designed to keep the flow of guests moving whenever there was a ball," Justin said instinctively. "Not for the purpose you have in mind."

"Nonetheless, I believe it best we stay as far apart as possible, lest one decide to trip the other in passing."

Justin chuckled. "Ah, I see we have a lust for blood on our mind. Whose death do you prefer, yours or mine?"

"Neither," Aidan stated sharply, stepping away from him.

"Well, let's see if we can make at least one journey up them without some sort of mishap."

Justin grabbed Aidan's hand and pulled his reluctant wife toward the stairs, his coat falling to the floor as he did so. When she refused to lift her foot, Justin swept her up into his arms and bounded up the steps, pretending to lose his grip on her twice. Frightened by the action, Aidan looped her arms around his neck, tightening them like a vise, nearly choking Justin in the process. Once they'd reached the landing, he dropped her knees and she slid against him, her feet barely touching the floor.

Pressed together as they were, their gazes instantly locked and held. For an enduring moment, violet eyes studied those of liquid silver; then Aidan noted how Justin's wicked smile faded slowly. The arm at her waist tightened for a brief moment, drawing her closer, then suddenly withdrew. Long fingers pulled her arms away from his neck, and he stepped back. Strangely, Aidan felt an emptiness invade her.

"We survived, madam," he said in an oddly taut voice. "I no more want your death on my conscience than you do mine. If we are wise, we shall try to work through this in whatever way the law affords us."

Recovering from the shock of his nearness, his silvery gaze searching hers intently, Aidan whispered, "Then you believe me when I say I had no knowledge of my father's plans to marry us—"

"I haven't decided on that yet," he countered abrasively, for he suddenly realized his unsteady breathing had little to do with his fast trek up the stairs. The knowledge angered him. Taking her arm, he guided her toward a lighted room just across the hall. "I have, however, concluded we shall make whatever effort it takes to divest ourselves of one another. I do not wish to be married to you. Take it as fact."

As he deposited her in a chair opposite the large mahogany desk in his study, Aidan wondered if he thought her such a vile creature that in no manner of speaking would he be able to tolerate her. Her pride rebelled, for she knew she was quite passable in looks, she bathed and groomed herself regularly, and dressed fashionably. She even had the best of manners when she put her mind to it. Why, then, did the man seem so repulsed by her?

Apparently Justin had read her mind. "Don't take any of this personally, Aidan," he said as he seated himself behind his desk, "but I was quite happy with my life the way it was before we married."

"So was I," she countered.

"Were you?"

"Yes, I was."

"Then explain why you didn't marry Sedgewinn like your father planned."

Instantly she wondered if the man was a complete imbecile. Angered that he dared ask such a thing, she lashed back, "Perhaps I should have. At least then I wouldn't have to be sitting here listening to you."

"If you'd like, I can drop you off at Lord Sedgewinn's now. If we hurry, I'll be able to have you there within the quarter-hour."

"No!" she cried, believing he just might do it. "I don't ever want to see that odious man again."

Justin viewed her for a long moment. "Then don't ever

say you'd rather be linked to him than to me. I assure you I'm far more understanding than he is." Aidan didn't respond and he reached for the container of brandy which sat on a tray atop the smooth surface of his desk. "May I offer you some?" he asked, raising the crystal decanter for her inspection.

"I'd prefer some wine."

"Sorry, this is all I have at the moment."

Realizing she needed something to steady her jumpy nerves, Aidan decided the brandy was better than nothing at all. "A small amount, please."

Justin sloshed the liquid into their glasses and handed Aidan's over the desk to her. "To your health," he said in way of a toast.

"And to yours," Aidan returned, wondering if he'd meant for it to be ill or well. Lowering the glass from her salute, she put it to her lips and swallowed a dram of the amber liquid. The brandy burned its way to her stomach. Instantly she made a sour-looking face. "How can you abide this?" she asked, shaking her head. "It's disgusting."

"Nonetheless, it shall keep you from fidgeting in your seat," he said, reserving a smile. "Drink the rest."

"Never."

"Would you like for me to assist you?"

Eyeing him, Aidan realized he would pour it down her throat if she refused to do so herself. Raising her glass, she swallowed what was left, but amazingly she found she rather enjoyed it this time around. The liquor descended smoothly, and a sensation of warmth immediately overtook her, spreading through her limbs and to her brain. The tension that had coiled itself up inside her these past several days seemed to unwind, then drain from her body. Breathing deeply, she gave off a contented sigh.

Hearing it, Justin smiled. "That's why I 'abide it,' as you say," he commented with a chuckle. He swallowed the contents of his own glass and began to refill it; Aidan's glass slid toward his. Frowning, Justin looked at it. "Are you certain you want more?"

"Very certain," she said, smiling.

His brow rose and his lips twitched. "As you wish." He set her full glass in front of her and watched as she sipped thirstily. "I suggest you go easy on that. If you're not used to it, you'll feel like you've been kicked by a horse in the morning."

Twaddle! she thought in disagreement, unable to believe that anything which made a person feel this good could possibly do one harm. "Now, you wanted to discuss our options," she said, a serious note to her voice. "Have you considered we might seek an annulment?"

"I have," he replied as he watched her sip her brandy anew. "In fact, I've already had an audience with the Queen."

"And?" Aidan asked, interrupting, then swallowed another gulp from her glass.

"And she has denied my request."

"Why? For heaven's sake, can't she understand we loathe one another?"

"Loathe?" he questioned Aidan's term, believing the word a bit overly strong. In truth, her confession briefly stung his ego. "Apparently she sees it differently; she was quite pleased to hear we were married. She believes—in her words—'we are well-suited.' "

Aidan again took a long sip from the glass, then said, "I really think, for some reason, Vi-hic—excuse me—Victoria holds a grudge against me. Sh-hic—excuse me again. She ordered me married, and now that it's done, she won't li-hic—listen to an appeal. Wh-hic—what do you pro . . . propose we do?"

Justin chuckled and shook his head. "I propose we put you to bed."

"You, s-hic-ir—sir, are being too for . . . forward. I sh-hic—shall do s-so on my ow-own. Besides, I'm m-hic—mad at you," she said, trying her best to glare at him, but his image refused to stay in one place. In fact, she could have sworn there were two of him!

A perplexed frown settled on Justin's brow. "Why?"

"Why? I'll t-hic—tell you why!" Suddenly Aidan realized she'd almost let it slip about the orphans and the ring. Fortunately she still retained enough sense to catch herself before she did. She frowned. "I forget why. But I'm still mad at you." Then, draining her glass, she aimed it for the desk, but it fell from her hand about a foot short of its destination, landing on the carpet with a thud. "Goo . . . good night."

Amazed, Justin watched as she weaved up out of her chair to smooth the skirt of her dress. With a toss of her head, she turned on her heel, then teetered wildly. "I feel like I'm on a merry-go-round," she said, giggling. "Everything's spinning."

Jumping from his seat, Justin caught hold of her as she toppled toward his desk; then he gently eased her across its surface. With his hand plastered to the center of Aidan's back so she wouldn't slip to the floor, he worked his way around until he was beside her. "An experienced drinker, I see," he said, lifting her into his arms. He strode toward the door. "Tomorrow, madam, you'll wish you'd never been born."

"A lie you tell," she said, smiling, her words slurred less than they were a moment ago. She lifted her hand to brush a dark lock of hair from Justin's brow. "You have very nice hair," she said, the brandy having loosened her tongue. Her fingers threaded through his thick tresses. "Clean and rich. And your lashes, they're *sooo* long!" She giggled again. "Men shouldn't have such long lashes. They make a woman envious, you know."

"And are you envious?" Justin asked, chuckling at her.

"Of you? Never . . . well, perhaps just a little."

His smile widened. "Why so?"

"Because you're a man. Men get to do anything they want, whenever they want."

Justin started up the stairs, heading toward the floor above and the bedrooms. "I seriously doubt that, madam."

"If I had been a man, my father would never have ordered me to marry Sedgewinn . . . and I wouldn't have had to ask George to marry me—I wonder what ever happened to him. I like George, you know. He was always a gentleman, just like you're being now. But I doubt he's as strong as you. He pads his shoulders, you know," she whispered in confidence, then babbled on. "You have good shoulders—broad, muscular. I thought of joining a convent, then George happened along. I even thought of joining it after I proposed —no, he proposed—whichever," she said, frowning, confused as to who asked whom. "But Eugenia said the good sisters would probably boot me out within a week—or was it a month? Anyway, she was certain they wouldn't be able to tolerate me for very long."

"Eugenia may have had a point," he said, again chuckling.

"No one likes me," she said, suddenly becoming quite melancholy. "Not my father, not the Queen, not even my husband. Indeed, if I'd been a man, you wouldn't be married to someone you hated," she concluded, petulantly.

Justin smiled at her. So, he thought, certain a drunk was less likely to lie, she did intend to marry Edmonds. Therefore, she was innocent of being party to the plot that had trapped him. "I don't hate you, Aidan. I simply don't wish to be married to you. Or anyone else, for that matter."

"Am I that ugly?" she asked, her eyes searching his.

"No, sweet," he said, taking pity on her, for he knew if she remembered any of this tomorrow, she'd be more than just a bit embarrassed by what she was saying. "Shocked" would be a better term, but he still thought the word too mild. "You are far from ugly." He strode through his bedroom door, Pitkin having left a lamp burning within; then he set his heel to it, kicking it shut. None of the other rooms were made up, and he didn't wish to rouse the house to do so. Carrying her to his bed, he sat her on its edge.

"Then what am I?" Aidan asked.

"You are a very beautiful woman," he stated, his eyes grazing over her upturned face, his hand still steadying her. "In fact, you're one of the most beautiful I've ever beheld."

Aidan smiled. "And you're the most handsome man I've ever beheld. Too handsome—and arrogant as well."

"I agree on both points. Now, will you be able to take care of yourself?"

"Certainly. Why shouldn't I?"

Justin released his hold, and Aidan immediately slid from the mattress with a plop. "That's why," he said, lifting her upward from the floor. "Never in my life have I seen anyone become so inebriated in such a short time."

"I'm not inebri . . . inebri—whatever you said."

"Try 'tight.' "

"Tight," she repeated. "I'm not tight. In fact, I feel very loose." She lifted her arm, showing him how it dropped to her side. "See, it won't stay up."

"Obviously, neither will you." He leaned her against the bedpost, angling his hips to hers to keep her there, and began unbuttoning her dress.

"You're putting me to bed, just like the night at the inn," she stated, her cheek stuck to the cool wood of the upright post, her arms dangling at her sides. "That's so considerate of you."

As Justin released the last button, he pulled Aidan back against him, then slipped her dress down her arms. "I had less trouble on the particular night in question, madam. Henceforth, you shall be limited to one glass of wine at supper."

"I'm not inebri . . . tight," she insisted.

"Sorry, love, but you are indeed that."

"I am not. You're simply getting rusty."

"Rusty?" he questioned.

"Yes. You've forgotten how to remove a woman's clothing."

"And what gives you cause to think I make a habit of doing so on a regular basis?"

"Everyone knows you do," she said, frowning at him over her shoulder. "They all talk about you, you know."

"And what else do *they* have to say?" he questioned as he loosened her corset strings.

She smiled conspiratorially. "They say you are the best lover in all of England."

Justin threw back his head and laughed. "They do, do they?"

"Yes. But I doubt there's any substance to the rumors."

He released the corset, then pulled it, her dress, and her numerous petticoats down her legs to the floor, leaving her in her chemise and drawers. Lifting her slight form into his arms, he kicked the garments aside. "What *they* say, Aidan, is mostly that—rumor. Don't take any of it to heart," he told her as he laid her on his bed, extracting the covers from under her. He quickly whisked them up to her neck, secreting her soft form from his eyes. "I'm not unfamiliar with a woman's body, but at the same time, I've not explored the scores and scores the gossips like to imply. If I had, I'd most likely be dead," he said, smiling. "No man could survive, I assure you."

As Aidan's head rested on the pillow where Justin had

once imagined it to be, he noted her hair was still coiled in its intricate style. He wanted to release the coppery tresses and feel their silky texture, letting them glide through his hands. Lightly edging his hip onto the mattress, he pulled the pins free, then threaded his fingers through the lustrous strands and gently raked them outward, as though they were a brush.

His actions were quite soothing to Aidan, and she moaned contentedly. "That feels wonderful," she whispered, and moved closer to his magical hands as they massaged her scalp.

The covers slipped down as she did so, and Justin's gaze took in her beauty. Eyes closed, her lips softly parted, the tops of her youthful breasts exposed for his hungry gaze to devour at will, she appeared content to allow his touch. To his masculine eye, she seemed like a virginal sacrifice, offering herself freely.

Hot desire suddenly shot through him, and he fought to tame his raging passion. It would be so easy to take advantage of her, he knew, especially when the brandy had released her inhibitions, relaxed her guard. Rightfully she was his to do with as he wished, and a few softly spoken words of endearment, coupled with several heated kisses, would have her turning in his arms, pleading for more. Although his body desired her, wanted her more than he could ever remember wanting any woman before, he did not want to be chained to her emotionally.

Knowing it was so, Justin freed his hands from Aidan's hair. "Get some sleep," he said in a husky whisper, and Aidan's eyes opened slowly to see him leaning over her. Rings of dark amethyst surrounded ebony pools, and Justin felt as though he were drowning in them. "If you should start to feel ill," he said, almost certain she would, "I'll be here in the corner the night through."

Aidan's hand lifted and her finger lightly traced over his lips. "Thank you," she said dreamily. "I shall remember." Then her hand slipped behind his head. "I imagine you would be a good lover," she said, smiling, "but then, I shall never know. I'm merely your unwanted wife." She drew his head down. "Good night," she said, innocently offering her lips.

So intoxicating, Justin thought of her beauty, of her naiveté, and smiled. And so totally intoxicated. His gaze traveled to her inviting lips, and he remembered his harsh words, words said in extreme anger, telling her he'd never touch her mouth again. A foolish statement, he decided as he checked his masculine desires and briefly, tenderly pressed his mouth to hers. Then the tip of Aidan's tongue trailed lightly over his lips and he felt his resolve to keep himself at bay tearing itself apart.

"Don't, sweet," he whispered as he tried to release her hand from his neck, but she held fast. "You have no idea what risk you're taking . . . what could happen."

"Kiss me," she pleaded, her fingers threading upward through his hair. Had she not been under the influence of the brandy, Aidan would never have uttered those words, but as it was, her reserve had fled, and she wanted more of him. She cared not what the consequences might be. "Please?"

At the soft plea, Justin's restraint snapped, and like a starving man, he emitted a famished groan, lowered his head, and ravenously partook of the bountiful feast before him.

As Justin's mouth hungrily devoured hers, Aidan's senses took flight. She felt as though she were suddenly drifting high above the bed, circling the room, like a wildly spinning kite caught on a draft of air, lifted upward, then pushed downward. Her heart soared beyond its bounds, dizzily, crazily, until it seemed to sweep her to the edge of oblivion.

In turn, as his eager lips traversed Aidan's, Justin's own senses were sailing free. But whereas she felt as though she were flying, he felt like he'd plunged into a turbulent sea. Great rolling waves of desire washed over him, pulling him downward into a roiling eddy, whirling him into a danger-ous maelstrom of no return. His tongue plunged the depths of her mouth. Deeper and deeper he sank, drawing what life he could from her, needing it to replenish his own. Then he was certain he was drowning in her, and he dragged his mouth aside.

"Something's happening, sweet," he breathed on a rasp of air. "Something I can't control." Then, knowing he had to somehow stop this madness before it consumed them both, he drew back. His desire-filled gaze lightly raked over his wife's tranquil features, and immediately he realized she had fallen asleep.

Inhaling deeply, he expelled a long arduous breath as he fought to master his wildly raging passion; then a derisive laugh escaped his lips. Whether she'd swooned from his kisses or had passed out from the drink, he'd never know. No doubt it had been a combination of both, he decided, shaking his head and tucking the covers around her. But, thankfully, she had done so when she had. Otherwise there was no telling what might have happened. He snorted at the thought, for he knew precisely what the end result would have been. But for a stroke of luck, he'd be doomed.

Rising from the bed, Justin strode to the chair which stood in the corner. He sank into it and stretched his long legs outward, his arms crossed over his chest. Surveying the gold-and-white decor of his room, then the small form nestled in his bed, he pondered the powerful emotions that had seized him only moments before. For hours he sat there, thinking on what it had all meant, never finding an answer—except that something inside him had tripped close to his heart, like a key turning in a rusty lock. And he feared what would pour forth if he gave her the chance to open the door completely.

Fool! he vehemently admonished himself. He needed no one, least of all the violet-eyed vixen who'd stolen her way into his life. But as he tried to reinforce that thought, a thousand arguments bursting forth in his mind to prove his case, he found only one that said he was wrong. And she lay in his bed, swaddled deep in its covers, like an innocently sleeping babe: his sweet, alluring, unwanted wife— *Aidan*.

9

Aidan awakened the next morning, feeling as though her head had been pressed between two boulders. Sluggishly she rose from the bed; an agonized moan escaped her lips. With cautious steps she carefully made her way to the basin, where she rinsed her face with cool water poured from the pitcher. All the while she wondered what had happened to make her feel so dreadfully awful.

Dabbing her face with a clean towel, she looked around the large room. Its fine furnishings her only companions, she experienced a great deal of confusion over how she'd gotten there. Slowly bits and pieces of the prior evening's events came slithering into focus. Suddenly the full picture of where she was and of what she'd done hit her like a giant wave. Doused by the shock of it, she steadied herself against the washstand.

Sweet Lord! She'd never be able to face Justin Warfield again! But as she thought about it, her embarrassment quickly turned to anger. He'd been the one who'd fed her the brandy, knowing its effect, deliberately priming her to loosen her tongue! If anyone were to blame for last night's debacle, it was him, not her. The insufferable rogue!

Taking great care not to jostle her pounding head or her overly sensitive stomach, Aidan washed and dressed herself. Several buttons, which were unreachable to her hands, remained unfastened on her gown. Then she gingerly pulled her fingers through her hair, removing the worst of the tangles. Without a brush, little could be done with the unruly mass, so she twisted its coppery length atop her head and pinned it. When she glanced in the small mirror above the washstand, she noted her pallor and bloodshot eyes and decided she'd looked far better on other occasions. But at the moment, her appearance was the least of her worries. Right now, her only concern was confronting Justin Warfield, head-on, and finding a way to dissolve their marriage once and for all.

As Aidan entered the hallway, leaving what she assumed was Justin's room, she noticed a maid stepping through a door at the end of the corridor and called out to her, then instantly wished she hadn't. Pressing her fingers to her throbbing temples, she slowly approached the young woman. "Could you please tell me where I might find the duke?" she asked.

"Why, he's probably breakfasting in the morning room, miss," the girl answered, a light blush creeping up over her already rosy cheeks.

Miss? Aidan questioned silently, then realized the maid had no inkling of who Aidan was. A natural mistake, for she doubted Justin had told anyone in his household he was now married. "And where is the morning room?"

"It be down the steps and to the back of the house by the terrace which leads out into the gardens."

"Thank you," Aidan said, then started to turn. "Oh, I almost forgot. Would you please fasten these buttons? I couldn't reach them."

The young woman looked at Aidan, her blush growing deeper. "Why, certainly, miss," she said, setting to work on them. "His Grace usually tells me when he's brought a lady home with him, so I can help her with her needs the next morning. I suppose he forgot."

Aidan's lips compressed into a tight line. Obviously the girl thought she was one of Justin's lovers. Like a prowling cat, the man probably dragged his willingly snared playthings through the door on a regular basis. "I suppose he did," she said, smiling coolly. "And your name is . . . ?"

"Millie, miss."

"Thank you, Millie. I appreciate your help," she said, then headed for the stairs.

Finding what she thought was the morning room, Aidan stepped inside to see Justin seated at a cheerfully dressed table. Bright sunlight poured through the large windows to surround him. Why, of all days, couldn't it be cloudy? she wondered, squinting her eyes against the intense glare. Then he rattled the newspaper he held, turning the page. The sound crackled through her head and down her spine, spreading outward through every nerve she possessed. Swallowing hard, she took a tentative step toward him, dreading what might ensue, then quickly prayed he'd forgotten last night altogether. Yet, hopelessly, she knew he hadn't.

Justin glanced up from his paper to bestow a knowing look on Aidan. He could tell immediately she was suffering greatly from the effects of the drink. "Ah, I see you've arisen," he said in a sunny voice, getting up from his chair, only to be presented with an intense stare. The harsh look bespoke annihilation—*his* in particular! "How do you feel?" he asked in a low, concerned voice as he seated her.

"Like Lazarus when he stepped from his tomb."

Wisely, Justin swallowed his rising chuckle. "That bad, huh?"

"Worse. Why did you let me drink so much?" she snapped, pinpointing him with her narrowed gaze.

"I warned you, but you seemed content not to listen. Now you know what I said was true."

"Which was?"

"You'd feel like you'd been kicked by a horse."

"I'd say more like an elephant." She frowned at him while rubbing her temple. "Why is it so bright in here?"

"Probably because it's eight o'clock in the morning and the room faces east. If you hadn't noticed, it's also a clear day."

"I've noticed," she grumbled, continuing to massage her head. "Everyone and everything seems to conspire against me."

Gazing down on her, Justin let loose his rumbling laughter, and Aidan cringed. "At last there's a truth we both can agree upon, for I've felt the same of late." Taking pity on her, he moved behind her. "Here, let's see if I can offer you some relief."

She stiffened at his touch. "What are you doing?"

"Relax," he commanded softly, his hands working gently along her shoulders, then up her neck. "I'm merely going to loosen the tension and hopefully relieve the pain."

Aidan opened her mouth in protest, but the wizardry he performed—his soothing hands expertly kneading her tight muscles, fingers splayed upward from the nape of her neck, into her hair, tenderly massaging away the pain—was tantamount to heaven. Of that, she was certain. Her eyelids fluttered closed, and she breathed deeply, letting the strain, knotted inside her, flow outward as she exhaled.

No man ever possessed such wondrous hands, she thought, giving herself up to their mastery, wanting the magic to continue. Then Justin eased her head back, to support it against his taut stomach, and his fingers lightly circled her temples. Bewitched, Aidan moaned softly, then whispered, "More."

As his hands ministered to her, Justin's eyes devoured the sight of her. Once again he was struck by her alluring beauty. Blue-veined eyelids lay closed, their long dark lashes brushing the delicate skin above her cheeks. Softly parted lips enticed him, and he remembered their sweet taste from the night before. He was falling deeper under her womanly spell; he wanted her, but this time the need was far greater than ever before. Swallowing the groan of longing which had suddenly welled up inside him, he quickly dropped his hands and stepped to his chair. "Hopefully, your ills have been eased. We have some things to discuss," he said tautly, seating himself.

Aidan's eyes came open. Miraculously, the sunlight no longer intruded on her senses to cause her misery; however, the tone of Justin's voice did. "Thank you," she stated in a husky whisper. A strange feeling of abandonment had overcome her the instant he'd moved away. "I, too, wish to discuss some important matters, mainly, how to dissolve this ridiculous marriage in which we've found ourselves trapped," she stated abruptly. Desperately, she tried to fight off the wild array of emotions spinning inside her. "If Victoria refuses to support us in getting an annulment, I presume we should seek a divorce."

Justin's lips cracked into a wicked grin; his brow rose ever so slightly. "What? You don't hold to the vow which said 'until death do us part'?"

Viewing his handsome face, Aidan wondered how he could affect her so. "I certainly do not—at least not with you, I don't," she snapped, her anger rising. But her anger was aimed at herself, not Justin.

"And what happens if we're also denied a divorce?"

"Then I suppose we're stuck with one another, as unappealing as it may seem."

His pride suffered the effects of her priggish slam, for she'd sounded as though no woman with a modicum of intelligence would want to be saddled with the likes of him; Justin smiled coldly. "Unappealing?" he asked. "Are you certain about that, Aidan?"

Catching his look, which stated she hadn't thought so last night, Aidan instantly dropped her gaze from his. He didn't have to remind her of it! she fumed silently, embarrassed by the memory.

"I'm afraid *stuck* is exactly what we'll be, dear wife," he said harshly, his ego not yet recovered. "If our Queen said she would not support an annulment, do you think she'd turn around and support a divorce and the resulting scandal? I sincerely doubt it. Since Victoria frowns upon the dissolution of our vows, neither the church nor the courts are likely to go against her wishes, no matter what form our personal requests may take. However, I shall try my damnedest to see what can be done to rid ourselves of each other."

Still unable to look at him, she asked, "What happens if we can't find a way out of this?"

"There is always a way out, sweet Aidan. But I doubt either of us has the nerve to choose it."

Aidan's gaze snapped to his face. "Surely you're not suggesting . . . You must be insane!"

"I've not yet come to the limits of my sanity. However, if we find we cannot abide one another, we can always agree to a duel. Pistols at ten paces, perhaps?"

Aidan glared at him. Having fired a pistol only twice, she certainly didn't consider herself an expert marksman. Yet, he was. "That would still be tantamount to murder."

"Yours or mine, love?" he questioned, chuckling, knowing precisely who the victor would be.

"You'd best watch your step, sir," she said haughtily. "You may be far better with a pistol than I, but a woman has been instructed on the usage of certain leaves and berries. Of course, their application is intended for medicinal purposes in order to cure whatever ails the members of her family. If they are mixed incorrectly or if a dash of something extra is added, however, the concoction could prove quite lethal."

He found himself intrigued with their game of wits. Where he was straightforward, she was equally so. Unlike other women, there seemed to be no need to deny her true feelings, masking them with false-hearted modesty, and he admired her for it. "Then shall we call a truce?" he asked, eyeing her with a new respect.

Aidan smiled. "A truce is welcome, sir. But I believe it shall be better served if you were to allow me to return to Lord and Lady Manley's. That way, if we were to break our agreement, we would be less likely to commit the act to which you've alluded. As you have said, neither of us has the courage to follow through on it now. However, given time, we may gladly use any means available to us to divest ourselves of the other."

Dancing silver eyes appraised her. "Although I may agree with your assessment of the situation, I will have to deny your request." He noted her instant look of rebellion. "There has already been enough talk among our peers. To quiet the gossips, I think it is best we reside under the same roof. At least the rumblings on that particular issue will be laid to rest. As a result, we'll be able to put our energies toward more important things, like securing our liberation, instead of wasting our time fending off the bevy of questions that are certain to greet us."

Aidan wondered why he wasn't bent on sending her back to Warfield Manor. "Then I assume you want me to stay in London."

"I do," Justin stated, "merely because I don't want to be bothered with the whispered speculations as to why you are at Warfield Manor and not at Westover House."

Relieved to hear he was against imprisoning her at his estate, Aidan still hoped she could negotiate as much freedom for herself as possible. "I will do as you've asked, on one condition."

"Which is?"

"That I am allowed to lead a separate life, free from your

edicts. I have my own circle of friends, as you have yours. I'm certain neither of us wishes to be encumbered with the other when we have the opportunity to attend a dinner party or the like, especially if one of us is not particularly fond of the company we shall be made to keep."

Justin perused her a long moment. "I will allow you to have your freedom in that respect, but only up to a certain point."

"What point?"

"The point where your actions might start the tongues to wagging again. If you'll agree to conduct yourself in such a manner that won't cause me any embarrassment, I shall allow you to travel in whatever social circle you wish. But remember, Aidan, should you manage to generate a stir of any kind, I will be forced to call off our agreement. Understood?" He saw her nod. "And should our request for a divorce be denied, remember, love, one day I shall want an heir. It's best you realize we may not be separated forever. If and when that time comes, I shall expect my bride to be unsoiled. Any relationships you might entertain with the male gender had best be strictly platonic. I won't be very understanding if I discover otherwise."

An incensed Aidan gaped at him. How dare he imply she was a woman of loose moral character! Before he started casting stones, perhaps he should first look to himself. If anyone were inclined to be unfaithful in this farce of a marriage, she was certain it would be Justin, not her.

Noting her accusing look, Justin chuckled. "Although I've been tempted, I've not yet broken my vows, sweet."

"I care little what you do or with whom you do it!" she retorted, then wondered if she spoke the truth.

"But I care a great deal about what you do," he responded, the tone of his voice sounding ominous. "I'll not be made a laughingstock by you or any woman. Least of all do I want to hear the gossips spreading the news that the notorious Duke of Westover has been cuckolded by some limp-kneed milquetoast like George Edmonds. So, love, be careful you don't do anything that might be considered the least bit improper. You'll regret it if you do." Justin rose from his chair and tossed his newspaper on top of his untouched plate of food. His eyes caught sight of her left hand, which lay upon the table. "Where, madam, is your wedding ring?" he asked, having just noticed it was missing from her finger.

Aidan felt her stomach jump; her heart leapt into her throat. Dear God, the ring! she thought. Her mind raced, wondering what she should say. "I've put it in a safe place," she countered quickly, praying her lie would not be exposed. With luck, she'd be able to visit the jeweler and buy the thing back, Justin none the wiser. But without funds, Aidan thought the prospect of doing so looked dim.

"I thought, my dear bride," Justin said, regaining her attention, "I told you never to take it off."

Was he going to force her to wear it? Quickly Aidan hoped to dissuade him of any such thought. "I may have many faults, sir, but hypocrisy is not one of them. The significance of a wedding ring means far more to me than some bauble to display on my hand. It was given in anger, not love, so I will not wear it."

Justin gazed at her a long, assessing moment. "The ring is to do with as you wish. But, remember, Aidan, your body is not. Disobey me on that accord and you'll pay dearly." He shoved his chair against the table, rattling the tableware. "I now bid you good day."

Aidan stared after him as his long strides carried him from the room. For a man who'd stated he had no desire to be saddled with her, she thought he'd certainly acted unduly possessive. She ruminated over Justin's words and finally decided he cared nothing for her, personally. It was her untarnished reputation, as well as her unsullied body that held itself uppermost in his mind.

The memory of her parents' shared joy filled her, and she lamented anew over not being blessed with a loving mate. Pushing herself away from the table, she rose and walked through the open French doors onto the terrace, above the perfectly manicured gardens. A profusion of sunlight danced off the velvet-soft rosebushes lining the pathways that wound themselves toward a high stone wall. Whereas once she would have enjoyed such a display, she now felt immune to its glory.

Dark thoughts suddenly crossed her mind as her anger rose anew. If she weren't such a coward, she'd throw his words back into his face. Cuckold, indeed! she seethed inwardly, wishing she were the type of woman who could easily and readily have an affair behind her husband's back. But Aidan realized she wasn't that sort of woman. Not because she feared Justin's wrath. No, it was her moral values, those which her father—and her mother—had instilled in her from birth, and they prevented such decadent behavior.

Yet, if she were to remain trapped in a loveless marriage, she considered whether she'd be any different from the scores of women who, under similar circumstances, were engaged in adulterous affairs. Although, at this point in time, she still was unable to condone such liaisons, she thought she understood how they had come about. Loneliness and despair could make even the most pious fall from grace. Of that she was certain.

Knowing she was far from godly, especially when her father had implied she possessed a streak of the devil in her, Aidan sighed. If only she hadn't been so impetuous, so headstrong, so rebellious . . . No, she had to stop worrying over the past and learn to put her faith in Justin, believing somehow he could find a way to absolve them of their marriage vows. Yet she found she couldn't help wonder what would happen if they remained trapped.

She thought about her new husband and had to admit he was indeed a fine catch. He was wealthy, extremely good-looking, held a lofty title, and when he wanted to be, was quite charming. Plus, he was vitally masculine and sensual, she conceded.

A sudden feeling of breathlessness overtook her as an image of last night's encounter between Justin and herself clearly etched itself in her mind; Aidan blushed profusely, embarrassed by her remembered wantonness. She could easily blame her lack of inhibition on the drink, but she wondered if she would have actually held back, even without the brandy.

In truth, Justin intrigued her, while at the same time, he frightened her. Never before had she lost her sense of self, her ability to control her emotions with a man—not until Justin Warfield had come into her life. And despite his many sins—especially his unfeeling treatment of Dr. Brenner's orphans—she held an unexplainable fascination for him. It was, she imagined, the same dizzying sort of attraction most women suffered when he was near. But she realized she had to somehow break his spell. Otherwise, she'd be lost.

Separate lives, she thought, encouraged by the concept, certain the greater the distance kept between them, the better for all concerned. Fortunately he'd granted her that one request: he'd go his way; she, hers. But the agreement was conditional. To keep herself as far from him as possible, she needed to be very careful in what she said and did. By being on her best behavior, she could become the epitome of what London society deemed a true lady. Without censure from her peers, surely her husband would find no fault with her. At least, she hoped not.

Resolved to the fact that her fate lay upon her own shoulders, Aidan turned and made her way back into the morning room, where she sat at the table. Surprisingly, she discovered she was famished. Her mood had lightened considerably, and amazingly, her headache was cured. With luck, she would soon be a divorced woman, no longer under anyone's control. Praying it would be so, Aidan smiled at the prospect. Then, strangely, an odd little ache centered itself near her heart. Denying its meaning, she quickly attributed it to the aftereffects of last night's brandy.

By eight o'clock that evening, Aidan found herself comfortably situated in her new room, which was decorated in soft blues and light cream colors. By choice, it was located far down the hallway from Justin's. If she could have picked a more distant place, she would have. But her next option had been the window ledge. Since she didn't particularly relish perching like a pigeon on the sill, she'd opted for the last bedroom in a line of ten which ran along the third-floor corridor.

With her possessions having arrived earlier in the day, her maid along with them, Aidan now sat at the dressing table while Penny carefully wove the wealth of coppery locks into an intricate style atop her mistress's head, adorning it with deep pink rosebuds.

"I've missed having your help," Aidan said, viewing

Penny through the mirror, smiling. "You have such magical hands."

The moment the words left her mouth, Aidan wished she hadn't said them. Reminders of this morning and last night flashed through her mind—Justin's gentle fingers working their sorcery on her, his masterful lips taking possession of hers—and an unbearable heat instantly rose throughout her body.

"Are you feelin' all right?" Penny asked, her eyes surveying her mistress in the mirror. "You look like you got a ragin' fever."

"I'm fine," Aidan snapped, angered by her lack of control. She rose from the small stool where she sat in front of the mirror. "Help me into my dress, Penny. I'm late."

"If you be comin' down with somethin', you shouldn't be goin' out," Penny said, assisting her mistress into the rose-colored satin gown trimmed with black Brussels lace. "His Grace wouldn't be too happy if you were to up and die on him."

Aidan laughed. "At this point, Penny, I believe he'd be ecstatic if I did." She noted her maid's surprised look. "Never mind. Just do me up so I can be on my way."

With the last tiny button slipped through its hole, Aidan turned in front of the mirror, surveying herself. Satisfied with her appearance, she draped a black lace shawl over her arms and, with her fan in hand, headed for the door. "Don't wait up for me," she said to her maid. "I'll be out until the early hours."

As she traversed the hall, striking out toward the stairs, Aidan prayed she wouldn't meet up with Justin, but her hopes were quickly dashed.

With his hip edged onto the marble balustrade, his shoulder leaning against a marble column, his arms crossed over his solid chest, he'd obviously been awaiting her. "Ah, you are ready at last." He rose to his feet. "Shall we go?"

Surprisingly, Aidan's step hadn't faltered. "Go?" she questioned, watching as he extended his arm, offering to escort her. "Perhaps I missed something, but I hadn't realized *we* were going anywhere, least of all together."

"Unless you had originally planned to walk to your destination, I thought I might offer to drop you off wherever it is you're headed. Potts and the carriage are awaiting us. Of course, the choice is yours." When she did not move, he shrugged and his arm fell to his side. "It'll be your feet that suffer, not mine," he called over his shoulder as he descended the stairs, heading toward the foyer and the door.

Aidan watched his retreating back. She'd never once considered how she might get herself to the Staffords', where she intended to meet David and Eugenia. If she'd thought of it earlier, she could have asked them to stop by for her. As she now saw it, she had a choice. It was either walk or ride with Justin.

"Wait!" she called, hiking her skirts and rushing down the stairs after him, for she didn't particularly like the thought of trekking across London alone at night.

Reserving a chuckle, Justin stopped and slowly turned toward her. "I presume you've decided sharing a carriage with me is somewhat less of a hazard than the perils which might greet you if you went afoot."

"I imagine the dangers are equal, sir. However, by accepting your offer, I shall reach my destination much faster than if I were to walk. In truth, I don't relish the idea of being stalked through the streets by some unknown felon. At least with you I have a fair idea of what to expect."

Justin's laughter filled the air. "Madam, with me, you should then know to always expect the unexpected."

As he took her arm in his, escorting her down the stairs, Aidan perused him with a feminine eye. His black evening coat spread itself across his broad shoulders and clung to his narrow waist, emphasizing his masculine proportions. Long legs were encased in matching black trousers, hiding what she imagined was hard sinew beneath, while his stark white shirt, cravat, and waistcoat set off his sun-bronzed complexion and silvery eyes. No woman could ever deny wanting to be seen with him, not even herself. He was positively magnificent!

"Do I pass inspection?" Justin asked, grinning down at her; Aidan's gaze jumped to his face. "A woman's opinion is always welcome, sweet."

"You'll do," she said, trying to hide her embarrassment over being caught ogling him. She saw his raised brow.

"But it's not my opinion which matters. You have a legion of admirers all over London. Ask one of them."

"Dear wife," Justin teased, chuckling, "it's your opinion I value most. The others see only my title and wealth. You could give a fig for either one. The truth, now."

Aidan couldn't help but smile; Justin felt his heart skip. "You are extremely handsome, sir," she said, then noticed they'd come down the entire length of stairs without incident. "But I believe you already know that to be fact."

"I do," he admitted a bit conceitedly. "And might I say you are extremely beautiful."

Aidan gazed up at him as Pitkin opened the door. Then, as Justin led her out to the awaiting carriage, she thought his sudden teasing manner rather . . . strange. "You certainly seem to be in a good mood tonight," she commented.

"Do I?" he countered, settling next to her on the seat, surprising Aidan. "Let's hope I remain such by night's end."

Aidan wondered what he'd meant by his statement; then she heard his voice.

"Where shall I drop you?"

"The Staffords' on Park Lane."

As the carriage made its way west across London, Aidan and Justin entertained themselves with small talk, coupled with light banter, which set Aidan's nerves at ease. Finally Potts slowly maneuvered their conveyance through the iron gates and up the short circular drive, stopping at the lighted entry.

Excited voices streamed through the open doorway of Stafford House, a conclave of boisterous activity beyond. Men in formal evening attire and women in colorful but elegant dresses, fashioned of expensive silks and satins, formed a line outside the brightly lit place. Each couple paused momentarily as they were inspected by a liveried footman, then allowed to join the throng inside.

For a brief moment Aidan wondered what sort of greeting she might receive tonight; then she watched Justin rise and step from the carriage. "Thank you," she said as he offered her his strong hand, helping her alight. "I shall find a ride back with Lord and Lady Manley."

"No need," he said, looping her arm through his, leading her up the steps toward the front door.

Aidan frowned, then tried to remove her hand, but Justin held it tight against his sleeve. "I believe I'm capable of seeing myself through the door," she whispered heatedly, not wanting anyone to overhear.

"I'm certain you can. But since we are both going inside, I merely thought to escort you. I have no reservations about playing the part of attentive husband—at least for the time being."

Aidan's feet came to an abrupt halt, which stopped Justin's forward motion as well. While the Duke of Westover smiled and nodded to several couples, motioning them around his wife and himself, Aidan glared up at him. "You had intended to come to the Staffords' all along, hadn't you?"

"I did," he admitted, pulling Aidan over to the side, for a line had formed behind them.

"You'd agreed to separate lives, but you've already gone back on your word," she accused hotly.

"I have an invitation to this party." He retrieved an envelope from his inside coat pocket. "You can't exactly say I'm an unwelcome guest. By the way, where's yours?"

"I don't have it with me. I imagine it's at Atwood House." She saw Justin's dubious look. "I've always been invited to the Staffords' parties." His brow arched higher. "I'm telling the truth."

"*Tsk, tsk*, Aidan. You should know that no one gets through the front door at the Staffords' without one of their specially engraved invitations. How, might I ask, did you propose to do so?"

"I had planned to explain I'd left it behind by mistake."

Just then a man's voice rose in anger. "I tell you we've been invited," he insisted, frantically searching his pockets again. "I must have left the blasted thing at home."

"I'm sorry, sir," the towering footman said as he looked down his long nose while blocking the doorway. "Without an invitation, I cannot allow you in. Now, please move aside. You're holding up the invited guests."

"Forgive me, dearest," the man said in a defeated tone as he escorted a disappointed-looking young woman back down the steps. "I suppose we should return home and have a look for it."

"Sir James!" a man cried, running up the drive, waving an envelope. "You left this behind on the seat."

A smiling Sir James patted his coachman's shoulder, then escorted his wife back up the steps and handed the footman their invitation.

"You'd never have made it over the threshold," Justin whispered near Aidan's ear. "Of course, if you have a mind to, you may share my invitation." He dangled the envelope in front of her. "Care to join me?"

Aidan looked at the lone name on the front of the envelope. "You know as well as I do, both our names have to be on it."

"Aren't they?" he asked, looking surprised, then checked the envelope himself. "My mistake." He reached into his coat pocket and withdrew a second envelope. "Ah, I believe we're in luck," he said, handing it over to Aidan.

Looking at the invitation, she noted it was addressed to the Most Noble Duke and Duchess of Westover. She glanced at Justin, weighing whether or not she should trust him.

He sighed. "Of course, I could always go it alone." His thumb and forefinger slipped around the envelope, but Aidan held on to it.

"You'll not leave me out here by myself," she stated, then marched toward the door, a grinning Justin close on her heels. "We are together," she announced curtly, handing the surprised footman their invitation.

As they stepped through the doorway of Stafford House, Justin quickly wiped the smile from his face before Aidan noticed it, but a humorous glint remained in his eyes. Then he whisked her up the stairs to the grand ballroom.

While they waited to be announced, Aidan silently fretted over the questions and innuendo that were certain to come her way. Gazing out over the glittering crowd, she felt her knees start to quake; the sudden urge to run bubbled up inside her. Had Justin not retained a firm grip on her hand, where it rested along his sleeve, she would have hiked her skirts and fled down the steps, out into the night.

"Smile, sweet," he whispered close to her ear as the footman stepped forward to make known their presence. "This is being done for your benefit. Head high. That's right."

"I wish I were anywhere but here," she said through smiling lips.

"You had your chance to escape at the front door." He felt the slight tremor of her body as she stood close to him, and he instantly took pity on her. "Perhaps it would help, sweet, if you were to imagine the entire lot naked," he said, smiling down at her while gently squeezing her hand. "That way, they'll seem less formidable."

Aidan looked out at her peers, and in her mind's eye, their clothing fell away. A giggle escaped her throat as dancing violet eyes climbed to Justin's laughing silver gaze. "It works," she said, a genuine smile lighting her face.

Strangely, Justin felt his breath catch somewhere in his chest. Beautiful, he thought. "We're on," he said, realizing the footman had already announced them. "Ready?"

Aidan nodded; then, with a regal tilt of her head and a squaring of her slim shoulders, she walked beside her husband into the ballroom. As before, the crowd seemed to come to a standstill, all eyes centering themselves on the handsome couple. Unexpectedly, a smattering of applause erupted, then spread throughout the room. Confused, Aidan looked to Justin.

"They're congratulating us on our marriage," he said, then inclined his head toward the crowd, acknowledging their salute; Aidan followed suit.

"A bit hypocritical of us, don't you think, to be putting on an act like this," she said, trying to keep her smile in place. "Especially when we're hoping for a speedy divorce."

"Until one is granted, madam, we shall play the part of the happy couple. Doing so will keep the tongues from wagging. We can then lead our separate lives without fear of censure."

"Live a lie, you mean," Aidan said, her smile fading slightly.

"If that is what it takes to keep the speculation down, we shall do so, and it will be done as convincingly as possible."

Aidan looked up at Justin while he guided her deeper into the crowd. A slight frown marred her brow as she wondered if she could play the charade. What difference it made, she did not know, for they were already living a lie. But to pretend to be blissfully married, she doubted she could do it.

Suddenly the orchestra struck the chords of a waltz, and like the Red Sea, the crowd parted, forming a circle around the large dance floor. Again Aidan heard her peers applaud.

"I believe they wish for us to begin this dance," Justin said, and Aidan glanced at the group to see their smiles and nods.

Then Lord Stafford's voice came from behind them. "Go on. They've been waiting all evening for the two of you to show. Now give them what they want."

Like the night at the Rothschilds', Aidan felt tempted to flee. Sensing her mood, Justin quickly slipped his arm around her waist and whirled her into the open area, expertly gliding her around the floor. "Smile, sweet. They're watching us."

"I don't feel like smiling," she snapped while keeping perfect time with his step.

"You're defeating the purpose," he stated, pulling her closer, for her rebellion nettled him. He'd staged this farce for her benefit, and hers alone. He cared little what anyone thought or said about him. But he knew Aidan felt differently. "I'd heard what had happened at the Rothschilds'," he told her, his head bending close to her ear. To those looking on, the duke and duchess seemed absorbed in an intimate conversation. Several young women, tears glistening in their eyes, fought their way from the crowd, heading in opposite directions, their hopes dashed that they'd ever capture Justin Warfield's heart, for it obviously belonged to his wife. "If you don't wish to suffer the bite of their tongues while you go about leading your so-called *separate life,* then I suggest you play the game!"

"And what shall they say when we've gotten our divorce?" she questioned, mutinous eyes pinpointing him.

"They may say nothing at all, madam, for we may never be granted our wish."

Suddenly the crowd seemed to close in on them, and Aidan noticed their peers had joined them. With a false smile pasted across her face, she viewed the towering man who held her. If she'd only had the good sense to run off to a nunnery, like she'd planned to do in the first place, instead of relying on one man to help her escape the clutches of another, she wouldn't be trapped in Justin Warfield's now!

The music ended, and Justin sailed Aidan off the floor to lead her to a quiet corner, where he deposited her into a vacant chair. "I'll find us some refreshments," he stated, then strode off without asking her what she would like.

Startled by his abruptness, Aidan watched as Justin made his way around the room, stopping several times to speak to someone who'd drawn his attention. From all that had been said and done, he'd seemed as though he genuinely wanted to protect her. Yet she wondered whether his insistence on portraying the happy couple was actually for her benefit. He would certainly be made a laughingstock if the lot were to learn how he'd been "tricked" into marriage, especially when he'd prided his state of bachelorhood as he had. Thinking it was his vanity he was protecting, she viewed him through distrustful eyes until he disappeared into the colorfully dressed gathering; then she decided perhaps she was making too much of it all.

"Is everything all right?" Eugenia asked, startling Aidan from her dark thoughts.

A weak smile claimed Aidan's lips. "As well as can be expected."

Eugenia lowered herself into the chair next to Aidan's. "Where's Westover? He hasn't harmed you in any way, has he?"

"He's off to get us some refreshments. And no, he hasn't harmed me. Other than verbal sparring, we've managed to keep from each other's throats. I only wish—"

Aidan felt a presence and looked up to see a pair of melancholy brown eyes gazing down at her. Instantly she wished she could disappear into the ether, but no magician's trick could save her, she knew. Their inevitable encounter, which she'd secretly dreaded, had finally come to pass.

10

"Why, Aidan?" George Edmonds questioned. "I waited for you—waited two long days at the inn—but you never showed. You and Westover—I don't understand. I—"

Abruptly George fell silent, and Aidan realized the man was embarrassed, for they were not alone. As she viewed the forlorn-looking man, she couldn't help but feel pity for him, especially when she'd assisted in the destruction of his hopes, his dreams. Knowing she had to somehow make amends, she looked to Eugenia. "Lord Edmonds and I need a private moment together," she said, her eyes pleading with her friend to make up an excuse for her should Justin return and find her gone. "I'll be back shortly."

"I understand," Eugenia replied, placing her hand on Aidan's and giving it a light squeeze, wishing Aidan luck.

Aidan acknowledged her friend's show of concern with a gentle squeeze in return, then rose from her chair. "If you will allow me a moment, George, I'd like to explain how all this happened."

"I think that would be appropriate," he said formally, offering his arm, and the two made their way through the open French doors, out onto the wide balcony, which stretched the length of the ballroom, and into the moonless night.

Leading George to a quiet corner where they would not be disturbed, and hopefully not overheard, Aidan wondered what she might say, do, to assuage the man's hurt pride. Tell the truth and apologize was all that anyone could do, she knew. With gentle words, she planned to explain what had happened and beg his forgiveness for involving him. With luck, he would understand.

"Do you love him?" George asked the instant they'd found a secluded spot.

"No, I don't. George—"

"Then why did you marry him? Was it his title? His money? Did you find me lacking in those areas?"

"No, George. I—"

"Why did you do it, then?"

"George, please give me a chance to explain," Aidan pleaded, but he seemed not to hear her.

"Aidan, you were to be mine—*mine,*" he said, his arms awkwardly going round her, pulling her close. His chin rested atop her head as he held her to his slim chest; Aidan felt as though she were suffocating. "From the moment I left London, I dreamed of the hour when you would finally become my bride. It seemed to consume my every waking thought. I couldn't sleep at night because I was anxious to have you with me. I needed you, Aidan. I need you now. Why did you betray me?"

Frightened by the intensity of his words, his crushing embrace, Aidan frantically pushed away from George's chest. "Listen to me," she whispered harshly, trying without success to break free of his hold. "George, I didn't betray you. I was forced into marrying Justin." His arms slackened, and Aidan was able to escape his grasp. Quickly she stepped back.

"Westover stole you away from me?" George questioned. "I should call him out for his treachery!"

Realizing the man had not only misunderstood, but was bent on getting himself killed as well, Aidan placed both hands on the sides of George's face so she might have his undivided attention. "George, hear me out. Justin had nothing to do with our being forced to marry. It was my father."

"Your father!"

"Yes, my father." She dropped her hands, but George caught them, pressing them to his chest. Aidan paid no attention to their placement, for she felt the information that she had to impart was far more important. "My father had somehow discovered our plan to elope, and enlisted some men to help him stop the marriage. He caught up with

Justin and me near the Scottish border. For some perverse reason, he refused to listen to either of us. Perhaps it was because he felt my reputation was at stake," she offered in way of explanation, not wishing to tell George that she believed Alastair Prescott thought the Duke of Westover to be a far better catch than a mere viscount. "All I know is that he closed his ears to both Justin's and my pleas and had his men escort us to the nearest marriage agent, forcing us to say our vows."

"Couldn't Westover have stopped it?" George asked accusingly.

"With at least a half-dozen pistols aimed at my head," Justin said through the darkness, startling both George and Aidan apart, "I found it rather difficult to do anything at all—except to repeat the words which have linked Aidan and myself as man and wife." He moved closer to the couple; Aidan felt overpowered by him. "Had there been any way for me to have stopped it, George, I would have," Justin said, knowing he owed the man an explanation. "I apologize for what happened. But you have to realize that, for better or for worse, Aidan and I are now married. And it would go better for you if you'd simply accept it."

"But you don't love her," George objected. "She cares for me." Aidan would have protested his statement, but the viscount quickly interjected, "Under the circumstances, one would think you'd do the decent thing and press for an annulment. You haven't sullied her, have you?" he asked in afterthought, surprising Aidan.

Justin's eyes narrowed. Although he felt he'd owed the man an explanation and an apology, he was quickly becoming annoyed with the viscount's demands, as well as his tactless queries. "The request for such has been denied."

"A divorce, then," George stated.

"Unlikely," Justin replied firmly.

"But she cares for me, not you!" George insisted. "Tell him, Aidan. Tell him, darling."

Aidan could only gape at the man. What she felt for George, at the moment, was pity, nothing more. He appeared to be on the brink of an emotional collapse, and her heart went out to him, for she knew it had been her fault that he believed her feelings ran much deeper. Perhaps if she explained that she thought of him only as a friend, he would then accept it as so and put any thoughts of her loving him to rest. "George, I care deeply—"

"There, you see! She's just confirmed it!" Again Aidan would have denied George's mistaken utterances, but the man's insistent words overrode any cry of protest she was about to make. "Aidan was to be my wife. Why won't you release her to me?"

Upon having heard Aidan's words, Justin felt an emotion he could only deem as raging jealousy streak through him; the foreign feeling infuriated him. Suddenly all his anger over what had transpired in the last two weeks unleashed itself upon George Edmonds. "The key word here, George, is 'was.' You seem to forget you put Aidan in my care." He pulled Aidan away from George's side and placed her behind him, intending to deal with her later. "Had you not been so concerned over your father's musty old house and shown a bit more interest in your forthcoming marriage, you would not be standing here now, acting the injured party. If anyone can be considered the wounded fool in this entire farce, it's me, not you!"

Justin heard Aidan's incensed gasp, but he ignored it. "Remember, George, since the matter of our marriage is no one's concern, except Aidan's and mine, I suggest you quell any further notions you may have about meddling in it. She is under my protection. And as her husband, under my rule. The only one who holds any claim to her is me," he said, his cold eyes threatening as he unknowingly backed the cowering viscount up against the stone balustrade. Justin felt Aidan's tug on his sleeve, but he shook her off. "Keep far away from her, George, or you shall be the recipient of my full-blown ire. And I can assure you, *friend*, that is something you would not wish on anyone, least of all yourself."

Throaty laughter sailed through the air, drawing everyone's attention; Aidan turned to see Cynthia Danvers not more than two yards away. "Really, Justin," the blond said, swaying seductively up to the object of her words. With Aidan's and Justin's attention on the newcomer, George saw his chance and escaped back into the house. "I had thought we had come out here to find a quiet place where we might . . . uh, talk," Cynthia interjected, "not for you to cause a scene."

Aidan watched as Cynthia placed her hand on Justin's chest, but then, of course, the woman *was* his mistress. For some unexplained reason, the knowledge infuriated Aidan.

Justin's own hand caught the wandering appendage and removed it from his chest. "Go inside, Cynthia. I need to have a private word with Aidan."

The blond turned assessing eyes on the young woman in question; then a long sigh escaped her lips. "As you wish. But don't be long." She turned and glided off toward the door.

Through narrowed eyes Aidan watched the alluring swing of the blond's hips and realized it was meant to entice Justin into following after her. The brazen hussy, Aidan thought, her fury rising. For someone who's said he wanted to protect his new bride from the gossips, he certainly had a strange way of showing it! Parading his mistress onto the balcony, in full view of his peers, was bound to create a flurry of insinuation. Was the man so dense not to realize it would? Or perhaps his overzealous libido had stunted his thought processes. The lecherous rogue!

While Aidan fumed over what was and was not considered proper conduct for a man of her husband's station, Justin's fiery gaze pinpointed itself on her. His anger flared anew as he remembered coming upon his wife and George Edmonds. Seeing her hands pressed to Edmonds's chest, her lovely face upturned to the viscount's, then hearing the pleading quality of her voice, the content of her words obscured by the distance between his bride and himself, had set him off. He'd instantly dropped Cynthia's arm and stridden the dozen or so steps toward the pair, before he'd realized he'd done so.

Now, as he gazed down at her, Justin attempted to convince himself that his immediate rage resulted from his wife's rebellious actions. All that he'd striven to accomplish tonight by attending the Staffords' ball with Aidan on his arm, his warm smiles meant only for her, hoping to keep the gossips at bay, had been done for naught. "I had thought," he said coldly, drawing Aidan's attention, "we had agreed to play the part of devoted newlyweds. Might I ask what inspired you to escape into the night with Edmonds sniffing at your skirts? Have you any idea at all the round of conjectures your actions may have produced?"

Aidan bristled at his accusing tone. "While I was waiting for *you,* George suddenly appeared," she retorted in defense. "You may confirm that with Eugenia, for she was also there. I felt I owed George the courtesy of an explanation as to why I am married to you and not him. Had you stayed by my side, instead of traipsing off with the excuse of getting us some refreshments, we both could have explained to him what had gone wrong."

Justin snorted. "Don't fool yourself. George would never have approached you with me there."

"Perhaps not. But just the same, he deserved to be told the truth."

"Since he's been informed of the circumstances, you'll not have any further need to speak with him. Henceforth, you'll shun all contact with him. Understood?"

Aidan did not answer immediately. Why, she wondered, was she expected to keep away from George—which she was willing to do of her own accord—while he was allowed the luxury of cavorting publicly with his mistress? "Since we are on the topic of explanations," Aidan said in a sarcastically sweet tone, "would you please tell me why you feel you have a right to condemn me for supposedly causing a stir, when you've obviously created one yourself by sauntering out onto a darkened balcony with a woman who's known by all to be your mistress? It seems, sir, that's rather like the pot calling the kettle black, wouldn't you agree?"

Justin gazed at her a long moment, then released his breath. "Cynthia approached me while I was waiting in line for our refreshments. Since I feared she'd make some sort of scene, I opted for a more private place for her to do so," he stated truthfully, but Aidan would have none of it.

"Refreshments? Ha! No doubt the only refreshments you went after were those which would instantly satisfy your rutting lusts!" she accused in a heated whisper, not knowing why she did so, for she refused to believe she might be jealous.

"Rutting lusts?" Justin repeated, instantly angered by

her unwarranted attack. His purpose had been to break completely with Cynthia, for he feared, given the chance, the vindictive blond would do Aidan emotional and mental harm. Although Aidan was independent, high-spirited, and forthright, he knew she lacked the experience to deal with a woman like Cynthia. The blond, on the other hand, was the type who would go straight for the jugular; Aidan would never survive one of Cynthia's calculated attacks. Forgetting his young bride knew nothing of his desire to protect her, Justin drew Aidan against him. "Take care, sweet, that I don't make you the object of my so-called 'rutting lusts.' One would think you'd be grateful that another has to suffer what you undoubtedly believe to be a loathsome act. Someday, love, I'll show you just how wrong you are."

He released her, and Aidan stumbled back. Glaring her dislike, she turned on her heel and headed inside; Justin followed at a slower pace. Angered and hurt, Aidan quickly brushed past Cynthia Danvers, who was purposely standing in the doorway. Her eyes refusing to look at the blond, the young duchess headed toward the area where she'd last seen Eugenia.

As Justin stepped in by the French doors, his gaze following Aidan's progression across the room, his mistress looked up at him. "For a man who claims he doesn't wish to be married, you certainly act as though you're becoming attached to the little baggage. I thought you were bent on getting rid of her."

"I am."

"Did you file the necessary papers requesting the divorce?"

"I did," Justin replied, his eyes still on Aidan as she spoke to Lord and Lady Manley. Their expressions seemed concerned. Undoubtedly she was relaying all that had transpired between his wife and himself on the balcony, eliciting their sympathies. Damn her for making him seem the ogre! Although in her eyes that's exactly what he was, for he'd certainly acted the part, she had no right discussing their private lives with anyone!

"And?" Cynthia asked, becoming annoyed that he wasn't paying attention to her.

"And what?" Justin asked, not looking at her.

"Do you think you'll be granted the divorce?"

"I doubt it. I was told it didn't look very promising. Apparently Victoria had already anticipated my next step. Right now, it's a matter of wait-and-see. Other than doing away with her completely, I may as well accept the fact that I'm stuck."

Light laughter bubbled from the blond's throat. "You could always arrange an accident, Justin," Cynthia suggested, easing up to him, her full breasts pressing against his arm, but to her surprise, Justin showed no masculine response.

"I could, but unlike you, Cynthia, I do have some scruples. If the edict comes down that Aidan and I are to remain married, I will accept my fate."

"You're joking," the blond replied incredulously.

"No, I'm not." He finally looked at her. "And, Cynthia, you may consider our little trysts at an end." He noted her instant surprise. "I will caution you only once. Don't attempt to harm Aidan in any way. If you so much as breathe her name, I'll see that you pay dearly. The house, carriage, jewels, gowns, and whatever else I bought for you will remain yours. Just don't attempt to cross me."

Although she was seething inside, Cynthia was careful not to show it. In time, Justin might change his mind, and she didn't wish to do anything that would permanently keep him from her doorstep. "Whatever you say, Your Grace," she said tonelessly. "I wish you well."

Justin viewed her with a cynical eye, then said, "Good night, Cynthia. And good-bye."

The blond watched as the Duke of Westover angled his way around the room, heading toward his young bride. Never had Cynthia thought that Justin Warfield would take the route of love, but she was beginning to believe that's exactly where he was headed. What seemed ridiculous to her was that he most likely didn't even know it himself. With luck, the little slut would be frigid, and he'd soon be back in her own arms. Until then, she was willing to sit back and watch the man make a complete fool of himself. Espying a particularly handsome young earl, Cynthia sauntered off, deciding the evening shouldn't be a total waste.

*   *   *

"He was extremely upset, Eugenia," Aidan said in answer to her friend's question about George's reaction to the news. "I can't blame him for being so. All this is my fault."

"And mine," Eugenia replied.

"Agreed," said David, then fell silent, for his wife had bestowed on him one of her censuring looks.

"The duke never returned with your refreshments. You didn't happen to run into him, did you?"

"No," Aidan lied, not wanting to share what had transpired between her husband and herself on the balcony. "Perhaps he became sidetracked."

Suddenly Aidan felt a magnetic presence near her; her whole body seemed pulled by its forcefulness. Turning her head, she saw Justin standing directly behind her. Instantly she shifted her gaze forward.

"Lord and Lady Manley," he said, his words flowing over her shoulder, "it's good to see you again."

Respectively David and Eugenia offered a slight bow and a small curtsy. "Your Grace," David said as Eugenia mimicked the words.

Justin inclined his head, acknowledging their formal salute. "If you'll forgive us," he said as the strains of a waltz filled the air, "I'd like to dance one last dance with my bride. Afterward we shall be headed home."

Before Aidan could open her mouth, she was whirled onto the floor. "I'd prefer to sit this one out," she snapped, her fiery gaze searing his face.

"Smile, sweet. We're being watched."

"I wouldn't wonder, with the way you've behaved this evening."

"And you also, sweet," he said, a stilted grin on his face. "Now, smile."

"Hypocrite," she accused, refusing to do so.

Justin tightened his hold on Aidan, then twirled her toward the door. Within moments the pair was seated in his carriage, heading back to Westover House.

Silver eyes assessed the young beauty who sat in the opposite seat, while the memory of seeing her pressed closely to George Edmonds filled the field of Justin's mind. Had it been only an explanation that she'd been offering the viscount?

The thought induced a cold fury to rise within Justin. "Remember my words on keeping yourself away from Edmonds," he said finally. Aidan glared her rebellion through the darkness. Although Justin could not see the flaming mutiny blazing in her eyes, he could feel its combustible force. "Consider it one of my rules," he announced. "One that you'll follow to the letter, especially if you wish to lead your so-called separate life. Or else, dear wife, you will find yourself chained to me day and night. Something I'm sure you'd truly abhor." She did not answer. "Aidan, don't let your anger with me ruin what rapport we do have. Now, will you promise me you'll stay away from George?"

She searched the shadows, knowing she had little choice but to accede to his wishes. Otherwise, she'd be made his prisoner. The thought of losing her freedom prompted her reply. "You leave me no alternative. Either I do as you say or I'm doomed."

Justin chuckled. "I fear you are already," he said, certain their divorce would be denied.

Aidan's brow furrowed. "What?"

"Nothing," he answered, not wanting to hear another round of angry protests over the issue. "Do I have your promise, then?"

"Yes," she hissed, piqued that he held such control over her. "I will stay away from George."

"Good. You now have my permission to travel about town on your own. Of course, I shall do the same. Occasionally, though, we will need to make an appearance together. You may choose the time and place."

"How about St. Paul's on Sunday mornings?" she countered, and a shout of laughter burst forth from Justin.

"Are you planning on making me look pious? I presume you'll next have me confessing my sins."

An impish smile crossed Aidan's face. "I'd never be that cruel. Your confessor would surely have grown a beard nearly three feet long by the time you finished uttering all your transgressions."

Justin chuckled. "And I suppose your sins can all be whispered within a single breath." Aidan didn't answer. "Beware, sweet, you don't add any wrongs to your list. I'm not as forgiving as our Maker."

"Nor am I. But you, sir, should take your own advice. Already the weight of your list would break a camel's back. One more and you might sink into perdition."

"I'm already headed in that direction, sweet," Justin said as their carriage stopped in front of Westover House. He stepped down and offered Aidan his hand. "Would you care to join me?"

Through narrowed eyes Aidan viewed his extended hand, then slipped her fingers over his slightly callused palm, for she feared if she didn't accept his help, she might get caught up in her voluminous skirts and end up on the ground. "This doesn't mean I shall willingly follow you to the nether regions," she said, nodding at their joined hands.

"But I'm certain we shall meet there, nonetheless," Justin said in a teasing whisper, his heated breath caressing her ear; an exciting warmth raced down Aidan's spine, leaving her breathless, as well as confused.

After silently making their way through the door and up the stairs, for Aidan was pondering her unexplained reaction to the man, Justin drew her into his arms.

"Good night, sweet," he said, and, stunned, Aidan watched as his face lowered itself toward hers. Quick and hard, his lips took control of hers; then suddenly he released her. "I'll see you in the morning."

Staring after him as he strode off toward his room, Aidan wondered about his abrupt changes in mood. The man was impossible to understand. Perhaps he purposely meant to keep her off-balance, her emotions tossed one way, then another.

Maybe, she decided, her eyes narrowing on his back, he was trying to drive her insane. It was a logical way for him to be rid of her. In fact, one might call it a forced bachelorhood. Once he had her institutionalized, which was fairly simple for a husband to achieve, she would remain there for life, thereby assuring him his freedom. He could not divorce her; therefore, no woman could trap him in marriage again. Yet the law stated nothing about him cavorting about town with as many women as he wished, taking them all to his bed if he liked! Too bad her own gender wasn't afforded the same privilege, she fumed silently, turning on her heel and heading for her separate quarters. If it was, she'd have him committed tomorrow!

Not realizing Justin's seesawing reactions to her resulted from the riotous emotions she'd evoked in him, keeping him equally off-balance, Aidan was certain he was up to some sort of underhanded trickery and decided to watch him carefully, lest she find herself permanently established in Bedlam!

Two days after the Staffords' ball, Justin was called to Buckingham Palace for a private audience with the Queen. The instant the doors closed behind him, offering them privacy, Victoria let loose her royal tirade. "I had thought, Westover, that I'd made myself clear when I told you there would be no annulment. Divorce is even more distasteful to me! I will have nothing to do with anyone who is even remotely connected with the word. Let it be known, here and now, if you continue to pursue this ridiculous notion about dissolving your marriage, I shall do everything in my power to strip you of all you have! Is that clear?"

"It is, Your Majesty," he said, inclining his head.

"Good. Now go home and start a family. The reward you will receive from such will be greater than anything you've ever known."

"As you wish, madam." Justin offered her one of his notably devastating smiles, then bowed and strode from the room. Strangely, he felt no anger over the episode. His resulting temper, however, was over how he should break the news to Aidan.

Justin had just stepped through his front door, his mind on Her Majesty's words, when Aidan came sweeping down the steps toward him. "I'm going to the races with David and Eugenia," she announced, pulling on her gloves. "Afterward I plan to share a private supper with them."

"What, no balls to attend tonight?" he asked sarcastically, tossing his hat and gloves onto the table near the door. "Perhaps we should entertain having one ourselves. That way, you shall be kept busy and your boredom will be appeased."

For some reason the prospect of having a ball here at Westover House excited Aidan. "Do you really think we could?" she asked, a smile lighting her face. "There is so much to do. I can't imagine where I'd begin. Perhaps Eugenia—"

"It's too late in the season to even attempt such an enormous undertaking," Justin stated in irritation. "Begin making your plans for next year."

"Next year? I don't plan on being here then," she retorted, certain they'd no longer be married. Abruptly she wondered if there had been any progress along those lines. "Has any headway been made toward our divorce?"

"I'm working on it, madam!" he snapped, a dark scowl marking his face. "Now, good day."

Aidan watched as he marched up the stairs and across the hall; the door to his study slammed shut with a loud bang. Reviewing the peculiar scene which had just taken place, she thought her husband's temperament more dangerous than that of an injured boar.

Over the ensuing week, Aidan went about leading her separate life, attending the numerous parties and balls that were scattered throughout London. She hardly ever saw Justin, which was just as well, for when they did encounter each other, his greeting was surly. Not being one to hold her tongue, she found herself to be equally ugly in her exchange of words with him. A dour mood had settled over Westover House, and Aidan was determined to keep herself from within its sullen walls as much as possible.

While Aidan set herself to enjoying her numerous social engagements—not so much that she relished the company of her peers, for she still thought them a stuffy lot, but mainly that the constant activity seemed to relieve some of the tension which had again coiled inside her—she impishly discovered that she rather liked being called "Your Grace." Those who were the most critical of her actions while she was simply Lady Aidan Prescott were now the most supportive since she'd become the Duchess of Westover. In their eyes, she could do no wrong!

Of course, Aidan instantly saw through their artifices, knowing it was not her friendship they sought, but that of her husband. No doubt they believed, through her, the Duke of Westover could somehow give them a higher standing in society or pad their paltry purses. Whatever their reasoning, Aidan played the part, always being most gracious to them all in public, while giggling with Eugenia in private over their blatant hypocrisy.

"I cannot believe they think I'm swallowing all this," she would say. Whereupon Eugenia would reply, "I suppose it's because they have yet to see you choke!" Then they would fall into the giggles, David's confused expression fueling their laughter.

Fortunately she saw George only twice. Both times, when he approached her, she was seated with a group of people, so his greeting was quite formal, their conversation polite. Once he requested a dance, but Aidan begged off, pleading a slight headache. Although her dance card was nearly full, she told each of her partners the same story, not wishing to hurt George's feelings any more than she already had.

As the days passed, she became much braver in her escapades, temporarily forgetting her husband's warning about being on her best behavior. A fast horse race across Hyde Park, where Aidan had been declared the winner, garnering her a hefty purse; large wagers placed on thoroughbreds, simply because she liked their names or the color of their coats, whereupon the nags would win the race; and shinnying up a large tree in her skirts to replace a small bird in its nest, which would have once drawn raised eyebrows, but now drew applause—all this came filtering back to the Duke of Westover's ears. While at White's or at a local coffeehouse—even in the House of Lords!—he would listen to the tales, smiling at his wife's antics, but seething inside, for he was being made a laughingstock. It was in that most noble House that Justin's patience finally snapped.

"I see you're having as much luck with her as I did," Alastair Prescott said, coming up behind Justin after the quorum had adjourned for the day. He chuckled. "I had thought you could control her. Perhaps I was mistaken."

Justin turned steely eyes on the man. "Since I didn't ask for the problem which you've settled on me, I see no reason why I should be the one to correct the flaws in her upbringing."

"Coward, Westover?" Alastair needled, again chuckling. "Perhaps you're not man enough to take her on?"

"Obviously, sir, you were not man enough to mold her into a proper lady in the first place. If you're so worried over her antics, I suggest you have a word with her."

"She won't speak to me," Alastair conceded. "She's still angry over your sudden elopement."

"I can't imagine why," Justin replied sarcastically.

"You seem rather testy yourself. A bit of advice, son," Alastair said, placing his hand on Justin's shoulder, leaning his head toward his son-in-law as though sharing a confidence. "Get her with child and she'll quickly settle down. Who knows? The act in itself might help soothe your jangled nerves and put a smile on your dour-looking face. It's worth a try."

Before a startled Justin could reply, the Duke of Atwood retreated, calling out to another member of the peerage, intent on making conversation. But as Justin brooded over Atwood's words, he began to see the sense of them. The facts, as he saw them, were thus: he'd been saddled with a bride and had every right to lay claim to her; as the Duke of Westover, he had need of an heir; and as a husband, he had to somehow stop his wife from making a complete fool of him! What better way to solve his dilemma than to seduce her and get her pregnant?

With his solution in mind, Justin quit the walls of Parliament and set off to find his errant bride.

Justin cursed his luck and strode into his study. Not only had Potts neglected to show with the carriage, but Aidan was again gone from the house. He poured himself a brandy, settled back in his chair, and loosened his cravat. No sooner had he raised the glass to his lips, his thoughts on his missing wife, than Pitkin appeared in the doorway.

"Sir, there's a Mr. Riley here to see you. He says it's most urgent. He's a local jeweler and thinks you might be interested in a ring he has."

"A ring?" Justin questioned, annoyed over the disturbance. "I have enough rings, Pitkin. Tell him I'm not interested in acquiring another."

"As you wish, Your Grace. But I believe he said something about your ducal crest being inscribed on the one he wanted to show you."

His curiosity piqued, Justin sat forward in his chair. "My crest?"

"Yes, sir, your crest."

"Send this Mr. Riley up, Pitkin." As Justin waited, his father-in-law's chiding words rolled through his head. Again he wondered where Aidan might be, then became even more annoyed by her absence. No doubt, he decided, she was shinnying up another tree! He noted a movement at the door and rose from his seat. "Enter, Mr. Riley. My man tells me you're interested in showing me a ring."

"Indeed, Your Grace," the jeweler said, stopping a few paces from Justin. "I'm very interested in doing so, and I think you might be equally interested in seeing it." The portly man withdrew the circlet from his pocket. "I'm not certain, but I believe this might be yours. At least, the inscribed crest indicates as much."

The heavy gold ring settled onto Justin's palm. Its ruby flashed in his suddenly steely eyes. "You're correct, sir," he said between clenched teeth. "Precisely how did you get this?"

"My clerk acquired it several weeks ago when a young woman brought it in and asked for a loan against it. Had I not been out of London, I would have questioned her on how she'd come to have it in her possession. But, unfortunately, that was not the case. When I finally returned and looked it over, I saw the crest. Thinking it might have been stolen, I brought it straight to you."

"By chance, did your clerk give you a description of this woman?"

"He did, sir. He described her as being about so high." The jeweler's hand stood several inches above five feet from the floor. "She was very appealing to look upon, and he said she had violet eyes." A red hue had inched up over the duke's face beneath his bronzed complexion, and the jeweler thought the man was about to explode; he stepped back a pace. "Do you know this woman, Your Grace?"

Hard gray eyes pierced the jeweler. "I do."

"Then it wasn't stolen?"

"That depends on how one looks at it," Justin snapped. "How much does this woman owe you?" The jeweler promptly named the figure, and Justin strode to his desk.

Taking the amount from inside a metal box, which sat in a lower drawer, he gave the large bills to the jeweler, plus one extra for good measure. "I'm most appreciative, sir, of your astuteness. Thank you for bringing this to my attention."

"It is I who must thank you, Your Grace," Mr. Riley stated, eyeing the gratuity he'd received while Justin ushered him toward the door. "If I can ever be of further service to you, please don't hesitate to call." He handed the duke one of his cards just as he was urged into the hallway; the door abruptly slammed in his face.

On the other side of the panel, Justin raked his hand through his thick hair. Blast it all! Why had she pawned his ring? *Money, you fool!* But why would she need it? Hadn't he supported her in the manner to which she'd been accustomed, exactly like he'd promised? All she needed do was ask and he'd have given it to her. But that was the problem. She'd never asked for anything, except to live separate lives. Was that her plan? Did she hope to sneak off and make him the laughingstock of all London? The ring clenched in his hand, Justin suddenly wondered if she'd done that already. *Dammit!* Where was she?

A knock sounded on the door, and he jerked it open. "What is it, Pitkin?"

The man blinked at his employer's abruptness. "There's an urchin downstairs on the doorstep who says he has news from Potts."

Frowning, Justin brushed past Pitkin and descended the stairs, where he found an ill-kempt towheaded lad standing just outside his front door. The boy's huge blue eyes gazed into the house with awe. "Young man," Justin said, hunkering down, "my butler said you have a message for me."

"Sure do, yer dukeship, sir." He smiled, exposing a toothless gap. "But yer man told me I was to get me money first, afore I told ye anythin'."

Justin chuckled, then withdrew several coins from his pocket. Fast as lightning, a grubby little hand snatched at them. "Whoa, not so fast, lad," Justin admonished, catching the boy's wrist and holding it. "First, tell me what Potts had to say."

The urchin looked at Justin distrustfully. "Ye ain't gonna pull a fast one on me, is ye?"

Justin held back his smile. "Do I look dishonest?"

"Well"—he frowned—"maybe not a bunch."

"Then give me the message, and I'll give you the coins."

"Yer man said to get yourself over past the Tower, 'cause yer missus is holed up in some big old buildin' and yer man be watchin' her."

"And where exactly is my man?" Justin asked, wondering what the hell Aidan was doing in the slums of London.

The boy saw his chance. "Well, if ye be wantin' some exercise, ye could step on along behind me, and I'll be glad to show ye—fer a price, o' course."

"I thought as much," Justin said, chuckling. "All right, boy. But we'll take a hired coach and save our feet."

"Gosh, yer dukeship, ye sure must got lots o' money."

"When we finally part, young man, I have a definite feeling I'll have a lot less."

The boy bestowed a gaping grin on Justin. "Cain't say yer stupid—not like some of them other uppity rich folks is."

Justin followed the shabby-looking urchin down the steps, and before long the two were headed toward London's East End. While they traveled the thoroughfares in the hired coach, Justin learned the boy's name was Tim. He was an orphan; the streets were his home. As Justin studied the bright, energetic Tim, he wondered what would become of the lad when finally they went their separate ways.

Soon they turned the corner at Mudlings Row, and Tim cried out, "There's your man, just like I told ye." His finger pointed toward Potts and the carriage. "Do I get me pay now?"

Justin knew, if he gave the boy his stipend, the tyke would be off like a frightened hare, losing himself in the rabble that occupied the streets. "In a moment, Tim. First, we'll see what Potts wants."

"Yer tryin' to cheat me, ye is!"

Justin grabbed the scruff of Tim's neck, and after paying the driver, led the boy to the waiting carriage. "Get inside and stay put," he ordered, lifting Tim from the ground. Dusting off his hands just in case some unseemly vermin had latched themselves onto him, Justin noticed how Tim glared his malcontent. Until he could figure out what to do with the waif, he wanted the boy close at hand. "You move and I'll break your leg," Justin threatened, hoping to put some fear into him.

With a pout, Tim fell back into the seat, his arms crossing over his chest. Satisfied, Justin turned to Potts. "Where is she?"

"In that old building with the stone wall around it."

Justin's gaze followed the line of Potts's finger. He frowned, for he recognized the structure as one of his own. He'd thought the place had been condemned and torn down long ago. At least, Dawson had informed him as much. "Why in hell did you bring her here?"

"I didn't, sir," Potts defended. "Her Grace instructed me to take her to her dressmaker's. I did, but when I dropped her off, she said I should go on home—that she was to meet Lady Manley and that Lady Manley would take her home. I left, intending to fetch you, sir, but when I traveled no more than a block, I noticed she'd left her parasol on the seat. I rounded the corner to see her stepping into a hired coach, so I followed her. She went in there an hour ago and hasn't come out since. There's something else, sir. Her Grace . . ." Potts hesitated.

"Go on."

His man drew a deep breath. "I saw Her Grace meet a tall man at the gate. Did I do the wrong thing by telling you, sir?"

Justin felt red-hot anger shoot through him. And something else—something he was unwilling to call by its true name. *Jealousy!* "No, Potts, you did the *right* thing." Justin looked back at Tim. "Mr. Potts will get you a hot meal, lad. I have business to attend to. Stay with Mr. Potts, and if you behave, I'll add an extra shilling to the sum I already owe you. Agreed?"

Tim smiled. "Yer pockets are gettin' lighter and lighter all the time."

Justin smiled back at him. "So they are, Tim. So they are."

He gave Potts instructions to be back within the hour, then turned toward the neglected building. A puff of wind could tumble it, he thought. Trying to restrain his fury, Justin strode through the gate and up the walk, then set his fist to the door more than once. Finally it creaked open, and a white-haired woman presented herself.

"May I help you, sir?"

"You may," Justin said, stepping inside. "For starters, you can tell me who leases this building." He glanced around, noting it was clean but in desperate need of repair.

"Dr. Brenner leases it," the woman stated.

Justin forcefully held his temper. "Is he here?"

"He is." Mrs. Hampstead viewed the tall stranger carefully. "Might I ask, sir, that you state your business."

"You may. I wish to see this Dr. Brenner."

"And who shall I say is calling?"

Justin reached into his breast pocket. "My card," he said, handing it to her.

Mrs. Hampstead read the name. Instantly her manner became overtly cool. "I shall tell the doctor you're here."

Justin watched as the woman turned on her heel and marched up the stairs, her starched skirts crackling with each angry stride. More interested in finding his errant wife, he waited until the woman disappeared from sight, then followed after her.

Reaching the second floor, he strode down the hallway, the sounds of children's laughter drawing him. From beyond a partially open doorway, a stunned Justin hid in the shadows, viewing the scene as it played itself out before him.

Near the opposite wall, by a filth-smeared window, Aidan sat in a rickety straight-backed chair, relaying a story about a not-so-fierce dragon, a bumbling knight, and his swaybacked steed. A tattered bunch of moppets, most of whom were several years younger than the seven-year-old Tim, sat at her feet, enthralled by her every word. Laughter rebounded from the colorless room on several occasions when Aidan added some particularly humorous embellishments to her tale. Justin couldn't help but smile himself.

Then her own laughter chimed forth, her eyes sparkling with merriment. Seeing her thus, he felt a strange sort of tenderness well up inside him. Never would he have imagined his spoiled, headstrong wife devoting her time to a passel of homeless waifs, assuming that's what they were. Obviously there were a lot of things he didn't know about

Aidan. Nor about himself, he decided, remembering his fury upon hearing she'd met up with a man.

"Sir," Dr. Brenner addressed his visitor frostily. "Mrs. Hampstead said you wanted to see me."

His eyes still on Aidan, Justin responded, "I do, sir." Another burst of laughter filled the air, and the young duke smiled again.

Noting Westover's reaction, Dr. Brenner decided to take advantage of it. "Our Miss Prescott is very good with the children," he stated, and Justin finally looked at him.

"Miss Prescott?" he asked.

"Yes. She's been a godsend to us all. She's given much of herself—her time, her money. She buys the children clothes, medicine, and whatever else is needed. In fact, they would be out on the streets now if she hadn't intervened on my behalf and negotiated a six-month lease with your business agent. But six months will go very quickly, sir. By then we'll be in the dead of winter. With your having doubled the rent, I doubt I can raise the funds again. Throwing children out into the cold is merciless, sir. Positively merciless."

Justin frowned. "Dr. Brenner, I believe we have some very important business to discuss."

"If you've come to withdraw the present contract, I shall resist your efforts in whatever way I can."

"On the contrary, sir. I've come to make you an offer that will benefit us both," Justin said, leading Dr. Brenner away from the door before Aidan overheard them. "First of all, my visit here must remain a guarded secret. No one is to know about it, except Mrs. Hampstead. Especially not your Miss Prescott. In return, I shall allow you to stay here rent-free for as long as you wish. The place is in extreme disrepair, so I want you to make a list of what needs the greatest attention. Obviously, the roof leaks," he said, his eyes scanning the ceiling. "It shall be replaced immediately. The rest will be done in due time. Also, there's a young lad by the name of Tim who lives somewhere on the streets near here. I'd like for you to take him in, making certain he receives a good education. My man will bring him to you shortly. If at all possible, keep the tyke away from Miss Prescott." Justin slipped some bills from his wallet. "This should help with your funding," he stated, handing them over to his tenant. "Now, are there any questions?"

Recovering from his shock, Dr. Brenner snapped his jaw shut. "Only one. Why is it so imperative that Miss Prescott not know all this?"

"Because, my good man, *your* Miss Prescott happens to me *my* duchess. She believes I'm the most ignoble beast she's ever met in her life. I certainly wouldn't want to change her viewpoint about my flawed character—at least, not yet," Justin said, chuckling. "If you can give me your word she'll never learn of my involvement in this and if you do what I've asked about Tim, then I'll gladly fulfill my promises to you."

Dr. Brenner weighed the request to keep Miss Prescott ignorant of the duke's benevolence against the needs of his wards, and he decided very quickly there was no contest. "I'll not say a word. Nor will Mrs. Hampstead. And Tim will be taken care of for as long as you like. But what should I tell Miss . . . uh, the duchess if she asks about the refurbishments that are taking place? She's bound to notice."

"Tell her the place has been sold to a kindhearted gentleman who has a great deal of compassion for any child who has lost his parents. Whatever the circumstance, the waif needs to feel secure. That's all she need know."

"I'll do as you say."

"Good. Then I shall be on my way."

The men shook hands, and Justin descended the stairs. Within a short while, a petulant Tim, his pockets jangling with new coins, was handed over to Dr. Brenner's care, with orders to behave himself. Knowing the duke would most likely whop him one should he disobey, Tim decided he'd play the part of a young gentleman—for a while, at least.

With the lad safely off the streets, Justin set a course for Mr. Dawson's. But first he had Potts drive by several of his properties that were supposedly little more than vacant lots. When he discovered the buildings still stood, Justin's eyes turned cold as slate.

Dawson turned the color of chalk the instant Justin confronted him. With the threat of prosecution if Dawson didn't repay the skimmed monies immediately, Justin dismissed the man from his employ. His books in hand, the young duke headed back to Westover House, his thoughts on his violet-eyed wife once more.

An enigma, she was, and Justin found her perplexities to be extremely intriguing. Spoiled and headstrong, she flouted propriety, caring little what her peers might think. Yet, at the same time, she gave most benevolently to those who were less fortunate than herself. He knew of no woman like her.

Thinking of his crested ring, he chuckled. Upon discovering he was the owner of the old building, she'd probably been extremely delighted to pawn the thing and, with its proceeds, pay the rent. He was sort of like a fat greedy cat having been made to swallow his own tail, he thought, smiling to himself.

For now, he didn't want her to know he'd been unaware of Dawson's double-dealing. Praise and affection were not what he desired from her. And to paint his character in a color other than what it really was might make her believe him to be a different man. Because of her naiveté, her innocent heart might see his own as caring and loving, not the jaded piece of stone he knew it to be.

No, he didn't desire her affection. But he did desire her body. Since there was no hope of ever dissolving their marriage, he was determined to have his wife where he wanted her—in his bed! She could continue her charity work, but her other antics would be made to stop. Again Alastair Prescott's needling voice rebounded through his head, and Justin became even more determined to put a leash on his wife's rebellious nature. And there was only one way he knew how to do it: *seduce her*.

11

Aidan stood at the open wardrobe, trying to decide what gown to wear, when a light knock sounded on her bedroom door. "Come in," she called, believing it was Penny; the panel opened, then closed. "Which dress do you think will look best—the blue silk or the green satin?"

"I liked the one you wore the night we first met," Justin said, and Aidan spun around, nearly colliding with him. "Here—this one." He reached around her, his arm brushing her shoulder as he did so, and drew the ivory creation, with its black-lace embellishments, from the wardrobe. "You looked beautiful in it."

"Wh-what are you doing here?" Aidan asked, just finding her voice, cautiously watching his every move.

"I knocked and you bade me enter."

He's too close, she thought, his clean masculine scent filling her nostrils. And why was he looking at her like that? "Well, now you can leave," she snapped, moving back a step.

Noting her quick retreat, Justin grinned down at her. "I came to talk about the ball you said you wanted to give. But if you're no longer interested"—he shrugged—"I'll just let it drop."

Frowning, Aidan watched as he turned and headed toward the door. "Wait!" Justin pivoted in her direction. "I thought you said it was too late in the season to plan one. What has made you change your mind?"

To seduce his wife, Justin realized he needed a viable reason to approach her without rousing her suspicions. Had she been any other woman, he knew he'd have her melting in his arms within a trice. But Aidan was different.

As wary as she was of him, she would never have fallen for his masculine attempts to lure her into his arms, no matter how seductively overpowering his advances might have been. Therefore, he needed a ruse; one that would throw them together so he might subtly break down her defenses without her suspecting he was doing so. Instantly their discussion on having a ball at Westover House had come to mind. If he could only get her interested in arranging the large affair, he felt certain it would be the needed catalyst to put his plan into motion and Aidan into his bed.

"You seem disappointed when I told you we couldn't possibly have one. After some deliberation, I've reconsidered. Westover House has not seen a ball in years. I thought it might be nice to throw open its doors and give an elegant party."

Suspicious of his explanation, Aidan viewed him with a calculating eye, only to discover his silvery gaze reflected what appeared to be complete sincerity. Yet, she remained cautious. "And what if I said I no longer desired to play hostess?" she probed, carefully examining his face.

Justin's guarded expression did not change. "Then, madam, I shall accede to your wishes. Not having the thing will save me an enormous expense. The decision is yours."

Not since she was a child had she participated in such a grand affair. When her mother was alive, Atwood House presented one of the finest balls of the season, and Aidan had been asked to help, though it was in the smallest of ways. But upon her mother's death, the Duke of Atwood had closed his doors, and the ballroom had remained unused from that day to this, the haunting echoes of happier times the only reminders of the gaiety and the laughter it once housed.

Remembering the joy her mother had received from planning such a magnificent affair, sharing in it afterward, Aidan had always wanted to arrange one herself, one that would have made her mother proud. Instantly she realized this might be her only chance. Her next husband—*if* she ever remarried—might not have the resources for such a grandiose feat. Why not take advantage of it while she had the backing to do so? Besides, Justin had said he was willing to comply. "I shall think about it," she said, suddenly fearing she would never be able to pull it off.

"When you've made your decision, let me know. I'll be in my study," he said, then turned and left the room.

Having paced her bedroom floor for an hour, first telling herself there was nothing to it—after all, balls were successfully given nearly every day of the week—then telling herself her efforts were bound to flop—she had absolutely no experience in such areas, other than folding napkins or polishing silver—Aidan had finally made her decision and gone in search of Justin.

The door to his study was slightly ajar, and Aidan sounded a light rap before stepping into the room. Justin glanced up to see her somewhat pensive look. "Have you decided what course you'd like to take?" When she didn't answer immediately, he subtly searched her face for a clue. If she said no to the ball, he'd have to find another ploy so he could maneuver her into a willing surrender. Suddenly he envisioned her sweet body lying in his large bed, he beside her, his masterful hands exploring her silken flesh. "Well?" he asked, a husky crackle strangely altering his voice.

"I would like to give it a try," Aidan said, "but I'm not quite certain how to go about it. There's so much to do."

The trapped breath in Justin's lungs released itself on a chuckle. "Perhaps if I were to offer my assistance, we could both set ourselves to getting it done."

"You'd help me with this?" she asked, surprised.

"Certainly, but only if that's what you want. I have some free time ahead of me, and whatever it is you need, I'd be willing to do." He noted her mildly confused look. "You seem a bit puzzled," he said, smiling at her.

"I am," she admitted. "For a man who has staunchly prided himself on his bachelorhood, you suddenly seem quite . . . domesticated."

"Since it is my money, my home, and my name that are lending themselves to the proceedings, I want it to be the very best it can possibly be. I have no fears that you cannot make it into a work of perfection. I'm simply offering my time and energy to facilitate whatever it is you think needs to be done."

Aidan wondered if she'd heard him correctly. Yet, nothing in his face revealed he was insincere. Quickly she decided she could not afford to turn down his offer. He was a man of impeccable taste, and Aidan thought his opinion might be of value.

"I accept your offer," she said, and Justin held back a grin. "Now, I suppose we should decide upon a date."

Feeling a heady sense of victory racing through his veins, Justin fought to contain his glee. "While you were upstairs, I sorted through all the invitations I—forgive me, madam—*we* have received for the various upcoming events. There appears to be one opening. It's on a Friday, three weeks hence."

"Three weeks!" Aidan cried. "That's simply not enough time!"

"I don't see why not."

"But the caterers are most likely booked."

"If they are, I'll enlist some from France. English cuisine is far too bland anyway."

"But there are the floral arrangements, and the table linens—do we have enough chairs?—the china and silver . . . the ballroom! The floors should be waxed and polished, the walls and windows cleaned—the chandeliers too! There's so much to do!"

Justin chuckled. "Aidan, it shall be done. I'll have part of my staff sent from Warfield Manor and hire competent help to assist them. Don't get yourself into a dither. Everything will work out fine."

"Do you think Aunt Patti might come along as well? She's so knowledgeable on these matters. I know she'd be a great help to me."

Justin frowned. He hadn't counted on Aidan asking for his aunt's assistance. Perhaps it was because he thought the two were still at odds with each other. Obviously, he'd been mistaken.

"I'll invite her, but sometimes her health prevents her from traveling great distances. A quick jaunt around the countryside in the phaeton is usually all she can manage."

"She's really quite good at the reins," Aidan said without thinking, then realized her mistake. She watched Justin for his reaction.

The chit has escaped!

The words rolled through his mind, and Justin felt like he'd been knocked in the head. *Deuce!* He'd been gulled by his own aunt, for he was suddenly certain the way of Aidan's escape had been beneath Aunt Patti's feet in the phaeton. And the note! Her message had been sent, not merely to inform him of his wife's running off, but to make certain he'd gone after her! And he'd played right into the old dowager's hands! Knowing it, Justin chuckled to himself.

He'd wanted to be alone with his wife so he could charm her, but if his aunt was trying to play matchmaker, like he thought she was, then perhaps the woman could give Aidan the needed shove, straight into his arms. With two Warfields working on her, she was bound to succumb.

"I think our first move," he said, masking his features so Aidan wouldn't know he'd come upon the truth about his aunt, "is to set the date, decide whom we shall invite, and then have the invitations engraved. We can both make out a list of what we think needs to be done. What one might miss, the other will hopefully catch. Is the date I mentioned acceptable?"

Aidan looked at him a long searching moment. "Do you think we shall still be together then?"

"If you are speaking of the divorce, I have no doubt we will," he said after carefully choosing his words. "The legalities of such take time. I've warned you not to become overly anxious. Or to get your hopes up too high. Instead of fretting about it, I suggest you put your energies toward planning this ball. Being occupied, as you will be, time will go much faster. By then, we might know something."

"Perhaps we can announce the dissolution of our marriage at our first ball," she said, then giggled.

"Perhaps," Justin said, wondering if he were truly that repulsive to her. "But I doubt it would be proper. One doesn't normally create a scandal at one's own party."

"Well, if we were to do so, I'm certain it would not soon be forgotten."

"Not likely, madam. It would be the talk of London for years to come."

Her light laughter filled the air, as well as Justin's ears; yet strangely, it stung his heart. "I suppose I should start making my lists," she said, then turned and made her way toward the door. "Oh!" Justin watched as she twirled toward him, his eyes never having left her. "Thank you," she breathed, smiling at him. "Let's hope we can make this the grandest affair London has ever seen. We shall stun them all—a sort of coup, if you will."

"Let's hope so, madam," he replied, returning her captivating smile with one of his own. "Success in this matter is quite important to me," he said, but it was not the ball to which he referred.

As the days progressed, Justin watched his wife throw herself into the ball's preparation, which greatly eased his nerves. At least she was no longer out among their peers, creating a stir with her coltish antics, thereby saving him the dissatisfaction of having to listen to the exaggerated accounts, which were immediately followed by mirthful chortles. Satisfied that one part of his plan was working, Justin set himself to the second part: seducing his wife.

True to his word, Justin transferred a large number of his staff from Warfield Manor to Westover House, then hired a small contingent of capable individuals to fill any need that remained. Aunt Patti had sent word she was suffering a minor flare-up with her arthritis, but planned to arrive a week before the event to help Aidan put the final touches on her work.

Upon inspecting the ballroom, Aidan found it simply needed a good cleaning. Having set a crew to doing so, she envisioned the enormous room on the night of the ball. With its three massive crystal chandeliers set aglow, flames dancing merrily on tapered white candles, the gold-and-white decor would glisten like a fairy kingdom. Regally, as though they were king and queen, Justin and she would welcome their guests. Unexpectedly, she discovered the thought excited her. Perhaps it was because she'd begun to enjoy her husband's company.

From the moment Justin had renewed the idea of having the ball, Aidan had been amazed by his willingness to help. Whenever she approached him on a matter concerning the plans, he would stop whatever it was he was doing, allowing her his undivided attention. His suggestions were, she discovered, most useful and always given with the understanding that she had the final choice on the matter.

What also surprised her was the way his money flowed freely. No matter what it took to make this lavish undertaking work, he seemed willing to pay it. Yet, Aidan remained cautious, picking and choosing carefully, protecting her husband's purse as she did so, keeping it safe from those who thought to weigh down their pockets with a few more shillings here and there. If she found a merchant to be disreputable, she would quickly discontinue all dealings with the person. Such devious actions were sternly frowned upon by the Duchess of Westover, and all London soon realized it.

Like his money, Justin's laughter began to flow freely. One day, while she sat cleaning a silver bowl, he chuckled jovially, teasing her about the dark smudge on her nose. "You look like a street urchin," he commented, merriment dancing in his silvery gaze. When his laughter calmed, to her amazement and that of those close by, he rolled up his sleeves and set to cleaning the candelabra, which was next on her list of things to do.

Seeing the Duke of Westover polishing the silver at first startled his staff, but then the group decided his desire to be near his lovely young duchess had precipitated the action. After all, she was laboring as hard as any of them, never complaining, and her husband undoubtedly felt left out. After a private discussion in the kitchen, the servants all agreed to work more strenuously, hoping to give the newlyweds greater freedom, which they were certain their master would welcome with glee.

Always a gentleman, Justin treated Aidan with the utmost show of kindness and respect. Yet at the most unexpected moments, she would catch his lazy silvery eyes upon her, assessing her in a vitally masculine way. When that happened, a rush of excitement raced along Aidan's veins, leaving her breathless. Never did he make an improper move, yet strangely Aidan felt as though she were somehow being seduced. Oddly, in a womanly way, the thought appealed to her; slowly her guard began to drop.

Had Justin known as much, he'd have been ecstatic. As the days had passed, he found an odd thing happening to him. Admittedly, he was most intrigued by Aidan. Her beauty drew him, certainly, but it was her wit and personality that attracted him most. Bright, charming, giving, she'd set his heart to tripping wildly with the softest of smiles aimed his way. Whenever he looked at her, he remembered her at the orphanage, bestowing happiness on a ragged-looking bunch of waifs, smiles lighting their pale, scarred faces, his lovely young Aidan the center of their attention. And, strangely, he felt very much the same way, for he'd found himself enthralled by her. Suddenly his lost freedom no longer mattered to him as it once had. In fact, as ludicrous as it may have seemed, any thought of his revered bachelorhood became extremely unappealing to him. Without Aidan's companionship, he would be lost.

One afternoon as she sat at the desk in Justin's study, the room having been set aside for her use, Aidan quickly ran through her checklist. New livery had been ordered for the servants, with the promise it would be delivered the day prior to the ball, as had the new table linens. The floral arrangements had been selected; the crystal washed; the silver polished; the china, displaying the Westover ducal crest, unpacked; the guest list decided upon; and the great house was on its way to being cleaned from top to bottom. Everything seemed to be going smoothly.

"You've looked over that list at least two dozen times," Justin said, surprising Aidan. He smiled down at her as he slid a hip onto the desk near her. "I've brought a present for you."

Aidan watched as he withdrew a card from his coat pocket. "The invitation!" she cried, her violet eyes showing their excitement as she took it from his hand. "Oh, Justin, it's beautiful!" Her finger lightly touched the ducal crest gracing the top of the invitation, then traced the gold lettering, which read: "The Most Noble Duke and Duchess of Westover request your presence . . ."

"They're being delivered by messenger at this very moment."

"D-do you think anyone will come?" she asked, suddenly fearful all her work would be for naught.

"Undoubtedly we shall be turning them away at the door." He saw her questioning look. "The house may not hold them all."

"Did we invite too many?"

"Perhaps we didn't invite enough."

"Surely we haven't forgotten someone."

"Yes, madam, we have. Your father."

A disjointed laugh erupted from Aidan. "Are you serious? After what he's done to you—to us—one would think you'd never wish to see him again."

"He is your father, Aidan, and we cannot continue to ignore him." She appeared unconvinced by his words. "I think we should invite him. Otherwise, our guests will wonder why he's not here."

Aidan doubted the wisdom of inviting her father to the ball. It would be her first time seeing him since she'd been forced to marry, and it was bound to spell disaster. "I'll think about it," she said finally, realizing Justin was awaiting her answer.

His brow arched as he looked down at her, but he held his tongue on the matter. "Have you finished checking your list?" he chided, retrieving it from the desk where it lay. "It seems everything has been . . . Wait! You've forgotten something."

"I have?" She snatched the paper from his hand and rechecked it. "I can't see a thing I could have possibly missed. It's all been checked off—twice."

"What you have forgotten isn't on the list, madam." He caught hold of her hand and urged her from the chair. "We shall go see about correcting the error now." He guided her toward the door, then down the stairs.

A frown settled on Aidan's forehead as she followed his lead. "Where are we going?"

"Out."

"But I'm not properly dressed! My gloves and bonnet!" she protested as he swept her out the front door to the awaiting carriage. Suddenly her heels dug into the pavement. "I'll not go another step until you've told me where we're headed."

Justin chuckled and lifted her into his arms, then playfully tossed her into the seat. "You will go . . . and it is a surprise."

While the carriage rolled toward their destination, Aidan raised a delicate eyebrow in haughty speculation as she stared across the span separating Justin and herself. "And we were getting along so nicely, too," she accused finally.

"Bear with me, sweet. Once you've discovered where we are going, I'm certain you'll be more than happy to renew our friendship."

When the carriage stopped outside Madame Bouchard's, the most famous couturiere in all London, Aidan gasped. Madame catered only to a select clientele, she knew, and it was purported that Madame herself chose which individual would wear her latest creation, and no amount of money could change her policy. To wear a Bouchard gown was to be envied by all.

"We are here," Justin said, smiling at her round-eyed expression, then stepped from the carriage. "Madam."

Aidan absentmindedly slipped her hand into Justin's. She felt his gentle squeeze; then he helped her alight. "I . . . I don't understand," she said, still awestruck.

He chuckled as he led her toward the door. "You will, madam," he said, opening the wood-and-glass panel; a bell sounded as he did so.

"Ah, Your Grace," an attractive redhead, whom Aidan thought to be in her mid-thirties, said in a sultry French accent, curtsying. "As always, you are on time." She turned her attention to Aidan and smiled. "And this must be your lovely young bride."

Something akin to jealousy streaked through Aidan, for the woman had sounded as though she knew Justin *personally*. Quickly Aidan denied its name and squared her shoulders.

"Madame Bouchard," Justin returned, bowing slightly. "May I present Her Grace, the Duchess of Westover."

Aidan inclined her head. "Madame."

"I am happy you have chosen my establishment for your needs," the woman said, then turned and clapped her hands. "Bridget, come!"

A shapely brunette appeared from nowhere; the young beauty's admiring gaze raked over the handsome duke as a coy smile teased her full lips. If Aidan hadn't known better, she would have sworn that she'd stepped into the middle of a French brothel and not the exclusive fashion house that Madame Bouchard's was purported to be. Indeed, the two women seemed more than willing to please Justin Warfield, in whatever way possible.

"Your Grace," Madame Bouchard addressed Justin, "please have a seat. I shall attend to your wife in a moment." The woman moved away toward the back of the shop.

Justin folded his long body into a dainty giltwood armchair, then gazed up at Aidan to find her staring down at him.

"Perhaps it is time you tell me why we are here," she snapped ungraciously.

"If you do not know by now, sweet, I'll not try to explain."

Narrowed eyes scanned his face; then Aidan blurted, "Madame acts as though she knows you quite well."

Justin let loose a knowing chuckle. "That is because Madame *does* know me quite well."

Again jealousy flamed within Aidan, but this time she could not deny it. Drawing a breath, she was about to ask if the word "know" was meant in the biblical sense, when suddenly Madame reappeared. "Come," the woman said, "we are ready."

As Aidan followed the Frenchwoman into the dressing area, she was thankful the couturiere had interrupted her retort. Never would she let the man think she felt anything for him but contempt!

While Bridget assisted a stiff Aidan from her blue silk day dress, Madame Bouchard regarded the violet-eyed beauty at length. "He said you were exceptionally beautiful, with eyes the color of a Scottish moor when the heather was in bloom. As always, he is right."

"And what else did he say?" Aidan queried sarcastically, suddenly resentful her husband would discuss her with this woman, never mind his words had been extremely complimentary.

A sultry whisper of a laugh escaped Madame Bouchard's throat. "Not much—except he wished to have the most striking woman in all London at his side the night of the ball." She turned and called through the curtain, "Yvette, bring it!"

Aidan watched as a slender young woman backed herself

through the draperies. When the girl turned around, Aidan gasped with pleasure, for in Yvette's arms was the loveliest satin ball gown Aidan had ever seen.

Deep orchid in color, the dress appeared bathed in twilight; Aidan discovered she was eager to try it on. With Bridget's and Yvette's help, she found herself encased in the beautiful creation in moments. "You may go," Madame Bouchard said, waving off her assistants, then set to fastening the last dozen satin-covered buttons, which ran up the back. With a quick tug, Madame pulled the puffed sleeves down, exposing Aidan's creamy white shoulders. "There," she said, satisfied. "What do you think of it?"

"It's gorgeous," Aidan whispered, then blushed as she eyed the indecently low décolletage through the mirror, for her young breasts were exposed more than she thought proper. Her hands climbed to each shoulder to adjust the sleeves, and with them her décolletage, but Madame stopped her.

"No, no! You must leave it to attract the eye of your husband," she admonished, pulling the small sleeves down again. "He will be pleased with your beauty." Madame saw Aidan's skeptical look. "It is true. He chose this style himself—the color as well. Ah, he has done well. Never before has he purchased a gown from me. There was no one he cared to dress so beautifully—not until you."

Aidan's questioning eyes met Madame Bouchard's in the mirror, and Madame smiled knowingly. "You thought perhaps he brought his lovers here?" Madame asked, and Aidan's gaze dropped away from the older woman's. "He has never brought anyone here, except you."

Hearing the words, Aidan again assumed that Justin and Madame Bouchard had been . . . *intimate*. Why else would he know her?

"You are wrong, *chérie*," the redhead said, and Aidan's eyes met Madame's again. "It is not your husband who has shared my bed, but his father."

"His father?"

"*Oui*. Ten years ago, when his father died, I thought I would be cast out of my little shop, which Malcolm had purchased for me. I was wrong. At eighteen, Justin was quite mature. Instead of tossing me out, he proposed we continue with a business relationship. We are partners, and my shop is what it is today because of him."

Aidan believed the woman. "I apologize," she said in a small voice, "for making such a presumption. But I . . . I—"

"With a man as virile and as handsome as your husband, the mistake is understandable. Any woman would wish to have him in her bed." She laughed throatily. "The bedroom, *chérie,* is where it counts. You can be as proper a lady as you wish in public, but once you have closed that door, always remember to play the part of the *femme fatale.* You must be a paramour for your husband. As long as you continue to please him, you will not lose him." Seeing Aidan's wide-eyed look, Madame shrugged. "But then, I may be wrong. He has never gazed at a woman as he does you. I know, for I have seen him with many. He may love you no matter what happens in his bed." Madame fluffed the sleeves again. "Now, are you ready to show him how truly beautiful you are?"

He may love you . . . The words rolled through Aidan's head over and over again. Ridiculous! she thought. But then, he did seem different: kinder, more attentive—more affectionate? No! She was imagining it. He wanted to be free. Their divorce was imminent. Yet, for some reason, the knowledge saddened Aidan. Could it be she was falling in love with him? The thought frightened her, for she discovered she was no longer able to state a definite no to the question.

"*Chérie?*" Madame inquired. "Do you wish to show His Grace your beautiful gown?"

"No!" Aidan said forcefully, then realized it was not Madame's query to which she responded, but her own. *Liar!* a piece of her heart protested, but Aidan ignored it. "I mean," she said more gently, "I'd like to surprise him."

Madame smiled. "A wonderful idea, *chérie.* You shall dazzle him."

"How, Madame Bouchard, did you know my size?" Aidan asked, suddenly curious as to how the gown managed to be a perfect fit.

"His Grace brought me one of your old gowns—an ivory satin with black lace. I took your measurement from it."

"Oh." Then, as Aidan slipped from her new gown to don

her day dress, she again thought about what Madame Bouchard had said, but refused to believe there was any truth to the couturiere's words. Justin could never love her.

As the couple made their way back to Westover House, Aidan sat next to Justin, deep in thought. Shortly she felt Justin's silvery gaze upon her and turned questioning eyes toward him.

"You seem unhappy," he said after a long searching moment. He slipped his arm behind her, resting it along the top of the seat, his hand only inches from her head. Forcefully he fought the urge to touch the silken mass of hair. "Has my surprise disappointed you?"

"No, not at all."

"Well, I was disappointed."

"Why ever should you be disappointed?"

"The gown, madam. I did not have the chance to see you in it."

"You will, sir, the night of the ball."

"Ho!" Justin cried, pretending to sulk. "After all the trouble I've gone through, you plan to make me wait until then?"

"I do," she answered saucily. "But remember, the excitement is in the anticipation, not the actual event."

Justin threw back his head and laughed. "Aidan, love," he said as his hand rose from his lap. His knuckles brushed lightly across her cheek, while his dancing eyes beamed down at her. "You are a woman unlike any I have ever known."

As her smiling gaze locked with his, Aidan felt a delicious warmth spread through her, all the way to her toes. Handsomely charming, she thought, the last of the barriers she'd erected cracking, to slowly slip away. She was caught in his spell, and Aidan suddenly realized she cared little that she was.

True to her promise, Aunt Pattie marched through the front door of Westover House precisely one week before the ball. Her sharp orders rang upward to echo through the great house as she directed her footmen on the placement of her luggage, her cane pointing to the exact spot each piece should go. Upon hearing the commotion, Aidan smiled and sailed from Justin's study, down the stairs. "Aunt Patti!" she cried, rushing to the woman's side.

The dowager marchioness offered her cheek for Aidan's kiss, then patted the younger woman's hand. Inspecting her niece's lovely features, she looked for that certain telltale glow, then was instantly disappointed to find it was not there. Anxious to hear what was happening, Aunt Patti asked in a conspiratorial whisper, "How goes it?"

The pair moved toward the stairs to slowly climb upward. "Wonderfully well," Aidan replied, a smile lighting her face. "The plans are all set for the ball and everything seems to be running smoothly."

"Not the ball," the dowager marchioness snapped impatiently. "How goes it with Westover? Does he suspect my part in your escape?"

"You're safe, Aunt Patti. He knows nothing of our duplicity. At least, he's shown nothing which says he does. As for Justin and myself, we are managing quite nicely. We are no longer arguing at every turn, but are working together toward a common end. Since the Queen has denied our request for an annulment, we've decided to petition for a divorce."

Startled, Aunt Patti instantly stopped her upward movement. The word "annulment" jolted her, but she'd been quite pleased to hear that Victoria had refused the request. Upon hearing the word "divorce," however, she'd nearly toppled back down the steps. "Have the two of you lost your minds? The scandal will ruin both of you!"

Seeing the woman's stern look, Aidan bit her lip. "I know what you're saying is true . . . but Justin wants our marriage dissolved. He's willing to do anything to see it at an end."

"Are you certain of that?"

Was she? Aidan wondered, especially when she'd noticed a marked change in him over the past few weeks. "You'll have to ask him: I cannot answer in his place."

"But you can answer for yourself," Aunt Patti stated, a censuring frown on her brow. "Do *you* wish to dissolve this marriage?"

"I can't say anymore. Sometimes I think it's best we do.

Then at other times I'm not so certain. In truth, I no longer know what I want."

"Well, then, *I* shall tell you what you want. Should the two of you persist in attempting to terminate this marriage, you shall both suffer for it. Allow my nephew to divorce you, and Victoria will strip him of his title, his lands, and whatever else he has. You, dear girl, will be scourged at every turn. Since it was your father who caused this loathsome mess in the first place, I'd hope that you would have the decency to save my nephew any further pain and embarrassment. It's time you cease this ridiculous ploy— divorce, indeed!—and start working toward getting yourself into your husband's bed!"

Instantly Aidan shot red; her mouth worked several times, but her words of protest refused to exit.

"Stop blushing like a schoolgirl," Aunt Patti admonished. "You're a woman now, and if there is any man in this town who can make you feel like one, it is Westover. Take my advice and stop playing these childish games. It is about time you set your mind to seducing your own husband, for it is unlikely that you'll ever have another!"

With her mouth agape, Aidan watched as the dowager marchioness ambled up the remaining stairs, all the while wondering what had precipitated the woman's sudden tirade. She'd simply answered Lady Falvey's question, but Justin's aunt had acted as though Aidan had committed an act of treason!

"Well, are you coming?" Aunt Patti called; Aidan looked up to see the dowager standing regally at the top of the stairs, gazing down on her. "You asked for my help, now let's be about whatever it is that needs to be done."

Not wishing to be the recipient of another one of the dowager's scoldings, Aidan lifted her skirts and scurried up the stairs. Once they were settled in the study, where Aidan thought they might begin their discussion of the ball and what still needed to be done, she ordered up some tea and cakes. Within moments Justin strode into the room, greeting his aunt warmly.

As Aidan watched aunt and nephew bantering back and forth, her gaze finally settled on Justin's handsome profile. His throaty laughter filled the air, and a warm feeling of excitement rioted through her, which was abruptly replaced by guilt. Was she indeed acting the child, like Aunt Patti had said? Admittedly, all that had happened was her fault, and to allow him to set a course toward ruin would be exceedingly callous of her. The notion of a divorce had suddenly become very distasteful. But it was not the thought of the resulting scandal which upset her. No, it was the fierce realization that she would never find a finer husband than the one she already had. And never one who was as attractive!

Instantly Aidan realized the truth. She was falling in love with Justin! The revelation nearly knocked her from her chair. But to hope he might feel the same way toward her would be a wasted effort.

The thought struck her that perhaps he truly was willing to lose all he had, simply to be rid of her! Surely he knew what the Queen's reaction would be—he'd be stripped of everything! But his kindness, his thoughtfulness, his teasing displays of affection—were they merely an optimistic response, knowing he'd soon have her out of his way? Bewildered by it all, Aidan conceded she was caught in an extremely perplexing dilemma—one, she feared, that was bound to break her heart.

12

Luminous violet eyes gazed into the mirror, and Aidan wondered if the woman she saw there was indeed herself.

"Oooh," Penny gushed, looking over her mistress's shoulder and into the silver glass. "I've never seen you look so lovely." She pulled the puffy satin sleeves upward, covering ther crests of Aidan's shoulders; instantly they were pulled down.

"Madame Bouchard said it is to be worn thus," Aidan stated, fluffing the sleeves, which now lay below the crowns of her shoulders.

Penny frowned at her mistress. "A mite daring, to be sure. Since you already got yourself a husband, whose attention are you tryin' to catch?"

Aidan noted her maid's censuring look, and her laughter bubbled forth. Although most would say, as a servant, the girl was far too outspoken, Aidan thought Penny's honesty refreshing. "I'm hoping to capture the eye of the most handsome man at the ball, Penny. You don't approve?"

The young maid sniffed disdainfully. "With the duke bein' the best-lookin' man for a long ways around, I'd think you'd . . . Oh! You mean it's *his* eye you're hopin' to snare."

"Yes, it's *his* eye, Penny, and his alone. Do you think I shall succeed?"

"Unless he's suddenly gone blind, you've nothin' to fear."

Panic surged upward in Aidan. What if Penny were wrong? What if Justin thought her the ugliest creature he'd ever seen? Then all would be lost!

Over the past week, Aidan had found herself in a constant battle. Her head kept denying that she loved Justin, while at the same time, her heart protested just the opposite. Yet how could she explain the wild excitement she felt whenever he was near, or the monumental emptiness which seemed to overtake her whenever he was away. The thought occurred to Aidan that what she felt was simply physical attraction, a magnetic pull, drawing her body to his. But the explanation left her unconvinced. There was more to it; something that ran much, much deeper. To her it felt like a joining of the souls, for she knew if she were never to lie with him, she would still desire his company, wanting always to be near him.

Once she'd finally admitted her true feelings for Justin, and had considered Aunt Patti's words, forcefully suggesting she seduce her own husband, Aidan planned to do just that. And tonight was the night! She no longer wanted a divorce. On the contrary, she wished to become his wife in every way possible. Yet she realized Justin might feel otherwise. Sadly, she knew she could offer herself and he'd take her willingly, then still seek the divorce. Virginity was not a prerequisite in obtaining a legal dissolution of one's marriage. Ultimately, she could end up making a fool of herself, and Aidan feared it was precisely what she was about to do.

"Is there a special necklace or brooch you want to wear?" Penny asked, examining Aidan's jewel case. "The gown is beautiful, but it needs—I don't know—an added somethin'."

"I've tried everything . . . nothing seems to look right. Perhaps it's best we leave it plain. Understating the gown may be far better than my looking like a peacock."

After inspecting her coppery hair, a sprig of violets woven into the intricate style, Aidan smoothed the skirt of the shimmering orchid gown, drew a deep breath, released it, and smiled weakly at her maid. "Wish me good fortune, Penny."

"You shall have it, Your Grace."

Noting the time, Aidan turned to leave the room. She glimpsed the open jewel case on the table beside her. An empty space caught her eye. Strangely, the missing ring haunted her, and she suddenly wished that the heavy gold circlet, its large ruby always mocking her, was still nestled atop the velvet where it once sat. Why, she was unable to say, for she knew that she would never wear it—not unless her husband vowed his love to her. In itself, the probability of his doing so seemed extremely remote. Yet, from experience, Aidan knew all things were possible. Justin's love as well? she wondered.

Sighing, she closed the lid to her jewel case. Her first payment was due in a little over a week, and Aidan decided to take several expensive pieces of her own, thus trading the jeweler outright. Her loan paid, Justin's ring would soon be back where it belonged. Or almost, she thought, gazing at her unadorned finger. Realizing she might never wear it again, she left the room and headed toward the stairs.

Two red-coated servants, looking dashing in their new livery, climbed the steps toward Aidan. One suddenly stopped his ascent to elbow the other. Awestruck, they stared at her. Then, remembering their social stations, they quickly moved to the rail, lowered their eyes, and bowed. "Your Grace," they said in unison.

Realizing the two young men at first had viewed her strictly as a woman, Aidan smiled, inclined her head, then moved past them and down the stairs, anxious to discover what Justin's reaction would be.

The Duke of Westover stood just outside the ballroom, growing impatient. With a quick flick of his wrist, he adjusted his cuff, then smoothed his hand along his taut stomach, over the white satin waistcoat he wore. His emotions in a turmoil, he wondered where Aidan could be, then scoffed at himself, for he realized he was acting like an untried schoolboy. Since the day he'd taken her to Madame Bouchard's, he'd been avidly awaiting the sight of her in her new gown. Hearing the rustle of skirts, She turned toward the sound. An electrical charge shot through him as his hungry eyes settled on his wife.

Aidan felt her husband's burning gaze sweep the length of her. Excitement riddled through her, and her breath caught as her heart skipped erratically. Their eyes locked, Justin's silvery gaze drawing her like a magnet, and she continued toward him, her step never faltering. Then she stopped before him.

"The anticipation of seeing you has been most taxing, madam," he said huskily, his heavy-lidded gaze sweeping over her once more; Aidan nearly swooned from the effects of it. "I was certain my heart could not take another moment of waiting." He smiled down at her lazily. "But you were wrong, love. The actual event has almost been more than I can endure. You are even more beautiful than I had ever imagined."

"And you, sir, are more handsome than I had envisioned," she countered, flirtatiously tapping his arm with her fan. "As you have said, the actual event is almost beyond endurance. I must admit, I feel overwhelmed."

No more had the words left Aidan's mouth than she realized how utterly ridiculous she'd sounded. Never had she been so bold with a man, and she wondered if she were being overly coy.

"You are tempting fate, sweet," he said, chuckling. "Perhaps our guests will not miss us if we were to sneak off and discuss this more thoroughly."

"They haven't even arrived as yet," she blurted.

"All the better for us," Justin countered, his tone teasing.

Confused, Aidan frowned. "How so?"

"Because they couldn't possibly forget such a stunning image as you are tonight." Then he took her arm and propelled her toward the alcove several yards down the corridor. Once inside, he withdrew a velvet-covered box from his inside coat pocket. "This is for you."

Her questioning eyes measured his as Aidan took the box; its top crested to reveal a necklace. Wide violet eyes gazed at the three large teardrop amethysts set in gold and surrounded by diamonds. They were suspended on a narrow collar of gold studded with amethysts and diamonds as well. "Oh, Justin, it's beautiful! Is it really mine?" she asked, not understanding why he'd given her such a lovely gift.

Moist eyes climbed to his face; seeing their soft luminescence, Justin felt a sudden jolt near his heart. "It was my grandmother's, and now it is yours. I thought it would go nicely with your gown." *And your alluring eyes,* he thought, feeling as though he were drowning in them. He plucked the necklace from its satin bed. "Turn around, love," he said, then fastened the necklace after she'd done so. "It's beautiful on you."

Aidan saw hers and Justin's reflection in the alcove's darkened windowpanes. After a long moment, her gaze finally dropped to the necklace. Penny had said the gown needed an added touch; the effect was now complete. "Thank you," she said, turning, and Justin captured her hands.

Silver eyes delved deeply into violet ones, and for an endless moment they gazed at one another. Aidan saw Justin's head move. Fear mingled with excitement as she waited in breathless anticipation. Her lips parted ever so slightly as his face slowly lowered toward hers. Then, just when she thought she could not bear the expectancy a second longer, Justin suddenly lifted her hand; his lips touched her fingers.

"You're welcome, sweet," he said huskily, lowering her hand; still dizzy with want, Aidan thought she would drop to her knees. He smiled gently. "I believe I hear our guests arriving."

Suddenly Aidan realized the buzzing sound, which seemed to fill her entire head, was that of voices. Disappointed, she smiled weakly. "I suppose we must go."

Justin's hand climbed to her face. "Yes, we must." His thumb brushed lightly over her soft lips; the urgent need to master them with his own was overwhelming, but he quickly tamed his cravings. "When we have a quiet moment, we shall sneak away. Then you can thank me properly."

His hand fell away, and he guided her from the security of the alcove, along the corridor, and into the receiving line, where Aunt Patti was greeting the first of the arrivals.

Unknown to Aidan, high color marked her cheeks; her eyes retained a look of womanly fascination about them. As she greeted Justin's aunt, the dowager marchioness's small but regal frame draped in black satin, Aidan espied Aunt Patti's knowing smile. "We could always chase the lot off," Lady Falvey whispered to her, and Aidan's face seemed to flame a brighter red.

A light chortle trickled through the older woman's lips; then she turned her attention to a stately-looking earl, a widower, a half-dozen years younger than herself, and commenced to bedazzle him. Within moments, she excused herself and strolled off, her hand on the man's arm.

"She's right, you know," Justin whispered close to Aidan's ear, drawing her immediate attention. "We could try yelling fire. I'd estimate thirty seconds and they'd all be gone."

"Or we could be trampled in the rush." Aidan gestured to their position in the doorway. "I would say it might be safer to wait it out."

As he took in her lovely face, his gaze slowly descending to the exposed tops of her full breasts, lingering pleasurably, an audible groan escaped Justin's throat. "And I say to hell with them all!"

A guest appeared before them, and Aidan quickly masked her startled look, then smiled, greeting the person warmly. Despite his agitation, Justin did the same. The crush became nearly unbearable, voices rising loudly in the great hall outside the ballroom. Several times the Duke of Westover thought to escape the press by sweeping his lovely duchess into his arms and striding up the stairs to his room. But he tamped down the erratic feelings and pretended to play the perfect host. *Later!* he told himself, convinced that if all went well, she'd soon be lying next to him in his bed, her silken skin replacing her satin gown.

Lord and Lady Manley suddenly appeared.

"Oh, Aidan," Eugenia bubbled excitedly, "you're simply stunning in that gown. And your necklace, is it new?"

"It was my husband's grandmother's," Aidan rejoined, gentle fingers lightly caressing the amethysts lying at the base of her throat. "Justin gave it to me tonight—I shall treasure it always."

Eugenia looked from Aidan to the duke; a knowing light entered her eyes as she smiled inwardly. "Well, David, the duchess has outdone herself, don't you agree?"

"I do," her husband replied, his eyes examining the perfection they beheld. "My compliments to the hostess."

Aidan's gaze had followed the sweep of Eugenia's arm, indicating the sparkling ballroom. Giltwood chairs, their gold-and-white-striped silk covers newly refurbished, lined the freshly cleaned walls. A light breeze flowed from the balcony to brush the three enormous chandeliers, hundreds of candles lit and glowing. Teardrop prisms chimed musically while they shimmered with a profusion of color, reflecting the beauty of the ballroom and the gaily dressed people within. Huge baskets of blood-red roses stood on marble pedestals near the open French doors, as well as in every corner, while a matching centerpiece, of enormous proportions, graced the lengthy serving table along the far wall, its pristine white tablecloth touching the highly polished floor. The Westover china and gleaming crystal goblets stood ready for the large quantity of food and champagne that would be served later. Roasted ducklings, capons, and pheasant, and boiled lobster and baked salmon were being heaped onto huge silver platters this very moment in the kitchen. Fruits and vegetables were being arranged in the most intricate of designs, while French pastries waited on the sideboards for their grand entrance. Still Aidan worried that there would not be enough to satisfy their guests' appetites.

"Thank you, Eugenia, David," she said, smiling. She turned her attention to Justin. "But none of this would have been possible without His Grace's help. He's been most cooperative—in every way possible."

"And I shall remain so," Justin replied, keeping his wife under his rapt regard. "I want nothing more, Aidan, than to please you—in *every* way."

Aidan understood his meaning all too clearly. Blushing, she quickly renewed her conversation with Eugenia and David. While Aidan spoke with them, Justin's eyes lingered on his wife. She excited him as no woman ever had, for she possessed the power to rouse not only his body but also his inner passions. His jealousy would flame inside him unexpectedly; his laughter would burst forth with ease. His tenderness would well up, filling every space within him, while just as quickly his temper would rise to its limits.

At first, he'd thought to seduce her in order to control her. But now he realized the feelings that had evolved within him were far more than physical. On no account was he willing to call it love, for he still thought the emotion for fools—his parents' marriage had proved that—yet he recognized the quickening sensation as something very much akin to the feeling which he'd always scoffed at so cynically. Dammit all! Like it or not, he was trapped. And he had no desire to be freed.

Aidan felt Justin's eyes upon her; she smiled up at him. "I think we are a success," she said of the party.

"Indeed, madam, we are," he said of themselves.

The intensity of his gaze caused a delicious warmth to spread through Aidan's body. The line of guests was dwindling, and as she continued to greet the few who remained, Aidan discovered she longed to be in Justin's arms, leading off the first dance. Equally as thrilling to her was the thought of them finding that special moment when they could slip away and she could thank him properly for his lovely gift. Her hand moved to the amethyst-and-diamond necklace, which had received as many compliments as had her gown. She caressed it lightly, reverently.

Seeing the motion, Justin smiled down at her. "The first chance we get, sweet, I promise we shall secret ourselves away from them all." He winked. "The anticipation, of course, will make the event far more exciting."

The expectation of such was already making Aidan's heart skip in nervous delight, and she blushed responsively. Then she heard Justin's chuckle.

"At least I know now I do not repulse you."

"Did you ever?" she asked without thought.

He grinned widely, knowingly. "That, love, is for you to decide—soon."

The challenging look in his eyes almost toppled Aidan. Her heart had already succumbed to him, which now left her body. She was lost, she knew. No woman could ever resist his masculine charms. Not even herself. Nor did she want to. But she wanted much more than a physical relationship with him. Their hearts must join as well. Yet the teasing light in Justin's eyes told her nothing of what he felt inside, only that he desired her. Undoubtedly many women had seen that same look. The thought depressed her, and she wondered if he were capable of loving any woman, especially herself.

She felt a presence and turned her attention to the next guest; instantly she stiffened.

"You look lovely, daughter," Alastair Prescott said, smiling down at her. "I see he is taking good care of you."

Her gaze ran over her father's familiar features to lock with his blue eyes. Strangely she discovered she was glad to see him, yet her latent anger, which had suddenly swirled to life inside her, refused to let her say so. In truth, she was unable to admit that her father's final selection of a mate for her was the most marvelous of all. "So far we have managed not to kill the other off," she snapped finally, then wished she hadn't been so abrupt.

Undaunted by her brusqueness, Alastair chuckled. "Someday you shall forgive me, daughter. Most likely it will come once he's finally bedded you."

Aidan's eyes widened comically. Having heard the exchange, Justin bit the inside of his lip to keep from laughing aloud. "Your Grace," he greeted his father-in-law, inclining his head. "We are pleased you could come."

"I am most pleased to have been invited," Alastair replied, bowing, then moved off into the ballroom.

"I thought we agreed not to invite him," Aidan accused in a hot whisper, knowing they had purposely deleted four names from the list.

One had been her father's, which she'd crossed off herself. Next came the Earl of Sedgewinn's, which they'd both marked out. Justin had struck a line through George Edmonds's name, while Aidan had nearly broken the pen point when she'd come upon Cynthia Danvers's, a large blob of ink staining the paper as she did so. Upon seeing the deletion, Justin had raised a brow, then presented her a roguish smile.

"But you sent him an invitation anyway, didn't you," she finished.

"I did."

"Why?"

"Because it's time you pardoned him. Although I've not completely excused him, I no longer feel the need for revenge. Perhaps after tonight, you will feel the same way."

"Tonight? Why tonight?"

Justin chuckled. "You'll see, madam. You'll see."

As they greeted the last of their guests, Aidan wondered what Justin had meant by "after tonight." *Most likely it will come once he's finally bedded you.* Her father's words bounced through her mind like a rubber ball; Aidan's head swiveled round. Staring at her husband, who continued speaking with a guest, she wondered if that was his intent. To bed her. *Tonight.*

Justin felt his wife's gaze upon him, but he purposely ignored her. The instant the final straggler came through the line, he took her hand, guided her through the teeming crowd, and out into the dance area. As they stood in the center of the floor, their guests holding to the perimeter, his hand settled at her waist. His free hand captured hers, lifting it into position. "After tonight, love, I hope your forgiveness will extend itself," he said, thinking of her reaction once she'd learned there would be no divorce.

Confused by his words, Aidan gazed up at him, but nothing in his eyes gave her the slightest clue as to their meaning. His head inclined and the orchestra came to life, the strains of a waltz flowing through the room. As they whirled around the floor, others finally joining in, Aidan again considered his statement. At first she'd thought he'd been referring to her father. But now, as she reviewed his words a second time, she was positive he spoke of himself. Had he done something that would require her forgiveness? Did it perhaps pertain to his mistress? Surely, besides her father, he hadn't invited Cynthia Danvers as well!

Aidan would have asked if it hadn't been for the fact that an elderly earl and his countess had found themselves in Justin's and Aidan's path. Justin instantly pulled them up short, avoiding a collision. After profuse apologies were extended, they all discovered the music had stopped. When it started up again, Aidan found herself in the shaky arms of the earl, while Justin slowly glided the aged countess across the dance floor.

From that moment on, the duties of playing host and hostess claimed Justin's and Aidan's attention. It seemed that everything conspired to keep the young duke and duchess apart. Yet Aidan realized she'd been the one who'd wanted to give this ball, so it was up to her to make it a success. And as the night wore on, she knew, if her mother had been here with her, she would have seen great pride in the eyes which had matched her own.

Several times during the evening, Aidan felt a pair of eyes upon her. While engaged in conversation, pretending interest, she would search out their owner to find they were her husband's. A thrill of delight would shiver through her, and she found herself wishing they could somehow slip away. But he, too, was caught in the press of their guests. Propriety simply didn't allow one to stalk away in the middle of a conversation, especially when each guest expected to feel equally important to the next. Yet Aidan found herself wishing a magician would suddenly appear, and with a stroke of his wand, everyone would be gone, leaving only Justin and herself in the glittering enchantment of the golden ballroom.

Her anticipation of being alone with Justin grew to the point where Aidan thought she would surely explode, but she maintained the facade of the ideal hostess, dancing whenever asked, conversing whenever approached, smiling until her jaws ached.

Finally, when her feet had been trodden upon one too many times, she found she simply had to escape. Her gaze skipping around the ballroom, searching for Justin and not finding him anywhere, she routed herself toward the open French doors and out onto the balcony for a breath of fresh air. Suddenly a hand snaked out of the darkness, catching her own, drawing her to a secluded corner, behind a potted plant.

"I thought you'd never give it up," Justin said, his strong arms going round her, his silvery gaze raking over her upturned features. "You've done well by them all. Now do the same for me."

Justin's head suddenly sank and his lips opened fully over hers, taking them in an eagerly persuasive kiss. The joy of being near him once more flooded through her body, and Aidan responded to him with a fervor which startled them both. Boldly she pressed herself to the length of his hard frame while her tongue traced his lips, then touched his own.

With a groan Justin drew it into his mouth to wildly mate and play. Sweet Lord! How he wanted her! A great shiver of longing racked through his body, emphasizing his need; blazing desire erupted from his core.

Realizing how powerful his passions were, Justin tore his mouth away; his lips sliced across Aidan's cheek to her ear.

"If we don't stop this madness, sweet, I shall lay you upon the cold stone and take you here and now."

His harshly grated words startled Aidan; she pulled back as frightened eyes searched his.

Seeing her confusion, Justin let loose a derisive laugh. "You have no idea, madam, what you do to a man's body," he said, releasing her and stepping back, hoping his arousal would quickly fade. "Especially mine."

"Is that good or bad?" Aidan asked, knowing he made her feel strangely wonderful, but naively unsure of how she affected him.

A deep chuckle rumbled from his chest. "Let's just say, sweet, that what I feel cannot be described in words alone. To explain, I must show you, and this is not the time or place to do it." Then suddenly he felt the need to tell her how he felt about her—that he wanted her to remain his wife. Not because his hopes of a divorce had been quashed, but because he desired that she stay near him. Again he denied love had anything to do with it. Companionship, friendship, and respect were his motives, and to fill those needs, he could never find a better wife. Besides, he desired her soft virginal body, wanted her in his bed. "Aidan, we need to have a serious talk. I think you should know—"

"Oh, excuse me," a feminine voice declared, its tone filled with mock surprise. "I had no idea you were out here, Your Grace."

Justin's towering form hid Aidan from the woman, and conversely, the woman from Aidan. Poking her head around Justin's arm, Aidan noted it was one of Justin's admirers. She remembered her as being the one who, on the night of the Rothschilds' ball, had bluntly informed Aidan she had thought Justin preferred true redheads.

Anger boiled up inside her, for the brazen hussy had been chasing her husband around the ballroom all evening. From all appearances, Justin had tried valiantly to escape her, but it was obvious to Aidan that the girl had thought to trap him on the balcony in hopes of soliciting . . . What? A kiss? Or perhaps the presumptuous little twit had thought to receive far more for her dogged pursuit.

Aidan offered the girl a superior smile. "My husband and I were just leaving." She took Justin's arm. "You may have this area to yourself. I hope you enjoy the night air *alone,*" she stated in a sickeningly sweet tone. Nudging him forward, Aidan whisked Justin away, back into the ballroom, leaving the redhead staring after them, her mouth agape.

"I'm forever in your debt, madam," Justin said, smiling down at his wife, his hand squeezing her fingers, which lay along his arm. "Her persistence this night has been like that of a bawling cow in heat. If she had found me first, I fear my only recourse would have been to jump the rail. The fall, no doubt, would have killed me."

Aidan's laughter erupted like a crystal bell, filling Justin's head with its perfect sound. "Next time, sir, don't escape into the night without first making certain you aren't being followed. It will save you the worry of having to choose life over death."

Throughout the rest of the evening and into the early hours of the morning, Justin kept Aidan by his side. Doing so not only bridled the duke's simpering admirers, but also thwarted any attempt on the part of an overzealous suitor, of which Justin noted there were many, to make an urgent confession of eternal heartbreak to his duchess. As Westover and his bride traversed the dance floor, the duke's laughter flying freely, his earth-shattering smiles bestowed themselves solely on his duchess, while she directed hers exclusively to him. The couple, it was said by all who had noticed, were wildly and madly in love.

"Well, Alastair," Lady Falvey stated as the pair watched the couple from the periphery of the dance floor, "I may not agree with how you went about snagging my nephew for your daughter, but I'm certainly pleased with the end result."

"Thank you, Pattina," the duke said, smiling. "I thought it rather a stroke of luck to find him in the coach with her. Only a fool would have passed up the opportunity that was given me."

"No one ever said you were a fool, sir. Devious, perhaps, but never a fool."

"Thank you, madam. But it remains to be seen if anything shall come of my maneuvering. I've planted a seed in his mind, telling him the only way he'll be able to control her is to impregnate her. Now its up to him to bring it to fruition and issue the bud."

"By the looks of it, sir, I predict the next invitation to bear the Westover crest shall be that of a christening."

"Then, madam, perhaps it would be wise if we were to discuss some names. Maybe they shall decide on one we've suggested."

"Excellent idea, Atwood," the dowager marchioness said as they moved toward a quiet corner, a lengthy list already forming in her head.

Feeling impish, Aidan smiled up at Justin as he waltzed her around the floor. "Do you think it's too late?"

"Too late for what, sweet?" he asked, returning her smile.

"To yell fire?"

Justin threw back his head and laughed. "Indeed, it is, madam." He noted her look of mock disappointment. "My body and soul are already ablaze for you, sweet. And I fear nothing could ever reduce the intensity of the flame."

The passionate fire which burned in Justin's silvery gaze seemed to ignite the fetters that held Aidan's inhibitions intact, instantly turning them to ash; she melted in his arms.

A wicked smile claimed his face. "Love," he whispered huskily into her ear as he held her close. "We seem to be drawing an inquisitive eye or two."

Aidan blinked. Noting that she was pressed to her husband's long body, she quickly drew back. As she looked around, to see the lot staring at her, she berated herself angrily. Another *faux pas* to add to her list!

Thankfully the music stopped, and Justin guided her toward the door leading into the great hall. "I suppose my one mistake of the night will be the only dialogue that anyone shall hear for weeks to come of this whole affair," she said pettishly. "After all my attempts to make this the grandest ball London has ever seen, I've managed to botch it."

"Since it is I who was the recipient of your affectionate display, I doubt they will have too much to quibble over. At least they seem to have taken the hint. Let's tell our guests good night, shall we?"

Indeed the crowd had started a voluminous exodus toward the doorway, and Aidan blushed anew. As she said her farewells, she espied the knowing smiles and comprehending looks and fervently wished the floor would somehow open beneath her feet and swallow her completely. Had it not been for Justin's restrictive hand, which held fast at her waist, she'd have fled the room and all who remained inside. To Aidan's relief, within a quarter hour Westover House had emptied of its guests.

"Well, my dears, you two were quite the talk of the evening," Aunt Patti said, chuckling. "I believe the festivities can be considered a grand success. I shall bid you both a pleasant good night." The dowager marchioness strode up the hall to the stairs, then up to her room.

With Aunt Patti gone off to bed, Aidan suddenly felt extremely apprehensive. Save for the few servants, who were busily carting tray after tray of soiled glasses, plates, and silverware down to the kitchen area, she was now alone with her husband. The flirtatious game they had played the evening long was now at its most crucial point, and she feared that he'd actually ask her to join him in his bed. Why not? She loved him. Or did she? Well, she wanted him, then. No, she did not. Unable to make up her mind, she bit her lower lip while she fretted over her indecisiveness.

Attuned to Aidan's wavering emotions, Justin realized the turn of her thoughts. "Sweet," he said, his tender smile upon her, "I think we should find a quiet place where we might talk."

"Yes, we need to talk," she agreed in a small voice, then allowed herself to be led down the hall to the sitting room, all the while wondering what else this night might bring her way.

13

Justin drew Aidan into the dimly lit sitting room and closed the door. Escorting her to the deep-blue-and-white-striped silk-covered settee, he gestured for her to sit; nervously Aidan poised herself on the cushion's edge.

Gazing down at her a long, silent moment, he studied her upturned face, noting her innocent beauty, and he wondered how he could explain that he wanted her to stay. He debated whether to tell her of Victoria's threats, but decided against doing so. His loyalty belonged to his Queen, but if he truly wished to be rid of Aidan, nothing Victoria said would have stopped him from doing so. His Queen knew that as well, but Aidan did not. So to prevent a misunderstanding between them, he elected to keep silent on the issue, at least for now.

Justin finally released Aidan's searching gaze and moved to the fireplace, where he braced an elbow on the mantel. "Before this night ends," he said, "I feel we must come to a decision on what's to be done about us—where we're to go from here."

Aidan felt the bite of her nails as her clenched hands tightened in her lap. Intent on hearing his next words, she was oblivious of the pain.

"After all my threats, all my denials, what I'm about to say may seem laughable." Justin did laugh, its harsh quality turning itself inward. "I would like for you to reconsider the matter of our divorce. It can serve no purpose but to bring us both to ruin. Your reputation would be irreparably damaged. Neither of us would retain the acceptance of our peers. We'd become social outcasts. On the other hand, if you choose to stay with me, I can give you everything and anything you may desire. Aidan, I'm asking that you remain here as my wife."

She carefully studied his face, then finally asked, "Do you propose this because you fear censure? Or because you truly want me to stay with you?"

Again Justin laughed. "You should know by now I could give a damn what the whole of Britain says about me. My reputation already precedes me wherever I go."

"No doubt because of your many affairs."

He smiled. "Yes, but there haven't been as many as you may think. However, my marked ability with a pistol and a sword is equally well-noted—as is my temper."

Aidan's eyes widened. "You've dueled! Have you ever k-killed someone?"

"I've been challenged several times. And I've been offered the opportunity to place my shot square into a man's chest. Likewise, my opponents have been offered the same chance. Fortunately they were all bad marksmen, each having missed me by a yard. All except one. I carry a scar on my arm as a reminder of that day. In return, he sports a similar scar. His intent may have been to kill; mine was not. But that does not go to say, if I had a valid reason to challenge someone, I would not see it to its end. As I've said, my reputation precedes me. But it's not my notoriety that is in question here. It's your name I fear will be tarnished."

Certain it was the social ramifications which bothered him most, Aidan hid her disappointment. "Then it's the censure that you fear, if not for yourself, then for me."

"Yes, sweet. I've grown to care about what happens to you," he said, unable to admit to her that what he felt went much deeper. "I want you to remain as my wife. Doing so can be quite advantageous for us both. But, you must know, if you decide to stay, when I refer to the term 'wife,' I also mean 'lover.' "

No reply came forth, for the words seemed to have stuck in Aidan's throat. He'd asked her to stay, and in doing so, said she was expected to share his bed. But he'd mentioned nothing of love. Sadly she wondered if he ever would.

Noting her air of withdrawal, Justin realized he was

making a mess of it. But the right words refused to come forth. She needed time to make her decision, he knew. God, after constantly telling her he wanted to be rid of her, would she now stay? "I'll not press for an answer right now," he said finally. "You are free to tell me what you've decided whenever you are ready. Remember, Aidan, the choice remains solely yours." He then angled himself toward the door; Aidan heard it close softly behind him.

For what seemed an eternity, she sat there reviewing his words. Many women of her class entered into marriages, the men not particularly of their own choosing, to eventually find they'd made a suitable match, for as the couple had grown to know one another, a fondness for the companion had blossomed forth, some discovering true love. Yet an equal number of her peers had found themselves caught in a loathsome situation. They became bored with their circumstance, and their hearts simply withered and died; only their lifeless shells remained.

She thought of Justin, his kindness, his tenderness, his wit, his masterfully seductive charm. Boredom would never claim her while he was near, she knew. Never! But suddenly she feared what might happen if she could not satiate his passions. Would he quickly turn to someone else?

Another thought occurred to her, which upset her equally as much. His masculine urges might be such that he could never be content with only one woman. Physical pleasure, derived from many willing sources, might be something he craved. Her heart ached to think he'd be so deceptive: using her while using someone else, all for his own personal satisfaction.

A light blush crept up Aidan's cheeks as she remembered Madame Bouchard's words: "The bedroom, *chérie,* is where it counts. As long as you continue to please him, you will not lose him."

As inexperienced as Aidan was, she wondered if she could possibly play the part of expert lover, like the couturiere said she must, thereby keeping her husband solely in her own bed. Oh, bother! She could only try her best, she decided, not knowing in the least what was expected of her.

Unsure of herself, Aidan finally contended that should she consent to stay with him, then an agreement must pass between them. He'd have to promise his fidelity to her, as she would vow hers to him. Then, and only then, would their marriage have a chance. Perhaps in time, love might flower within him, rivaling the feelings that had already bloomed forth within her.

In the end, Aidan knew she had to take the chance. She would stay as his wife. As her eyes sought the clock on the mantel, she realized it was nearly half an hour since Justin had left the room, no doubt taking himself off to bed. Yawning, she thought to do the same, and left the sitting room, following the hall toward the stairs. Her eyes caught sight of the light coming from Justin's study, and she moved toward the partially open door. Nervously she hesitated.

Justin's taut backside retained a position on the corner of his desk, his coat, cravat, and waistcoat carelessly thrown across its top. His thoughts on Aidan, he slowly released the studs from his shirt, down to his breastbone, exposing the thatch of curly dark hair on his chest. Would she spurn him? he wondered, dropping the studs alongside his discarded clothing. He scoffed at himself for acting the jittery schoolboy, then reached for the brandy decanter and poured himself a healthy glass. Raising his drink to his lips, he saw Aidan standing in the doorway; his breath caught. *God, she's beautiful!*

"I hope you haven't come seeking out a nightcap," he said, trying to hide his uncertainty, his fear. "If so, madam, I'll have to refuse. The last time you imbibed from my stock, you became rather—"

"Tight?" she asked, moving unsteadily toward him, praying he didn't notice. She stopped only an arm's length away.

Justin chuckled, relieving his tension. "I was about to say 'soused,' but 'tight' is equally appropriate. Although I'd very much enjoy undressing you tonight, as I did then," he teased, "I do not wish to have you passing out on me. Making love to an unconscious woman is most unappealing and ruins one of the greatest of all pleasures known to man."

"And what, sir, is *the* greatest of all pleasures known to woman?" she asked boldly.

"The same, madam, plus the knowledge that a new life

forms within her. But for the latter to come about, she must first experience the former."

"Unfortunately I'm inexperienced at both."

"But that does not say you have to remain so." His silvery gaze locked with her soft amethyst eyes. "The choice, as I've said, is yours."

Unable to hold his gaze, she dropped her concentration to his chest, a decided mistake. Tanned skin covering hard muscle and generously sprinkled with dark curly hair claimed her attention. Staring at his manly chest, an incredible feeling of warmth flowed through her. Then her gaze quickly skittered back to his to see his knowing smile.

"Have you come to a decision?" he asked.

"Yes," she whispered; Justin's breath caught anew. "I shall stay as your wife—but it is done with a condition."

"And what is that condition, love?" he asked, taking her hand, drawing her toward him, nestling her between his outstretched thighs.

"That you . . ." She hesitated and drew a steadying breath. "That you promise me your fidelity." Having expected a derisive snort from him, she noted instead his tender regard. His arms looped around her, hands linking loosely at her waist, urging her even closer. "W-will you promise me such?"

Justin smiled to himself. Had his own parents made that same pledge and kept it, he most likely wouldn't view love so cynically. But as it was, the two had acted like a pair of rutting swine. They'd been obsessed with one another, yet never faithful. Jealousy had driven Malcolm Warfield to murder his wife; then he'd taken his own life in despair. Why, Justin was unable to fathom, for his father had been as faithless as his mother. And for that, Justin despised them both.

"I will, madam," he said finally. "But only if you swear the same."

"I will."

"Good. We have now struck a bargain. Make certain it is never broken."

Besides hearing the subtle threat which had laced itself through his words, Aidan saw the same warning written in the steely depths of his eyes. A small chill ran down her

spine, for she was certain it spelled certain death to whoever trespassed on that which he'd named as his. "I'm not
a common trollop, sir," she defended sharply, angered because he believed she'd break her word. "Nor am I of the
nature to go seeking another man's favors."

"That remains to be seen, love. Understandable or not,
some women, once they've experienced sexual gratification, cannot do without that particular physical pleasure for
very long. They become obsessed with their need, and
when one man can no longer fulfill their voracious desires,
they turn to another and another, searching but never finding what it is they seek." His hand splayed outward, sliding
down her spine to her bottom, pressing her closer, trapping
her between his thighs. "Once we've made love, sweet,
you will have no reason to go to anyone else. My hands and
mouth will worship your silken body—all of it. I will fulfill
the sum of your desires, see to all your needs, and teach
you not only what pleasures you but also what pleasures
me. And when our bodies join, they will ignite with such
passion our souls will transcend all human bounds. This,
love, I promise you."

Caught up in his seductive words, Aidan found she wanted
to experience everything he'd promised. Unknowingly she
moved against him; Justin's indrawn breath hissed through
his teeth as she briefly surrendered her lips to his.

She pulled away, and with a power he never knew he
possessed, Justin fought his primal urge to pull her hard
against him and lay claim to her mouth, ravishing it with his
tongue. "Come to me again, sweet," he enticed, his unsteady breath rasping against her beautiful face, which appeared so near, yet seemed so far. "Don't hold back. I
want to taste you, feel you."

Smoky pewter eyes pleaded for her return, and with a
soft whimper, Aidan fell against him. Her satiny lips opened
fully under his, her velvety tongue darting lightly, seeking
entry, wanting to taste him, feel him, every bit as much as
he wanted to experience the same of her. Raw desire shot
through Justin, snapping his restraint, and he drew the
moist sliver deep into his mouth to play a wildly erotic
game of love. Responsively, Aidan pressed herself into the
V created by his outstretched thighs; a violent tremor of

longing racked through Justin. With a full-throated curse, he suddenly pulled away.

Aidan was startled by his harsh oath and his abrupt withdrawal, and her eyes flew wide. "Wh-what's wrong?" she asked weakly, fearing she'd somehow repulsed him.

Ragged laughter erupted from Justin as he came to his feet. "I told you before, sweet, that you have no idea what you do to a man's body. Unless you wish to discover yourself sprawled on the floor with your skirts thrown over your head, I suggest we find the comfort of my bed."

A small cry escaped Aidan's lips as Justin swept her up into his arms. He strode from the study into the hall and up the stairs to his room. Crossing its threshold, he kicked the door shut with his foot.

Aidan felt herself floating to the floor as Justin slowly released her. Balancing on shaky legs, she nervously stared up at him. Her heart pounded erratically while her breath seemed suspended somewhere between her throat and lungs. Fear laced with desire spiraled through her, leaving her weak.

"Relax, sweet," Justin said, a gentle smile curving his handsome lips. "Breathe slowly, deeply."

Not until that moment did Aidan realize she'd been starved for air; she drew a steadying breath. Instantly she became dizzy with Justin's masculine scent. Spicy cologne mingled with a hint of brandy, the pair underscored by his own special male fragrance. The combination piqued her feminine senses, and Aidan could no longer deny her womanly desires. "I want you," she whispered throatily, not realizing she did so.

"And you shall have me, love."

Aidan felt herself turning, then deft fingers freed the long row of buttons on her gown; the heavy satin dress fell to the floor. Satin ribbons came loose, then along with her petticoats her corset descended to meet the dress. The feel of his strong but gentle hands upon her reminded her that she'd been intoxicated with brandy the last time he'd undressed her. This time, however, she was intoxicated by the man. She was drunk with the smell of him, drunk with his touch, drunk with his nearness, which had left her in a delicious stupor over which she had no control.

The last of her clothing slipped away, as did the diamond-studded amethyst necklace, which carelessly dropped from his fingers. Molten-silver eyes raked over her straight shoulders, down the gentle curve of her spine, branding the rounded fullness of her firm bottom, then swept her long shapely legs, stopping at slim ankles. At the sight of her, Justin felt raw desire shoot through him; he hardened, agonizingly so. Drawing a ragged breath, he forcibly controlled his raging urge to lay her on the carpet, spread her silken thighs, and bury himself deep within her with one driving thrust. She was a virgin, coming to him pure, untouched, and his prurient lusts had to be subdued. Otherwise, he'd frighten and injure her.

Instead, he sought to gentle her, seduce her slowly. Then, like a flower laved in warm sunshine, she would blossom under his expert touch as he tenderly persuaded her into opening to him, receiving him willingly, her carnal passions burning as hotly as his. Suddenly his fingers ached to feel her silken hair, and the pins slipped from her coppery mass to fall onto the carpet. Draping the heavy tresses around her, Justin whispered, his voice quaking, "Let me see you, sweet."

Slowly, shyly, Aidan turned toward him. Would he like what he saw? she wondered, knowing she was not the first woman he'd ever viewed unclothed. Nervously she gazed up at him, awaiting his approval.

The lamp near his bed burned on a low wick, bathing her in a soft stream of amber, and Justin's smoky eyes traveled her unveiled grace, hungrily devouring every exposed inch of the golden-skinned goddess who stood before him. Breathtakingly beautiful, he thought, not remembering any of his women as having been so perfectly formed as was Aidan.

Slowly his hand rose, and his fingers lightly grazed the gilded slopes of her high, full breasts; fire singed Aidan's veins and her breath caught in her throat. With a harsh groan, Justin scooped her up into his quivering arms and carried her the few short steps to his bed.

Cradled in the center of the down-filled mattress, Aidan watched curiously as Justin stripped his clothing away. Magnificent, she thought, as more and more of his masculine form revealed itself to her. Then he stood before her, the long sinewy planes of his muscular body hard and erect, his desire for her evident. Her virginal shyness begged her to look away, but Aidan's womanly interest refused to allow it. Then suddenly he was beside her, his throbbing member pressing itself against her sleek hip. A small shudder trembled through Aidan as his eyes locked with hers in a poignant embrace. For an eternity Justin gazed down at her; then he finally whispered, "Tonight, love, you will be mine."

His head slowly descended and Aidan's heart tripped wildly in her chest. Burning, slanting lips covered hers in hot, open possession, and Aidan felt a heady excitement surge through her, making her dizzy with longing. Her own lips played lightly beneath his; then her tongue daringly darted against his supple lips in a tantalizingly rhythmic foray, unknowingly imitating the centuries-old ritual which bonded male and female in an elemental joining of need.

Justin drew the teasing sliver deep into his mouth, mating with it in a wildly exotic dance; then his own tongue plunged between her lips to taste the honey-flavored nectar within. With a throaty mewl Aidan rolled toward him, her arms encircling his corded shoulders; searchingly, she bore herself against him. Heated passion instantly streamed from Justin's every pore. Hot, hard, and wet, he moved against her taut belly, his hair-roughened thigh sliding over the satiny softness of her own, trapping her.

Instantly Aidan drew back, wary violet eyes probing his face. "Don't shy away from me, love," Justin said hoarsely. "You're no longer a girl. You're a woman with a woman's desires. Let your passions sail free."

Feverish silver eyes watched her intently while his lightly callused palm slowly edged upward from where it held fast at her small waist, gliding ever closer to an invitingly full breast. A shiver of delight shook Aidan as his hand finally captured the taut globe, long fingers reverently enclosing it to squeeze gently.

"My lips want to worship you, Aidan. Will you allow them to do so?" he questioned seductively as his heated gaze mesmerized her.

"I . . . Oh, yes," she said on an emancipated sigh, all her inhibitions discharging themselves as she did so.

She watched as his head lowered to the aching mound, his lips opening over its peak. A hot current bolted deep into the pit of her stomach as he drew the pink bud between his teeth, teasing it with rapid flicks of his rough, wet tongue until it flowered completely, fully in his mouth. A fervid sigh escaped Aidan's parted lips as her fingers wound themselves through his thick wavy hair, settling at the nape of his neck, forcing him closer, rising to meet him.

Justin chuckled, then pulled back slightly, and a tortured cry protested his abandonment, sounding like music to his ears. Soon she'd be his. "Easy, sweet," he crooned. "I'm simply leaving one lovely sphere to explore the other." His fingers captured the perfect mate, his lips and tongue savoring the ripe summit in the same reverent fashion they had its twin.

As his adept hand paid homage to one vibrantly aching breast, his masterful mouth worshiped the other; a nearly delirious Aidan felt certain she would swoon. Her head rolled against the satin-encased pillow as she arched upward, wanting more of him. Justin's hands slid down her sides to claim her waist, his swirling tongue following to her navel to dip into the small depression, teasing it mercilessly.

"Justin! What are you doing?" she breathed raggedly. "Stop it, or I swear I shall faint."

Again his knowing chuckle erupted. His hot tongue withdrew, and Aidan relaxed, drawing a steadying breath. But suddenly she felt his lips start their foraging anew, grazing down her tense stomach, brushing lightly in her tight mass of coppery curls, moving lower and lower. She jerked and shoved at his shoulder, but Justin persisted. "Let me, sweet," he breathed against the downy wisps, his hand urging her rigid thighs apart. "I want to worship all of you."

Alarmed by his desires, certain this strange invasion was indecent, Aidan grabbed his hair and tugged hard.

Justin's scalp tingled sharply. He'd frightened her. With one last, almost imperceptible kiss, he moved up over her, his hard body raking deliberately along hers. Slow and easy, he reminded silently, telling himself to remember she was a virgin. Finally his silvery gaze met hers. "When we've grown to know each other better, we shall try it again."

Aidan's eyes widened. "Surely you don't mean that people . . . that—"

"Yes, love," he replied, smiling down at her innocence from where his head rested against his level hand, "and they enjoy it immensely." Color rose high on her cheeks as Aidan cast him a disbelieving frown; Justin let out a low laugh. "When we know each other better, you will discover the truth of it. For now, you will have to be satisfied with the traditional way." His fingertips brushed lightly over her breasts, making ever-wider circles, fanning outward in a bedeviling sweep of playfulness. Then they sluggishly trailed down her stomach into the tight curls; again Aidan stiffened. "Sweet, you must relax. There is no other way to prepare you for what is to come. If you're not ready, I might hurt you."

Gray eyes said he spoke the truth; Aidan had no other choice but to believe him. "I . . ."

"Hush, sweet. Just close your eyes and let me guide you."

Again her violet eyes examined his; then slowly her long lashes fell against her cheeks. As Justin surveyed her, he again thought her the most beautiful creature he'd ever seen. And she was his. All his. Slowly his head lowered, and he covered her lips with his own. Gently, persuasively, he toyed with them by way of soft caresses, teasing her with his experienced mouth until she was anxiously seeking his full slanting kiss. Frantically their tongues mated, soft whimpers mixed with low throaty groans, then slowly Justin's fingers slipped between her thighs in a gentle quest for the satiny folds hidden within her curls.

At his first light touch, Aidan felt herself withdraw, but his fiery lips continued their onslaught while his skillful hand urged her to open to him. A small tingling sensation erupted deep in her stomach, and she felt herself melt against the sheets. Tenderly, methodically, he wooed her with his fingers as they sought all her secret places, seducing a rich, moist flow from within her. A spark ignited, and Justin became master of the flame, making it flare higher and higher, until Aidan thought she'd be consumed by the blazing inferno that was ravaging her entire body. Her hips writhed as his probing fingers found the untapped entry, exploring the velvet smoothness inside; his thumb pressed gently against the slumberous bud of her womanhood, enticing it into a taut edifice. Insane with want, Aidan tore her lips from his, her small teeth nipping lightly at his throat. "Justin . . . oh, God, I . . . I need . . ."

"What do you need, love?" he rasped, but her voice had suspended itself in her throat. Unable to answer, Aidan gazed up at him, her eyes begging for the unknown.

His insistent knee urged her to open wider for him; then he cradled himself in the gap she created, his own sinewy thighs holding hers wide apart. His quicksilver gaze met hers. "Soon, love, we shall find a pleasure only you and I will ever know," he whispered as he easily positioned himself in the center of her dewy petals, easing himself slowly upward until he met her maidenhead. "Give me your lips, Aidan," he commanded as he leaned over her, hands on either side of her head, fingers coiling through her silken hair as it fanned out over the pillows. "Kiss me, love."

He lowered himself to her on muscular yet strangely unstable arms, and as her mouth met his in a ravenous kiss, Justin thrust upward, breaching the thin barrier that blocked his way. Her short cry of pain lost itself in his throat; he stopped, allowing her time to adjust to the rigid fullness within her. Then he moved slowly, deliberately, his mouth lifting from hers. "Now we will know each other, love. Know the ecstasy of our own pleasure. You can release your passions now, love. Give yourself to me."

With slow rhythmic thrusts, Justin drove himself ever deeper until she enveloped him fully. His passion-glazed eyes took in the glorious sight of her as her slumberous gaze met his. A myriad of expressions painted themselves across her lovely face while she savored each new driving force. The world spun crazily for Aidan, tilting madly, threatening to fall off its axis. In savage sweet splendor her anticipation grew. The bite of her nails dug softly, then almost painfully into Justin's back as she tried to meet him thrust for thrust, heartbeat for heartbeat, until she was certain she'd disintegrate. She loved him, loved him with all her soul, and she strained against him, offering all of herself, wanting to pleasure his body as much as he did hers.

Instantly a pulsing throb started deep inside her, growing

with each endless second. Nothing could ever be this wondrous, she thought, feeling herself twirling outward into another dimension, somewhere beyond earth's bounds. Seeing her rapturous look, noting her fervent response as her hips eagerly rose to meet his suddenly demanding plunges, Justin felt the pressure in his loins quaver; desperately he fought for control. A fiery vortex whirled up inside, spinning him ever closer to the edge of perdition. The fires of hell could not burn any hotter than the flames that were presently blazing through him, he knew. He was lost in her, his body and soul doomed to her forever. No longer the master, he was now the slave. Only Aidan could fulfill his needs, his desires. He'd become his father's son—obsessed with the woman he'd married.

A sudden anger filled him and his strong hand slipped beneath Aidan's soft undulating hips, lifting her to him as he rammed deep into her, hopelessly trying to purge himself of the hold she'd suddenly gained over him. A cry erupted from her softly parted lips; instantly he stopped, fearing he'd injured her. But the minute caressing spasms, which quickly grew in intensity, coaxed him to move again, urging him onward. And with a final driving thrust, a great shudder racked his entire body; her name escaped him with a triumphant shout, his seed spilling forth into her womb.

Slowly Justin's harsh breathing settled into an easier mode, his wildly pounding heart beat at a more normal pace, and his face finally lifted from the pillow where it was buried in her fragrant hair. Silver eyes looked down at the small woman still trapped beneath him. Questioning violet eyes gazed upward, reflecting an uncertain shyness. "What is it, sweet?" he asked, levering himself up onto his forearms, fearing his superior weight would crush her; his body remained connected to hers. "You seem a bit puzzled."

Unable to hold his gaze, her own moved toward the wall. A small frown marred her brow as she wondered if she'd imagined it or if she'd truly heard the words that were torn from his lips, losing themselves somewhere in her name. *I love you!* Her mind heard the phrase again, but she couldn't decide if the endearment had come from him or if it was her own confession that had rebounded in her ears, sailing straight to her heart. Sadly, Aidan believed the pledge had been nothing more than a fanciful hope, stemming from her need to hear it from Justin's own lips.

"Sweet," Justin said, studying her face, which seemed filled with confusion, "if you are troubled about something, ask the question and I shall try to answer it."

Her eyes claimed his once more, searching for the answer. Undoubtedly, if the words had been his, he was unaware he'd said them. Since he'd once told her that love was an emotion reserved for fools, he'd most likely scoff at her, denying he'd ever said them. In the end, Aidan decided she'd be a fool to ask.

Tucking her hopes away into a hidden place within her heart, she smiled up at him. "I was simply wondering if you really enjoyed what we did. I mean . . . at the end, you sounded as though you were . . . uh . . . that you were in agony."

A deep rumble of laughter flowed from Justin's chest; he rolled to his side, bringing Aidan with him. "*Sweet* agony—that's the only way to describe it, love. But the feeling is something I'll crave my whole life through," he said, his gray eyes turning to molten silver. "I hunger for it now."

Renewed excitement quivered through her, and Aidan's heart threatened to burst as Justin began to worship her again, fully, completely. Eager to please him, she gave herself up to him willingly.

His desires satiated, his mind perplexed, Justin cradled his drowsy wife against him. Within minutes she was asleep. He gazed at the small hand which centered itself on his chest, over his heart, and his own hand covered its smoothness, holding it tenderly, protecting it in his gentle embrace.

Something had happened to him. Something he couldn't explain. *Nor* deny! he admitted silently. Just now, when they'd been making love, he'd felt his heart open, and somehow Aidan had slipped inside. He'd fallen in love with her. It seemed impossible, but it was true.

A mocking smile spread across Justin's lips. He'd thought himself immune to the emotion which presently claimed him. All his ranting and raving on wanting to be free, he now knew, had been a lie to appease his own pride. How stupid of him to believe he was any different from his male counterparts! he thought, finally realizing he was as human as the next man. Stupid, indeed!

His harsh smile relaxed into one of adoration, and as his silvery gaze traversed Aidan's tranquil face, Justin felt his heart swell. In truth, she'd captured him with her beauty, her stubbornness, her wit, her innocence. And now that he was caught—body, heart, and soul—he vowed he'd never let her go. She was his.

Yet, strangely, Justin discovered he was afraid to voice his feelings aloud. For now, he was content to hold this newfound sentiment inside, its faint glow growing steadily brighter. Settling a gentle kiss on Aidan's brow, he pulled her securely against him in a protective embrace. And as the soft rays of dawn scattered themselves across the horizon, his eyes slowly closed, his once burdened heart feeling eased at last.

14

Horse hooves hit the cobblestones with a smart click as Justin guided the phaeton through the sunlit streets of London, his young wife at his side. "Are you certain you don't want me to join you?" he asked, gazing down at Aidan in tender regard. "And extra hand might be needed for your packages. I'd be willing to offer mine."

Aidan smiled up at him. "Today is Eugenia's and my day out, sir. No men are allowed." The light in her eyes turned teasing. "Besides, Eugenia's couturiere may not appreciate your being in her shop." She saw a dark brow arch in question. "Fascinated by your presence, dear husband, her clientele will, no doubt, lend their full attention to you and not the bolts of fine material the poor woman will be trying to show. You're too much of a distraction, sir, and the entire outing could only end in disharmony.''

Justin chuckled. "Madam, I already detect a sour note in your usually melodious voice. Are you certain it is the couturiere who will object to my drawing an interested feminine eye? Or could it be it's really you who object to my doing so?''

"Are you accusing me of being jealous, sir?" she asked in mock peevishness. "If so, you are mistaken.''

"Am I?" he teased. "Correct me if I'm wrong, madam, but I believe it was only a week ago today, when a certain persistent young woman thought she had cornered me alone on a darkened balcony, that you instantly went on the attack. Had I not been there, I shudder to think what might have happened to the poor unsuspecting creature.''

"Had you not been there, the entire incident wouldn't have taken place. And as I remember it, you were extremely relieved to have me play the role of protector. I believe it had something to do with a sudden fall," she returned, smiling prettily.

Deep, rumbling laughter flowed from Justin's chest. "True, madam, your protection was indeed most welcome," he admitted, grinning at her. "Had you not been there, I would have taken that sudden ill-fated plunge, never to have experienced the euphoria we shared later that night, and every night since.''

A light blush crept up over Aidan's face. "Euphoria" hardly described what they'd shared over the past week. And Justin certainly hadn't restricted his lovemaking to those hours between sunset and dawn!

Aidan felt a thrill of warmth course through her as she remembered their last encounter, possibly no more than an hour ago. Strangely, she realized she never grew tired of his continuous pursuit. Behind any locked door, night or day, in any logical or illogical spot where he was able to trap her, she'd willingly allowed him whatever he desired.

In her naiveté, Aidan never realized one could make love in so many varying ways, but she was quickly learning, with Justin her ardent tutor. Whether they were clothed or unclothed, seated or standing or lying down, it made little difference, and she discovered she looked forward to each new experience. She craved his physical mastery, desired it, like a parched desert thirsted for a replenishing rain. Already she longed to feel the length of his hard body stealing up over hers, taking all she offered, rewarding her in return. Admittedly she never had enough of him!

Viewing her, Justin had read her every thought; a spark of mischief centered itself in his eyes. "When you come home, love," he whispered seductively, his hot breath tickling her ear, "I'll be waiting for you. We've not yet initiated the gardens. Imagine it, love. The warm, rich aroma rising from the earth, mixed with the scent of roses, intermingling with our own special fragrances, our bare limbs stretching, entwining, on a cool, thick carpet of grass—already my body aches to savor the experience. Does yours, love?"

Her mouth agape, Aidan stared at her husband. "Rutting out in the open like . . . like animals!" she cried in disbelief. "Y-you must be insane!"

As Justin shifted his gaze to the street, he fought to contain his mirth. "Not insane, love, just daring."

With feminine curiosity, Aidan gazed up at the virile man next to her, wondering if he could ever be satisfied. For that matter, could she? "Are all men as lusty as you?" she inquired innocently.

Justin's head snapped around, his gaze suddenly gone hard. "Other men's passions aren't your concern, madam. So you may put your curiosity to rest, for no man will ever vent his lusts on you, except me."

Taken aback by the strength of his words, Aidan stared up at him, curious about his abruptness. He acted as though she'd planned on cuckolding him. What had provoked the ridiculous notion in him, she couldn't say. But his accusatory manner, which had been laced with a subtle threat, upset her.

The phaeton slowed, and Aidan turned her attention to the street, noting they had arrived at Madame Sophie's. David and Eugenia waited on the walkway outside the small shop, absorbed in an intimate conversation.

Under Justin's skillful guidance the horse came to a halt, and Aidan looked back to her husband. "David has promised to have me home by three o'clock," she said, a slight coolness reflecting in her voice as she reminded him of the prearranged schedule. "I shall see you then."

The skirt of her blue silk dress slid across the leather as Aidan edged forward in her seat, but Justin's hand stopped her. "Haven't you forgotten something, sweet?" he asked.

As she noted that she had her reticule, her confused gaze met his. "I don't believe so."

"But you have," he countered as he pulled her toward him.

Realizing his intent, Aidan pushed against his chest in a feeble attempt to keep him at bay. "We're in the middle of a public street," she whispered frantically.

"We could be sitting in the Queen's own lap for all I care, madam," he retorted, his clean breath fanning her face. "No matter the time or place, when I decide to show you my affection, I'll do so."

Instantly his open mouth took hers in a brief, hard kiss, his tongue slicing between her lips to quickly withdraw; he released her. Feeling somewhat breathless, Aidan stepped from the phaeton.

"I shall see you at three, madam," Justin said as he snapped the reins, setting the horse into motion.

Still dazed, Aidan watched as her husband disappeared around the corner; then she turned to see David and Eugenia smiling at her, a knowing look on both their faces. "It appears the notorious Duke of Westover has become the most attentive of husbands," Eugenia needled her friend, her blue eyes dancing mischievously. "What do you say, David?"

A grinning Lord Manley noted the Duchess of Westover's censuring glare; abruptly he sobered. "I say it's time for me to be on my way. I'll meet you both here at two-thirty, sharp." Settling a light peck on his wife's cheek, he strode to his awaiting carriage, climbed inside, then ordered his driver to move on.

"Does he suspect anything?" Aidan asked as soon as the vehicle had turned the corner.

"No. With any luck, David will be completely surprised by it all," Eugenia said of the small birthday celebration she was planning for her husband, which was only a week away. "Let's be going. We have so much to do and very little time to do it. David's always on time, and I don't want him to think we've been anywhere but Madame Sophie's.''

Reminiscent of their schoolgirl days, the two marched off down the street, arm in arm, their giggles erupting periodically. Their unladylike display managed to raise an eyebrow or two along the way, but neither one cared a bit.

Stopping outside the caterer's, Eugenia gazed at her friend. "How are you, Aidan? I mean, are you as happy as you seem?"

"Happy? In what way?"

Eugenia felt a bit awkward in asking, but she had to know. "Have you finally found those wondrous feelings you'd longed for—much like your parents once shared? Are you in love with your attentive young duke?"

Aidan frowned and gazed off in the distance. "I am in love, Eugenia," she answered finally. "But I don't think the feeling is shared by Justin. He's been good to me. Most attentive and caring, but he's never said anything about love. I doubt he ever will."

"The word may not have passed his lips," her friend said after a long pause. "But what he feels for you is clearly written in his actions. Give him time and he'll open up. I'm certain of it."

Aidan wished she were as positive about that as Eugenia was. But as she reviewed what Justin and she had shared this past month, she realized there had indeed been a marked change in him, especially over the last week. His passions were insatiable, and so were hers. Blushing slightly, she urged Eugenia toward the door of the shop. "We'd best be moving or we'll never make it back in time to meet David."

Leaving the caterer's, they made their way to the baker's, then on to a quaint little shop in hopes of finding some attractive decorations. As they reached the entry, Eugenia suddenly wobbled on her legs; a soft cry escaped her lips. Reflexively Aidan caught hold of her friend before she fell.

"What's wrong?" Aidan asked anxiously, her worried eyes searching Eugenia's pale face. "Is it the heat?"

Dabbing her brow and upper lip with her handkerchief, Eugenia offered Aidan a weak smile. "Partially, I suppose. But I do this, of late, in the cool of the evening as well."

She saw Aidan's concerned frown. "I'm not seriously ill, my friend. I think I'm expecting."

Excited by the news, Aidan hugged her. "Oh, Eugenia, I'm so happy for you. Does David know?"

"No . . . it was to be part of his birthday surprise. I plan on telling him after the party." Another bout of light-headedness claimed Eugenia. "I fear I can't go on. Do you think you can find some way to get me home? I really must rest."

It would be another hour before David arrived back at Madame Sophie's, and Aidan found herself in a quandary over what she should do. Supporting Eugenia against her as she did, she couldn't very well rush into the street to hail a passing cabby. Besides, there wasn't one to be seen.

Anxious eyes caught sight of what Aidan thought was a familiar face. The man drove a sparkling new phaeton, which thankfully was headed in their direction. "Lord Edmonds! George!" she shouted, waving a frantic hand in the air; relief rushed through her as the vehicle quickly stopped beside the two women. "Lady Manley has suddenly taken ill," she told the young viscount as he hopped from the phaeton. "We need to get her home."

Without a word, George helped Eugenia into the vehicle, then handed Aidan up. Settling next to the pair, he whipped the reins and the horse trotted off. By the time they had arrived at Portman Square, Aidan was relieved to see Eugenia's color had improved greatly. As Aidan and George assisted the countess up the stairs and into the house, Eugenia assured them she felt better and pleaded with them to stop fussing over her. Fortunately, David was not at home. Had he been, it might have ruined Eugenia's surprise, but then Lady Manley became concerned.

"He had an appointment with his banker," she said between sips of lemon water. "I suppose he's still there. Most likely he plans on going directly to Madame Sophie's. If he doesn't find us, he'll worry. Aidan, you know how strongly he reacts to the slightest things where I am concerned. Would you very much mind going back to Madame Sophie's and explaining what has happened?"

Aidan quickly masked her frown. To honor Eugenia's request, she'd have to rely on George to get her back to

Madame Sophie's, something she preferred not to do. Certainly, she could ask George to go back alone and relay the message himself to Lord Manley, but like Eugenia, Aidan feared that David might react foolishly. Aidan thought it best she meet David herself. Hopefully she'd be able to keep him calm.

"I'll go," she said finally.

"Thank you," Eugenia replied. "And remember, don't say anything about . . . you know."

"Your secret is safe," Aidan promised.

Having left her friend in the care of a maid, Aidan nervously set off with her escort. As she sat next to a rather quiet Lord Edmonds, she wouldn't permit herself to contemplate the outcome should Justin catch her with George. Instead, she fervently prayed he'd remain oblivious of the fact.

When Aidan and George arrived at the couturiere's, Lord Manley's carriage had already taken a stance outside the establishment. David, his back to the pair, struck a leisurely pose as he sat waiting for his absent wife; Aidan viewed him carefully while her mind selected her opening words. The instant George pulled the phaeton to a stop, she alighted, then walked the few steps to the carriage. "Hello, David," she said in a cheery manner.

He turned toward her, a smile on his face, but it slowly faded. "Where's Eugenia?"

Aidan retained her smile. "She's at home. I—"

"Home! What's happened to her?"

"Nothing. She was simply overcome by the heat and—"

"The baby, is . . . is it . . . ?"

Aidan blinked. "You know about the baby?"

"Certainly I know. Although I'm merely a man, I'm not a complete idiot where my wife's concerned!"

"But she'd hoped to sur—" Aidan chopped off the end of the word. "David, please believe me, Eugenia is fine. She purposely sent me here to tell you not to worry. She's—"

"My pardon, Aidan, but I must see for myself." He turned to his driver and instructed, "Take me home!"

The carriage quickly sped off. "Wait!" she cried, but David apparently hadn't heard her. Angered she'd been left behind, Aidan stamped her small foot.

"I'd be most happy to offer you a lift back to Lord and Lady Manley's," George said, coming up behind her. "Or I could drop you by Westover House. Whichever you choose."

Debating whether she should accept his offer or not, Aidan gazed up at the viscount. Her eyes traveled over his curly blond locks, then downward, stopping at his soft brown eyes. What harm could it possibly pose? she wondered, ignoring the small voice within her warning her to decline his kind overture. As she saw it, she had two options: either she went it alone on foot, thereby leaving herself open to the possibility of being accosted by thugs, for again there were no cabbys in sight, or she could accept the viscount's show of kindness. George, she insisted silently, was always the gentleman. Nothing untoward would happen to her while she remained under his protection. Her decision made, she smiled up at him.

"I accept your offer, George. You've been a godsend more than once today." But as the viscount assisted her up into the phaeton, Justin's dark countenance suddenly loomed before her mind's eye; dread shivered through her as she thought of her husband's reaction should he learn of her association with George, innocent as it might be. Surely he wouldn't object once she'd explained the situation to him! Yet she decided that a shred of caution might be wise. Although they were several blocks closer to Westover House, she thought twice of George taking her there. "If it's not out of your way, you may drop me by Lord and Lady Manley's. I'd like to see how she's faring."

As George maneuvered the gelding out into the thoroughfare, joining his new phaeton in with the varied assortment of horse-drawn vehicles already claiming the roadway, Cynthia Danvers exited Madame Sophie's shop. Her rounded hips swayed in their usual provocative motion as she walked to her awaiting coach. "Follow that phaeton," Justin's former lover said to her coachman, motioning at the retreating couple as they made their way toward Park Lane. With a vengeful smile on her face, she stepped inside the vehicle.

Justin sat in his study, watching the hand on the French clock which stood on the mantel. A chime struck the quarter-hour. Three-forty-five, and his wife was not home. The hand slowly crept upward toward the hour; then the chimes finally struck four times. Rising from his seat, he left the room.

"George, please believe me when I tell you how sorry I am that all this has happened," Aidan repeated her apology for the umpteenth time, hoping to gain her freedom from the man's insistent arms. For what seemed like an eternity, she'd been trying to convince the agitated viscount, who'd suddenly veered his phaeton off Park Lane and into Hyde Park, driving it across the grass and into a remote stand of trees, that she and Justin had been thrown together by her father's treachery. "No one conspired against you, least of all Justin," she said, struggling to keep the desperation and the fear within her from manifesting itself in her voice. Again he appeared not to hear her. "Justin and I had little control over the situation. My father's men were holding loaded pistols on him. What else could he do but marry me? I swear to you, had he had any way of avoiding the situation, he'd have done so. He didn't purposely break your trust."

His hold on her tightened as George pulled Aidan closer; she stiffened, but he seemed not to notice. "And what of you, Aidan, did you make known your desire not to wed him?" he asked, burning brown eyes searching her face.

"I did," she answered truthfully, her slender arms wedged between them, hands trying to keep him at bay. "I even threatened to kill myself," she blurted, hoping he'd let her go. She noted a strange glimmer in George's eyes, flaring brighter and brighter. *Lust!* her mind screamed, suddenly recognizing the look he cast upon her. Instantly she feared he might do something terrible. *Oh, God, why had she come with him!* Loathing the thought of his touch, she cried, "Truly I shall kill myself!"

"No!" George stated sharply. "If anyone is to die, it will be Westover. I can't lose you again, Aidan. I can't." Then his face slowly lowered toward hers.

Stormy gray eyes resembling a roiling thunderhead pinpointed themselves on the pavement as Justin piloted the charging phaeton down the street. Having gone to the couturiere's, where he'd last seen his wife, he was told by Madame Sophie she'd not seen Aidan at all that day. A dour look had settled on his face as he headed straight to Lord and Lady Manley's, whereupon their butler informed him, "Her Grace is not here."

As Justin remembered it, his virulent curse had rung through the house, drawing the earl and his countess from the sitting room. One look at the Duke of Westover, and they'd both stopped in their tracks.

"Where the hell is she?" he'd questioned, hands balled into fists at his side.

"Sh-she went back to Madame Sophie's to tell David I'd taken ill," Eugenia had replied. "I had thought David had taken her home."

"She's not there. And she's not at Madame Sophie's, nor has she been at any time this day, madam!"

"David, you didn't just leave her there on the sidewalk!" Eugenia had accused.

"I . . . I guess I did," he'd said. "Viscount Edmonds was with her—" Hearing the name, Justin had slammed out of the house.

Swearing aloud, he whipped the reins against the lathered horse, driving the steed faster. When he found them, by God, they'd both suffer for their treachery. That much he promised.

Suddenly a coach veered from the curbing into his path; Justin hastily reined in, and the phaeton jolted to a wobbly halt. "*Goddammit*, Cynthia! Are you trying to kill us both!" he bellowed, fighting to control his horse. The steed reared, but a quick jerk on the reins brought him down. "What in blazes are you up to?"

"Hello, Justin," the blond said, smiling at him through the coach window. "My, you seem to be in a bit of a hurry." Stormy eyes raked over her. Undaunted by her former lover's fierce stare, Cynthia cooed, "Could it be you've lost your precious little wife? If so, I believe I know where you might find her."

Cynthia fell silent, and Justin's hands tightened on the reins as though her neck were beneath them; the phaeton lurched backward. "Out with it, woman!" he commanded, glaring at her. "Or would you like for me to step inside the coach with you for a moment."

Cynthia's throaty laughter erupted. "A few months ago, Your Grace, I would have invited you to join me. But today, I fear your intentions may run along a different line than they once did." She sighed. "Such a pity. We were so good together, too." She noted his glare become even more virulent. "You might check for your errant bride inside the park. I believe she and Lord Edmonds are secreted away in some trees, right down there."

Justin's gaze followed the slant of Cynthia's hand; he noted a flash of blue among the trees. It was the color of Aidan's gown. Reining the horse backward so the phaeton could clear the coach, Justin set the small vehicle into a forward motion.

"George, don't," Aidan pleaded, struggling against his hold. But he ignored her, moving ever closer to her; Aidan tried to draw away. "Stop it!"

"Don't fight me, dearest. You're mine. Mine, I say. Come to me," he coaxed softly, pressing himself upon her.

Fear leaping through her, Aidan desperately tried to escape him. With her hands trapped between them, her feet hit against the floor of the phaeton, her bottom sliding across the smooth leather. Suddenly she found herself caught against the corner. His weight crushed down on her as his slim body awkwardly covered her. "Please, don't!" she cried ineffectually as he pressed her deeper into the seat.

A scream bubbled up into her throat, but just as Aidan thought to open her mouth and let it fly, thin lips instantly swooped down, catching hers in an inept kiss. Nausea filled her as her attacker's slick tongue traced her tautly held mouth. Attempting to twist her face aside, Aidan discovered that she was unable to move. *Oh, God, get him off me!* she cried silently, a despondent whimper wrenching itself from her throat.

As if a thousand saints had heard her anxious plea, Aidan was instantly freed. Pulling herself up, she saw George lying on the ground; blood flowed from the unconscious man's split lip, down across his bruised jaw. Elated violet eyes snared steely gray ones. "Oh, Justin, thank God you're here!"

Joyously Aidan leapt at her savior, her arms flinging themselves around his sinewy neck. Strong hands jerked them down, then one clamped itself around her wrist, and with long, hard strides, Justin dragged her up the small incline, away from the shielding trees, to his awaiting phaeton. Tripping over her skirts, Aidan stared up at him.

Stony of face, Justin forcefully checked his roiling temper, but a tic pulsed along his clamped jaw, betraying the intensity of his anger. A different sort of fear suddenly riddled through Aidan's tremulous body, and she hurriedly said a new round of prayers, asking that she be protected from the forbidding stranger beside her. Then, with a startled cry, she was suddenly lifted and tossed into the seat of the phaeton; Justin settled in next to her and snapped the reins.

"Justin," Aidan said after a long moment, "will you allow me to explain? I—"

"Unless you wish for me to vent my fury on you at this precise moment," he snarled at her, "I suggest you hold your tongue. Most men beat their wives behind closed doors. Say one word more, and you'll take your punishment in the middle of a public street for all London to see."

"You think to beat me!" she cried incredulously. "You'll pay hell trying to do so, sir. I won't allow it!"

On a slow pivot, Justin's head turned toward her; the feral gleam in his eyes stunned Aidan. He's truly after blood, she thought wildly.

"Won't you, madam?" he questioned coldly. "Soon enough, we'll see who ends up the victor. Don't count on its being you."

By the time they'd reached Westover House, Aidan was trembling through and through. Her legs would hardly support her, which made little difference, for Justin had virtually dragged her through the front door. To Aidan's relief, they came face-to-face with Pitkin.

"The Queen's messenger was just here. He left a letter for Your Grace," he said to his master, pointing at the missive which lay on the silver tray.

"Leave it," Justin snapped, his abrupt manner startling the man. Angling around his butler, Justin pulled Aidan toward the stairs. Her feet skidding across the marble floor, she refused to cooperate, and Justin turned on her. "By the gods, woman, you're sorely testing my patience!"

"Let loose of me!" she commanded, struggling against his hurtful grip. "I've done nothing wrong!" she said, frantically trying to unwrap his steely fingers from her wrist. "If you'd only give me a chance to explain, I—" Her nails inadvertently slashed his flesh and blood oozed from the imprints.

Startled violet eyes climbed to Justin's face; with a curse he grabbed hold of her, slinging her over his shoulder like a sack of grain, and marched up the stairs.

"Pitkin!" she cried, her face bobbing against Justin's lower back. "Call the constable! Get help! Please!"

"You move one foot, Pitkin," Justin said over his shoulder, continuing his trek up the stairs, "and I shall come down there and step on you like I would a bug."

Pitkin swallowed convulsively. "Whatever Your Grace wishes. I'll not move. Not an inch, sir. Anything else, sir?"

"Dammit, Pitkin!" Justin snarled, knowing the man would stand on the same spot until he dropped from exhaustion. "Go to the kitchen and make yourself a cup of tea. Should we need anything, I'll ring you."

Aidan kicked her feet while she pounded Justin's back. "Pit— Ouch!" she cried as a firm hand swatted her backside.

"Be still," Justin threatened, "or I'll dump you down these stairs. With any luck, the fall will kill you, madam, saving me the trouble of doing the job myself."

The Duke of Westover's words rang down the stairway straight into his butler's ears. A frown marked Pitkin's aged brow; then he shook his head in disagreement. His master would never do such a thing, not to the duchess. Not when the duke loved her like he did. Shrugging, the man hobbled off into the kitchen intent on brewing himself some tea.

The door to their room was flung open with the force of Justin's kick; then with a flick of his wrist the panel crashed back into a closed position. A half-dozen steps, and Aidan was tossed onto their bed, her skirts flying up over her head.

The sight of Edmonds's long body covering Aidan's smaller one, their lips pressed together, filled Justin's head. "You've learned quickly how to strike a provocative pose, madam—

much like that of a common whore displaying her wares,"
he lashed out at her, his temper rising anew; Aidan tore the
skirts of her blue silk dress away from her face. Violet eyes
angrily clashed with gray. "Prepare yourself to be mounted,"
Justin finished, his hand moving to release himself.

"You *ass!*" she hissed, attempting to bound from the
bed, but he was on her in a trice. "Get off me! You have no
right to—"

"Right? I have every right, madam," he said, his heated
breath searing her face. "By law, I can do whatever I want
to you, whenever I desire to do so." His hard body covered
the length of hers fully, pressing her deeper into the mattress. Aidan endeavored to free herself, but Justin was far
too powerful for her to throw him off. "Cease your struggles! This is all I'm after." He growled, his hand swooping
beneath her skirts to clamp itself between her legs; Aidan
jerked. "Does my touch suddenly offend you?" he asked,
his hand working seductively against her. "Or is it George
Edmonds's caresses you now prefer? Have you allowed him
that luxury, Aidan? Has he already violated what is mine?"

"No!" she cried, fighting against him anew. "Justin,
please. I gave him nothing that was yours. I want nothing
from him."

"Then why where you hidden in the trees, locked in his
arms, love? Why was his knee caught between your thighs,
your moans of pleasure filling the air around you?"

"They weren't!" she cried. "Dear God, Justin, he forced
himself on me. He offered to take me home from Madame
Sophie's. He—"

"And somehow you ended up in the park, which, madam,
is in the opposite direction from where you live."

"I asked him to take me to Eugenia's. I thought if you saw
us together—"

"I'd what? Kill you both?" Grating laughter escaped his
throat. Just like his mother, he thought, remembering her
lies, her wheedling voice, trying to explain to his father
where she'd been half the night through. "So right you
were. I should have finished the bastard off when I had the
chance," he said of George. "But first, Aidan, I shall deal
with you."

Her breath caught as his hand made its way from under

her skirts, up over her quaking belly, then past her quivering breasts to caress her throat. Did he mean to kill her? Dear God, no! she cried silently as she thought she felt his fingers tighten. Tears suddenly filled her eyes as her head rolled on the pillow. "Please believe me," she whimpered. "Nothing happened. Nothing was meant to happen. I didn't do anything. I swear."

Justin's gaze caught sight of the lone tear that slashed from the corner of her eye into her hair. Something inside him begged him to listen to her, but his anger overrode the plea. He released her and drew himself on his knees. "Sit up," he said, his voice devoid of emotion. Eyeing him carefully, Aidan complied. "Turn around," he ordered, and when she did so, the buttons on her gown flew in all directions, his hands tearing through the silk.

"No!" Aidan cried as he tore at the corset strings.

"Yes, madam," he said, pulling her gown down over her arms, to her waist. Then he ripped his shirt wide, baring his chest. "You'll make ready for your punishment."

Perhaps she was too frightened or perhaps she no longer cared, but Aidan discovered she was unable to fight his dominance. Within moments she was stripped of her clothing. "Don't defile something that was beautiful between us, Justin," she said as she tried to cover herself with her arms. "Please, I beg you not to ruin what we had."

Whether he'd heard her or not, Aidan couldn't say. But there was no response from him. His burning eyes raked the length of her, and the intensity of his hot gaze seemed to set her skin ablaze. A small cry escaped her as he suddenly pulled her against him and lowered her to the bed, pressing her into the mattress. The hair-roughened flesh on his hard, expansive chest scraped against her exposed breasts as his fully clothed body moved over her; a linen-clad knee spread her quivering thighs apart. Then he reached to free himself, and Aidan's heart wrenched in her breast. "Justin, no! I didn't betray you. Please, I . . ." Positioned, he hesitated, then suddenly drove himself into her; she jerked. ". . . love you," she cried on a sob.

Pained silver eyes absorbed the hurt look on her face; a knife seemed to slash into Justin's chest, her confession of love tearing deep into him. He'd wanted to punish her, but instead, he'd punished himself. God, would she ever forgive him? As he gazed at her lovely features, unshed tears glistening in her huge violet eyes, her soft lips trembled, wanting to be soothed. God in heaven, he *loved* her! Too late, he understood not all women were like his mother. Yet he'd acted the part of persecutor, just as his father had before him. Why wouldn't he listen to her? Why had he felt compelled to castigate her for something he knew all along she hadn't done? Then the question tore itself from his lips. "Why, Aidan? Why, love? Oh, sweet, I . . ."

To Aidan, Justin's words seemed ripped from his heart. She had no time to discover the rest of his unspoken request, for his mouth claimed hers in a purging kiss. He drew from her, begged her response, begged her forgiveness. Wanting to prove her love to him, she found she couldn't deny him. Their searching tongues touched, then surrendered. She heard his groan of pleasure; then slowly he moved, expertly seducing that delicious warm flow from within her, his mouth never leaving hers. The rough material of his clothed hips chafed against her soft thighs, yet Aidan cared not, for it was a gratifying sensation. She envisioned herself the seductress, captivating him, luring him with her nude, vitally willing body as it played a siren's song of love.

Eagerly her legs locked around him, her hips rising to meet his every thrust, and Justin drove deeper and deeper into her, trying to lose himself in her soft alluring body, her naked limbs urging him onward. He felt like the master, then the slave, then master to her again. Greedily they clung to each other, tongues, lips, bodies joining in a dance of desire. Then suddenly, just as that familiar spinning sensation overtook Aidan, her spasms erupting with rapturous delight, Justin's cry of exaltation sounded above her, his hard body jerked uncontrollably, and he spilled his hot fluid deep inside her.

Slowly they spun back to the here and now; Justin, feeling the sting of its harsh reality, rolled to his side. He felt his wife's soft violet eyes upon him, but he was unable to look at her. "We'll talk tomorrow," he said in a broken whisper, needing time to sort through all his emotions.

Pulling the cover from the edge of the bed, he draped it

over Aidan, then held her close against him. For an eternity he stared up at the bed's canopy, hating himself for his cruelty, his brutality, praying she would somehow forgive him, until finally his eyelids drooped. He slept deeply.

For a long, long time Aidan listened to Justin's soft slumberous sounds, her gaze roving over his handsome face. In sleep, with all his anger falling somewhere behind, he resembled a young boy. Yet, she remembered him only a short time ago, his face filled with fury, his tormented gaze raking over her while deaf ears refused to believe her truthful cries of protest. He'd used his body to punish her, but after that one quick chastising thrust, he'd relented, she knew, and he'd made love to her with a furious passion as he'd tried to purge himself of his guilt, his worshiping yet demanding body begging her forgiveness.

Something had been driving him—something beyond what had happened today. Of that she was certain. But what it could be, she had no idea. Tomorrow they would talk. Perhaps then she would learn the truth.

Yet, Aidan realized, although their bodies communicated in the sweetest of melodies, she and Justin seemed incapable of expressing themselves with the simplest of words. That constant disharmony would destroy them, she knew. Hopefully they would be able to find a mutual accord, allowing them to live together in complete unity.

"I love you, Justin," she whispered, permitting herself to speak freely of the wondrous emotion she felt. No longer would she hold back the utterance of that feeling. She loved him—always would. Knowing it, Aidan slowly closed her eyes, and her mind immersed itself in an oddly gentle sleep.

15

Aidan awakened the next morning and found herself alone in the huge bed. Deciding against calling Penny, she bathed and groomed herself, then donned a soft lavender silk dress. Retrieving from the floor the torn blue silk gown she'd worn yesterday, she placed it in the wardrobe with hopes it could be repaired. With one last check in the mirror, she set off to find Justin.

Meeting Pitkin on the stairs, she was informed that the duke had gone out for a short while, so she breakfasted alone, then walked out into the gardens to enjoy the morning sunshine. As she sat on a low stone bench, inhaling the rose-scented air, she heard a sudden rustle in the bushes; a shrill, piteous cry erupted.

Aidan bounded from the bench as a cat abruptly loped off across the grass, scampering up the stone wall, disappearing over the barrier. Searching through the thorn-laden rosebushes, her eyes caught sight of a small rabbit, its flesh lacerated, its back leg badly mangled. Carefully she stretched an arm through the thick stalks and reached for the injured creature while she tried to evade the bite of the treacherous thorns. Like razors, the pointed barbs sliced into her arm and tore at her bodice, yet Aidan persisted until she gently drew the quivering rabbit from within its spiny den.

"Poor thing," she said, holding it close to her breast, petting it lightly with soft, tender strokes, knowing it would not survive. After a few minutes the furry thing's rapid breathing slowed; then, with a great racking shudder, the life drained from its small body, and the light in its tiny eyes snuffed out.

Aidan carried the rabbit to a secluded spot in the garden. Using her hands, she scooped out a small grave in the soft, rich earth and placed the rabbit's limp body inside. With the dirt mounded over it, she felt a single tear drop from her eye. Life, she thought, was so precious, so delicate; in a twinkling it could be gone.

As she stood, she noted the bloodstains on her torn bodice and headed for the house. Upstairs, she washed her hands and changed her gown, then dropped the newly ruined dress into a basket which was reserved for sweepings and waste. Afterward she decided to see if Justin had returned, and made her way to his study.

Inside the room, she inhaled deeply; her head filled itself with the smells of oiled wood, a hint of cigar smoke, and a lingering manly fragrance, exclusively Justin's. Unfortunately he was not there.

Since her husband spent much of his time in the study, she decided to leave him a note, which she hoped he would find immediately upon his return. Doing so would save her the bother of searching for him the morning through. As she rounded his desk in search for paper and a pen, she noted an open letter lying on the smooth wood surface. It was signed by their Queen!

Remembering Pitkin's announcement yesterday that the missive had arrived, and Justin's curt order to leave it, she quickly scanned the note's contents. Instantly she stiffened, and as though she'd been caught beneath a tumbling wall of stone, she crumpled into the chair, her hopes and dreams crushed by a slash of a pen.

The *bastard!* she thought, her eyes sparking purple fire as she hid behind her anger. He'd bedded her, not because he desired her, wanted her for herself, but for personal gain! So there would be no mistake, her frenzied eyes searched the letter for the passage that would confirm her silent accusation.

Since you wisely agreed with my edict of a month past that no divorce will take place, I applaud you. I would hate to see you cast into ruin. As I said, once you've become intimate with your new duchess, your reward shall be forthcoming. I promise it shall be substantial and ever-enduring.

Her fury rose anew when she realized Victoria's and

Justin's discussion had taken place on the day he'd sauntered into the great house telling her he'd changed his mind about giving the ball. His attentiveness, his kindness, his gently persuasive manner were all ploys in order to seduce her! And stupidly she'd allowed him to do it!

What precisely had he been promised? Lands? Money? A new title? What could better being a duke, she couldn't say! But something apparently had won his interest. For he'd lost no time in seeing that he'd become *intimate* with his new duchess! Where was he now? Out reporting the personal details of their lovemaking to their Queen so he could quickly collect his *reward?* Angered by the thought that she'd been used, Aidan bounded from the chair, marched to the door of the study, and headed toward the stairs. Had she had any sense in the first place, she'd have taken her own counsel and joined a nunnery!

Instantly she stopped her climb up the steps. Turning, she strode down their entire length to the foyer, stopping only long enough to retrieve her reticule, which she'd dropped last night and which now lay atop the table by the ever-present silver tray. The door opened, then banged shut behind her.

Justin strode in from the back of the house, the gift he'd purchased for his wife clutched in his hand. Not finding her in the gardens, where Pitkin reported last seeing her, he bounded up the stairs. "Aidan!" he called. "Where are you, love?"

Unable to find his wife, Justin went into his study. Folding himself into his chair, he set his gift on top of the open missive from the Queen. Lifting the lid to the velvet box, he again felt pleased with his selection and found he could hardly wait until Aidan returned to present it to her.

Where had she taken herself off to? he wondered, his heart skipping like that of an untried schoolboy enamored of his first love. Each time he thought of her, he was overwhelmed by the same delirious feeling, and Justin found he could no longer deny it. All these years, in which he'd fought to keep his heart secured, fearing someone would tear it to shreds, like his mother had his father's, were for naught. He'd masqueraded as a rogue and a womanizer, allowing people to believe he was shallow and a cheat, simply to build his barriers higher. He'd even denied the possibility of his ever permitting himself to feel anything for a woman by repeatedly telling himself that love was a wasted emotion and marriage a thing for fools, whereupon he vowed to keep himself apart.

Welcome to the masses, Justin thought, shaking his head, a derisive smile spreading across his lips. Cupid's arrow had finally found its mark, a violet-eyed vixen having strung the bow. Slowly, unknowingly, she'd chipped away at the sturdy wall he'd erected around his heart, until it had fallen with a resounding crash. No, he could no longer deny it. Aidan was his first love, his only love. Yet the feeling was so new to him, Justin wanted to savor the emotion, experience its growth. Were he to say the word aloud, he feared the sentiment might somehow vanish.

Anxious to see Aidan's beautiful face again, needing to speak with her about last night and beg her forgiveness for his bestial wounding of her mind and body, Justin waited and waited, until dusk had settled outside his window. Still his wife had not returned. Consumed with worry, he sent Potts out to make the rounds of Aidan's friends, subtly inquiring if they'd seen or heard from her. When the man returned, shaking his head in a negative response, Potts then told him a quick probe of the local authorities had turned up nothing either. As Justin heard the words, a strange coldness enveloped his recently trusting heart, freezing it solid.

Dismissing his man, he slowly rose. Icy gray eyes riveted themselves to the amethyst earrings he'd purchased that morning. Snapping the lid shut, he tossed the velvet case, along with the letter from the Queen, into a drawer, then closed and locked it.

If need be, he would tear London apart to find her. And he would start with George Edmonds. With long, hard strides, the Duke of Westover quit the room.

Alastair Prescott walked into the library. "Elsworth said it was imperative you see me, Penny. Has something happened?"

Penny gave a quick curtsy. "Oh, Your Grace, it's the young duchess, sir. She didn't come home last night."

"Why are you giving me this information, and not her husband?" Alastair asked. "She answers to him now."

"But, sir, I think somethin' bad has happened to her. And he's the one who did it to her!" She pulled the lavender silk day dress from an overly large cloth bag she carried. "I found this in the refuse bin. It's the duchess's. Look! There's blood all over the bodice." Alastair grabbed the dress from Penny's hands, his eyes inspecting it carefully. "I'm afraid he mighta done her in, just like he's threatened."

"What do you mean 'like he's threatened'? Has Westover made threats against her life?"

"Yes, sir. At least, I think so, sir. Once, when I thought she was comin' down with somethin', I told her His Grace wouldn't like it very much if she was to up and die on him. My mistress said she thought he'd be real happy if she did. Then, the night afore last, Pitkin—he's the butler there at Westover House—said somethin' about Her Grace wantin' him to fetch her a constable. Said that the duke was gonna kill her. Threatened to break her neck for somethin' she'd done. I found the dress this mornin' when I was dumpin' the bins. She ain't been home, and no one's seen her since early yesterday mornin'."

"Thank you, Penny," the duke said. "I'll keep the dress in a safe place. If Westover has had anything to do with my daughter's disappearance, we'll need it as evidence. Until I get to the bottom of all this, I want you to stay at the duke's home and keep your ears open. If you hear anything . . . even the slightest whisper about what may have happened to Aidan, I want you to report it to me."

"I will, sir," she said with more bravado than she felt. "I'll see what I can come up with. Good day to you, sir." Penny curtsied and quickly left the room.

Perplexed, Alastair shook his head. When he'd last seen his daughter, she'd seemed extremely happy. Westover appeared quite content as well. Now Aidan's maid had brought him a tale, virtually accusing the Duke of Westover of murdering his wife. Yet, what Penny had offered in way of proof was very little: a few threats and a bloodstained dress. The dress, however, created a convincing case. But the threats? Admittedly, when he'd reached the end of his own endurance with his daughter, he'd threatened several times to strangle her himself! However, he would not easily dismiss the charges that Penny had made. Aidan was missing, and if she didn't appear soon, he would take the information to the authorities. Right now, he planned to investigate the matter on his own.

"By God, man!" Alastair bellowed, his fist pounding the table, causing several dishes to jump into the air, "since you claim you had nothing to do with her disappearance, then I suggest you produce my daughter this instant! Or I'll see you charged with her murder!"

Trying to hold his temper in check, Justin kept his eyes devoid of emotion as he gazed at the Duke of Atwood and the four men who'd stormed his house and stridden into the dining room without preamble. "Gentlemen," he said to the constable and his men, "and, of course, Your Grace." Justin inclined his head ever so slightly as he casually leaned back in his chair. "When I last saw my wife, over a week ago, she was in perfect health. I've tried my best to locate her, but she seems to have disappeared without a trace. Where to, gentlemen, I have no idea."

Indeed, over the past week Justin had torn London upside-down in search of Aidan, but he'd had no luck in finding her. Eugenia knew nothing of her whereabouts, nor did David. Penny, her maid, had told him, in an accusatory tone, that she had no clue as to where her mistress might be. He'd even gone to see Aunt Patti, who'd traveled back to Warfield Manor the day after the ball, but like the others, his aunt hadn't had any communication with Aidan, in person or otherwise. Not even the enterprising young Tim, who had settled into the orphanage with ease and now ruled his peers like a king, had any information about his missing duchess. "She ain't been around here," he'd told Justin. "And I know everythin' there is to know about this place, inside and out."

George, the first person he'd questioned, had denied seeing her too. Fearing Justin might unleash his anger on him again, the man swore on bent knees that he'd not seen

Aidan since the day in Hyde Park. Disgusted with the whimpering sop, Justin had decided to leave George's face intact. As the days had passed, he'd become even more fed up when he'd been unable to discover the least little thing about his missing wife. His mood had grown darker and darker.

Apparently, while Justin had been trekking all over London in search of Aidan—first grieving over her loss, fearing the worst had somehow happened to her, then heaping curses upon her head because he was certain she'd run off and was very much alive and well—Alastair Prescott had conducted his own investigation into his daughter's disappearance, no doubt, culminating in this friendly little visit tonight.

"I assure you all," Justin finished, "I've had nothing to do with my wife's sudden vanishing act."

Or had he? Guilt suddenly rippled through Justin. More than once, he'd wondered if his brutal attack on her had caused her to take flight. If that were the case, could he blame her? No! he castigated himself, knowing she had every reason to renounce him. *God, Aidan, where are you?*

"Indeed, sir!" Alastair accused. "Although you deny any involvement in this rather bizarre affair, I strongly suspect you know exactly where she is."

His personal anguish having torn his heart to pieces, the old barriers surrounding it had been erected anew. "I do not!" Justin lashed back, coming to his feet, his linen napkin clutched in his balled fist. Because of his pain, he struck back, cruelly. "But when I do find her, sir, I'll send her your way, posthaste. I no longer want her as my wife!"

"You never did 'want her as your wife,' Westover," Alastair countered, trying to turn the man's hand.

"You should know, sir. You're the one who forced us into this disagreeable situation in the first place!" Justin blasted, his constraint on his temper finally shredding. "Had you not interfered in either of our lives, you'd need not be here now, tossing about accusations which cannot be proved. I repeat, though sorely tempted on several occasions, I did not murder your daughter!"

"Constable," Alastair said, his eyes locked with Justin's, "show the duke my proof."

One of the men stepped forward, then unrolled a long sheet of paper, revealing a blood-splattered gown.

"That's Aidan's dress! Where did you find it?" Justin asked, his heart pounding wildly, his hand clutching at the lavender silk. "God! The blood! What's happened to her?"

"That, sir, will be revealed at your trial," Alastair stated. "Unless, of course, you'd like to make your confession now."

Justin glared at the man. "If you know something about her, tell me! Where did you get this dress?"

"From a refuse bin within this very house, sir." The Duke of Atwood turned to the constable. "Do you have enough evidence to charge this man with murder?"

"We do, Your Grace."

"Then get on with it!"

"Yes, sir." The constable turned his attention to Justin. "By authority of the Crown and the laws of Great Britain, I arrest you, Justin Alexander Malcolm Warfield, Duke of Westover, for the murder of one Aidan Elizabeth Prescott Warfield, Duchess of Westover. Will you come peaceably, sir?"

Hard steely eyes stared through the man; then Justin tossed his napkin onto his untouched plate and strode through the doorway into the hall. Fearing he might escape, the constable and his three men quickly shuffled after him. "Pitkin!" the young duke shouted, and stopped short; the four men bumped into Justin, nearly knocking themselves down. The elderly butler appeared, arching a brow at the indecorous foursome and their overly close proximity to his master. "Until further notice," the Duke of Westover informed his man, "I shall be on holiday at Newgate! Should my errant *wife* decide to return, tell her she may find me there!"

". . . She was afraid of him," Eugenia confessed as she stood in the witness box. "But I doubt very much Westover murdered her. Aidan is most impetuous. She—"

"That will be all, Lady Manley," the prosecutor stated.

". . . When he took her from our house," David said, "Westover's temper seemed to be held by a thread. But I presume his anger stemmed from her disobedience. He—"

"Thank you, Lord Manley," the prosecutor interrupted, and looked toward the stony-faced, white-wigged justices. "I have no further questions of this witness, milords."

". . . When Her Majesty denied him the annulment, His Grace decided to seek a divorce," Cynthia Danvers said. "But he told me he thought Her Majesty would block that option as well."

"And?" the prosecutor prompted.

Cynthia looked at Justin's hardened face, then back to the prosecutor. "Other than doing away with her, he saw no way out of their marriage."

"Thank you," the prosecutor said. "That will be all."

". . . Her Grace told me to call a constable," Pitkin admitted stiffly.

"And did you?" the prosecutor asked.

"No."

"Why not?"

"Because His Grace told me if I moved, he'd step on me like he would a bug."

"What else did His Grace say?"

Pitkin looked to his employer; then his gaze dropped. "As he carried his wife up the stairs, he threatened to drop the duchess back down them . . ."

"Go on, sir," the man urged. "In Westover's exact words, what did he say?"

Pitkin swallowed hard. "He said: 'With any luck, the fall will kill you, saving me the trouble of doing the job myself.' "

Several gasps echoed through the House of Lords, now convened as the Court of the Lord High Steward. A low rumble of speculative voices quickly followed. "Thank you, Mr. Pitkin," the prosecutor said while he looked directly at the accused.

As gray eyes held themselves steady on the prosecutor, Justin wondered how the hell his manservant had been able to quote, verbatim, what had been said that night, especially when Pitkin couldn't remember anything else! Obviously fate was against him.

"She was fine the next morning!" Pitkin protested quickly. "Not even a bruise or a scratch that I could see!"

"That will be all, sir!" the prosecutor snapped.

His head downcast, Pitkin stepped from the witness box.

". . . Now, Your Grace," the prosecutor addressed the Duke of Atwood, "you've stated that, at pistol point, you forced a rather reluctant Duke of Westover to marry your daughter, is that correct?"

"It is, sir. He'd compromised my daughter's reputation. I had no other choice but to correct the situation."

"And what was your daughter's response to the forced marriage?"

"She was very upset."

"And the duke's response?"

"He had murder in his eye!"

Justin shot from his seat; his hard gaze locked with that of his father-in-law. "By God, if I did, it was directed at you, sir!" he shouted, his hands balling into angry fists.

"And I say you are your father's seed," Alastair lashed back.

At their sudden outbursts, a loud questioning rumble passed through the room. So, Justin thought, Atwood wanted to bring up the long-extinct conjectures about his parents' deaths. After the initial shock of finding their bodies, Justin had quickly removed the weapon that was clutched in his father's hand. Then he'd stripped his parents of their valuables, intent on making their deaths appear the result of being set upon by highwaymen, hoping to prevent a scandal. Yet there were those who had surmised the truth. Apparently Alastair Prescott was one of them.

Noting the two men's hostile stares, the prosecutor turned fully toward the Duke of Westover, extremely pleased that someone had finally elicited a response from the man. "Thank you, Your Grace," he said, smiling at Justin.

Justin's steely gaze turned from Atwood's to pierce the prosecutor's face; slowly he fell back into his chair.

". . . I found her dress in the waste bin on the mornin' after she disappeared," Penny stated, eyes wide. "The bodice is torn, like you sees it. There's blood on it!"

"Thank you," the prosecutor said. "That will be all." He waited until the wobbly-kneed girl stepped from the box, then pronounced, "If it will please the court, I now call the Duke of Westover, who, of his own volition, has agreed to testify."

When Justin was situated in the box, the prosecutor

asked, "Your Grace, are you able to deny any of the testimony presented thus far, specifically that of your butler?"

His emotionless gaze on the prosecutor, Justin studied the man intently. He'd agreed to give testimony because he had nothing to hide. But now he thought his decision foolish. Finally he said, "I cannot." Another rumble of voices filled the room.

"Then you admit you were forcibly carrying your wife up the stairs, as your butler has stated."

"I do."

"Why?"

"Because I was intent on bedding her!" Justin snapped, which was not a lie.

The peers' laughter trickled through the large room, and the prosecutor cleared his throat. "From the testimony already presented, you confirmed that your wife pleaded with your butler to get help, you threatened his life if he did so, then you also spoke of killing the duchess. My question is, why?"

"I was simply warning her to behave. She is an extremely high-spirited and headstrong woman. I was merely trying to control her."

"Control her? Or were you intent on punishing her for some imagined indiscretion? Did she give you cause to want to kill her?"

Justin refused to answer. Were he to confess the incident in Hyde Park, Aidan might suffer further reproach. The truth about their forced marriage had damaged her enough.

"Have you no answer?" the man asked.

"My wife did nothing improper, if that's what you're implying."

"Then, since you say she committed no indiscriminate act which may have drawn your ire, I propose to you, sir, that when faced with an unwanted marriage, in which you were soundly and permanently trapped, you took it upon yourself to do away with your wife, and that you've hidden the body in an effort to escape punishment for your heinous act!"

"That's a lie!" Justin shot back. "She's alive!"

"If that be so, produce her, sir."

Justin glared at his accuser. "I cannot," he said finally.

"I have no further questions of the defendant," the prosecutor announced, and Justin stepped from the witness box. "If it will please the court," the man said when Justin was seated, "I now call Viscount George Edmonds to testify."

As Justin listened to George's testimony, he realized he was doomed. Two scenarios had been created by the prosecutor: one, the Duke of Westover was trapped in an unwanted marriage that he desperately wished to be freed from; two, Westover's wife had attempted to cuckold him. Either of the two might be construed as a cause for murder. *Dammit, Aidan! Where are you?*

Aidan rubbed the back of her hand across her itchy nose, then set the wet, soapy brush to the floor again, scrubbing in a circular motion. How many times had she cleaned her small room and those of the good Anglican sisters over these past six weeks, she could not say. But it was far and away one time too many.

Wearily she tossed the brush into the wooden bucket. Dirty water sloshed onto the clean floor. Ignoring it, she leaned back on her knees. Her once soft hands were cracked and rough, her nails broken and split, her back ached unmercifully, and her knees were bruised from their constant wear on the stone floors. Admittedly, the only thing that kept her from leaving the cloistered convent and going back to London was her pride. "Damn my pride!" she chastised herself aloud as she came to her feet. Instantly someone cleared her throat behind her, and Aidan turned to see the abbess standing in the doorway.

"Elizabeth," the abbess said, addressing Aidan as she was now known, "profane language is not used here. Please remember it."

"I apologize for my blasphemy. It will not happen again."

The abbess arched a skeptical brow, then posed a gentle smile. "I'm certain you will be most careful in the future. But it is readily understood why one might denounce pride. As it is written, 'Pride goeth before destruction, and a haughty spirit before a fall.' It is certainly something to ponder."

"Yes, Abbess. Pride can be most destructive." Especially her own, Aidan thought. And her haughty spirit as well.

"If you are through here, I'd like for you to take a letter into the village to post."

Aidan's eyes suddenly brightened. She hadn't been beyond the walls of the small convent since the day she'd arrived. Very little communication flowed in or out of the ancient stone fortress, and like a butterfly, Aidan felt she was about to be released from her cocoon.

"Brush your hair and wash your face," the abbess said. "By then I shall have finished my letter."

Aidan watched as the abbess slowly walked away. Quickly she went to the basin and scrubbed her hands and face. Next she pulled a hard bristle brush through her hair, pinning it into a stark-looking bun at the nape of her neck. Rolling her sleeves down, she smoothed her skirts, then strode from her small cell, down the hallway to the abbess's room.

Guilty of murder as charged! The proclamation rebounded through Justin's mind. A fierce shake of his head negated the verdict; he groaned. *To be hanged by the neck until dead!* A burly black-hooded man dragged him forward on the scaffold. The crowd cheered wildly as the thick hemp was placed around his neck; the heavy noose tightened. The floor suddenly dropped from beneath his feet, and he fell straight downward. A hideous noise escaped his throat. *Air! Air! God, I need air!*

Justin sat up with a jerk. A violent shudder racked through his sweat-soaked body as he realized he'd been trapped in another one of his nightmares—a nightmare that would come to fruition in scarcely two days.

"Goddammit! Where is she!" he snarled, jumping from his bug-infested cot to pace the dank cell. A candle burned low on a small table, his only source of light. "She's not dead! I know it!"

A key scraped in the ancient iron lock and the thick wooden door swung open. "Ye gots a visitor," his jailer informed him.

"Out of my way, young man!" Lady Falvey snapped,

prodding the guard with her cane. "I'll call you when I'm ready to leave. Now, off with you!"

The door squeaked on its hinges; the key twisted in the lock. Justin's tired eyes searched his aunt's face. "Any luck?" he asked in a dull tone.

"No. One thing's certain, she's not with George Edmonds, nor has she ever been. I've had a man on him constantly. He's reported nothing. The others that I hired are spread out all over England, looking for her. If she's to be found, she will be."

A strangled laugh erupted from his throat. "That's what you said during the trial. Dammit all! How can this be happening? I didn't kill her. Why won't anyone believe me?"

"Calm yourself, Westover," his aunt said, patting his arm. "I believe you. So do Eugenia and David. You were convicted on circumstantial evidence. Hearsay. A torn dress with blood on it, and Edmonds's rambling testimony about the incident in Hyde Park. Your Warfield temper has gotten you into this. Had you held your tongue about wanting to be rid of Aidan when you first found yourself unwillingly wedded to her, you wouldn't be in this little scrape now."

"Little scrape! I'm to be gibbeted in less than two days and you speak of it as though some bully were going to call me out into the schoolyard to box my ears!"

"Keep your wits about you, nephew! You'll need a clear head to help me figure out where she has gone."

"For six weeks I've been pondering that question and I'm no closer to an answer now than I was then. Had I even an inkling of where I might find her, I'd break through that blasted door and drag her back here for all London to see. It's useless."

Aunt Patti thumped her cane. "No Warfield, except one, has ever yielded when faced with insurmountable odds. And you'll not follow your father's cowardly path, sir. You'll fight this to the end! Is that understood?" She saw Justin's curt nod. "Now, tell me everything that has happened between the two of you from the time you retrieved Aidan from Lord and Lady Manley's to the day you last saw her."

"That could take weeks," Justin said.

"Then I suggest you talk fast. We haven't that much time."

Justin settled on his cot while his aunt claimed the small wooden chair next to the table, the only rudiments in his small cell, except for the chamber pot positioned in the corner. Then in a low tone he related everything to his aunt, every detail, including the punishment he'd instituted on Aidan the night before she'd disappeared.

"She's not dead," he said, his hand raking through his tousled hair. "I know it."

"How do you know it?" Aunt Patti questioned, her faded blue eyes searching his face.

"I just know." He saw her arched brow and drew a deep breath, but rejected the chance to explain himself.

"So, you still refuse to confess your feelings aloud. Had you dropped that arrogant facade of yours and told her that you loved her, I doubt she would have dashed off as she did. Eugenia believes Aidan may have become incensed over something and that she's off somewhere collecting her thoughts in order to face you again."

"Well, I hope to God she's gotten them together by now, for if she hasn't, she'll be facing me in hell!"

"It's always much simpler to blame someone else for your own failings," Aunt Patti said on a weary sigh. "You've too much pride, Westover. And it has led you to the threshold of your destruction." He didn't answer. "I shall keep searching. And you shall keep praying. I'll see you on the morrow." She rose from the chair, then walked to the door and thumped it with her cane; quickly the guard opened it. "I've an audience with Her Majesty late tomorrow," she said to Justin. "I'll come here directly afterward."

"Till tomorrow," he said without emotion. When the door closed, the key bolting it anew, he sank to his cot. Troubled gray eyes searched his bleak surroundings. Unless his wife returned, he would have no future. But even if by some miracle of miracles he were saved and she still did not return, he knew he'd still have no future. Without her he was dead.

"Aidan, I love you," he whispered fervently to the stone walls, the pain of her loss tearing through him. "Come back to me. Come back, love."

16

The late-afternoon sun flowed over Aidan as she traipsed down the craggy lane toward the small village which lay nearly a mile from the convent. But the golden rays of sunshine did little to lighten her spirits, for a dark emptiness remained deep inside her. *Justin,* she thought, wanting to be near him again, desiring to see him beyond anyone else in the world. Impetuously, she'd run off, not allowing him the opportunity to explain the meaning of their Queen's letter. Yet she feared, if she were to return now, he'd only shun her, for his pride was as lofty as her own. In truth, neither one was willing to admit his or her mistakes and beg the other's forgiveness.

Pride goeth before destruction and a haughty spirit before a fall. The words rolled through her mind, and Aidan could not deny their meaning. If she could only learn to be less hasty in her actions and more thoughtful of mind, she'd be far better off than she was now. Perhaps, in time, the good sisters would be able to teach her prudence in all she did. But she feared their tutelage might take a very long time.

Her feet finally hit the main road leading into the village, and within moments Aidan ducked inside the small posting station. Allowing her eyes to adjust to the dimness within, she noted several men milled about, one near the counter, so she stood aside to wait her turn.

". . . He's to be hanged—let's see—the day after tomorrow at sunrise," the posting agent commented to the man nearest him, pointing to the newspaper in his hand; Aidan felt a cold shiver run through her at hearing such depressing talk. "That's if Her Majesty don't stop it. Nope, never remember a duke being gibbeted afore. Probably will draw a crowd from all round London."

"Well, if he was cuckolded, like the papers hinted he mighta been," the man commented, "I cain't say I blame him for doin' away with the little slattern. O' course, they ain't found her body. And he keeps insistin' she's alive. But I guess that there viscount's testimony was what sealed his doom. Cavortin' in broad daylight in the middle of Hyde Park for everyone to see. Had I found my missus sprawled under some man, like he was to have found her, I wouldn't have been so nice about it all—bustin' her lover's jaw! I'd have killed them both, then and there!"

"I know what ye mean," the posting agent replied, refolding the tattered newspaper. "That Westover bloke sure bagged himself a passel of bad luck, he did."

Aidan shakily pulled herself away from the wall that she'd fallen against. Activating her legs, she dashed to the counter and grabbed the paper from the startled man's hands.

"Hey, missy," the man said, trying to snatch it back. "What do ye think ye'r doin'?"

"Leave it, sir!" she commanded abruptly as her eyes scanned the article, which was dated nearly a week ago. "My God!" she cried as her trembling hands lowered the paper. "They think he's murdered me!" Aidan's legs buckled; luckily the man beside her caught hold of her before she hit the floor. Drawing her up, he steadied her until she was able to stand on her own. "Please, I have to get back to London. Is there a public coach coming this way soon?"

The posting agent frowned. "Sorry, miss, but there ain't no coach that comes here. Ye should know that. Ye'll have to go over to the Boar's Inn to catch one."

Aidan *didn't* know that, for she'd hired a private coach to carry her to the remote village which lay in the English countryside well north of London. Having instructed the driver to drop her at the lane leading up to the convent, she'd paid him his fee, then set off alone to ask for shelter from the Anglican nuns.

"Where's the Boar's Inn?" she asked, although she doubted, if she were somehow to reach the inn, the few coins hidden in her pocket would pay her fare back to London. "How do the mails get from here to there?"

"The inn is 'bout twelve miles east of here. And old John Taylor takes what's to be posted over to the inn every Friday." He eyed the plain rough-linen gown the abbess had given her, his gaze settling on her work-roughened hands. "Ye ain't really that duchess they're talkin' 'bout in the papers, is ye?" he asked skeptically, a dubious brow arching. "Ye sure don't look like no duchess to me."

Aidan bit back an angry retort. "I *am* that duchess, sir, and I have to get back to London! Please, can someone help me?" No one answered, and her annoyance grew. "Where's this John Taylor you spoke of?"

"He's gone off to visit his wife's folks. Won't be back till the mails have to run again. Ain't no one goin' that way for a couple of days, miss, so maybe you'd best set off walkin'."

Several of the men chuckled; instantly Aidan was filled with both fear and fury. "Sirs, my name is Aidan Elizabeth Prescott Warfield, and I am the Duchess of Westover. My husband is about to be executed for a crime he did not commit," she said in a low, barely controlled voice, "and not one of you seems willing to help me. Should my husband be put to death because of your lack of compassion, I shall see that all of you are brought to ruin." Hard violet eyes pinpointed each man there. "Now, I repeat, will someone help me?"

After a lengthy silence, Aidan glared her malcontent at the men, then turned and fled the building. Hiking her skirts, she ran up the road to the rutted lane; frantic feet pulled her up the hill toward the convent. As she reached the heavy wooden gates, Aidan fell against them, gasping for air; then her fist pounded the aged timber.

"Let me in!" she sobbed as her emotions spun wildly inside her. After what seemed an eternity, an old nun released the bolt and opened the panel; Aidan rushed inside. "Wh-where's the abbess?" she asked, her breath still coming unsteadily.

"She's in the chapel."

Aidan didn't tarry. Traversing the small courtyard at a full run, she bolted toward the chapel. She stopped short several steps inside the holy sanctuary where the abbess knelt before the altar repeating her prayers. Knowing the silent litany might take forever, Aidan asked God's forgiveness and rushed the short distance to the altar. "Abbess, I must speak to you."

As though she'd not heard Aidan, the woman continued with her prayer, head bowed, eyes closed.

"Please, Abbess," Aidan cried, violet eyes spilling forth their tears. "It's a matter of life and death!"

After a few moments the woman opened her eyes, then stood. "What is so urgent, my child?"

"I must get back to London. They're going to hang him for something he didn't do!"

"Calm yourself. Of whom do you speak, child?"

"My husband, the Duke of Westover—they think that he's murdered me! I must get back to London to stop his execution! It's all my fault," she lamented, a sob jerking from her chest. "I should never have run off."

"Was it your pride that carried you to our door?" the abbess asked, gentle eyes searching Aidan's.

"Yes," Aidan confessed. "And it's going to lead to Justin's destruction. I can't let it happen."

"Come, we shall see what can be done."

Aidan quickly followed the abbess to her quarters.

"Do you have any money?" the nun asked.

"Very little—only a few shillings."

"Then you shall need some for the coach to London. Take this," the abbess said, having withdrawn a small pouch from the drawer of the writing table, placing it in Aidan's hand. "It's not much, but it should see you through."

Aidan eyed the small leather bag. "But this is all you have. How will you survive? You and the others need food."

"Our Lord will give us what we need," the abbess said. "Come, now we must find a way to get you to the Boar's Inn."

Aidan followed the abbess to the gates. "I'd almost forgotten what it was like outside our walls," the older woman said as they stepped through. She smiled, breathing in the sweet air. Then the two set off down the lane to the road.

As they reached the narrow thoroughfare, a young man, a few seasons lesser in age than Aidan, guided a small cart along the roadway, a swaybacked gelding harnessed at its front.

"You, there!" the abbess called. "Come here!"

Thinking the nun was speaking to someone else, the lad looked around him. Not seeing anyone on the road, he routed the cart over to the woman. "Yes, ma'am?"

"I need for you to take this young woman to the Boar's Inn."

"Ain't goin' that far, ma'am."

Taking the pouch from Aidan, the abbess withdrew several coins. "That may not have been your intent, young man, but you'll do so now."

The lad eyed the money in his hand; a crooked grin spread across his unwhiskered face. "If ye say so, ma'am."

"Let me know what happens," the abbess said as she turned toward Aidan. She hugged the young woman, known to her as Elizabeth, then urged Aidan into the back of the cart. "Godspeed, my child."

"Thank you, Abbess. Pray for me. And above all, pray for my husband." As the cart was set into motion, Aidan remembered the letter. "I shall post your letter in London!" she called, waving at the older woman, the abbess waving in return. The small conveyance rounded the bend and the abbess disappeared from sight.

Seated in the back of the rickety cart, Aidan realized that she had less than thirty-six hours to get to London and stop Justin's execution. Under the best of conditions, a good day's travel lay ahead of her, she knew. Suddenly she grew anxious. Should something go wrong . . . Palpable anxiety leapt through her, and she became annoyed with the slow pace of the old gelding. "Please! Can't you make him go faster?" she asked impatiently.

Instantly the young man set the ancient steed into a notably quicker gait, which shook the wobbly cart and jarred Aidan's spine. Certain the conveyance was about to fall apart at its seams, she prayed most fervently it would hold together. Dear God, please, *please* let me get there in time!

Dark slowly descended upon the open fields and the tall forests framing the roadway. Along the blackened path, the ancient gelding kept to his lumbering pace. Miraculously the cart held together, and nearly four hours later it pulled to a stop at the Boar's Inn. Aidan didn't wait for the young man, whose name she'd learned was Stephen, to help her alight. She jumped from the vehicle and rushed through the door into the dimly lit inn. "I need to get to London!" she said to the sleepy man at the desk. "When's the next public coach out?"

He yawned. "Tomorrow at two in the afternoon, miss."

"There's nothing sooner? Please, it's imperative I get there without delay!"

"No. That's the only coach we got. But it don't go direct to London. It sorta weaves around—"

"If I should book passage, what time will I get into London?"

The man scratched his head. "Well, if there ain't no delays, you should be there by three o'clock."

Aidan breathed a sigh of relief, for she had been certain the trip would take far longer. "Thirteen hours isn't so bad," she said, smiling, knowing she'd be in London with time to spare.

"Thirteen hours?" the man repeated. "You misunderstood, miss. It won't get to London until three the *next* afternoon."

Suddenly feeling light-headed, Aidan steadied herself against the counter. "Wh-where can I catch a coach that will get me to London without delay? I must be there before sunup, a day hence."

"Probably Lincoln."

"How far is Lincoln?"

" 'Bout fifteen miles."

Aidan turned and rushed back through the door to find Stephen and explain the situation to him. The young man agreed to take her on to Lincoln. Would this night ever end? she wondered as the ungainly gelding hauled the shaky cart toward her next destination. *Oh, Justin!* her heart cried. *Forgive me, love. I'm coming!* And again she prayed for her husband's safety.

At nearly four in the morning, the pair entered the town of Lincoln. Finding the coaching inn, Stephen helped Aidan from the cart, then accompanied her through the doorway into the inn. Aidan was assured that the next coach to

London would have her there in plenty of time, so she purchased her ticket, then bade farewell to the young man who'd assisted her.

"In a few weeks, Stephen, you shall have yourself a fine new cart and a grand horse to pull it," she said, smiling her gratitude while fighting the urge to rub her aching back and sore bottom.

"Whatever ye say, ma'am," he replied, a doubtful frown marking his brow. "Good luck to ye." He walked from the inn, then pulled himself up into the rickety conveyance and set the gelding back onto the road, heading off toward the little village whence they'd come.

With the few coins she had left, Aidan had herself a light meal, then waited for the public stage, pledging to repay the abbess a thousand times more than what the woman had given her. As promised, the stage arrived at ten o'clock, and within moments Aidan was finally on her way back to London.

Aunt Patti entered the small cell to look at her nephew's bedeviled face. "Her Majesty sends her regrets," she said. "She truly grieves over what has happened to you—what will happen to you—but she cannot reverse the sentence of the court. The most she will do is keep the deed private. There are to be no crowds. Except for a few who have been granted special concessions, only those close to you will be allowed to share your final moments."

"So I am to be hanged, is it?" he asked tonelessly. "And for a crime I did not commit. What a travesty of justice."

"Her Majesty felt your trial was fair and quite expeditious. She—"

"Expeditious!" Justin shouted. "In the history of all Britain, nothing has taken place with such speed as did my trial. No doubt Atwood's influence played a large part in its swift end, as well as in my conviction. In the loss of my appeals too! Damn the man and damn his daughter!"

Aunt Patti's harsh gaze affixed itself to Justin's. "Were she to step through that door now, would you still wish to send her to perdition?" She watched as her nephew's troubled gaze fell from hers. "Instead of damning your wife, I suggest you pray for her immediate return. Perhaps your Maker will hear your pleas and send her to you, posthaste.''

"It's useless, Aunt. I've been praying for her return since the moment I found her missing. Obviously she does not want to come back to me. The question is, why?" Had it been his brutality? he wondered, thinking of how he'd punished her with his body, knowing she had good reason to leave him, never to return. God, why had he shown such anger, such cruelty?

"Perhaps she is unable to come back. She could be dead—not by your hand, but by another's. A thief may have—''

"No!" he cried, discounting the theory. "I'd know if she no longer lived! I'd feel it in my soul if she were gone from me forever. The gallows would be a welcome end to the torture I would feel over my loss. No, Aunt, she lives. I know it!''

Pattina reserved a knowing smile. He loves her, she thought. But his admission may have come too late. A pity for them both. "I shall wait with you, nephew. We shall not give up hope. There's still a chance—''

Justin's dark laughter erupted. "Always hopeful, eh? Earlier, Aunt, a bell was rung outside my door. It's the custom—the Execution Toll, as it is called—for those who are to die on the morrow.''

"You seem to have become even more jaded than you already were, Westover. Forget the bell," she snapped, already knowing of the custom. In her numerous investigations, she'd learned of the secret tunnel which connected the condemned hold at Newgate to the old St. Sepulchre's Church. A hand bell was carried through the passageway and rung outside a prisoner's cell on the eve of his execution. If it was done to remind the one who was to die to seek penitence, she could not say. But since there was a way into the prison, there was also a way out. "Perhaps a two-handed game of whist will perk you up," she said, withdrawing a deck of cards from her reticule. "Put the table over there so we might gain some comfort.''

The wooden legs scraped against the stone floor as Justin moved it toward his cot; the chair followed. "And what are the stakes, Aunt?" he asked, seating her.

"I shall wager you will live to be an old, old man, sir."

"Then I shall allow you to win each hand, Aunt. For my own bet would be, in less than twelve hours, I'd be swinging from the end of a rope. A gruesome thought, if you ask me."

"You must have faith, sir. Except for your father, no Warfield has ever gone down without a fight. And you shall not imitate your sire. Now, deal."

As Justin sat on the edge of his cot, shuffling the deck of cards, he eyed the aged Pattina suspiciously. "You know, Aunt, I'd swear you had another game besides whist in mind—one filled with intrigue, and of a deadly nature as well. Take care you don't find yourself at the end of a short rope with a long fall ahead of you, the same as me."

"You should know, nephew, the only rope I shall ever allow myself to wear is one made of pearls." She placed her hand on her withered thigh, repositioning the loaded pistol which was securely tucked into her garter and hidden beneath her skirts. "Now, on with the game."

"Indeed, madam," Justin replied, certain his aunt had a cunning yet solid plan in mind for his escape. "And may it end successfully for us both."

Raised torches lit the deserted roadway, casting eerie shadows on a small group of men. Taut muscles strained in unison as chests heaved outward in weighty effort while labored grunts escaped distended throats. Anxiously Aidan watched as the four men tried, without success, to lift the coach from the ditch where it had landed over an hour ago.

Lulled by the steady roll of the wheels, she'd stupidly gained a false sense of security. London was less than two hours away. Certain her worries were over, she'd thought Justin would be saved. Yet fate had reared its malicious head, and the instrument of its sordidness lay within inches of her.

A fallen tree limb had blocked the darkened roadway. Too late, the driver had caught sight of it. Reining in, he'd turned the galloping bays, sending them all into the ditch. Angrily Aidan kicked the gnarled limb; hot pain instantly shot through her toe and up her leg. Glaring her hatred at the thing, she hobbled back to where the small group of passengers stood watch, an enormous feeling of dread filling her soul.

"Give it up, men!" the coachman ordered, a low curse rolling through his lips as he rose and massaged his aching back. "There ain't no way we can move it. 'Sides that, the wheel's busted. Couldn't get another five yards on it even if we had to."

Anxiety screamed through her as Aidan extracted herself from the weary group of passengers. "Sir!" she cried wildly. "It's imperative I get to London before sunrise. Please, it's a matter of life and death!"

"Look, miss," the coachman said, wiping the sweat from his brow on the back of his forearm, "if ye want to set off walkin', fine. Otherwise there's not a thing I can do to help ye. I'm sendin' one of my men on ahead to the next village. It'll be daybreak or a little after afore he gets back."

"But that will be too late!"

"Sorry, but there ain't nothin' to be done." He turned toward one of the guards assigned to protect the coach. "Tom, break one of those bays free and head on into the next village. Have 'em send a smithy out with a new wheel."

Aidan snatched at the coachman's sleeve. "Can I go with him?"

"No, miss," he said, shaking her hand free. "It's against company rules."

Hysteria bubbled up within Aidan as she watched the man retrieve his coat and pistol from the ground. He tucked the weapon into his belt. "Please!" she whispered, forcibly fighting the riotous emotion which threatened to send her into a screaming rage. "There's no time. He'll be—"

His back aching unbearably, the coachman's nerves had gone suddenly raw with anger; he turned on her. "The word is no! So don't bother me none about it again!"

Foolishly Aidan pressed on. "Sir, I'm the Duchess of Westover— "

"And I'm Prince Albert!" the coachman snapped back, his eyes raking over her paltry garb. "The answer is no!"

Aidan bit her lip and watched as one of the bays was unharnessed, then led away from the others. If she could only find a way to procure the beast, she thought, her narrowed eyes settling on the loaded pistol in the coachman's belt. It was do or die, she decided, then rushed up to the man.

"Oh, sir, please hear me out!" she cried in a piteous voice, throwing herself full against him.

"Here, girlie! Stand back!" he ordered, grabbing her shoulders, thrusting her away. Aidan stumbled back, and the coachman's eyes widened. His pistol was pointed straight at his heart. "Give me that, miss," he said, slowly stretching his hand toward her. "You'll come to no good by doin' this. They'll stretch your neck for sure."

With a steady hand, Aidan kept the barrel leveled at the man's chest. "And you, sir, will find a lead shot in your heart. So keep yourself back." The coachman obeyed. "Now," she ordered, "have your man bring that horse over here."

"Tom," he called, "bring the bay to me."

The guard ambled toward the coachman, a length of leather lead held in his fist. "Does ye wants me to go or don't ye?" he asked in a perturbed voice.

"The little lady, here, has decided to take your place."

The man nodded toward Aidan, and Tom's eyes slowly followed; he blinked. "Don't get excited now, missy," the guard said. "Just hand me that there pistol."

"Instead, sir," Aidan rejoined, "you can hand me yours."

"Do as she says," the coachman commanded when the guard hesitated. "She's bent on gettin' to London. So don't nettle her none."

Tom slowly passed his weapon, butt-first, to Aidan, then he quickly stepped back. "Now, get on your knees," she ordered, pointing the weapons, one at each man.

Although she'd been speaking to the one called Tom, both men instantly fell to the ground, their noses bent to the earth. All the better for her, she thought, smiling to herself. Quickly she lowered the pistols. Hiking her skirts, she used their backs as stepping-stones as she vaulted astride the huge gelding.

"You may collect your horse at Westover House, London," she called as she grabbed up the leads, her heels kicking the gelding's flank. "And thanks for the loan of your weapons."

A double explosion ripped through the air; then the spent pistols fell to the ground beside the quavering men. Aidan was off down the road, a round of oaths following her into the night. With a little over two hours until sunrise, she began her litany anew, praying that she would make the old London gates before the rays of dawn scattered themselves across the sky.

Justin threw his cards on the table and rubbed the back of his neck. Even his loosened shirt collar, the buttons left undone to mid-chest, suddenly seemed too tight. "What time is it?" he asked.

"It grows close to dawn," Aunt Patti replied, her blue eyes scanning her nephew's tired face. "Perhaps you should rest."

"*Rest?*" He laughed raucously. "I shall soon be doing that for eternity."

The key rattled in the old lock; the door opened. "Ye have some visitors," the guard said. "A Lord and Lady Manley, they says."

Justin released a long breath, then came to his feet. "Send them in."

"Your Grace," Eugenia said, curtsying. "David and I came to—" Her eyes suddenly filled with tears. They choked her throat, and she shook her head, for she was unable to go on.

"There's no need for tears, Lady Manley," Justin said, taking pity on her. "Sometimes life deals us an unlucky hand. It appears I've been dealt mine."

"But it's not fair!" she cried anxiously. "I know she's still alive!"

"Has there been any word?" Aunt Pattina asked, looking to David.

"None, Lady Falvey," he replied despondently. "Your men have been unable to find a trace of her."

"We must not give up hope!" Eugenia cried. "There's still a chance . . . Oh, God! How foolish she is!"

A great sob overtook her, and as Justin and Pattina watched, David led his wife from the small cell. "Well, nephew," his aunt said. "I hear France is lovely this time of year."

Justin cracked a cynical smile. "And I've heard that hell is hotter than blazes."

"I'd much prefer France," his aunt countered, "but whatever the outcome might be, we shall go the distance together, nephew.''

Justin frowned. "I can't allow you to—"

"Don't argue with me. The Warfields have always championed one another, no matter what opposition they might face. It shall remain so this time, sir. I'll not be left without family to sustain me in my old age."

Justin shook his head. "You're a fiery old baggage, Aunt. Tenacious as they come. Too bad I didn't marry a woman exactly like you."

"You did, sir. You simply overlooked the fact."

The door squeaked open anew, drawing both Warfields' attention. "Ye has another visitor," the guard said, but before he could announce the name, Cynthia Danvers swept into the dank little room.

"Oh, Justin," she said, coming up to him. She raised herself up on tiptoes to press herself against him; her red lips touched his. When she received no response, she lowered her heels to the floor. "I can't believe this is really happening," she lamented soulfully.

"Believe it, Cynthia," Justin said without emotion. "The deed shall soon be done."

"My testimony—I couldn't lie, Justin!" she insisted, her fingers climbing up his chest, brushing the dark hair peeking through his open shirt.

"I never asked you to do so," Justin stated, removing her hand. "If you've come here to seek my forgiveness, then you've wasted your time. You only repeated my own words, as did everyone else. You see, Cynthia, I managed to convict myself. Now, I must beg your forgiveness, for I wish to spend my last moments with my aunt."

Taken aback by his dismissal, Cynthia scanned her former lover's face one last time, then quickly fled the cell. When the door closed, Justin turned to Aunt Patti. "I suppose you won't reconsider your plan?"

"I will not."

"Then hand me the pistol, Aunt. In your haste, you may very well blow off your own foot." He saw her questioning look and smiled. "Where else would a lady hide a weapon but beneath her skirts?"

Just as the dowager marchioness started to lift her gown,

the door burst open anew. Several men came through. "It's time, Your Grace," one of the men said as the great bell began to toll, summoning Justin to his execution. "Ye've a long walk ahead of ye to the gallows, so we'd best be goin'." The man produced a set of manacles and cuffed Justin's wrists behind him. "Sorry, but we cain't take no chances," he said, making certain the irons were secured.

Gray eyes settled on faded blue ones as Justin looked to his aunt. A message passed between them in what could very well be their last good-bye. Then Justin felt the guard's prodding hand on his shoulder, and he walked toward his cell door. *God! Where are you, Aidan! Save me, love!*

Aidan urged the lathered bay onward. The gelding's breath drew and released itself in great racking snorts as the nearly spent horse broke past the ruins of the old Roman wall and what was once a secured entry into London known as Bishopsgate. A violet hue painted itself across the sky, and within a short time the soft purple would turn to pink; then the fiery sun would top the eastern horizon to mark the beginning of a new day and the end of Justin's life.

Aidan kicked the steed's sides, and flying hooves hit the cobblestones at a frantic pace. Reining the horse to the right, Aidan turned onto Corn Hill. In the near distance, the dome of St. Paul's Cathedral loomed before her. Newgate Prison was just beyond, and Aidan's heart sang, for the sky was barely pink.

Suddenly the great steed faltered; it slowed, then toppled beneath her, throwing Aidan into the street. Dazed and badly bruised, she slowly drew herself up to her knees, then shook the buzzing sound from her head. There before her lay the bay. With a great blow from its lungs, it released its last breath.

Oh, God! she thought, coming to her feet. Why? She was so close, yet so far. Hiking her skirts, she stumbled across the street, then down the sidewalk. Tears blurred her vision as great sobs broke through her lips. *Oh, Justin!* her heart cried. *I'm coming, love! Please, God, keep him safe!*

Blindly she ran around a corner, the cathedral dome her guiding landmark; then she rushed into the street, where she caught sight of a conveyance only yards ahead of her. "Wait!" she screamed, then chased after it.

The vehicle pulled to a stop, and the man inside turned toward the disheveled woman. "Aidan!" George Edmonds cried in disbelief. By special consent, he'd been on his way to watch the life being choked from the blackguard who'd killed his beloved Aidan. But now? "My God! You're alive!"

Aidan leapt into the phaeton. "Get me to Newgate!" When the stunned George hesitated, she grabbed the reins and whip, then set the horse into a full gallop, throwing Lord Edmonds back into his seat. On the last turn, which led to the prison gate, Aidan glanced up at the sky. Riotous streaks of pink fanned out across its magnificent width. Dawn, she thought, praying it wasn't too late.

Pulling the reins, Aidan violently jerked the horse's head back, and before the phaeton had stopped, she leapt from the seat; George fought the beast down as it reared, then he, too, hopped to the ground.

Frantically Aidan's fists pounded the weathered gate. "Open up! Hurry!"

A small door opened within the larger one, and a man's head appeared. "Here! What's all the noise about!"

"Let me in!" she cried, noting the sky was lighter still. "My husband, the Duke of Westover, is about to be hanged! I have to stop it!"

Doubtful eyes scanned the woman in front of him. "Eh, go on with ye. This here ain't no public hangin'—Queen's orders."

"Sir, I'm the Duchess of Westover. Open that gate this instant!"

The man snorted. "So says ye! Move along, girlie."

Infuriated, Aidan glared at the man. A great bell began to toll, startling her. "What's that?" she cried, eyes wide.

"The duke's bein' summoned to his execution. In a few minutes it'll all be over."

Aidan felt certain she'd swoon. "Please, you must believe me. George, tell him," she pleaded, uncontrollable tears falling from her wild eyes. "Make him believe me!"

His brown gaze ran over her face. "It's too late, Aidan. The bell. I—"

"Won't anyone help me!" she screamed.

"Open that gate, sir!" a familiar voice bellowed from behind her, and Aidan spun around. "She's who she says she is!" Alastair stated. "Now, by God, do as I say!"

"Aye, Your Grace," the guard said, instantly recognizing the Duke of Atwood, for the man had been here several times, checking the workings of the gallows, and was one of the few to be granted permission to watch the hanging. "As you wish, sir." The door creaked open, and the threesome rushed inside.

"Get me to him," Aidan ordered the guard. "Hurry!"

"It's too risky," Justin whispered to his aunt as she stepped through the cell door into the dank corridor which led to the gallows; Eugenia, David, and Cynthia stood close by. "Someone could get hurt."

"Hurt!" Pattina lashed out in a low voice. "You're about to be gibbeted, sir. Do you think there's no pain involved?"

Two men suddenly grabbed Justin's arms while the third informed the others, "If ye are all goin' with him, ye'll have to follow a length behind." He wedged his girth between the small group and his condemned prisoner. "Now, move back."

Infuriated, Aunt Patti leaned one hand on her cane and, with the other, reached for her skirts. Seeing her movement, Justin yelled, "Pattina—don't!"

His cry erupted too late, for a withered hand had already pulled the pistol from her garter; cocking the pistol, she pointed it at the guard's head.

"Here, what do ye think ye'r doin'?"

"You'll not hang my nephew, sir," she stated coldly, her hand wobbling uncontrollably from the weight of the weapon. "Now, release him."

The guard eyed the frail woman. Suddenly his foot kicked out, striking the cane. Knocked off-balance, Aunt Patti stumbled; the pistol fell from her hand as she hit her head against the stone wall, rendering her unconscious. Eugenia and Cynthia screamed as a deafening explosion erupted. A volley of sparks flashed as the lead shot ricocheted down the narrow corridor.

Seeing his injured aunt lying on the filthy stone floor, Justin was filled with instant rage. With a feral cry he fought against his guards, but they held fast to his chained arms. "Aunt Patti!" he cried, his anxious eyes traveling over her fragile form. He noted her silver hair was turning red. "Someone help her!"

Eugenia moved, but the head guard, his own pistol drawn, motioned her back. "Stay put, all of ye!" He looked to his men. "Get him to the gallows!"

"I'll see all of you in hell!" Justin shouted, struggling against his bonds.

At the pistol's discharge, followed by screams, Aidan's heart had nearly stopped. Recovering, she rushed past the guard who was leading her to Justin, and ran down the lengthy corridor, George Edmonds at her heels. Finally rounding the corner she heard Justin's damning pronouncement. "Release him!" she cried, running toward him.

Hearing his wife's voice, Justin spun around. Silver eyes riveted themselves to Aidan. His heart swelled with momentary elation as he took in her disheveled appearance. Her hair tumbled wildly around her shoulders, her dress was tattered and dirty, but she was the most beautiful sight he'd ever seen. Then his gaze leapt to George Edmonds, and instantly his chest felt as though it had been crushed by a heavy stone.

What deception was this? he wondered, certain that he'd been made to suffer for naught. Cheat! he thought, a silent curse rolling through his mind. His aunt had risked her life to save him, while all along his wife had been alive and well, no doubt tucked away somewhere by her lover. Damn her for her subterfuge!

Forthwith he was hit by the force of Aidan's body as she threw herself against him, her arms encircling his neck. "Oh, Justin, I thought I'd be too late," she said, her joyous kisses raining themselves over his emotionless face. "Oh, love, thank God you're safe."

Abruptly she was jerked free of him. "Here, what do ye think ye'r doin'?" the head guard asked, his meaty hand bruising her arm. "Who do ye think ye are?"

"This, gentlemen," Justin said coldly, "is my deceased wife. Apparently her conscience has gotten the better of her, for she seems to have suddenly arisen from the dead."

Startled by the iciness of his words, Aidan stared up at her husband. Her troubled gaze traveled his stoic face; then she heard her father's words as they rebounded through the tunnel.

"Release that man!" Alastair commanded. "There will be no execution. He is innocent of the deed."

"Aye, Your Grace," the guard said, taking the keys from his belt.

As the manacles were released from his wrists, her husband's steely gaze attached itself to Aidan; a cold shiver ran the length of her body. "Justin, I—"

"Don't say a word, madam," he ordered in a frigid tone, his hands breaking free of their bonds. He turned and walked the few steps to his aunt, who was being attended by Eugenia. "Aunt Patti," he whispered almost painfully as he squatted beside her. She moaned, and he gently lifted her into his arms. "Lead me from this hellhole!" he ordered of his jailer.

"What's happened to her?" Aidan asked with an anxious cry when she noticed the blood. Justin remained impassive. "Aunt Patti?" she inquired of the unconscious woman; then her gaze rose to her husband. "Will she be all right?"

Forcefully, wordlessly, Justin brushed past Aidan, knocking her aside, his hard gaze centered on the guard who was leading him from the depths of the prison.

Dread filled Aidan's soul. "Justin, wait!"

"You've managed to create enough havoc to last him through eternity," Cynthia Danvers stated in a condemning voice. "The kindest thing you could possibly do now is to leave him in peace."

A wealth of tears flooded Aidan's eyes as she watched the blond rush off after Justin. They disappeared around the corner, and Aidan fell back against the wall. "Oh, God, will he ever forgive me?" Slowly she sank to the cold stone floor, her tormented sobs echoing upward through the unfeeling passageways of Newgate. Although his life had been spared, Aidan knew Justin's love was lost to her forever.

17

"Do you wish for one of us to come with you?" Eugenia asked as the carriage came to a stop. Her concerned gaze searched Aidan's pale face. "Perhaps if David and I were to speak to him—"

"No," Aidan cut in, troubled violet eyes viewing the elegant exterior of Westover House. Suddenly the place seemed cold and foreboding. "I must do this alone," she said, offering a weak smile. "Hopefully he will listen to me."

"We will wait for you here." A smile of encouragement crossed Eugenia's lips, letting Aidan know that they would not desert her. "I shall say a prayer that all goes well."

"Say more than one, Eugenia. I have a feeling the entire prayer book will be needed." Aidan stepped from the carriage, smoothed the skirt of the rough linen dress she still wore, then walked up the steps and set the knocker to the door.

As she waited in the small sitting room off the foyer, Aidan started to tremble. Less than an hour ago, she'd been ecstatic to see her husband, alive and well. Now she feared coming face-to-face with him and being the recipient of an impersonal look, cast upon her by his hard gray eyes—that was, if he consented to see her at all.

The events at Newgate seemed a blur to Aidan. One moment Justin had appeared overjoyed to see her; the next, he'd turned frigid, his glacial stare freezing her to the spot where she'd stood. Emotionlessly, indifferently, he'd rejected her. Yet she felt compelled to come here, so she might somehow explain, somehow beg his forgiveness, somehow make things right between them.

She felt a strange chill shiver along her spine. She turned to discover Justin in the doorway. His wintry gaze inspected her from head to foot. He seemed to be repelled by the sight of her.

"Why are you here?" he asked finally, his voice toneless.

Aidan drew a shaky breath. "Aunt Patti—is she. . . ?"

"She'll recover. The physician is with her now. Tell me, why are you here?"

"This is my home, and you are my husband. Where else should I be but with you?" she questioned with more bravado than she felt. On unsteady legs she moved closer to him. *Please don't reject me!* her heart cried. He remained silent, aloof. "Justin, I feel I must explain. I—" *Oh, God, how she wanted to throw herself at him, have his familiar arms surround her, hold her close, and to feel his masterful lips devour hers once more!* "I'm sorry for the pain, the torment I've caused you. I—"

A cold laugh erupted from his throat, silencing her. "Pain? Torment? You nearly caused my death!"

"I know that!" she cried, fearing he'd turn on his heel and leave her before she had the chance to explain. "I was wrong to run off like I did, but my pride wouldn't allow me to ask about the letter. I read it and I—"

"What goddamned letter!" he exploded.

"The one from Victoria—the one that said you'd receive your reward once you'd become intimate with me. I thought you only made love to me for your own personal gain. I know now, by running away, I was overly impetuous. The good sisters taught me—"

Sisters? The word rebounded through his head. "where the hell were you?"

"I was at a convent near Lincoln."

Justin digested the word. "A convent!" he shouted in disbelief, his hard gaze boring into her; Aidan felt as though she'd been speared straight through the heart. "I should have known," he said, just now remembering her shared thoughts about joining one on the night he'd carried her up the stairs, her tongue loosened by the drink. "No wonder you had managed to evade everyone who searched for you." His hand raked through his hair. "Damn you!" he denounced vehemently. Again he experienced the feelings of dread that had claimed him: fearing she might be dead, certain she wasn't, but unable to prove it. He thought of the trial, the accusations, the charges laid upon his head by her father, the Duke of Atwood, that he, Justin Warfield, the sixth Duke of Westover, was his own father's seed—a cold-blooded murderer! Then Justin remembered the sentence that had been imposed upon him all because of her impetuousness.

His head spun as he relived the fears he'd felt; his mind's eye envisioned the noose tightening around his throat, his feet dropping into endless space, and his neck cracking as the hemp jerked taut against it. Suddenly his ire rose to choke him. "Damn you!" he spat at her anew.

Aidan felt the force of his anger, and she instantly stepped back. "Justin, please listen to me. This is all my fault, I know. The letter . . . the mention of a reward . . . Oh, God! I love—"

"Silence." The word hissed through his clenched teeth. "No more of your lies!" His cold gaze pinpointed her; he steeled himself against the emotional pain etched on her face. "All this because of a letter. Had you stayed around to ask me what the word 'reward' meant, I would have told you our Queen referred to our forthcoming children! Since Victoria is ecstatic over the near-arrival of her first issue, I suppose she believes everyone should be filled with jubilation over the prospect of having one of his own! But no, you had to run off!"

Justin moved toward her; although frightened, Aidan held her ground. Hard eyes glaring, he stopped within inches of her.

"Your little escapade has convinced me, dear wife, that this marriage is nothing more than a farce—has been from the onset. Because of your impetuosity, your immaturity, our private lives have been put on public display for all to see. I was nearly gibbeted because of your irresponsible behavior. And my aunt lies injured because of your callousness. Had I any way to rid myself of you, I would. But as it stands, I've no way out. Except, madam, to get you as far away from me as possible. Tomorrow, Potts will take you to Warfield Manor, where you'll henceforth remain. Now, get out of my sight!''

He turned on his heel, and Aidan rushed after him, her hand pulled at his arm. "Justin, please! I didn't mean—" With a harsh curse, Justin shook her free; she stumbled and nearly fell.

"Pitkin!" he ordered, once he'd hit the hall. "See Her Grace to the door!"

Afflicted violet eyes watched as Justin disappeared up the stairs, his strides firm, unrelenting; a scream of protest rose to Aidan's throat, where it quickly died. Sadly she realized his ears were eternally closed to her, along with his heart. Her vision blurred by a heavy film of tears, Aidan slowly left Westover House, forever banished from its walls by her husband.

A bright mid-October sun washed over Aidan as she sat on a long stone bench, her violet eyes staring lifelessly at the withering gardens behind Warfield Manor, where she'd been exiled. But the soft golden rays of sunshine gave her no warmth. Condemned to spend her life away from the man she loved, she felt dead inside, as dead as the falling leaves that swirled around her on a light autumn breeze.

Justin, she thought, the pain of his loss compressing her heart. A single tear slipped from her eye to drop onto the open letter which lay on her lap. Slowly her gaze fell to it, and she stared at Eugenia's neat handwriting, then read the missive again.

I'm sorry, dear friend, but he refuses to listen to anything anyone says. One mention of your name, and his eyes turn as cold as a gray winter's day. I understand he plans to stay in London, instead of retreating to the country, like most of us do this time of year. He's lost weight and his features have frozen themselves into a stoic mask. I've yet to see him smile, but others have; however, I've been told there's no light in his eyes when he does so. From all reports, he seems bent on his own destruction. Late nights and too much brandy seem to be the course he's set for himself of late. Although I hesitate to do so, I suppose I must tell you that he's been seen quite frequently in the company of Cynthia Danvers. Why, dearest Aidan, he re-

fuses to forgive you or to even hear your explanation, I cannot say. But I feel what troubles him goes much, much deeper than either of us really knows. I shall pray for you both. One day, I'm certain, he'll see the error of his ways. Until then, don't give up hope. Remember you must have faith.

Hope? Faith? An impossibility, Aidan thought dejectedly, remembering Justin's cold dismissal of her. He hated her, she was certain.

"If you sit there much longer, undoubtedly a pigeon will take to roosting in your hair."

Aidan spun around. "Aunt Patti!" she cried, coming to her feet, hugging the woman. "When did you arrive?"

"Nearly ten minutes ago. Most of that time I've been watching you." She noted how Aidan's hopeful gaze had centered itself on the house. "I came alone, dear," she said, gently patting her niece's hand. "Now, tell me how you are."

"I'm fine," Aidan lied, her gaze refusing to meet that of the dowager marchioness. "But what of you? Is your injury healed? Should you be moving about?"

"Quit popping off so many questions at me," Aunt Patti reproved, "and sit down." She motioned to the bench with her cane. "Ah, that's better," she said, once they were seated. She turned her eyes on Aidan. "Now, in answer to your inquiries, I'm in excellent condition. It will take more than a mere bump on the head to see me to my end. Had I spent another day lying about Westover House, as my nephew insisted I do, I'd have gone completely mad! Yes, I most surely should be up and moving about!"

Aidan's gaze traveled out over the gardens. "How is Justin?" she asked in a small voice.

"Temperamental, brooding—he's acting like a child of three, which unfortunately is a typical Warfield trait reserved mainly for the males in the family. I could no longer stand to be near him, so I escaped to the countryside to find some peace." Aunt Patti's gaze lowered to the letter lying on the ground. "What's this?" she asked, moving it toward her with her cane.

She stooped from the waist, intending to retrieve it, but

Aidan's hand snatched it up. "A letter from Eugenia," Aidan said, folding it over.

"And?"

"She sent me word on what's been happening in London."

"I suppose she's told you about Cynthia Danvers as well."

"She has," Aidan admitted as her concentration dropped to her hands and the letter they held. "Lady Manley has said that Justin has taken up with her again."

"Rubbish! The chit has tried to foist herself off on him. He uses her as an ornament to hang on his arm."

"I'm certain there's more to it than that, Aunt Patti. She was his mistress before I met him. No doubt she's his mistress again."

Pattina's blue eyes snapped with fire as she inspected her downtrodden niece. "For the sake of argument, let's say they *are* involved again. Are you willing to let some showy trollop like Cynthia Danvers win over your husband's affections without the slightest whimper of protest?"

"H-he doesn't want me," Aidan defended. "He's said so himself."

"Nonsense!" she retorted, her tone censuring. "You heard his pride talking, not his heart. But if you continue to sit here licking your wounds as you have been doing this past month, I've no doubt you'll lose him. He's a man, with a man's needs. So, dear niece, if you don't want him crawling back into that blond slattern's bed, where he'll bestow upon her the pleasures he once gave you, I suggest you make a stand! And it had best be done quickly!"

"I . . . I don't think I can do it," Aidan whispered, fearing Justin's rejection anew. "He was most adamant about never seeing me again."

Aunt Patti rose with a thump of her cane. "I thought you had more spunk than that, girl. Perhaps I was wrong. Maybe you're like all the other simpering little creatures my nephew has been trying to escape since he was of a marriageable age. I do know one thing, though," she said, her shoulders squaring, "if he were my husband, I'd be in London right now, fighting tooth and nail for him! Whatever it took, whether it be acting the obedient wife or playing the whore in his bed, I'd do it just so long as I won him back! Think on it, Aidan. You can either sit here the rest of your life, withering away like some old spinster, or you can get off your backside and go after him! You've nothing to lose by trying."

Aidan looked to Justin's aunt. She had nothing to lose—except her pride, she thought. Damn her pride! That was how she'd lost Justin in the first place. "You're right, Aunt Patti. I'll do it!" she said, coming to her feet, a smile lighting her face, the first in weeks. "I can't give him up without a fight."

"Clever girl," Aunt Pattina commented. "I knew you'd come to your senses."

"That's why you came here, isn't it?"

"I came to Warfield Manor to find some peace and quiet, not to be depressed by your overly morose mood. By the same token, I had to escape Westover House for the same reason. The two of you would make a perfect set of corpses," she said of Justin and Aidan. "Now, let's go into the house and have some tea."

The pair walked arm in arm up the path to the great house, Aidan's mood far lighter than it had been in days. As they had their tea and cakes, Aunt Patti suggested several possible ways of throwing the couple together again.

"You're really quite the matchmaker," Aidan said, laughing at the woman's last scenario. "I can see it now," Aidan said. "He'll come home and slip into his bed to find me lying there naked. If I know his temper, he'll probably toss me through the window."

"Or he may instantly succumb to your womanly beauty, dear. Despite what you might think, I'm certain he's not had carnal contact with a woman since you left him. As virile as my nephew is, I imagine he's feeling quite like a parched field that is suffering under hot sun and an extended drought. One look at your loveliness and his thirst will have to be slaked."

Aidan blushed. Most women Aunt Patti's age would die rather than speak of such things. She was quite then enigma, Aidan thought. One moment she was extremely concerned with propriety; the next, she was speaking her mind in whatever terms she chose. "I'll think about it," she said of the dowager marchioness's idea.

"Well, while you're doing that, I shall take myself off for a rest." She rose slowly, then headed for the doorway. "I'll see you at supper."

The young duchess watched from the sitting-room door as the older woman ambled up the stairs. When Aunt Patti had disappeared, Aidan turned and made her way back out into the gardens. Strolling the paths, she felt the sunshine warm her, rejuvenate her, and she breathed in the fresh clean air, happy to be alive.

Her movements eventually took her beyond the gardens and into a small copse, then out into a field, its long grasses gently waving in the breeze. Deep in thought on how she could possibly reclaim her husband, she discounted several pretentious schemes which Aunt Patti had suggested, then settled on what she thought was the best and most viable way to approach the problem—honesty. She would go back to London and ask Justin for a moment of his time, then maturely discuss their difficulties, confessing her love for him. If that didn't work, she'd do as Aunt Patti had proposed. Whatever it took, she had to get him back.

Suddenly Aidan heard movement behind her. She spun around; a relieved sigh escaped her lips. "Heavens, you gave me a start! What are you doing here?" No reply came forth as a hand clamped itself around her wrist and pulled her toward the awaiting horse. "Let go of me!" she cried, struggling against the force of the grip. "Let me loose or I shall scream!"

Aidan opened her mouth to liberate her shriek, when suddenly a hard fist clipped her on the jaw. Pain shot upward into her temples as her world spun wildly. Fighting for consciousness, she gave it up; blackness overtook her.

Justin lowered the missive which had just arrived by special messenger from his aunt. "Missing, huh? Another one of her tricks, no doubt."

"Did you say something, sir?" Pitkin inquired.

"No," the Duke of Westover replied, tossing the note onto the silver tray. "I'll be out all day—possibly past midnight. Don't bother waiting up."

With one last look at the note, he dismissed it as being

inconsequential, then strode through the door to his awaiting carriage to collect Cynthia Danvers for their outing.

Aunt Patti marched from the darkened doorstep into the candlelight elegance of Westover House. "Take me to my nephew," she announced to the butler, squaring her frail shoulders as she did so.

"He's not in," Pitkin replied.

Instantly the butler blanched as his master's deep chuckle filtered across the hallway from the small dining room, to be followed by a woman's seductive laughter.

"Not in?" Aunt Patti poked Pitkin with her cane. "Get out of my way." She walked across the hall, then stopped in the open doorway to see Cynthia Danvers, her chair angled close to Justin's, raising her mouth toward her nephew's. The young duke seemed to hesitate; then his head lowered in response. Her eyes narrowing, the dowager marchioness whacked her cane against the door, startling the couple apart before their lips met. "Have you no scruples, sir?" she asked, her censuring gaze riveted to her nephew.

"It's been stated, several times, I do not," he replied, leaning back in his chair. "In actuality, I believe you were the one who first informed me of the fact. Why are you here?" he asked, certain he would discover the reason whether he inquired or not.

"Since you ignored the message I sent you three days ago, telling you that your *wife* is missing, I decided to come to London to make certain you had received it."

"I did."

"Well?"

"I suggest you check the convents. She may have decided to take another sudden sabbatical."

Infuriated by her nephew's callous words, Aunt Patti struck her cane against the dining-room table; Cynthia jumped. "You pigheaded dolt!" she accused hotly. "While you sit here wining and dining this . . . this used piece of goods, your wife could be suffering great danger!"

Justin eyed his aunt at length. "Cynthia, will you please excuse us? The dowager marchioness and I have need of privacy."

Cynthia rose. "Since your aunt seems to have a lot on

her mind, I shall see you on the morrow," she said, then deliberately placed a kiss on Justin's cheek. "Good night, darling."

As the blond swayed past the dowager marchioness, Pattina squared her shoulders anew. "Mrs. Danvers," Lady Falvey said for their ears alone; Cynthia looked down on Justin's aunt. "You might have better luck in seeking your fortune if you were to search out a man who is not already married. Who is to say? The fool might just propose and give you a modicum of respectability—something you now lack."

Affronted, Cynthia glared her discontent at Aunt Patti, then tossed her head and swept through the open door.

Justin had noted the blond's sudden stiffness. "Passing judgment again, are we?" he asked sarcastically.

Aunt Patti ambled closer to her nephew. "As the saying goes, sir: 'If the cap fits, put it on.' "

His lips spread into a cool smile. "And I suppose you have a quaint little saying for me as well."

"Indeed, sir, I do. Like the dull-witted Nero, you seem content to sit and play your fiddle while all Rome burns. Your wife is missing and you do nothing to find her!"

"And I say she's cried wolf one too many times. Her penchant for deception is repulsive. I'll not play her games, Aunt."

"Games!" Pattina shrieked. "You foolish pup! You are a jaded, cynical, coldhearted man, Justin Warfield. You've allowed your parents' obsessions and jealousies to taint your views of what a real marriage and true love actually are. You speak of your wife's deception, sir. But I propose that the real deception is your own. Look deep into your heart, nephew. I doubt very much that you can truthfully say you don't love her. And if you persist in hiding your feelings, you shall pay for the gravity of your lies. This I promise you!" She turned on her heel. "I shall be at War-field Manor," she said over her shoulder. "If she still lives, I pray that you come to your senses before you've lost her forever."

Justin sat motionless, listening to his aunt's cane make a rapid tap across the marble floor. With a loud thump, the front door closed behind her. Love her? he questioned himself. Hell, yes, he loved her! But he refused to allow himself to suffer the heartache that was associated with the emotion. Jaded, cynical, coldhearted—in truth, he was all those things. Yet there was a reason behind that sordid side of his character. And he seemed unable—or unwilling—to abolish its presence from his soul.

Yet, if Aidan were in trouble . . . No! He'd not fall into that trap yet another time. She'd tricked him more than once. And he'd not allow himself to be duped again!

Throwing his napkin onto his untouched plate, Justin rose and strode from the small dining room into the foyer. Certain his sanity was on the verge of shattering, he decided to escape the house. The place was filled with memories of his wife, and he could no longer sit within its walls, constantly thinking of her. "I'll be out for a while, Pitkin," he announced curtly. "Don't wait up for me."

Not wanting to see Cynthia anytime soon, for the woman was beginning to wear on his nerves, he ordered Potts to take him to White's. No doubt he'd discover yet another ribald tale about the Duke of Westover being spread by his peers. Upon hearing it, he might have a laugh or two himself.

"I tell you, Westover, the man has gone completely mad," Sir Percival Filbert said with a sniff.

Justin watched as Sir Percival raised his drink to his lips, took a swallow of his brandy, then set himself to rocking back and forth on his feet; the habitual motion began to annoy Justin.

"He had taken to mumbling to himself—acting most peculiar," Filbert continued. "Then, about four or five, maybe six days ago, he paid off all his debts here at White's and has presumably left town. No one has seen him since. Lord Quigley said the man told him he was leaving London permanently . . . said something about 'claiming what was rightfully his,' I believe. I suppose he was speaking of an inheritance or something of that nature." Filbert swallowed another sip of brandy. "Anyway, I thought perhaps you should know about this. With his father off in India—although I'd thought the man was to have returned by now . . . oh, well—I assume your aunt would be the person responsible for him should the poor fellow have gone crackbrained on us. Most peculiar situation, indeed." He stopped his monotonous sway. "By the by, how goes it with your wife these days?" he inquired. "Hasn't run off on you again, has she?"

Sir Percival looked around him to see the Duke of Westover striding out the door. "Touchy fellow," he said to himself, then traipsed over to make conversation with another one of his peers.

Outside White's, Justin's feet hit the walkway at a full run. "Potts! Get me home fast!" he ordered, vaulting into his carriage.

Damn! Why had he ignored his aunt's warnings? he wondered as the conveyance careened through the London streets, Justin cursing his own stupidity, along with his abominable pride. Sir Percival's story was not the only one he'd heard this evening concerning George Edmonds's strange behavior of late. Like all the rest, though, he'd tried to ignore the obvious.

To claim what was rightfully his. Filbert's words rolled through his head. George had abducted Aidan! Or had she willingly run off with him? No! He remembered how she'd tried to confess her love, and his cold denial of it, telling her he didn't want to hear her lies, seeing the devastated look on her face when he'd done so. She'd been taken by George; he was certain of it. What had she been made to suffer because of his callousness, his refusal to believe that she was in danger? Oh, God! What a fool he was! *Aidan!* his heart cried, no longer able to deny his love for her. *Hold on, love!*

As soon as the carriage stopped at Westover House, Justin commanded Potts to have Apollo saddled and waiting. Once he was through the doorway, he barked orders at Pitkin, who had not yet retired, to procure him several days' worth of food. Then Justin bounded up the stairs to his rooms.

Dressed in black from head to foot, Justin watched as his stallion was led into the mews. A leather bag containing food and water, plus an extra weapon, along with shot and powder, was strapped to Apollo's saddle. With a loaded pistol tucked into his belt, Justin bounded to the steed's back.

"Pitkin," he stated, trying to control the prancing horse, "send word to my aunt that I'm on my way to Moorsfield. Tell her of my suspicions. And you'd best inform the Duke of Atwood as well. Should I not succeed, someone will need to win the duchess's safety." He looked to his coachman. "Potts, make sure he doesn't forget."

With a kick of his heels, Justin sent the horse into a restrained gallop through the London streets. But once they hit the Great North Road, he let Apollo pace himself at a hungry, mile-eating stride. Like two black souls intent on destruction, man and beast aimed themselves toward the Yorkshire moors.

18

Fierce gray clouds swept across the desolate moors, the evening sky growing darker and darker. Locked inside Moorsfield's impregnable turret, dampness seeping from its cold stone walls, Aidan pressed her forehead against the dirt-smudged windowpane, watching as the volatile thunderheads ripened in intensity beyond. The menacing elements sadly reminded her of Justin's eyes when she'd seen him last—roiling with contempt—and forlornly she wished, in that last shared moment of time, he had viewed her with gentle affection instead. But whether his silvery gaze had shone with tenderness or with anger, she was certain she'd never look upon his beloved countenance again.

A jagged sigh escaped her as she was overcome with a sudden bout of weakness. Her head spun crazily as her stomach rumbled in vicious protest over its lack of nourishment. How long had she been here? she wondered, fighting off the blackness which threatened to overtake her. Three days? Four? Yes, four, she decided, unable to fully remember the exact count. Everything had suspended itself in a deepening haze. To Aidan, nothing seemed real anymore.

Lightning volleyed above the darkened landscape, and Aidan blinked. Had she seen it? Or was she hallucinating again? More than once, she thought she'd espied someone on the barren wasteland, far below her, but she discovered the apparition had been nothing other than her hopeful imagination, which only added to her anguish. What sensibilities she could gather now told her it was a horseman. Both he and his steed appeared to be as black as night. Death! He was coming for her! Strangely she realized she'd welcome his arrival. Anything was better than being kept prisoner, day after day, only to be tortured by her crazed jailer, for George Edmonds had gone completely mad!

Feeling the sting of tears behind her eyes, Aidan eased herself down from the rough-hewn stool she stood upon, taking great care not to jostle herself. Quivering hands wiped the salty spillage from her cheeks, and she breathed deeply. Dear God, if only she could end this torment, she thought, gazing at her cold, heartless prison, all hope of salvation lost to her.

She shuddered as she viewed the depressing room, centuries of cobwebs knit high in the corners, years of dust overlying the timeworn stone floor. She noted how her footprints marked a narrow path through the powdery grime, where she continually traversed the space from window to door, then back again. Was someone else kept prisoner here? she wondered, certain she felt a ghostly presence always close by. Perhaps the poor unknown soul had died within the bounds of her cell, forever haunting it, as Aidan felt sure was to be her fate as well.

The key scraped into the lock, and Aidan's whole body jerked at the sound. What torment would he inflict on her this time? she wondered, wild violet eyes watching as the door slowly opened.

George stepped inside and pocketed the key. One hand balanced a tray, a lighted candle atop it. Instantly the aroma of hot food drifted across the small space to fill Aidan's nostrils, making her mouth water. But she knew the provender would come with a condition. As always, she'd be asked to submit to him—lie with him as though she were his wife. Then, and only then, would he feed her.

"Get out!" she screamed, not certain she could endure his calculated torture much longer. All that had sustained her each day was water—just barely enough to drink and to lightly bathe. Suddenly the pleasant odor of what she craved most turned sickening. Nausea overtook her and she rushed to the chamber pot. Her stomach twisted painfully as she retched futilely, and Aidan cursed George, cursed his parentage, and cursed herself for not ending her life by throwing herself from the galloping horse the day he'd abducted her. Finally she straightened to wipe a shaky hand over her face and hatred filled her eyes. "Get out, I said. The answer is still no!"

"Aidan, my darling," he coaxed, setting the tray and candle holder onto the small wooden table, "you must eat something. You're ruining your health."

"Don't call me darling! It is you, George, who are ruining my health. I'll not eat if the conditions are the same. There is no way I'll willingly share your bed. Now, leave me!"

"My darling, come sit," he said as though he hadn't heard her. "Your food grows cold."

"Get out and take it with you!"

His brown gaze slipped over her. "There are no longer any conditions, Aidan, darling. You must eat. You grow thin and overly weak. Now, come. Eat for me."

Aidan stared at him and instantly noted the strange glow in his eyes. A trick, she thought, her mind urging caution. Somehow she had to escape him. But in order to do so, she needed to regain her strength. "I will eat, but you must leave the room."

"My lovely, Aidan, I'll not leave, but I promise not to give you cause for alarm. I love you, Aidan. You should know I'd never hurt you. Now, come, sit . . . eat. I will remain away from you while you do so."

She watched as he moved over to the open door to lean a shoulder against its jamb. Slowly she moved toward her small cot, then wedged herself between the rough wooden table and the rickety little bed. Lowering herself to the rush-filled mattress, she lifted the linen napkin covering her fare.

Stale bread peered up at her, along with some moldy cheese; her stomach lurched, forcefully objecting to the unappealing offerings. Then she tipped the saucer, which capped a bowl, to find some hot broth. It was the best of the three, she decided, but as the steam rose upward, she realized it was far too hot to eat.

Through lowered lashes, she peered at George, then back to the hot broth; her heart leapt wildly in her chest. "George," she said cautiously, her hands centering themselves around the bowl. As she lifted it, the heat seared her fingers; valiantly, she held fast. "I can't eat this," she said, her face twisting with aversion. "Look! There's something most distasteful floating in my broth."

"That hag!" he exclaimed, referring to the old woman he'd hired as a cook. Shortly after he'd dismissed Moorsfield's meager staff several months ag0e. He moved toward the table. "She's half-blind, my darling. Were she still here, and not on her way home, I'd strap her one." He looked into the bowl. "I don't see anyth—"

Instantly the scalding broth flew into his face, and with a yell, George stumbled back and Aidan was out the door. Her head spun crazily as she ran down the spiral stone steps, blazing torches lighting her way. As she fought against her dizziness, she could hear George's heavy footsteps following close behind. *Oh, God, let met get free!* she cried silently, her feet rapidly slipping down the worn stone until a heavy door blocked her path. Frantic fingers grabbed the ancient handle, and she twisted, then pulled, but it would not move. Hitting her shoulder against the door, she tried to break free. Hysteria bubbled up inside her as she realized she was trapped.

"It's locked, my darling," George said, his fingers dangling the key on high; Aidan fell back against the door, her frightened eyes watching his every move. "I'm not a fool, Aidan," he said, a strange smile settling on his mottled face, his burns showing bright red in the torchlight. "I thought you might try to escape me. But your attempt has come to no avail."

He descended the last few steps and advanced on Aidan. "What are you going to do?" she cried, her fear rising to choke her.

"It's time I claim what is rightfully mine." He pulled her away from the door; then his long pale fingers twisted in her coppery hair, holding her in place so she wouldn't bolt. "Now, my darling," he said, inserting the key and releasing the lock, "we shall retire to my room."

"No!" she cried as he dragged her through the door and into the darkened hallway. "George, I don't belong to you. I belong to Justin."

"He stole you from me!" His hand tightened in her hair as his hard strides forced her toward his room. "Oh, had he only been hanged for his deceit, how very easy it would have been. I went there to watch it, you know. I'd hoped to glory in his struggles—hear his neck crack, watch his face turning black as he strangled. If you hadn't stopped it, we could have been married, my darling. Until I've found a way to permanently rid ourselves of him, we'll have to live together without the benefit of having said our vows," he said, stopping outside his room. In the dim light from the open door to the turret, his gaze ran hungrily over Aidan's face. "You're mine, darling, and shall remain so. No one will ever take you from me again."

Wide-eyed, Aidan watched as his face lowered toward hers. Startled into action, she thrust her head aside as her fists struck at his face and chest. "No!" she cried, attacking him. "Don't!"

Angered by her assault, George jerked against her hair; a distressed cry escaped her lips. With his full weight, he pinned her against the closed door. "Don't? You deny me what is mine?" His hand cupped a breast, squeezing it between his fingers, causing pain to shoot through Aidan. "This is mine . . . and so is this."

His hard hand thrust itself between her thighs to roughly paw at her, while his wet mouth pressed against her neck. The orchid silk dress and voluminous petticoats she wore obstructed his hold; he pulled back to tear at the encumbrance.

Riotous fear coursed through Aidan, for she knew, in his madness, he was intent on raping her! Wildly she fought against him; her scalp hurt unbearably as he tried to subdue her. Then with a frenzied effort she drew up her knee, hitting him in the groin; instantly he released her as he doubled over, his body racked in sick agony.

Aided by the light that bled through the turret door, Aidan struck a fast run for the stairs. Her hand grabbed the rail, and she rushed down the murky void, heading toward the lower level and hopefully her freedom.

Thunder clapped loudly, rattling the entire house, scaring Aidan. Lightning struck anew, flashing through the windowpanes. Its eerie light quickly died, a booming rumble replacing its blue glow. Bent on her downward flight, she rounded the landing and fled down a half-dozen steps toward the front door. She had to escape!

Suddenly she ran headlong into a sturdy form; a startled cry escaped her as a strong arm clamped itself around her waist. A scream rose to her throat, for in the blackness she crazily imagined it was George. Nearly hysterical, she struggled against the powerful hold. "Oh, God, no!" Intense light streaked from the sky outside the window, illuminating the stairs again. "Justin!" she cried in disbelief; then she instantly sobered. "I-is it really you?" she asked, fearing he was an illusion, another trick of her mind.

"Yes, sweet," he whispered throatily. His pistol held near her waist, he crushed her tight against his pounding chest. His heart threatened to burst with joy. Thank God she's safe, he thought; then he released her. "Apollo's waiting outside. Let's go."

"Stay where you are," George commanded from just above them. A blue glow lit the stairwell again as thunder clapped anew; in the brief flash, Justin saw a cocked pistol leveled on his wife's back. "Put your weapon aside," Edmonds ordered, motioning to the duke's hand; carefully Justin crouched and laid it on the step. "Release her, Westover," George said, satisfied his opponent no longer posed a threat to him. "Send her to me. Or she'll be lost to us both."

With Aidan caught between them, Justin knew he had no recourse but to do as George bade. "Go to him," he whispered, his hands turning her, urging her upward.

"No!" Aidan cried, hesitating.

"Do as I say!" he ordered harshly, fearing that George was just crazy enough to shoot her. Once she was with Edmonds, Justin had no doubt that George would fire the pistol at him. His weapon empty, the viscount could no longer threaten Aidan with it. With luck, she might be able to break free and flee the house to the awaiting Apollo. "Go!" he repeated.

On nervous legs Aidan climbed the four steps that separated George and herself. Instantly he grabbed her and spun her around, his arm pulling her tight against him. "Farewell, Westover," George said, aiming the pistol at Justin's heart.

Realizing his intent, Aidan hit his arm. Powder flashed as a deafening explosion ripped through the air. She saw her husband stagger. "Justin!"

He heard his wife's scream, then felt the sting on the outer edge of his cheek; blood trickled from the nick down to his clenched jaw. His eyes centered themselves on the shadowy George Edmonds, and with a snarl, Justin bounded up the steps after him.

Instantly fearing for his life, George shoved Aidan into the oncoming Duke of Westover. Catching her before she tumbled down the stairs, Justin pressed her against the banister, then scrambled up after the fleeing man, snagging him at the top of the stairs.

Through the shadows, Aidan watched as the two men struggled above her. Fists flew furiously; then suddenly the two combatants lost their balance. Rolling bodies, arms and legs entwined, tumbled toward her; a booted foot hit her own. With a cry, she felt herself falling; flailing arms reached out, her hand seizing the spindles supporting the smooth banister. Her bottom hit the steps twice, then stopped. A grateful sigh whispered through her lips; then she thought of Justin.

Frightened eyes caught sight of two sprawled forms at the bottom of the stairs. Which was her husband and which was her nemesis, she could not tell. Then, while she watched, one man slowly struggled to his knees. Fearing it was George, Aidan reached for the discarded weapon lying at her feet, and pointed it at the man.

"Justin?" she asked, but received no answer. "Answer me!" she cried as she cocked the pistol. Unsteady hands aimed the weapon at the man as he loomed upward, coming to his feet. "I'll shoot if you don't!"

"About now, madam, I wish you would. It should put me out of my misery."

Hearing his familiar voice, Aidan lowered the pistol and flew down the stairs. "Dear God! Are you all right?"

"I will be," Justin replied, taking the pistol and uncocking it, to lay it aside. Then he stooped down beside George. As he gazed at the motionless man, lightning flashed, its eerie glow exposing a gruesome sight. Justin came to his feet and sheltered Aidan from its ugliness. "He still lives, but he's broken his neck. I think his windpipe is crushed." Aidan tried to look around him, but Justin stopped her. "No, you don't need to see him. Take yourself into the other room. I'll call you when it's over."

Before Aidan could move, a strangled gasp gurgled from George's throat, drawing the couple's attention. Then, as the life drained from the man's body, blue fire lit the stairwell again, revealing Lord Edmonds' face—a hideous face that was swollen and appeared black as night.

Aidan quickly turned away. George had received what he'd meant for Justin. Realizing how close her husband had come to meeting a similar end, Aidan suddenly went weak. "Take me away from here," she pleaded, a sob rising within her chest.

"The storm—it's not safe."

"Please, Justin! I can't bear another minute in this horrid place."

Feeling her fear, Justin knew he had to get her away from Moorsfield. Quickly he led her into what he supposed was the sitting room. Easing her down into a chair, he strode to the window and detached the ties from the draperies. With a quick jerk, he ripped one free of its anchors; years of dust showered the air. "Stay here," he ordered Aidan, then strode into the hallway and covered George's lifeless body. Upon his return, he pulled the second drapery free. "The rains have begun. We'll use this for cover."

"Where are we going?" Aidan asked, coming to her feet.

"There's a stable out back. That's as far as I'm willing to take you in this storm."

"So long as it's away from the house," she said, moving alongside her husband to the front door.

Justin draped the heavy brocade over them. "Ready?"

"Yes."

At a twist of Justin's wrist, the door flew open and the

pelting rains blew in; with a burst of speed, the couple headed toward the stable, their way marked by a barrage of lightning. Once inside, Justin told Aidan he'd be back shortly; then he headed out into the downpour for Apollo. After what seemed an eternity, he finally returned.

Striking a flint, Justin lit several candles he'd procured from the house and placed them in their holders. As Aidan set them around on some high, level boards, brightening the interior of the building, Justin led a skittish Apollo to a distant stall. With the stallion attended to, he returned to the spot where his wife stood, a large leather bag, along with several quilts, tucked under one arm.

"What's all this?" she asked, her curious gaze climbing to her husband's handsome face. "You're bleeding!" she cried, just now noting the deep scratch high on his right cheekbone. "Let me have a look."

Justin caught her hand as it rose toward his face. "In a moment, sweet. First, let's make some comfort for ourselves."

Within minutes he'd mucked out a stall, then spread a fresh blanket of hay, whereupon he placed the quilts he'd taken from the house. Although they were a bit damp, he believed they would afford Aidan more comfort than the straw alone. Strangely, as he worked, he felt himself over-powered by a sense of awkwardness. Never had he been stricken with the inability to vocalize his thoughts, especially to a woman.

How could he explain his feelings to her, beg her forgiveness, and confess his love when the ghosts from his past stood between them? Somehow he had to purge himself of the anguish, the contempt, the distrust, and the hatred he'd borne inside him all these years. Because of those dark feelings, Aidan had suffered. So had he. Through it all, hers was a heart so innocent. Now it was time he set himself free of the encumbrances that had kept them apart.

Aidan's teeth edged themselves along her lower lip as she watched Justin smooth the covers over the straw. One moment he'd seemed glad to see her, hold her in his arms; the next, he'd become cool, pensive, a deep frown marking his brow. He'd been given his chance to be rid of her, but he hadn't taken it. Perhaps now he wished he had.

"Sweet," he said, looking up at her from where he rested on bent knees. "Welcome to your new abode."

In the dim candlelight, Aidan gazed at his outstretched hand, then slowly made her way toward him. She drew a steadying breath as her trembling hand slid over his roughened palm; gently his warm fingers wrapped themselves around hers in a reassuring embrace. Aidan lowered herself to the blanket.

Justin's silvery eyes ran over her face, then dropped to her torn bodice. Riotous anger filled him when he noticed the fingerlike bruises marking the top of one breast. His hard gaze snapped to her face. "Did he insinuate himself upon you, madam?"

Although her husband's accusing anger was actually centered on her abductor, Aidan felt certain he was charging her with precipitating the attack. "No!" she cried. "H-he tried, but I managed to get free of him. I was fleeing him when I ran into you. I swear I didn't do anything to provoke it. I—"

"Hush, sweet," Justin said, realizing the harsh tone of his words had given Aidan cause to believe he was indicting her for something she could not control. He drew her close in order to comfort her. "My anger is with Edmonds, not you, love. And with myself," he confessed. "I'd feared that he'd hurt you more than he had. The thought of him forcing himself on you . . . God! I couldn't repress the fury I felt, knowing it would have been my fault."

"Your fault?"

"Yes, Aidan—my fault. Stupidly I sent you away from me. I put you in danger. All because of my pride." A low curse hissed through his lips as he raked his hand through his hair; then he vented his anger on himself. "Damn my pride!"

Aidan couldn't help but smile up at him; her violet eyes twinkled in the candlelight. "I believe we are in mutual agreement on that particular subject, sir." Justin's brow arched in question. "I've cursed my own several times."

"Indeed, madam. We appear to be perfectly matched in that area." He bestowed a knowing look on her. "And in several others as well."

Realizing he referred to their insatiable desire for one another, Aidan blushed; instantly her stomach grumbled.

Justin's eyes widened; then he chuckled. "Hungry?" he inquired.

"Extremely," she replied, then decided not to tell him of George's method of torture. Justin already blamed himself for the ordeal she had been made to suffer. When things were right with them, she would share those hours of torment. "Thirsty, too," she added.

Justin drew the leather bag to him, then removed the cloth-wrapped fare inside. A flask of water followed. Greedily Aidan ate her fill, washing it down freely with the water. "I hadn't realized I'd married such a glutton," Justin commented, a smile teasing his lips.

Her stomach sated, she smiled up at him. "I missed Cook's delicious cakes, that's all."

Surveying her with a critical eye, Justin noted she seemed thinner than when he'd last seen her. This time he controlled his anger. "He tried to starve you into submission, didn't he?"

Aidan looked away. "Yes," she admitted in a soft voice. "I'd rather have died than let him touch me. Why did he change? He seemed so very much the gentleman. Did I do this to him?" she asked in a pained voice.

Feeling his heart lurch, Justin slipped his arm around her shoulders and held her fast. "He had much misery in his life, sweet. His father's cruelty was the greatest cause of what he suffered. The changes in him came through that. I'm certain of it."

"The earl—what will happen when he learns his son is dead."

Remembering the grisly sight he'd discovered upon returning to the house, Justin swallowed hard in an attempt to keep the bile from surging into his throat. As he'd searched the upstairs hallways, looking for candles and whatever else he thought he might need for the night, he'd been drawn by a putrid odor, which resembled decaying flesh. Finding the door he was certain the rancid smell lay behind, he'd pushed it open. Therein lay the earl, tucked neatly into his bed, his head bludgeoned.

When the man had returned from India, Justin had been unable to say. Yet noting the severity of rot, he'd estimated the earl had been dead well over two months. Quickly he'd fled the foul-smelling room, fearing he'd vomit. Then, upon finding what he thought was George's room, he'd discovered an open cask filled with gold. Seeing it, Justin had instantly understood the viscount's recent show of wealth, the sporty new phaeton one of George's ill-gotten treasures.

"Don't worry about the earl," he said finally, refusing to share what he'd found with her. "Just know that what changed George was not of your making. As I said, much of what he was at the end resulted from what happened before he met you." He paused and drew a deep breath. "And much of what I am, Aidan, is the result of my past as well."

Confused violet eyes stared up at him. "What do you mean?"

"I mean my actions toward you have a cause. There are things I must share with you. Things that I've kept hidden inside me for a very long time. Aunt Patti accused me of having become jaded, cynical, and coldhearted. I've been all three where you are concerned. Although I've always wanted you, Aidan, I purposely tried to reject you."

"Why?" she asked, her eyes searching his.

"Because I was afraid of you—of us. Of what might happen if I . . . cared too deeply," he said, unable to express the true word for what he actually felt. "But stupidly, I kept trying to deny the obvious."

Aidan felt her heart soar. "Then you do care for me?" she asked. Why couldn't he say the word "love" the way it was meant to be said? He called her by the endearment all the time.

He smiled tenderly. "I do care, deeply, and have done so since the moment I first saw you. But I wouldn't allow myself to believe what my heart said was true. I refused to make myself admit it. I suppose there was too much hatred and distrust built up inside me, all because of my parents."

"You hated your parents?" she asked uncomprehendingly.

"I hated what they'd done to one another, what they'd done to me by way of it. Seeing how they treated each other, I found myself unable to believe in marriage, in the bond of love. Theirs was a travesty."

"Tell me what happened," she said, her soft hand caressing his face, taking care not to touch his wound. "If you share it, the pain you've suffered may finally leave you. I love you, Justin," she confessed, her voice showing the strength of her commitment. "I'm not afraid to say it. If you share your uncertainties, then maybe you won't be afraid of saying it either."

His tormented gaze traveled her face; then after a long moment he began to speak of his parents. He told her of their obsessions, their jealousies, their inability to remain faithful to one another. Then he told her of the day he'd found them in the meadow, explaining how he'd made their deaths appear as though they'd both been murdered by thieves, hoping to protect their names.

"Although others suspected the truth, Aunt Patti was the only one who actually knew what had happened. She'd just recently lost her son and daughter-in-law from cholera. She had no one else, so she came to Warfield Manor to stay with me. At eighteen, I suppose she still thought I needed a guardian."

"And did you?" Aidan teased, her brow rising.

"Indeed I did," he admitted, a grin settling on his face. "Had it not been for her censuring attacks on my sudden lack of proper conduct, I'd most likely be dead by now from an overindulgence of wine and women." He noted her brow rise higher. "Aidan, there were women in my past, but not as many as you might think. I allowed everyone to believe I was a rake. It was my way of protecting myself, keeping young women, much like yourself, away. The few with whom I was intimate knew the rules. Love was never involved, only physical gratification. Believe me, I was far worse in my impetuous youth than in more recent years. The dowager marchioness managed to curb most of the baser side of my character in short order."

"How so?" Aidan asked.

"All it took was several angry whacks of her cane across my backside, and I quickly learned to behave myself." Justin noted her skeptical look. "The rest, love, was accomplished by you. Ever since we met, I've been on my best behavior." Her gaze instantly dropped from his. "What's wrong, sweet?" he asked, tipping her chin upward to meet his gaze.

Aidan sighed and looked him in the eye. "After you

exiled me to Warfield Manor, I'd heard you were seeing Cynthia Danvers again.''

"*Seeing* was all I was doing, love. Although to all outward appearances my actions may have stated otherwise, I've been faithful to you, Aidan. I promise you I have."

After carefully searching his eyes, Aidan believed him. "Perhaps, sir, you remained so because you feared Aunt Patti's cane," she teased with mock severity.

"Perhaps," he said with a smile, "but I think it's because no one else appealed to me except you."

"I've heard love does that to people."

He looked away. "Love does other things as well."

She heard the cynicism in his voice. "Justin, do you believe our marriage will be like your parents'?"

"I can't help but be afraid it will end up the same way." He looked to her again. "Aidan, I've never felt jealousy until I met you. I've never been angered enough to kill someone until I met you. Lately, all I have been able to think about is how much I want you, how much I need you—you've become an obsession with me. In myself, I see my own father, and I fear what might happen to us."

"There's a difference between your parents' love—if it was love—and what we share, Justin. I, too, have felt all the things that you've just described. And no matter how hard I tried, I've been unable to erase you from my mind. I want to be with you always, to have your children, to be a special part of you . . . your life. Our heartache has been that we haven't been honest with one another. We've been hiding our real feelings from the first day we met. I love you," she confessed, the emotion shining in her eyes. "I'd never purposely hurt you. Nor would I willingly leave you—never again. I'll always be faithful to you. Please, you must trust in what I say, for it's true."

His pained gazed raked over her, and to his wife it seemed even more tormented than before. "Oh, Aidan, make me believe it's true. Make me believe it, love."

Wanting her love, needing her to prove it, Justin quickly pulled Aidan into his arms. His mouth descended, capturing hers in a searching, hungry kiss. The taste of her sweet lips, opening themselves under his, showing their desire to please, inflamed him. His hand slipped up over the silk-clad middle to her breast. Tenderly he held it, marveling at how she fitted perfectly into his hand. Then, with a whimper of need, she pressed her aching body to his.

"Make love to me," she urgently breathed against his lips, and Justin could not deny her request.

Their clothing fell away, and gently, slowly, he laid her onto the quilts, his hard, hair-roughened thighs settling between her soft, sleek ones. The sweet smell of hay, plus her intoxicating fragrance, instantly filled his head, and an earthy form of excitement vibrated through him. Soft violet eyes, luminous in the dim candlelight, gazed up at him; then her open arms and legs surrounded him, urging him to her.

With an agonized groan, he went willingly into her accepting embrace; his silver gaze devoured her beauty as he positioned himself. "You feel like hot satin," he rasped as he slowly eased upward, settling deep inside her. "God, I want you."

"I'm yours, Justin," she whispered softly; then her hips moved enticingly against him and he was lost.

With long fluid movements he withdrew, then drove into her, again and again.

"Make me believe, Aidan," he demanded as his splayed hand lifted her rounded bottom, urging her closer. "Show me it's true."

"I love you, Justin," Aidan whispered near his ear. Fearing she might somehow lose him, she held fast to his sinewy neck and rose to meet each of his hard, purging thrusts. "I'll love you always. Love me too. Oh, please, say you will."

Her soft plea, which seemed torn from her heart, spun through Justin's head, then spiraled straight to his soul. Wildly, provocatively, poignantly, he laid claim to her. He wanted her, needed her, desired her with all that was in his being!

Frantically she writhed beneath him, her sweet voice calling to him, her soft form beckoning. He tried to hold back, but he found he couldn't. He was lost in her, lost to her. And with one last driving plunge, his hard body jerked convulsively. A shout climbed from his throat, and as the litany of her name ascended above them, his seed spilled forth. Miraculously, all the dark emotions he'd harbored deep inside him released themselves as well. Instantly his heart rejoiced. He believed! Oh, God, how he believed!

Say the words, his heart demanded. "I love you, Aidan," he whispered huskily, his silvery gaze reflecting that wondrous, exciting feeling. "Oh, how I love you." As his passion-glazed eyes slowly focused, he noticed her tears. "What's wrong, love? Why are you crying?"

Liquid violet stared up at him. "You said you loved me, Justin. But because of me, those words might never have been said. I . . . I almost caused your death. I'm so ashamed."

A deep chuckle rumbled from his chest, but noticing her seriousness, he sobered. Gently he wiped her tears from beneath her eyes. "Love, in truth, you did cause my death, but my old life came to a welcome end. I'm no longer the man I once was. Through your love, I've been given a new life—one filled with promise and hope." Suddenly a roguish grin spread across his face. "And one that will bring me great rewards. My Queen has ordered it so."

Smiling up at him, Aidan laughed; her crystal tone filled Justin's head. "Then, sir, we should not disobey your Queen. I hear she can be quite adamant about certain decrees which she has handed down. No one crosses her. So, unless you wish to lose your head, I suggest we go about fulfilling her wishes."

Justin's silvery gaze danced merrily. "My dear duchess, I've already lost my head—my heart as well. But in keeping with what is considered proper, I shall most happily make certain Her Majesty's wish is granted."

As his lips lowered toward his wife's, Justin grew serious. "I love you, Aidan. I will always love you." Then his mouth claimed hers in a poignantly endearing caress.

As the candles burned low on their wicks, Apollo blew a soft whinny, his hoof striking the straw-covered earth in his stall; a light rain beat against the roof in a gentle rhythm.

Justin lay awake, listening to the pacifying sounds, content to have his wife tucked close to his body. Lazily he gazed at Aidan's slumbering form; his heart expanded fully in his chest. Nothing could ever have prepared him for the marvelous feelings filling him now, in mind, in body, and in soul. Indeed, no one could ever have made him understand the true meaning of love—its gladness, its joy, its ecstasy. And, yes, its sorrow. Not until Aidan. Only she could bring about the change in him. Prior to meeting her, he had been only half a man, cynical and empty. But now, through her love, he was whole and happily complete.

While she lay under his tender regard, Justin thought of all the times he'd foolishly said he wanted to be rid of her. Through his own callousness, he'd almost lost her! Thank God, he hadn't. As his arms drew her closer to his heart, he placed a gentle kiss on her untroubled brow. Slowly his eyes drifted shut, and he decided, most adamantly, he would keep her.

Epilogue

Christmas 1840
Warfield Manor

"Well, Alastair," Aunt Patti said as she sat by the warmth of the crackling fire, "I'd say we've done a good job of it." Her gaze shifted to her nephew and his wife, who stood by the win-dow, watching the drifting snowflakes. "Wouldn't you agree?"

Alastair chuckled. "On occasion, I had my doubts, Pattina. But yes, I do believe we managed quite nicely in the end."

"Oh, tosh, there was never any uncertainty in my mind. They were meant for each other. Just needed a little prodding, that's all." She raised her glass of sherry. "A toast to you, sir, for having the wisdom to unite them."

"And a toast to you, madam," he returned, lifting his brandy glass high, "for having the wisdom to make certain they stayed united."

"Hear, hear!" they both cried in unison.

* * *

"By the New Year we'll be at Sommerfield. I can barely wait to see Eugenia and David again," Aidan said, snuggling deeper into her husband's arms, her back resting against his solid chest. "And to think, in two months I shall be a godmother."

"And I shall be a godfather," Justin returned, chuckling. "The term sounds a bit doddering to me. Whenever we visit the little scamp, I shall be tempted to lean upon a cane and chuck his chin."

"Or to kiss her cheek," Aidan countered, smiling up over her shoulder at her husband. Suddenly Pattina's and Alastair's salutes erupted into the air. "What do you think they're up to?" Aidan asked, frowning.

Justin's face lowered closer to hers. He nuzzled her ear, almost dislodging one of the amethyst earrings he'd given her. "They're probably making plans for us again," he said disinterestedly, for his wife's creamy neck seemed far more appealing. "Since my *reward* is on its way"—he smoothed his gentle hand over the purple velvet gown and Aidan's slightly rounded belly—"I suppose they're choosing a name for him."

"Her," Aidan countered haughtily.

"Him," Justin insisted, arching a brow.

Aidan smiled. "It matters not. Aunt Patti says, because of the way I'm blossoming, there might be one of each."

"*Twins!*" he exclaimed incredulously.

"A double reward, sir. Our Queen should be most pleased."

"Indeed, she should be. Perhaps I shall ask her for a loan so I might support my issue . . . uh, issues."

"The only loan you'll receive from our Queen is a wealth of advice. As I recall, it nearly tore us apart. Henceforth, I'd prefer you kept your own counsel."

"Had I done that, sweet wife, the two of us would not be standing here now. Nor would I soon be receiving my reward. It was she who suggested I bed you, love, and get you with child—along with your father."

Aidan sputtered. "My father!"

He grinned. "Yes . . . said it was the only way to control you."

"And I suppose Aunt Patti suggested something similar."

"She may have. I don't recall."

Violet eyes assessed him at length. "It took all those people to convince you to make love to me."

"Not really. Had your father not come upon us when he did, I most likely would have had you before we were married."

"In the coach?"

"I've heard that somewhere before," he said, grinning. "Yes, madam, in the coach."

"Sounds interesting," Aidan teased, returning his smile. "Shall we give it a try?"

"And risk frostbite?" he asked, affronted. "I assure you, madam, there are certain parts of my anatomy I'll not purposely expose to such a possibility."

"Oh, but, Justin," she cooed, a mischievous twinkle centering itself in her eyes, "where it will be nestled is like hot satin. You said so yourself."

An agonized groan vibrated in his throat, then flowed through his lips. "Behave, madam, or I'll discover the truth of it, here and now." His arms tightened around her, his hands linking at her waist. "Watch the snow, Aidan. It will cool us both—I hope."

Her light laughter filled the room as Aidan cuddled against Justin. While her hand caressed her husband's, a flash of red caught her eye, and she gazed down at the large ruby. Explaining how the ring had come into his possession again, he'd vowed his eternal love and returned it to her finger. There it would stay, forever.

Then, as serene violet eyes looked out over the snow-covered lawns of Warfield Manor, Justin's protective arms surrounding her, his love filling her heart, Aidan knew she was home at last.